JUSTICE for TOBY
a Fish Springs novel

What reviewers say about Manuel and Timbs' first novel
Fish Springs: Beneath the Surface

"A rare and intimate story with powerful and complex characters that bring out emotional elements we want to see move from page to screen." —Belle Avery, Exec. Producer of *Before the Devil Knows You're Dead*," with Philip Seymore Hoffman.

"Manuel and Timbs write honestly and sometimes humorously, easily gliding into back-stories about their mountain characters in a style reminiscent of Pat Conroy through his coastal characters and scenes. The dialect is fast paced and advances the plot so effectively that one would think he is watching the drama unfold in a mini-series. Romantics will love this tale, but so, too, will Civil War historians." —Bessie Meeks, *Lake Wylie Pilot*, Lake Wylie, S.C.

"The novel is entertaining and a little mysterious. It's easy to wonder what's true. —Dudley Brown, *Herald-Journal*, Spartanburg, S.C.

"It's a story about passion, pain, war and murder. But it's also a story about a little-known community in Northeast Tennessee that time and hundreds of thousands of gallons of water have almost washed away." —Max Hrenda, *Johnson City Press*, Johnson City, Tenn.

"Flows as steadily as the Watauga River where much of the story is centered. The reader can easily get a true sense of living through each moment right along with the characters. The characters are complex and the lives they lead are certain to keep readers glued to the pages wondering what will happen next." —Lacy Hilliard, *The Tomahawk*, Mountain City, Tenn.

"Beneath the surface lies the soul of every human being." —The Rev. Bruce Simcox, Mountain City, Tenn.

D1565652

ALSO BY

Michael Manuel &

Larry C. Timbs Jr

FISH SPRINGS
Beneath the Surface

JUSTICE for TOBY
a Fish Springs novel

Michael Manuel &
Larry C. Timbs Jr

Bearhaven  **Publishers**

Bearhaven  Publishers

www.fishspringsnovel.com

This book is a sequel to the novel
Fish Springs: Beneath the Surface
first published by
Ingalls Publishing Group (2014)

Cover photo by Michael Manuel, Watauga River
at Sycamore Shoals near Elizabethton
Book design by Luci Mott

ISBN-13: 978-0692740859 (Bearhaven Publishers)

ISBN-10: 0692740856

*For more details about the authors and the story, see the Acknowledgments
and notes in the back of the book, and the authors' website:*
www.fishspringsnovel.com

JUSTICE for TOBY
a Fish Springs novel

CHAPTER 1

Toby's Bones

On a warm, cloudless spring day in 1883, in the remote mountain community of Fish Springs, Tennessee, Isaiah Washington plowed a previously unused plot of his bottomland along the Watauga River.

The land was rich with only a few rocks, and Isaiah, a solidly built, dark skinned former slave, strained every muscle in his arms and shoulders to keep the mule-pulled plow in the right furrow. Every so often, the sharecropper and foreman for Daniel Smith, one of the most prominent landowners in Carter County, stopped to catch his breath and wipe the sweat off his brow. He swatted the pesky mountain gnats that seemed on this day to be especially bothersome.

Isaiah stuffed his old red handkerchief back in his overalls pocket and resumed his task, for he knew that barring a flood or other natural disaster, the rich river bottom soil would yield a fine crop of potatoes and corn. The earth-polished blade cut through the dark soil, occasionally jerking when it encountered a stone.

Isaiah held the plow upright and encouraged Sue, his big-eared mule, with voice commands.

"Gee!" Isaiah shouted when he wanted the animal to veer to the right. "Haw!" he barked when he'd rather the obedient mule veer to the left.

Half way down his tenth row the plow jerked again. Sue threw her head back, lunging forward at Isaiah's command and overcoming whatever obstacle the blade had encountered. Isaiah assumed it was the large round stone that had come to a rest on top of the overturned earth. He stopped, pulled the handkerchief from his back pocket and wiped the perspiration from his face. Stooping over, he picked up the round smooth object. Surprised it was not heavier, he turned it over and looked into the empty sockets of a human skull.

Isaiah hollered, dropped the skull and fell backwards, his rear end coming to rest in the soft, damp soil. He noticed other bones in the trench he had just plowed. Isaiah studied the skull and bones, thinking that these were probably not the remains of a Cherokee Indian that had inhabited the area because those would have been buried higher in a mound.

Arm bones and leg bones, along with smaller ones, were scattered about. Isaiah sifted through fragments and bits of rotted clothing and leather. Noticing a rotted leather cord, he pulled it from the soil, bringing whatever was attached to the surface. He cleaned the dirt off the object exposing a large tooth. Studying the tooth more closely, he recognized it as the tiger's tooth that his friend Toby Jackson had worn.

Isaiah turned the tooth over and over in his big brown hands as he sat down in the dirt and began to cry. *How could they do this to my old friend Toby? Toby never hurt nobody. Toby was gentle as a lamb!*

When he pulled the rotted boot off a skeletal right foot revealing two missing toes, Isaiah was convinced it was his friend Toby, who had been missing for the past thirteen years.

Toby had told Isaiah that his toes had been cut off when they turned black with frostbite. He had lost them as a young man because his slave master, Jake Edwards of the Valley Forge community, had made him work outside in freezing weather. This was well before the Emancipation Proclamation.

"Lawdy, Lawdy, what happen ta you my old friend?!"

Isaiah picked up the dirt-encrusted skull and turned it over and over, as if wishing somehow it would speak to him. Then he placed it gently—reverentially—back on the ground, among the other bones. But the tiger's tooth he held tightly in the palm of his hand.

The heartbroken Negro vowed right then and there to get justice for his friend. For he knew Toby hadn't died a peaceful, natural death. Isaiah surmised that Toby's last few seconds on this earth had been horrible. Something evil had befallen him..

He remembered Toby as a God-fearing gentle giant of a colored man, one who could lift your spirits with his ivory-white, toothy smile, who never complained, who had not had the easiest life—far from it—but had made the best of it.

As Isaiah stood there among the bones, he kept palming the tiger's tooth. He had a feeling that Jake Edwards probably had something to do with Toby's killing.

Toby had confided in him that he was determined to pay off his bill at the store owned by Edwards so he could finally be free to leave.

Toby had also shared with him that every time he tried to pay off his bill, the spiteful Edwards had added to the balance. To the despair of the hard-working Toby, he couldn't get his boss paid off. And Toby, being an honest man, would never leave without settling the debt.

It seemed Jake Edwards and his equally vicious wife Martha were determined to never let him leave. They had Toby where they wanted him: tending to their livestock, working their land, doing all manner of backbreaking chores—and for what?

Their worker was paid a monthly pittance and lived in their smelly, drafty old barn. His dreadful lot was not much better than that of a slave.

Fanny May Brown, who worked in Jake's store, was a former slave who had become too old to do field work. She landed the job at Edwards' little store when he found out she could read, write and make change—skills that very few Negroes had in those days.

Fanny May was paid a meager wage to manage the store that was located in the shade of Jenkins Mountain on a dirt road that ran along the Elk River. Having access to Jake's books, Fanny May was aware that he was inflating his helps' accounts to keep them indebted to him. She was extremely bothered by this but was afraid to say anything about it. She also knew that on many occasions Jake had taken advantage of the colored girls working for him on his farm.

Toby told Fanny May that Jake had once come within an inch

of laying his hands on the young former slave girl Prissy, who at the time was Martha and Jake Edwards' housekeeper.

Secretly Fannny May despised Jake Edwards and she had long suspected that he was a member of the Ku Klux Klan.

Thinking back, Isaiah recalled Toby telling him that he had scrimped and saved and had enough money to pay Fanny May Brown the balance at the store; and as soon as he did, he would stop by and see him and his new baby boy on the way to Alabama.

What Isaiah did not know was that the day Toby went to the store to pay off his bill, the compassionate, elderly Fanny May took his money and handed him a slip of paper.

"Toby, you take this and put it in a safe place. 'Cause dat devil Jake Edwards not be an honest man," she said.

"What it be, Fanny May?"

"It's a receipt, Toby, showing you paid off dis bill an' I signed and dated it."

"Thank ya, Fanny May. I find a good place for it. Fanny, has I got enough money left for dat corn cob pipe and a can'a dat 'bacca?"

"It be close enough, Toby. She handed him the pipe and a can of Old Virginia Smoke tobacco. "Where you be goin' now, Toby?"

"I'm gwine to Alabama where my little brother be. He works for da railroad. He be a foreman, and he said he can get me a job dere. Soon's I see my old friend Isaiah, I be on my way."

"Ok, Toby. I'll miss you. You has a safe trip."

Toby grinned as he walked with a bounce in his step from the little country store. He had felt good about himself and his future. *No more Mista Edwards! No more sleepin' in that stankin' barn. Nevva' agin! I's be truly a free man now.*

Toby was like many of Fanny May's customers. They loved her because of the way she treated them, always greeting everyone with a cheery smile and often coming from behind the counter to give a down and out colored customer a big warm hug. The Negroes affectionately referred to her as "Aunt Fanny."

She even embraced some of her white customers. Some, but not all of them, because she could sense which ones looked down on colored folks.

As a consequence, people came back, and Jake Edwards' store did well.

But a few years after Toby left, business dropped off when a large dry goods establishment opened in Valley Forge. So Jake closed his store and sent Fanny May on her way—without any severance pay, and with not so much as a "Good luck, thank you."

The old Negro woman bid all her friends and customers farewell, telling them she was on her way to Knoxville to live with her daughter Mattie, a school teacher.

Isaiah studied the bones and wondered what to do next. He was troubled. And where first did he always go when he was troubled?

Home to Prissy. Together, Isaiah figured, they would decide what to do. So he unhitched the plow, took the big brown mule by the reins and headed toward his barn. His hands were sore from gripping the plow, and his back ached. They would get better. His heart also ached, but it wouldn't get better, at least anytime soon.

The same questions kept nagging him: Why had Toby suffered such a terrible fate? What'd he ever done to be killed and buried, and his bones barely covered in a desolate field and if it wasn't Jake Edwards, who else could have done such a horrible thing?

Isaiah knew Prissy would be heartbroken because she had been like a little sister to Toby when they both worked for Jake Edwards. But unlike Toby, Prissy had survived the wrath of their employer.

As Isaiah walked Sue across the river bottom, he thought about where he was and how he had reached this point in his life.

He was free now, seemingly a hundred years removed from that painful time in Africa when white slavers, with the help of Africans who betrayed their own people, captured him. They had forced him into the bowels of a slave schooner, branded him like an animal and shipped him to Jekyll Island in America. He had survived the torturous voyage across the ocean, when many of his fellow captives had not. He had been shackled and sold on the auction block in Charleston, S.C. Then there were those years of miserable, gut-wrenching labor on a giant plantation in Virginia. All that happened before Daniel Smith bought him away from that plantation owner and brought him to Fish Springs. Isaiah had first worked for Daniel as a slave, but then, even before the Emancipation Proclamation, Daniel had granted the appreciative Negro his freedom.

Not so long after that, Isaiah married Daniel and Mary's housekeeper, Prissy. The pretty, light-skinned former slave become the mother to their three rambunctious, loving boys. Isaiah also became a proud landowner, one of the very few Negroes to be such in Fish Springs. He had been given a cabin, small as it was, by the good-hearted Daniel for his many years of service as a hard worker—first as a slave, then as a paid employee and now as a sharecropper and foreman.

Isaiah realized he had a lot to be grateful for. True, slavery had been banned by the law of the land years ago—immediately in the aftermath of the Civil War. But in East Tennessee, colored folks still had it plenty hard. Old prejudices died hard in predominantly white Fish Springs and in other remote mountain communities. And while many Negroes had paying jobs, in Tennessee and the rest of the South, they labored at the bottom of the heap. Hardly any colored man, unlike Isaiah, could boast of being a landowner, or of owning his home—completely paid for.

Yet, it still seemed that he and his family were looked down on by some white folks, like they were trespassing in Fish Springs.

Lawd, I ain't asked to come here. And yet we are here. This is our home. And I got ta make the best life I can for Prissy and our younguns'. And oh yeah, Willie. Lawd, help me. 'Cause Willie's four years old now and that little half white boy thinks I'm his daddy and my sons are his brothers.

CHAPTER 2

Mourning a Good Friend

Prissy was startled when Isaiah, mud on his boots, arrived at their cabin. It was hours before he was supposed to be home, and she hadn't gotten her household chores done.

She dried her hands on her faded apron and then, as she always did when her man returned from a hard day of labor, she gave him a big kiss and bear hug.

But even though he hugged her back and smiled slightly, Prissy could tell something was wrong. Isaiah seemed limp, dejected.

Prissy looked him straight in the eyes.

"Now Isaiah, you tell me right now what's troublin' you, and don't tell me nothin' because I knows something's not right. Why are you home so early taday? You feelin' bad?"

Prissy, pretty as a picture even in an old, tattered apron and faded cotton dress, put her hands on her hips. Her eyes stayed sternly focused on Isaiah's.

But when her mournful husband, in his dirt-stained, ragged overalls, said nothing, just stared back at her as if he'd lost his voice, Prissy became more adamant.

"Now you tell me what it is right this minute! I ain't askin' you again. You know we can talk 'bout anything."

Prissy put her arms around him, pressed her soft, curvy body up against his and held him tightly. For she had learned long ago that Isaiah loved to feel her from her head to toe.

Her husband, now perking up a bit, squeezed her back. As always to him, she felt wonderful, warm, loving. Then he ran his hands through Prissy's hair. It was not stiff like that of most Negro women, but full of soft curls that dangled on her shoulders, as if beckoning to be touched.

Prissy parted from her husband slightly and looked at him again. The man she loved deeply had been crying. So she dabbed his sad eyes with her apron.

Isaiah got a hold of himself and spoke, "Toby's dead. I found his bones in the field I was plowin' taday, Prissy. I think that old Jake Edwards killed'im. He murdered our friend Toby."

Isaiah explained to Prissy how he knew he had found Toby's remains. How the tiger's tooth and the missing toes on one skeletal foot were the telltale signs. How he'd remembered what Toby had told him about never being able to escape the wrath of his employer. How Toby, despite making all those payments on his bill at Jake Edwards' store, could never get his greedy, mean employer paid back in full.

Isaiah also reminded his wife about the letters they had received from Toby's brother asking if they knew anything about his whereabouts. They had asked around, but everyone who knew or might have known Toby had no ideas at all. And Isaiah could only recall what his old pal had shared with him all those years ago: "I's gwine ta stop by and see you on ma' way to Alabama."

But he had never stopped by. And when Isaiah, sensing the worst, mustered up the courage to ask Jake Edwards if he knew where Toby might be, Edwards said he had no idea. Isaiah pressed him, but the Valley Forge resident fumed with anger. Then, brandishing his shotgun, he launched into a tirade of racial slurs.

"Git your damn black ass off my property! I'm plum tard of puttin' up with niggers! Git on back up ta Fish Springs and ta your little nigger whore, and don't be showin' yourself here agin! Now scat before I blow your head clean off!"

Isaiah recounted all this venom to Prissy, and she took it in with little emotion—at first. Then she slumped down in a chair, closed her eyes and folded her hands, as in prayer.

It had been years since she'd laid eyes on Toby, but she hadn't forgotten about him. How they'd looked out for each other when they'd toiled, slavishly, for Jake and Martha Edwards. How, for instance, she'd once secretly brought the totally exhausted-from-work Toby a blanket on a particularly frigid night in the barn where, after covering himself up with hay, he shivered and tried his best to sleep; how she'd occasionally snuck him a few cookies, slices of cakes or pies and a hot cup of coffee; how Toby, in return, had once wrapped her swollen, sprained ankle—suffered when Prissy stumbled and twisted it with a too-heavy load of clothes she carried to a nearby creek to wash. He'd found some old rags in the barn, cut them into strips and wrapped them carefully around her ankle for support.

Toby promised he'd make sure nothing bad happened to her, and that he'd die, if need be, protecting her from Jake Edwards' wrath. He knew about the dreaded, ugly bull whip that their boss kept in the barn, for he had indeed felt the sting of the whip across his own back, and Toby would never *ever* have allowed their employer to thrash Prissy with it.

Although it had never come to Toby giving up his own life for Prissy's, it was a comfort to the former slave girl to know that Toby was like a protective big brother to her.

But though he might be in a better place, she grieved she'd never see him again in this life.

"Prissy, if we go see the sheriff, do you think that he will put ole' man Jake Edwards in jail?"

"I don't know, Isaiah. White folks looks after white folks. Besides, he might not believe your story."

"Then who can help us, Prissy? I want that devil Jake Edwards ta pay for what he done!" Isaiah knew that in Fish Springs and the rest of Carter County, coloreds were thought of by many whites as less than human. *No big loss if a colored man died. Jest one less nigger to worry 'bout. He was above his raisin' anyway.*

Prissy, the sparkle in her eyes beginning to return, rose from her chair, thrust her shoulders squarely back and put her hands on her husband's shoulders.

"We do what we always do when there's trouble, Isaiah. We go to the only man in Fish Springs we can trust. The only one we have faith in to help us. Mista Daniel Smith."

"You be right, Prissy. We go see Mista Smith. He'll know what to do." Isaiah was surprised that he himself hadn't thought of that idea. For they could always depend on Daniel Smith—respected, good to the core, the Fish Springs landowner and community leader who had, in essence, thirteen years ago brought

Isaiah and Prissy together. Prissy was confident that Daniel Smith would help them because he was a good man that did not judge people by the color of their skin. He, along with Isaiah while on a hay-buying trip to the Edwards farm, had stepped up and rescued Prissy when Jake hit her and tried to keep her from leaving because of her unpaid bill at his store, thus holding her in servitude.

No, Daniel hadn't tolerated any of that. He and a pleading Isaiah on behalf of Prissy had had a showdown with the snarling, angry Jake Edwards that day on his farm. The result—Prissy had left with them, never again to serve the heartless couple who had seemed so intent on permanently "owning" Prissy and nearly working her into the ground. All she had wanted was a chance at a better life, and that she would have.

From then on, Prissy worked for Daniel Smith and his beautiful wife Mary. They also had their hands full with four children—Izzy, Peter and Charlie, from Daniel's deceased first wife Polly, and "Little Danny," from Mary's deceased first husband, Alfred.

Prissy had been raised on the Shirley Plantation in Virginia where her mother was a house servant. Mary Carter, the Master's wife, took Prissy under her wing, teaching her how to read and write and speak properly. So Prissy became much more than just a housekeeper for the Smiths. She was almost like a member of the Smith family, helping look after and nurture their four children in addition to cooking, canning, cleaning, sewing and otherwise keeping the house in order.

Likewise, Daniel and Mary Smith and their children came to think of her as one of their own. She went to church with the Smiths. She bowed her head in prayer with them at the table before eating. She had her own little room in the attic of their house. And for the work she did, she was paid a decent wage.

And so, after a few years with Prissy in the Smith household and Isaiah living temptingly nearby in quarters provided to him by Daniel, it was only a matter of time before the inevitable happened. Isaiah, Daniel Smith's right hand man on the farm, and Prissy the house girl, became husband and wife. The big strong Negro had instantly fallen for her all those years ago on the day he and Daniel rescued Prissy from the Edwardses. Mary, Daniel's wife, had helped speed things up in their relationship when she gave Prissy advice on how to make the shy, romantically awkward Isaiah think that marriage was his idea. The plan worked, so Isaiah and Prissy were married, jumping the broom, on the Smith farm by the Rev. Horace Leftwich, pastor of the Colored Baptist Church in Elizabethton. After the marriage they moved into a little cabin with five acres, given to them by Daniel Smith.

After Prissy and Isaiah agreed to go see Daniel Smith, the couple prepared to head out to the Smith home. With help from his oldest son, 13-year-old Benjamin, Isaiah went to the barn and hooked Sue up to the wagon. Then they returned to the cabin.

"I know he did it. Jake Edwards killed our friend Toby, Isaiah. He's evil in the worst way," said Prissy, running a comb through her hair and putting a kerchief over it for the ride to the Smith home.

Benjamin, his faithful companion Shadow at his side, asked "Who's Toby, Pa?"

"Take Shadow outside, please."

"But MaMa, he—"

"Ben."

"Yes ma'am."

The eight-year-old gray and brown bluetick hound was the grandson of Blue, the cherished, devoted dog of Isaiah's boss Daniel and his wife Mary who took in the canine when his master died. Shadow followed Ben out onto the porch. He yawned, then plopped down on his favorite spot and closed his eyes.

Ben gave him a gentle pat on the head, but the dog paid him no mind. He seemed to be asleep almost instantly.

Returning to his mother, Ben asked again, "Who's Toby?"

"He was a good friend of ours, son," Isaiah said.

"What happened to him?"

"We don't rightly know, Ben."

Then Prissy, her emotions raring up again, interjected, "I know! That devil Jake Ed—"

Isaiah cut her off. "Prissy we cain't be sayin' that. He took hold of her hands and shook her. "Not 'til we know for sure."

The couple's two other boys, Jeb, 11, and Leroy, nine, just stood by by with confused looks on their faces.

But little Willie was whimpering. "Pa, Pa, Pa!"

Isaiah bent down and picked Willie up. "Not Pa. You call me Isaiah," Isaiah said, patting his own chest and kissing the little one on the forehead.

"Isaiah, you should be ashamed. You are the only Pa that child has now. He only wants to be like the other boys, Isaiah."

"He cain't never be like the other boys, Prissy," Isaiah responded.

Prissy corrected him. "He can never be, Isaiah. But he *is*."

"This is not the time, Prissy," an insistent Isaiah countered. "We be done talking 'bout this for now."

He carried Willie out to the porch, spoke to him gently and the two of them sat for a spell in the porch swing while Isaiah waited for Prissy. Willie nodded off. Isaiah handed the slumbering tyke over to his other children, putting Ben in charge, and asked them to tend to their youngest while he and their mother took a ride.

"Where you and Ma goin'?" Ben asked.

"To Mista Daniel Smith's house, Ben, but we be back soon," Isaiah said. "Now, you the boss, Ben, but Jeb and Leroy—y'all both have to help your big brother."

The anxious couple then set out on the dirt road that meandered along the Watauga River for the short ride to the Smith home.

CHAPTER 3

Seeking Help

"Is that a storm cloud I see over on the mountain?" Prissy pointed as she swung herself up on the wagon seat beside Isaiah.

"It a long way off," Isaiah said. "We be there plenty before it hits."

It wouldn't take long to get to their destination, and Prissy, sitting next to her husband, liked making the ride to the Smith residence. Their dusty and bumpy route wound through some of the most beautiful river bottomland in East Tennessee. Lush green meadows, dotted here and there with waxy leafed mountain laurel, chicory, columbines, trillium and other mountain wildflowers, lined the left side of the road. Deer, squirrels, chipmunks and rabbits were plentiful, as were bears recently coming out of winter hibernation, although they saw none of the latter this particular day.

Beyond the meadows was a virgin hardwood forest. Prissy and Isaiah had taken their family on picnics in that forest and knew it was full of pines, hemlocks, chestnuts and hickories.

Prissy's favorite tree had always been the birch. "Look at how the white bark of that tree just peels off," she had exclaimed to her husband. "And look how the birds build their nests way high up in it. They know nothing can git' to their babies up that high."

"Uh-huh," Isaiah countered, but he was really looking beyond the birch tips at the way the clouds were building.

As they continued along, the old growth forest seemed to close in on them. They followed the road under a thick canopy of huge tulip poplars and sprawling oak trees. If there had been

19

a sudden spring thunderstorm at that juncture in their trip, the two could have stayed put in their buggy under such a dense canopy of trees and felt hardly a drop of rain.

To the travelers' right, just a stone's throw away and flowing along their path practically all the way to Daniel Smith's farm, was the Watauga River. Daniel had told them that "Watauga"—in Cherokee—meant "broken waters."

Where they rode now, the river streamed quietly, mildly—*perfect*, Isaiah thought—*for fishing.* Because here you could keep your line in the water. And if you were lucky, and the Good Lord smiled down on you, the Watauga would yield its most prized catch, a rainbow trout. You could also land a catfish or bass.

But to Isaiah's taste, the best-eating catch of all was the horneyhead. Some folks used this little thorny, silver-bellied fish as bait for larger prey, but Isaiah swore there wasn't a better tasting fish in the river. "They are the best eatin' in the world," he said to Prissy. "I'd rather catch one horneyhead then two of those trout."

"Yea', but they are one boney little fish and you have to eat a whole bunch of em to fill you up," she countered.

On a good day, if Isaiah happened upon a school of horneyheads, he could catch the scrumptious little fish with his bare hands. Long ago, the Cherokees, thousands of whom had inhabited this rich land, taught the whites how to use only their hands to scoop the little fish up onto the bank. But you paid the price of getting stuck with their little horns on the top of their head.

But no fishing today, for Isaiah and Prissy had to keep on their way. And as they got closer to Daniel's home, the cliff-lined mighty Watauga changed—what had been a gently flowing body of water was now a fast-flowing, whitewater river with big, jagged boulders jutting out of the water.

As if standing vigil over the river, blue herons and king fishers were perched on some of those huge rocks. Soon enough the majestic-looking, voracious eating birds would have a trout or salamander in their beaks.

And always, in the distance, beyond the meadows and river, were the purple-hazed mountains. They framed this part of Tennessee like monuments, almost touching the clouds—which now were beginning to blacken.

Isaiah and Prissy heard what old time Fish Springers called a "thunder boomer" off in the distance.

"We better be gittin' along, Isaiah, before that storm hits."

A mule slogging along a muddy road was a slow mule. So, obliging his wife, Isaiah snapped the reins on Sue. As he did, he smelled the scent of the onsetting rain. The air had suddenly gotten cooler. A breeze rustled through the tree leaves.

Prissy, also sensing that the sky was about to open, pulled her kerchief more tightly around her head and draped a horse blanket around her and her husband.

"We're almost there, Prissy. This old mule'll get us there before the rain starts. Then we be sittin' under the roof on Mista Smith's poach, I hope."

They arrived at their destination, not a moment too soon, for the wind-whipped rain pounded, lightning crackled through the darkening sky and the road turned to slop.

"Mista Smith! Mista Smith! Mary?!" Prissy shouted as she climbed down from the wagon, shielding her head from the downpour with her hands. "Y'all home?"

She knocked on the door while Isaiah pulled their wagon in the barn. He untethered the mud-splattered mule so it could rest and made sure it had water and hay.

When he had gotten this done and hustled through the rain to Daniel Smith's front porch, Prissy, wet but relieved, was hugging Mary.

Tall, handsome, 63-year-old Daniel stood next to the two women, waving, beckoning Isaiah to hurry and get out of the rain.

"Hello, Mista Smith," Isaiah said to the only white man the Negro considered his friend.

The two men, one a former slave and now a sharecropper and foreman, the other one of the richest and most honorable farmers in Carter County, greeted one another as friends. Then looking down they all laughed at Isaiah's socks, one blue, one red as he pulled his muddy boots off.

"I can't do nothin' with that man, Mr. Smith. He just won't train."

Isaiah just rolled his eyes while the others snickered. Then Daniel invited Isaiah and his wife to join them inside in "the big house," as Prissy called it.

Inside, next to the massive stone fireplace, the four of them sat down in rocking chairs.

Mary, who would have still been a hotly pursued woman in Fish Springs if she weren't already taken, excused herself for a few moments and brought tea. She was now in her early forties, but her green eyes, as they always did, sparkled. The golden curls that escaped her bun framed her perfect physical features. She had a slender waist, peaches and cream complexion and square shoulders. Prissy had often said to Isaiah, "She as pretty as a mountain wildflower."

Years earlier, Mary had indeed been considered the prettiest girl in Fish Springs. Such designations were usually used on young single ladies. Nevertheless, at her age, Mary was still the envy of every woman and the desire of every man in Fish Springs.

"What brings you out'en this storm, Isaiah?" Daniel put the question to him after they'd exchanged pleasantries and taken a few sips of the hot brew.

"Well to say the truth, Mista Daniel, it was pretty when we left the house."

"Yea these spring storms can—" Boom! A crash of thunder interrupted Daniel and echoed through the mountains.

"We are here to ask a favor, Mista Smith."

"And what would that be, Isaiah? How can I help my right hand man?" Daniel noticed that Isaiah began breathing easier.

"There is a wicked devil livin' down Valley Forge way!" Prissy interrupted.

Isaiah shushed his wife. "Let me tell Mista Daniel, Prissy. You get too mad when you talk about it."

"Ok, Isaiah. You right."

His emotions sometimes getting the best of him, Isaiah spelled it all out. He told his boss about the bones he'd happened upon and plowed up. He described the missing toes in the skeletal foot, which he was sure was Toby's foot. He told Daniel about the tiger's tooth on the leather cord, found among the bones, that Toby always used to wear around his neck. He told about what Toby had confided in him concerning not being able to get his bill paid off at Jake Edwards' store tended to by Fanny May.

"Mista Smith, we think that evil man Mista Jake Edwards killed our friend Toby and covered him up with dirt and worms in that field!" Prissy angrily declared. "And we are here asking you, Mista Smith, to git him arrested."

Isaiah looked at Prissy sternly but said nothing.

Daniel, taking it all in, thought for a moment. Then he spoke. "I need to go see those bones for myself, Isaiah. And if it's like you say it is, we'll fetch Sheriff Nave. Can you take me to that skeleton at first light? Do you remember the exact spot in your field where the bones are?"

When Isaiah said the shallow grave site was at the spot where he quit plowing. Daniel nodded to his foreman and said he'd meet him at the cabin early in the morning.

Prissy said, "He will be ready, Mista Smith. Isaiah can show you Toby's bones. Toby was our friend. Me and Isaiah have got to make this right. We have to get justice for Toby."

Daniel awoke early the next day. He kissed Mary on the cheek, told her he loved her, and she needn't get up. She mumbled back, "I love you, too."

Then, suppressing his urges, he went downstairs and brewed himself a cup of coffee. He liked it strong and black. Mary slept peacefully, even though a rooster boldly announced the new day. The house was quiet, still—the way Daniel liked it when he had something serious on his mind.

He cradled his steaming coffee, sipping it while he planned his day. First he would ride to Isaiah's cabin, and the two of them would be off to the field where Isaiah had discovered the bones. Then they'd inspect Toby's makeshift grave site. *If those are truly Toby's bones and if it's really where someone disposed of his body, I'll have to do what I can to help Isaiah and Prissy. It's the only right thing to do.*

Daniel saddled his big black horse Black Jack and set off for the cabin, as a spectacular red sunrise was breaking over the mountains. Man and horse navigated the same narrow, winding road to Isaiah's home, the route still muddy from yesterday's storm. And when the road stretched alongside the Watauga River on Daniel's left, he noticed an osprey perched on a huge mossy rock. In its claws was a good-sized trout that had made the mistake of getting too close to the river's surface.

Farther down the river, and closer to the bank, Daniel spotted a beaver. The flat-tailed furry animal was hard at work building a stick-filled dam in an inlet from the Watauga. Soon enough it would have the dam and a teepee-like shelter near the structure complete. And then, Daniel thought, the beaver would be safer from some of its predators—eagles, bears, coyotes and wolves. But there was always man. For the beaver's fur was prized by mountain folk. And beaver meat? An old trapper had recently bragged to Daniel that a beaver's "some of the best eatin' you ever tasted." But when that same hunter had brought him and Mary a skinned and gutted beaver, they graciously accepted it then gave it to one of the hired help. Mary swore she'd never eat a beaver. "I'm not chewin' the meat of somethin' that looks like a big rat!" Daniel, smiling to himself now, recalled her exclaiming.

He knew Isaiah would be up by now, and Prissy would have already made sure her man had eaten.

In fact, Isaiah had just finished a biscuit with jam along with a tin cup of coffee when Daniel arrived at the cabin. Prissy gave Isaiah a quick hug and bid her husband's boss a hearty "Good mornin', Mista Daniel!" Then she waved goodbye as the men headed toward the field, Daniel on Black Jack and Isaiah on Charger, a horse gifted to him by Daniel.

It was only a few minutes ride to the freshly plowed rows that ended where the bones lay.

Both men dismounted and walked to the bone site.

"This is where Toby was buried, Mista Daniel."

They were unmistakably human—the skull, the big bones of the legs and arms and the rib cage.

Isaiah showed Daniel the skeletal foot with the missing two toes. Then he reached in his pocket, and handed Daniel the leather cord with the tiger's tooth. "Here is the tiger's tooth I plowed up too, Mista Daniel."

Daniel said nothing. He wondered what poor Toby must have endured his last minutes on this earth before being sent to eternity by whoever it was that killed him. Had there been a fatal, brutal argument, as Isaiah contended, between Toby and his employer? And if so, where? Had Toby been murdered, not here, but elsewhere? If Edwards had killed him away from this field, had he done the despicable act and hauled Toby's body to this spot? Had Toby's coffinless body been crudely covered up with dirt without even a few consoling words being said?

At last Daniel spoke. "I will help you, Isaiah."

"Thank you, Mista Daniel. You are the only one Prissy and I could go to."

"I will do what I can, Isaiah. Now it's time we go to Sheriff Nave. We can't do nothin' else here. The sheriff'll know how to handle this."

"You think Sheriff Nave will get justice for Toby, Mista Daniel?"

"We'll hope so, Isaiah. We'll hope so."

CHAPTER 4

Sheriff Nave Investigates

"Like this new bridge, Isaiah?" asked Daniel as they crossed the Doe River into Elizabethton.

"Sho' do. I didn't like goin' through the water. 'Specially when the river was high." Isaiah eyed the ducks and a gaggle of quacking, head bobbing geese below.

The river, fed by ice-cold gurgling springs from the mountains, flowed through the edge of town, and Daniel was thankful he could cross it on the newly finished covered bridge. That way, he didn't have to ford the swift current. "I know what you mean, Isaiah. There's been more then one buggy washed down stream. They say this bridge is one hundred thirty-four feet long. Look at the size of those white pine beams. They had to haul 'em down outa the mountains usin' draft horses and mules. Times is changin', Isaiah. Look at this beautiful courthouse. There's no limit to what man can accomplish when he puts his mind to it."

"You right, Mista Daniel. Times is changin'," said Isaiah as the two men in Daniel's buggy passed the courthouse.

The Doe River flowed near the stately old structure where justice was meted out in Carter County and where at least some lawyers in coats, ties and derby hats did their best to represent those in trouble.

Isaiah could see a lot of changes taking place all around him. In this bridge, and the courthouse. In the new fine homes going up and even in the community's older houses—some of them getting a renewal, with workers busily hammering and sawing away, repainting or re-roofing. He also noticed the large brick buildings under construction in town.

But the biggest change of all was the narrow-gauged East Tennessee and Western North Carolina Railroad that snaked its way from the west. On its tracks, a little coal-fired steam locomotive known locally as "Tweetsie," named after its high-pitched whistle. It carried passengers and freight—mainly iron ore and lumber from the forests—through East Tennessee. Tweetsie's whistle echoed throughout the mountains, and it was a treat to ride on the train. The fare was just a few pennies. It sure beat bumping along over ruts and through the dust and mud in a horse-drawn buggy.

Along with all the changes, Elizabethton was a beehive of activity. Busy peddlers in wagons, tried to sell their wares. Children stared raptly at toys on display in glass store windows or rolled hoops down the street. A bearded fat man with a fiddle strummed an old mountain tune as an inquisitive crowd gathered. Women in long cotton dresses, with their men in bib overalls, congregated on front stoops catching up on the latest news and gossip. A couple of bedraggled old men sat on a bench whittling.

What a difference from sleepy little Fish Springs, Isaiah thought. Whereas you could spend an entire day in Fish Springs and hardly see a soul, or only a little activity, Elizabethton—only about 10 miles to the west—was a bustling county seat town of stores, businesses, livery stables, private residences, boarding houses and government offices. Even the smell of the little town filled the senses. The pungent aroma of meat being cooked over an open fire, the smell of sweaty, unbathed, buckskin-clad trappers returning from the mountains, the scent of horses tied up to hitching posts outside the Black Bear Saloon. All were unmistakable signs of a town on the move.

What Isaiah didn't see in Elizabethton was a change in the way colored people were treated by most white folks.

As in Fish Springs, coloreds here did the heavy lifting and dirty work and were at the beck and call of white employers, leading a life of drudgery and hard labor. The white man bought the big sacks of feed and food, and the colored man carried them out to their wagons. The white man got down from his horse; the colored man unsaddled and watered the animal and led it to the stable. True, Negroes in Elizabethton were no longer slaves, but whereas whites owned land or businesses, coloreds owned hardly anything. Instead, they worked menial jobs as maids, servants and porters.

In Isaiah's mind, It was as if the words of President Abraham Lincoln in his Emancipation Proclamation— that all persons held as slaves shall be then forever free—had never been uttered or had fallen on deaf ears. At the time Isaiah had been comforted by those words, spoken as the law of the land after tens of thousands of young men spilled their blood in the Civil War. But he also sensed that they were only words. Unbekownst to Isaiah was the fact that, with all the hatred and prejudice against colored folks it would be an uphill battle, spanning many lifetimes, for his kind to get anything even faintly resembling respect as human beings.

If all white people treated coloreds like the Smiths did, this'd be a better world, and we'd all get along just fine, Isaiah thought. *But there sho' is some bad folks in this hea' world.*

There had been that news of the recent lynching of a young Negro man in East Tennessee, accused of inappropriately touching a white woman. The accused, thrown into jail, had not been given a trial by judge or jury. Instead the unfortunate fellow, who repeatedly proclaimed his innocence, had been taken from the jail by a swarm of whites and dragged to the outskirts of town where he was strung him up, kicking and struggling, from the limb of a massive oak tree.

He was a Negro man, one of hundreds in the South, who had been hanged not for punishment but as a spectacle—a harsh warning that coloreds had best stay in their place, lest they be sent to meet their maker.

Isaiah tried not to think about such bad times as he and Daniel passed the Black Bear Saloon.

But there, leaning against the wall outside the local watering hole, were Sheriff Nave's two deputies—the same two who years ago had accosted him.

Isaiah tried to look inconspicuous, as one of the lawmen nodded to Daniel, and Daniel reluctantly nodded back.

"Why, lookie yonder. There goes that there damned uppity nigger that almost got us fired," Duke Rayburn said. The venom-spewing deputy spat out a stream of tobacco juice. Then he turned his nose up, snarling.

His sidekick deputy and one of his very few friends was Hank Beeler. "I still say he was up to no good," Hank growled. "And I ain't carin' if he does work fer Daniel Smith. Me'an that nigger's got a score ta settle."

"Ever see that young'un his nigga woman drags around?"

"Yeah, I seen him a while back," Duke said. He spat out another stream of tobacco juice. "He don't look like the other ones, does he? Do you reckon it's hers?"

"'Tis now. Least that's what the sheriff said."

"Where'd she get it?" he asked, not taking his beady eyes off Isaiah and Daniel.

Hank, a whiff of alcohol on his breath, said, "You 'member that drifter that caused all that ruckus at the Black Bear Saloon? The one we run outta town? I reckon that was his pa."

But Duke was skeptical. "Well, how'd those darkies get him?"

"The sheriff tol' me that drifter gave the boy to'em, 'cause he couldn't keep'm."

"Well, who in tarnation'd wanta boy like that anyways?"

Isaiah always tried to avoid Duke and Hank when he came to Elizabethton because he knew they hated colored people and him more than most.

He still had painful memories from years earlier. For doing nothing at all, the deputies had thrown him against a wall and threatened him with his life. They had accused him of taking advantage of Daniel Smith's precious eight-year-old Izzy. It just wasn't right that a colored man was walking a little white girl through town holding her hand on the way to get some candy at the Dry Goods store.

The deputies claimed he had to have been guilty of something, but Isaiah at the time had simply been following Daniel's instructions. He was responsible for the little girl's safety, so he held Izzy's hand protectively as the two of them crossed the street in Elizabethton. A child could get run over there by a buckboard or a galloping horse.

But the overzealous deputies hadn't seen it that way. At least not until Daniel Smith, an influential man in Carter County, came looking for Isaiah and little Izzy just in the nick of time. Daniel had come down heavy on the two deputies and on the sheriff himself. The sheriff apologized, chastising his men that times had changed and that they had to treat colored people the same as white people. And he had promised Daniel that such a misstep would never occur again.

Daniel took the promise with a grain of salt and moved on.

Isaiah was aware of the two deputies lurking nearby. He thought of how close he had come, years earlier, to being imprisoned or worse for doing nothing but following his boss's order to protect his little daughter. It was as if, in some ways, Isaiah's clash with the deputies had happened only yesterday. He remembered waking up that telltale day, as he did most mornings, to a spectacular Tennessee mountain sunrise. It was supposed to have been a good day. Snuggled next to him, her body warm and soft, was Prissy. They laughed. They hugged. They made love. They ate breakfast together, chatted—oblivious to what would happen a few hours later in Elizabethton when Isaiah accompanied Daniel and Izzy. *We just never know what this ol' world goin'a deal us,* Isaiah thought.

Daniel pulled the buggy to a stop in front of Sheriff Nave's office.

"You want me to wait hea, Mista Daniel?"

"No, Isaiah. You come with me."

Sheriff Billy Nave shook hands with Daniel and nodded to Isaiah. The no-nonsense, play-it-by-the-book sheriff was a beefy, barrel-chested man with a thick neck, a full head of gray hair and a handlebar mustache. He wore a leather vest with a tin star. In a holster attached to his belt was a gleaming silver pistol.

Nave had a reputation for not being particularly fond of colored people, but his position made him treat them with a degree of respect. For he prided himself in being a man of integrity and honesty, and if someone did in fact kill Toby Jackson without due cause and that could be proven, they would be brought to justice. That is, if he decided to investigate the bones.

Daniel told the Carter County lawman about Isaiah's discovery and what his helper thought had happened to Toby.

Nave listened with skepticism.

"Now we all know, Daniel, that a lotta Indians are buried around here and from time to time their bones get plowed up," Nave said. He looked at Isaiah who seemed to be hanging on the sheriff's every word.

"That's true, Sheriff, but I don't think that's the case here," Daniel countered. "There's other factors involved, Billy, and I'd like you to take a look at those remains if you don't mind."

Carter County's chief law enforcement officer looked back at Daniel, removing his hat, wiping the sweat from his brow with the back of his hand and nervously scratching his head. He cleared his throat and took a deep breath. He would have to take this request seriously. Daniel Smith was one of the largest landowners and taxpayers in the county. You didn't want to get on the bad side of such a prominent, admired man from Fish Springs. Daniel expected action.

"Maybe in the next—"

"Sheriff—"

"Okay, Daniel, I reckon I'll take a look. We can go now if you like. Not much going on here in town anyway. I'll follow you on my horse so you won't have to bring me back." He took a swig of cold sassafras tea and offered Daniel and Isaiah a glass as well, but they declined. "Damned! That drink's good," Nave said. "It's got kinda'of a wang to it. They say it's good for what ails ya."Then the sheriff took one last gulp, smacked his lips, and the three men left the office.

Nave mounted his big chestnut horse and rode to where his deputies were standing.

"Boys, I'm gonna' ride over ta Fish Springs and have a look-see at some bones Mr. Smith's man plowed up. If anyone needs me, tell'em I should be back in a few hours."

As the sheriff rode out of sight behind Daniel's buggy, Hank turned to Duke.

"Whose bones you reckon that nigger plowed up?"

"I don't rightly know. Probably Indian bones."

It didn't take long for Isaiah, Daniel and the sheriff to reach the burial site, and they paid hardly any attention to the cool wind that made the trees bend almost to the ground. The air got colder, more ominous, and the whispy thin clouds of what had started out as a sunny spring day had quickly grown darker. Spring in East Tennessee could be unpredictable, with the brightest, sunniest weather suddenly being replaced by a vicious, spring storm of rain and hail.

"We best move a little faster," Daniel said. The sheriff, too, was taking stock of the wind-bent trees, the cooling air and the overall disquieting forest. Not a bird chirped. Not a rabbit or squirrel or groundhog, usually plentiful, could be seen. It was as if those creatures sensed nature was about to ravage.

They reached the plowed up bones, and, after hearing everything one more time, and seeing first hand the severed toes as well as the tiger's tooth that Daniel gave him, the man with the tin star conceded that it did indeed look suspicious.

The sheriff chose his words carefully. "I don't rightly know what happened here, but I'll come back tomorrow and bring the county coroner, Doc Rueben Bowers with me. Isaiah, I'd like you to be here, too. We might have a few more questions for you."

"I will be hea' in the mornin'. Sheriff, do you think you can arrest Jake Edwards for killin' my friend Toby?"

"We're a ways from doing that, Isaiah. All the evidence is hearsay but I'll work on it. I promise you that."

"Sheriff, Isaiah told me that Elijah Wood was a foreman for Jake Edwards back when Toby disappeared," Daniel said. "He still lives here with his wife, in a little shack at the back of Jake's property. He might be able to shed a little light on what happened here."

"I'll talk to 'em, Daniel, and then I'll find out what Jake Edwards has to say. I'll get back to you."

Nave, satisfied he had seen enough and heard enough for the time being, bid them farewell, mounted his horse and galloped away.

"This sky lookin' bad, Mista Daniel." Isaiah waved a hand at the gathering clouds. "I worry about Toby out here in the weather until tomorrow."

"I see what you're saying." Daniel reached into the back of the buggy and pulled out an oiled leather lap robe. "Let's cover Toby up with this, and weight it down with these stones."

The job done, Daniel and Isaiah climbed in the buggy and headed to Isaiah's cabin.

"Thank you, Mista Daniel," Isaiah said. "I don't think the sheriff wouldda' done nothin' for me."

"Well, he sure as hell will now, Isaiah. I'll see to that."

"Thank ya, Mista Daniel. I can't give up gettin' justice for my friend."

With the sky still darkening and the Tennessee mountain air beginning to chill, Daniel and Isaiah pulled to a stop in front of Isaiah's cabin. Three excited boys scampered up to greet them. And Prissy came out on the porch holding wide-eyed Willie's hand. Daniel noticed the little tyke was bigger then when he last saw him.

"Hello, Mista Smith. Come set a spell on da poach. I just made some tea."

"Thank you, Prissy, but I best be gettin' on home. This sky's not lookin' the best and Mary'll be expectin' me. Willie looks like he has put a little meat on his bones."

"Yes suh. He eats like a little baby bird."

"You have a good evening, Mista Daniel, and tell Miss Mary I said hello."

"I will Prissy. I'll be in touch, Isaiah. Now you take good care of your family."

The man who would make things happen then pulled away as rain, along with a few pellets of hail, pounded the top of his buggy. As he pulled onto the road that ran along the swift flowing Watauga, he thought about that shallow grave and what Isaiah had told him about his old friend Toby and that scoundrel Jake Edwards.

Daniel Smith wondered how it would all play out.

CHAPTER 5

Little Willie

Later that afternoon, dark clouds parted and the sun began shining again. Steam rose above the rich mountain soil, forming cloud-like puffs that drifted to the treetops. The air was cool and refreshing. Crows cawed and hawks screeched in the distance.

Isaiah sat on the porch. He had brooded about Toby the whole day. How hard it was during these times for a colored man to get a fair shake from the law—even from the grave.

Toby, like Isaiah, had been a slave. And like Isaiah, Toby had experienced unspeakable sorrow and pain in his life. He had been wrenched from his family in West Africa, had somehow survived starvation and disease, when many of the captives didn't, during the six-week trans-Atlantic voyage to America in the horrible, stinking, dank hold of a slave ship. Had been bullwhipped, branded and chained like an animal, and sold on an auction block in Charleston, S.C. He had been bought by a wealthy white plantation owner in Virginia. He was sold later to the merciless Jake Edwards and his equally harsh wife Martha of Valley Forge, a few miles from Fish Springs.

Toby had most likely never even slept in his own bed. Had never worn a new shirt or new pair of pants. Instead, Jake Edwards' colored man had worn hand-me-downs or rejects from his white employer. He had spent his nights in a smelly, cold and drafty barn in the winter. His boss, Edwards, had been a man who seemed to gloat over the misery of others. A man who by the grace of God and Daniel Smith had lost Prissy, a housekeeper at the ruthless beck and call of the Edwardses, to Isaiah.

"Isaiah, I know you are thinkin' about Toby," Prissy said, putting her consoling hand on her husband's big broad shoulder. "Now we have to have faith in the Lord and the law. Mista Daniel said the sheriff will get justice for Toby, and that's what we have to believe."

Isaiah smiled at his wife, for she always knew what was on his mind. *I sho' hope she is right this time.*

"Willie! What you have, baby?!" Prissy asked the little boy who had seemed to show up out of nowhere.

The rambunctious youngster scampered onto the porch with a spring frog that his brother Jeb had caught for him. There was always an abundance of the critters after a shower.

"Look, Pa! Fog!" Willie yelled. He held up the slimy, green creature, then gently laid it on the porch floor. The frog croaked and leaped on Willie's pant leg, making him squeal with delight.

"Fog!" Willie repeated. "He gwine home now."

"Yes, I see, Willie," Isaiah said. As the little croaker leaped down to the floor and off the porch, Isaiah picked the boy up and sat him on his lap.

Willie looked at Isaiah, pointed his finger at him and said "Pa."

Isaiah at first said nothing. Then he grinned and responded, "Yes, Pa."

Willie broke out into a big smile exposing a mouth full of baby teeth as he looked at his new Pa. Prissy, standing just inside the door, saw the exchange, and choked back tears.

It was a far better exchange than Prissy had experienced a year earlier when Willie was thrust upon the two sharecroppers.

Prissy remembered it well. It had been a warm spring day, much like this one, and their three boys— Jebediah, Leroy and Benjamin—were searching for arrowheads in a recently plowed field. Leroy wanted to add to his collection, and Jeb and Ben were helping. The best time to find arrowheads was after a rain shower in a plowed field because the dirt had been washed off, and the gray, black or dark brown quartz had a slight sheen to it. The plowed river bottom was a good place to look because it had also been a good hunting ground for the Cherokee Indians who had populated the area for centuries.

Prissy recalled seeing her three sons walking side by side in different rows, with their eyes glued to the ground while Shadow ran along ahead of them.

"Wow!" the sharp-eyed Jeb, nine at the time, hollered, running ahead and scooping up the perfectly shaped arrowhead. "Lookie hea' at this one, Leroy!" Jeb handed the shiny black artifact to his younger brother.

"That's the bestest one I ever seen. You sho' you want me to have it, Jeb?"

"Sho' do, Leroy," Jeb said. "You the one that has a arrowhead c'lection. I want you ta have it."

"You a good brother, Jeb," said 11-year-old Ben, as he patted his younger brother on the back.

Isaiah and Prissy, relaxing on the porch within view of the boys, had taken it all in. There was no mistaking their sons had found something when Jeb hollered with excitement.

"They found another one," Isaiah said.

"They are good at findin' them arrowheads," Prissy noted. She put down her knitting for a few moments, stood up and stretched and shaded her eyes so she could see better.

"I wish they could find dug up taters as good as they find them arrowheads," said Isaiah, laughing with Prissy.

"They find what they want to," Prissy said. She giggled harder, and the happy couple reminded each other how blessed they were that God had given them their sons.

They noticed the boys now seemed even more excited and eager to find more Indian artifacts.

"I bet there is a lot more outten' this field!" Jeb had shouted to his brothers. "We jest got ta find'em."

As Isaiah and Prissy were watching the boys they saw a large, bearded man coming over the hill, approaching the boys on horseback. Tied behind the man's mount, a big palomino, was a mule loaded down with beaver pelts. Shadow, his keen eyes, nose and long droopy ears always alert to strangers, ran toward the intruder. He growled. He barked. The fur on his back stood up. But he stopped and returned when Ben called him back.

The rider, who wore a duster and a western style hat, stopped and spoke with the boys. After a few minutes, Ben pointed him toward the cabin. The man, tilting his hat as if to oblige Ben, started up the incline toward the watchful parents.

"I wonder who that is," said Isaiah, a bit apprehensive.

"He's a trapper, but why he be comin' here?" Prissy wondered aloud to her husband.

The mystery visitor had a jug tied to the saddle on one side and a rifle in a scabbard on the other. Isaiah and Prissy noticed that nestled in front of him on the saddle was a small child. The infant was wrapped in a blanket and a length of rope bound the two together. The little one flapped its arms and squealed as the scruffy looking trapper pulled to a stop near the porch.

"Evenin', folks."

"Evenin'," Isaiah and Prissy replied in unison.

"I ain't meanin' ta bother ya'll on this bright spring day, but I was just talkin' to your boys, and they're right smart younguns. I can tell ya'll done a good jobba raisin'em."

Isaiah and Prissy breathed easier, because the stranger, far as they could tell, was just passing through and meant them no harm.

"Thank you, suh. We did our best," Isaiah said.

The bearded stranger smiled after paying them the compliment.

Then his tone and demeanor changed—from being a mere passerby who accidentally happened upon Isaiah and Prissy's family to someone who had serious business.

"I ain't rightly knowin' how ta say this, but I've been travelin' these hills fer weeks now, lookin' fer' a family such as yourn. And I'm plum tired and hurtin' and needin' your help."

Isaiah said, "I don't understand, suh."

The trapper said nothing for a few seconds. Then he put his hand on his jug, but decided not to take a drink. Instead, he spoke. "It ain't a purty story. Me and my woman and this here child was run outta the town where we lived, by so called God-fearin' Christians. Seemed them same Christians didn't take kind-lee' to a white man and colored woman havin' a baby.

"And they hated even more when we took our little'un with us to thar' church—even though his skin's purt-near white as mine."

The grizzled trapper untied the rope wrapped around the jostling child and gently lifted him from the blanket.

Then holding up the beautiful, caramel-colored boy, he said, "Ya' both can see he's almost white, but he ain't. 'Cause all them Christians claimed that if you has even one droppa' colored blood, then you ain't white. And his mother, well she was colored.

"And it made no diffrence at thar church that I was white 'cause they said she worn't; she was a nigger, and our child was a half-breed, and they wasn't allowin' no nigger with a half-breed child ta worship with'em."

Isaiah and Prissy took a closer look at the child. He had blue eyes, curly hair and skin even lighter brown than Prissy's.

He is a beautiful child of God, Prissy thought.

The trapper continued his sad tale about how he and his humiliated common law wife had been pressured to leave their little mountain community in North Carolina— because folks there, proud to call themselves Christians, couldn't accept them or their baby.

"Them so-called Christians got ta hatin' us sa bad we wasn't even able ta buy a sacka' flour from the store. Got downright mean an' ornery ta us. Wouldn't have nothin' ta do with us. All on account of the color of my woman's skin.

"And then this past winter, the woman I loved with all my heart got sick and died. God bless her soul. Not sure why, but it made it worse, the way all them Christians shamed her. She was a good woman and she and me made this here boy. She was a good mother to this boy. Now all he's got is a useless drunkin' father who cain't care fer him."

The trapper's words came harder now and with more emotion. He untied the jug and tilted it up, taking a big swig. "I've tried. God knows I've tried, but I cain't raise this boy. Cain't give'em a good life. And now I've come ta love this jug as much as I love my own flesh an' blood. And that ain't right. I'm not fit no more ta be a father.

"So I'm goin' ta leave him with you."

Isaiah and Prissy looked at each other incredulously, then back at the stranger with the child in his arms.

There was dead silence, broken only by the screaming of a hawk high above.

Isaiah mumbled nervously. "Suh, I sorry about your woman, but we cannot take this child. Besides, you need to find a white—"

"This child is a mulatto!" the trapper adamantly interrupted. His mother was colored. He will do better with a colored family. Your family!"

"Suh, I am sorry but—"

"You will take this child, so help me God, or I'll leave him on the side of the road!"

"We'll take him!" Prissy, clutching her husband's arm, interjected loudly.

"What is this child's name?" she asked.

"His name is William Frances McFarland, and he will be two years old on December first."

Isaiah shook his head, but he knew that Prissy had made up her mind, and nothing was going to change that. She was worried about the little boy, and she would see to it that he was cared for regardless of whatever hardship he brought with him. It had been the same way, Isaiah recalled, with Daniel Smith's children. Prissy had been the Smith family's housekeeper, but she had also come to love Izzie and the other children as she loved her own flesh and blood now. Isaiah knew that was it. What was done was done, regardless of the fact that the little boy, who could almost pass for white, had been born between two worlds, and neither one would likely ever accept him. His life would be a struggle at best.

"What should we tell this boy about his mother and father when he gets old enough ta understand?" Isaiah asked.

"Tell him his mother, Willa Sue McFarland, is in heaven and his father, Barnard McFarland, couldn't take care of him."

The devastated trapper's voice broke and he began crying. "And tell him I loved him very much, as did his mother, but I that knowed he'd have a better life with you folks."

Then the defeated man took another swig of whisky and tied the jug back to the saddle. He handed little Willie down to Prissy who took the whimpering child and cradled him in her arms.

Barnard McFarland took one long last, forlorn look at his now screaming son, who was reaching back, and shot a farewell glance at the new parents. He wiped the tears from his cheeks, slapped his horse on the rump and galloped away—figuring never again, this side of eternity, that he'd lay eyes on his son.

"Lordy, Lordy, what are we going do with this little boy, Prissy?"

"We'll keep this child, Isaiah. We have no choice. That's what we have ta do."

CHAPTER 6

The Coroner's Assessment

Isaiah awoke the next morning when Killer the Rooster crowed at the break of dawn. The children had named him Killer because he was such a fierce fighter. Killer had torn apart two other roosters on the farm in a competition for the job of servicing the twenty or so hens that provided eggs and meat for the family.

There was no rush for Isaiah to get to the site where his friend had been buried because Sheriff Nave and the coroner would be coming from Elizabethton and not arrive until late morning. So, wiping the sleep from his eyes, he rolled over and kissed Prissy on the cheek and whispered tenderly that he loved her. When she roused only slightly, he kissed her again, got out of bed and went to the dry sink where he poured water into the washbowl from the pitcher and washed his face.

Prissy by this time would have been in the kitchen making coffee.

But not this morning.

She was still in the bed. Naked and with her shining curls resting temptingly on her bosom, she had flipped the sheet back offering herself to him.

Her big strong man quietly closed the bedroom door and propped a chair against it—thinking, like most men, that this could last a while, prompting a giggle from Prissy.

Isaiah couldn't take his eyes off her. She was beautiful, looking much like she did—with her youthful, shapely figure—the day they married. The only clue that she was in her late thirties was a few wrinkles around her eyes. In fact, she looked so young that on one occasion while in Elizabethton with Benjamin, someone asked if she was his sister.

His heart now racing and his manhood thoroughly alive, Isaiah lay down next to Prissy and kissed her. Their lips and tongues became one. Their eager bodies folded into each other. In the minutes that followed Isaiah and his wife couldn't get enough of each other. Later they stayed wrapped drowsily and happily in each other's arms.

Isaiah had become, in those precious sensuous minutes, a much younger man again. How blessed he felt to have such a wonderful, passionate lover who was also his best friend.

When they first married, the only thing Isaiah knew about making love was what he had heard from his friends. But he had never forgotten what Reverend Leftwich, who had performed their wedding, told him. *Sex between a man and his wife is truly a gift from God and will grow and get better as does your love for one another. That's the way the Lord means it to be, Brother Isaiah.*

Isaiah thought now, as he cuddled with Prissy, that the reverend had never been more right about anything in his life.

"I'm gon'a take Ben with me today, Prissy."

"Why, Isaiah? That boy is only thirteen. He don't need ta see them bones. They might give him nightmares."

"He's a young man, Prissy, and I need his help. If they let me, I want ta put all Toby's bones in a box so he can be buried proper-like."

While Prissy prepared a big breakfast, Willie played on the kitchen floor with some little blocks of wood that Isaiah had cut out for Ben when he was a toddler. Isaiah and Ben went to the barn and found enough lumber to construct a box that would serve as Toby's casket. As they worked on the box, twelve-year-old Jeb pulled down hay from the loft for Bessie to munch on while he milked her, and ten-year-old Leroy fed the chickens.

Ben left his father to finish the box when his mom hollered out the back door that she needed a pail of water. He would go to the spring box and scoop out a pail of the cold spring water and take it to his mom. That was normally his job anyway, because he was the oldest and strongest of the three boys.

"Thank you, Ben. Tell your father and brothers that their breakfast is ready as soon as they finish their jobs."

A few minutes later, the man of the house came in with all three boys.

"Did Bessie give you much today, Jeb?" Prissy was curious about the milk because some days the cow seemed to give plentifully. On others, however, the milk that Prissy and Isaiah needed to keep their family strong and healthy was scarce. You never knew how much the cow would yield.

"I put about a full pail in the springhouse, Ma," said Jeb, eying the stack of biscuits and smacking his lips.

Isaiah said, "That ol' cow did good taday." He took his seat at the big table in the kitchen.

That satisfied Prissy, because now she knew that little Willie would have plenty of milk to last him through the day. She smiled when she considered how much Willie loved his milk.

"That Willie drinks more milk than all three you boys together. I'm glad I didn't have ta nurse him. He'd'a dried me up."

Isaiah and the boys looked at each other and no one spoke. They tried not to laugh but it was no use. Even Willie, sitting in Prissy's lap, joined in with the merriment. The little guy never wanted to be different or be left out, so if his brothers and parents were having a good time, he would, too.

"You embarrass these boys, Prissy."

"Well, they will just have ta get over it, Isaiah. It's part'a life."

Jeb reached for a biscuit, but Prissy grabbed his hand before he got it.

"Are we forgettin' something, Jebediah?"

"Sorry, Ma," he said meekly, staring apologetically at his mother.

Then they all bowed their heads, held hands and closed their eyes. Isaiah said a blessing. "This food is a blessin' to our family, Lord. It was cooked by Prissy but we know it really comes from your son, Jesus, who came from a little faraway place they called Nazreth. He made the sick better, and he fed the hungry. And he was only a carpenter, but he done good all his life, and they killed'em and nailed'im to a cross—"

Prissy gently kicked her fervent husband's foot with hers and whispered, "That is enough right now, Isaiah. We have to eat."

"Amen," he obediently ended.

The hearty eaters enjoyed a breakfast of eggs, crispy bacon

and crusty biscuits with rabbit gravy. Prissy had, the previous day, skinned and gutted a rabbit that a neighbor had given them. Then she had heated lard in a frying pan, dipped the rabbit in batter and fried it. After the meat was finished and removed from the pan, Prissy added milk, flour and a pinch of salt to the left-over juices. Then she stirred the concoction until it thickened in the pan, and there was her rabbit gravy.

"Ain't nothin' like ma's rabbit gravy!" Ben said.

Little Willie, not to be outdone, added, "Raby graby good!"

On the side were homemade blackberry jam and apple butter, all washed down with cold, delicious milk from the springhouse.

After a trip to the outhouse, Isaiah and Ben headed back to the barn to put the final touches on the box that would hold Toby's bones. Then they loaded the box into the work wagon. It was too early to leave for the site so Isaiah decided they could use the time to shuck some corn.

He and his oldest son went to the corncrib and filled several burlap sacks with the corn that had been picked and stored in the crib to dry the previous summer. They carried the sacks to a spot in the barn to work and sat down on two stools on opposite sides of a small tub.

As always, Shadow lay with his head on Ben's feet. The coonhound, appropriately named by Isaiah, had completely bonded with Benjaman when the boy was just five years old.

They stripped the shucks. Then, holding the corn over the tub, stripped kernels from the cob. The dried kernels would be put in sacks and taken to the mill in Butler, a little community just a few miles from the heart of Fish Springs. There it would be ground into cornmeal, and the shucks and stripped cobs would be fed to hogs. Every morsel was used. Nothing went to waste.

"Pa, you think the sheriff will find out what happen to your friend?"

"I sure hope so, Ben. We have Mista Daniel Smith helpin' us too, and if he cain't get somethin' done, nobody can." Isaiah considered what his bright-eyed, curious son had wondered about. *He is thinkin' a white man like the sheriff ain't goin to help us. But Prissy says all men have a good side an' a bad side, an' tha sheriff is mostly good. An' Mista Daniel says because I own land an' pay tax, tha sheriff is workin' fer me.*

"How long you knowed Mista Smith, Pa?"

"Known, Ben," Isaiah corrected. "I have known Mista Smith pert near ma' whole life. I was only about four years older than you when Mista Smith bought me from Jacob Tibbs, a mean ole' plantation owner in Virginia. He sold me so he could pay off a gamblin' debt.

"I was Mista Smith's slave about fifteen years. Then when he freed me I stayed here and went ta work for him." Isaiah knew the questions would keep coming because the lad only seemed to want more information as he got older. *But that's not a bad thing. He wants ta know more 'bout me an' Prissy ever' day.*

"Pa, I know you say Mista Smith be a good man, but how can you say that 'bout a man who owned you, like you own a dog or a mule an' you had ta do what he said? And if you didn't, he could whoop you. That just don't seem right, Pa."

"It wasn't right, Ben, and yeah, he could do that but he wouldn't. Mista Smith tol' me, even when I was his slave, that he come ta know it was wrong ta own another person. I think that's why he is so good ta us now. The good Lord taught us in the Bible that we must love ever body. We has ta have forgiveness in our heart. I made my peace with Mista Smith a long time ago, Ben."

"I wish all white folks treated us like the Smiths, Pa."

"I pray someday they will. I know it's hard ta love ever'body, Ben. But we have ta try. We have ta be kind and help others. That's what the Lord wants us ta do."

But the more he thought about it, the more Isaiah had trouble believing his own words to his son. *I'm glad Ben ain't askin' me if we have ta love that devil that murdered my friend Toby. 'Cause I can't feel one bit'a love for Jake Edwards.*

Isaiah and Ben hitched up Sue to the creaky old wagon, loaded the crafted box and headed out to Toby's burial site—a lonely piece of plowed fertile ground surrounded by a thick hardwood forest.

Later, as father and son stood at the site, Ben had a thousand questions about Toby and what had happened to him. Isaiah shared with him a few of the known facts but none of his speculation. Because he had faith that the ugly truth would come out;

it was just a matter of time. Meanwhile, he figured there was no need in telling Ben too much.

The unmistakable sound of a trotting horse on the road and Shadow's bark announced the arrival of visitors. And sure enough, when Isaiah looked over his left shoulder he noticed a buggy pulling off the road and into the field. Sheriff Billy Nave held the reins; beside him was Carter County Coroner Dr. Samuel Bowers, and in the back, staring back at Isaiah was his worst nightmare, Deputy Duke.

"Oh Lawd," Isaiah, grimacing, muttered.

"What's the matter, Pa?"

"Nothin', son."

Ben knew it had to be bad, because his father was clearly on edge.

Nave pulled the buggy to a stop and climbed down. He greeted Isaiah without shaking his hand and introduced Doc Bowers, who did not offer his hand, but nodded to Isaiah. It was a token, at best, but Isaiah thought the coroner had at least tried to be cordial.

"Nice to meet you, Isaiah."

"Is this your boy?" asked Sheriff Nave, smiling at Isaiah's son.

Ben looked back at Nave and returned the gesture.

"Yes suh. This is my boy Benjamin. He my oldest."

The sheriff tipped his hat slightly and gave Ben another smile.

"Isaiah, I think you know my deputy, Duke."

"Yeah, he knows me right good," said Duke, extending his right hand to Isaiah, just for spite.

The big colored man reluctantly shook hands—as if he were touching a snake. The bad blood between the two of them still simmered.

"Me an' Isaiah go way back. We had a little misunderstandin' a long time ago, but we got past it. Right, Isaiah?" The muscular, Duke had his back to Nave and a smirk on his face.

The sheriff was skeptical because he had caught Duke in lies before, but the wayward deputy had also come through in a pinch from time to time, and Nave didn't want to lose him. There had been occasions at the Black Bear Saloon where roughnecks had gotten angry over losing at poker or, their lustful ways getting the best of them, had fought for the affections of one of the bar gals. The place, a favorite watering hole in Elizabethton, would have been busted up, and folks would have gotten hurt or worse, had it not been for Duke arriving just in the nick of time and handcuffing the troublemakers. He never, it seemed to Sheriff Nave, ventured far from the saloon. Because Duke himself had a taste for good whiskey and wild women pandering to the passions of hungry men.

"Now let's get this investigation started," Nave snapped.

"Benjamin there looks like a strong buck. He can help us dig up the rest of them Indian bones," Duke offered.

Sheriff Nave looked sternly at his deputy.

"We'll make that determination, Duke. Now you just get on with the diggin'."

Later Doc Bowers and Nave studied the bones unearthed by Duke, Isaiah and Ben, and laid out on the ground by the plowed trench. By now the sun was high in the sky and the air was hardly stirring. Pesky gnats and deer flies aggravated the men. Beads of sweat formed on their foreheads and soaked their shirts.

"Take a break, fellows," Nave commanded. "That working in the dirt's a killer. You got water, Isaiah?" The sheriff held up a jug.

"Yes suh. We have some in our wagon," said Isaiah, heading toward the wagon with Ben and out of hearing range from the others.

Duke walked toward the edge of the field and peed.

The coroner had had dealings with Duke in earlier investigations and had grown to dislike him for his ruggedness and brashness. Duke, in one instance, choked a man to death in a headlock at the Black Bear Saloon.

"That deputy of yours seems to have a chip on his shoulder, Billy. Ain't ya' got nobody else better'n him to help you?"

"I know, Doc. I keep askin' myself why I keep puttin' up with his nonsense, but it takes a tough man to handle some of the scallywags we have to deal with. And if nothin' else he's tough as nails."

Nave went down on one of his knees and took a long swig of water. "I know we're not quite through digging yet, Doc, but looking at these bones laid out here, have you come to any conclusion at all?"

The venerable coroner pushed his derby slightly back on his head, wiped the sweat from his forehead with a handkerchief, and put it in his back pocket. He rubbed his chin with his right hand and turned to Nave, and without even a hint of a smile, responded, "Only one, Billy."

"Yeah?"

"This man's dead."

Nave had a hard time concealing his laughing from Isaiah and Ben, but with his hand and kerchief he managed.

Later, the sheriff, holding the skull, scraped off the dirt caked on back and noticed a finger-size hole.

"Looks like this man was shot in the backa' the head."

Isaiah wanted to shout out in anger at Jake Edwards but he restrained himself. Then he tried to imagine what Toby's last minutes had been like. Had he been shot here, at this desolate spot in a remote field in Fish Springs, or had his murderer done it elsewhere and hauled his body here? Isaiah could picture Jake Edwards grinning as he buried Toby.

"Could it a'been a no-good thievin' Indian tryin' to outrun a white man? I mean these damn bones look just like them other Indian bones we dug up. Hell, these hills is plum full'a ol' Indian bones."

If looks could kill, the angry one that Nave gave his brazen deputy would have done him in.

"Dammit, Duke! Just shut the hell up and let Doc Bowers do his investigation."

Isaiah felt a bit of satisfaction with Nave's outrage.

After Doc felt that all of the remains had been unearthed, it was about time to render his determination. But first he wanted to study the bones more closely and he had hoped to find one more clue.

"Come here, Ben. I have a little job for you. Now don't be afraid. Ain't nothin' here gonna' hurt you. Take this skull and work the dirt loose inside with this brass rod and shake it out on this flat board—like this." Bowers ran the small rod through the eye sockets and mouth and shook the loose dirt out on a thin board about a foot square. Then he held out the skull for Ben to take.

Ben hesitated and looked at his dad.

"It's okay, Ben. You can do that."

Ben mustered the courage, took the skull, sat down on the ground and started working the dirt loose inside with the small pointed tool as Shadow obediently sat near and watched.

A few minutes later, a grinning Duke snuck up behind the boy and shouted "BOO!"

The scare tactic startled Ben to no end. He screamed, his eyeballs bulged and he dropped the skull.

"Duke!" Nave shouted in anger. "Leave that boy alone, and take these shovels down to the river and wash 'em off! I need you to get your ass outta here—now dammit!"

Duke picked up the shovels and headed toward the Watauga, about 100 yards away. *I pert near scairt that nigger boy ta death,* he gloated as he walked away.

As Ben poked the rod in all the orifices of the head, Doc studied the other bones with a magnifying glass, trying to determine about how old they were.

"These bones is problee' ten to fifteen years old," Bowers surmised.

"I think these bones be thirteen years old, suh," said Isaiah, "cause my friend Toby was on his way ta my house to see my newborn son Ben, this boy hea, who is thirteen now. He tole' me when I saw him at the feed sto, he was gon'a leave soon as he had enough money ta pay his bill off at Mista Edwards' sto. He said he would have enough in a week. He told me he'd come ta see me before he left for Alabama but this is as close as he got."

Doc Bowers considered all this for a few seconds.

"Isaiah's story does make sense, Billy. And this man had two toes sawed off." The coroner, attentive to the smallest detail, had examined the foot bones with a magnifying glass and could see saw blade marks.

"Then there's the tiger's tooth, and how many Indians have you seen wearin' heavy boots like that? This was no Indian."

Doc Bowers stood up, took the handkerchief from his back pocket and started wiping the dry dirt from his hands. "Putting all this together leads me to believe this could very well be Isaiah's friend."

About that time, as Ben shook more loose dirt from the skull, out fell a lead slug.

"Look! What's this?" asked Ben.

Nave bent down and picked up the slug and studied it. He turned it over and over in the palm of his hand.

"It ain't a musket ball. Looks like it might be a slug from a 30-caliber rifle."

"A lot'a things point to foul play here, Billy. Looks like this man was trying to run away, or he was executed. I think you need to start an investigation into what happened here."

Sheriff Nave said he agreed, and he assured Isaiah, who felt better now, that he'd do his best to find out what happened to his good friend Toby.

"Thank you, Sheriff. Thank you, too, Doc," Isaiah said. He hugged his son, and patted him on the back.

"If you want," said the coroner, placing his instruments back into his black bag, "you can take these bones and give your friend a proper burial."

"Yes suh. I like ta do that. Me an' my boy hea' made a box ta put Toby's bones in."

As Isaiah watched the three men leave in the buggy, Duke, who was in the back and who had a scowl on his face, held his hand in the shape of a gun and pointed his trigger finger at the big Negro and his son.

Ben, frightened, looked up at his father.

Isaiah pulled his scared boy close to him. "It's okay, son."

CHAPTER 7

Horrific Voyage

Isaiah and Prissy sat on their porch with a cup of coffee right after sunup. No matter how hot the days, the early morning breeze coming off the Watauga River was always cool and refreshing. Isaiah had finally gotten a good night's sleep now that he knew his friend's murder would be investigated. He and Prissy vowed to help with that investigation. Isaiah also told Prissy about Deputy Duke's intimidation tactics and told her to be careful if she ever encountered Duke, who Isaiah believed was conniving and evil.

"I best go wake up Ben so we can get on the road. We need ta get those bones to the church and I'm gonna talk to Reverend Leftwich about havin' a little service next Sunday. Maybe he can say a few words when we bury Toby's bones in the cemetery behind the church."

"I'm sure he will do that, Isaiah. You know, Toby went to our church whenever Jake Edwards let'em."

Later, as Isaiah and Ben traveled along the road to Elizabethton, the box of Toby's bones and Shadow in the back of the work wagon, they talked about the beauty of the river, how the layer of morning fog lifted off the cold water and drifted to the mountain tops.

"Pa, where you lived as a boy in Africa, was it like this hea in Fish Springs?"

"A lot like this, Ben. But it was summer all the time. Very hot, never cool like this even in the mornin'."

"What was it like, Pa, to be taken from your momma and papa?"

At first, Isaiah did not respond to the question. He knew Ben was old enough to hear the painful story, but it would bring back feelings of suffering and misery. But Isaiah also figured that Ben needed to know about his heritage. As bad as it would hurt to tell the story, it needed to be told.

"I spose you are old enough ta hear this story, Ben."

Ben waited for his father to start but Isaiah just looked ahead down the road and his eyes got watery.

"Pa, if it hurts too much, you don't have ta tell me."

"No, it's okay. You need ta hear it."

"I remember you tol' me you were about my age when you got took but that's about all I know."

"Yes, I was aroun' your age," said Isaiah, gaining his composure. He went on to tell a softened version of the horrific story to his eldest son.

It came back to Isaiah slowly but surely. Isaiah told Ben he was about fourteen years old, a happy, rambunctious, free person roaming the jungles and beaches of his home.

Isaiah's gauzy memory of those years continued to return— more clear as he kept talking. He told his oldest son that he had been named Nwamaka (precious child) by his adoring parents. Even now, all these years later, Isaiah could still see himself wearing his loin cloth and with a small piece of ivory through his nose, a reward from his elders for his bravery in killing a huge white snake. Isaiah told Ben that he hunted and fished to his heart's content, and, even at a young age, helped provide meat for his family. And, of course, the pleasant memory now bringing a smile to his face, there had been all those pretty young girls in his village. He'd had a tough time taking his eyes off them, and they, him. Because the muscular, long-legged Nwamaka had been viewed as a catch by many a girl. To them, he was handsome, well mannered and surely verile—an ideal future husband. Even as a teenager, he had a lean, hardened physique.

"I sho did like the girls back then an' they like me," Isaiah confessed. "They be on my mind a lot."

Ben smiled and urged his dad to tell him more.

Isaiah grinned and thought about some of those good early years in his lush, beautiful homeland—about how with a spear and bow and pointed arrows, he hunted for wild pigs and other game. Once he and some friends had brought down an antelope that the entire tribe shared. He fished and often brought home a tasty catch. He had been considered a brave hunter because he had slain that dreaded giant white snake with his spear when he was thirteen.

"I kill' that big ol' snake and chop' his head off an' skinned'im an' brought tha meat home for my papa an' momma an' my little sister," Isaiah recalled proudly.

Ben's eyes got wider when he heard that he might have an aunt on a faraway continent.

"You ain't never' told me, Pa, 'bout you havin' a sister. What was she like?"

Isaiah didn't rightly know where to begin in describing his sister. For one thing, he hadn't laid eyes on her in more than twenty-five years. For another, he recollected her only as she was the last day he saw her, a giggling, playful little girl full of love.

"She jump inta my arms when I got home from huntin'. She loved her big brother ..." Isaiah's voice faded and became shakier as he tried to collect himself. He hadn't even thought about his little sister in forever, let alone tried to imagine what she was, where she was or how she was today.

"I guess tha Lord seen fit ta make us go our different paths, son. I just pray she is alive an' well."

Those glorious days with his family and friends in Africa now seemed like an eternity ago. But curiously, too, for Isaiah it was as if they were only yesterday.

He wondered, looking now at his son, why he hadn't thought more about his early years in Africa. Maybe, he thought, it had been for the best—to put the happy past *and* the painful past behind him. To focus only on the present and future. To keep the wounds hidden.

"So how did tha white men from the slave ship catch you, Pa? How did they find you an' take you from your home?"

Isaiah knew this part of his sordid past all too well. One day, he explained, it had all come to an end. His freedom, his family, his future as an African warrior and possibly a tribal leader taken away. Everything good in life gone. All because as a trusting, innocent lad he had ventured too close to the bearded white strangers with their irresistible bounty of brightly colored beads and necklaces, bells and other trinkets.

The strangers had beckoned him to come closer to them on the beach. To come and receive gifts from far across the sea. "Not always good ta trust a stranger, Ben," Isaiah cautioned.

Nwamaka, like so many other unsuspecting, naïve Africans, had taken the bait. He had no idea that the smirking shipmates who enticed him thought of him as nothing but flesh to buy and sell and work in the hot cotton fields of America.

And so, as he squatted unknowingly there on the beach draping their beaded necklaces around his neck, a net, seemingly from nowhere, was thrust upon him. The white slavers laughed as Nwamaka thrashed about and pleaded to be let go.

When Ben asked his father if he tried to escape, he said there was no way he could get himself free from the net.

Isaiah said he tried and tried but that net was too strong. The white men, some half drunken, raucously laughed and were delighted with themselves for capturing such a prized prey. He told how they dragged him into a small boat which they paddled to their ship, *Wanderer*.

Here the story took an even sadder twist. For, according to Isaiah, his friends and some of his family had heard about the terrible plight and rushed to the beach. They had cried, waved their arms, frantically jumped up and down imploring the whites to return their captive.

But the slavers just kept laughing and taunting them.

"Please return our son!" his mother yelled in her native African tongue.

But the white slavers ignored her cries.

A few of the more stalwart shouters manned a canoe and rowed desperately toward *Wanderer*. They had spears and long knives and arrows, but even if they'd caught up with the ship before it departed, it would have been useless—their crude weapons no match for the muskets.

Isaiah would never forget what happened next. The slavers had held him down and stripped him of his loin cloth while one white man, a hook replacing his missing left hand, branded him on his back with a hot iron. He screamed and writhed in pain, clawing the ship's deck until his fingers were bloody. Then he lost consciousness.

And when he came to, sometime later, he had been manacled and chained in the ship's hold.

"I ask' Ma about that place on your back. She said some day you would tell me. That hurt really bad, didn't it, Pa?"

He nodded to his son. Isaiah continued reciting what had happened to him all those years ago, skipping some of the more brutal or grisly parts.

He recalled how about 500 of them had been captured in West Africa by white slavers. The next thing they knew, they were en route, riding the choppy white-capped waves, to America. There they had sat or lain crammed in the filth of their own excrement and urine, the pungent smell of death filling their senses.

Upwards of one quarter of them would not survive the six-week trans-Atlantic voyage, Isaiah told his son. "They jest died in the dark belly'a that slave ship."

"What from?" Ben, hanging on every word, asked.

"From all kinds'a sicknesses, son." Isaiah did not tell Ben about how some of his fellow African captives became so sick they choked on their own vomit. Or how some, losing all hope, refused to eat or drink and commited suicide. Those and similar parts of the sad tale he kept to himself.

Isaiah recalled how he had crouched helplessly in chains below the deck of the slave schooner *Wanderer*—bound for Jekyll Island, Georgia. He winced as the nightmare came back to him. But again, his son urged him to keep talking.

"It not be a pretty story, Ben. You sure you want ta hear the rest of it?"

Ben nodded eagerly that he did.

Isaiah spoke of how he, like his fellow captives, had been chained in the sunless, stinking bowels of the slave ship. "Members of *Wanderer*'s crew fed us bits of rice, grains of corn, and sometimes a yam or a hard biscuit. But a lot'a times the biscuit had worms in it. When you be that hungry, you will eat most anythin'."

"So, Papa, did you get any water to drink down there in that dark place?"

They gave us 'bout two dippers of water a day. But I remember bein' thirsty all the time," Isaiah replied. All these years later, he could still picture a *Wanderer* crewmate, bearded and snarling, climbing down below the grated hatchway with a bucket of water and a ladle.

What he didn't tell Ben was how the slaves, their throats burning and lips parched, pleaded for the water. How sometimes they vomited the cool liquid up because they drank too quickly. How the knife-brandishing, slovenly crewmate sometimes cruelly teased them, grinning and smacking his lips when he poured a ladle of water over his own head.

Isaiah could still hear that crewmate's harsh words. "Watch this ya' black stinkin' heathens!" he had shouted, dousing himself with what the Africans begged for. The *Wanderer* crewman got perverse pleasure from depriving the poor suffering souls in chains.

Lying down there in the ship's hold in chains—naked, fighting hunger and thirst and feeling like you couldn't breathe, totally bereft of any kind of hope for something better—Nwamaka had almost given up.

He had never witnessed such wickedness. Only days before he had been proud, free, roaming the rain forests and rivers and fertile valleys of his Ibo homeland in West Africa.

"Pa, did they keep you in that dark hold tha whole time?"

"Ever' few days they bring us up on da deck in chains. They throw buckets of ocean water on us and make us dance. They called it 'exercisin'."

I don't understand, Pa. Why did they do that."

"You have to understand, son. We was like a cow or a horse ta them. They couldn' sell us, if we didn' look healthy. That why they gave us jus' enough food an' water an' make us exercise. 'Cause if we look sick we worn't worth as much money. And if we died they lost a lot'a money."

And in the pitch darkness of the hold, except for a few errant rays of sunlight that shone through cracks in the deck of the *Wanderer*, he heard terrifying stories that the whites were cannibals and would surely eat them.

"That's what the giant kettles are for," one manacled Negro

had grunted in his native tongue. "They are for cooking us. The whites will gut us, boil us in the big pots, separate our flesh from our bones and eat us. These are godless, savage people."

Nwamaka remembered the two huge black kettles he had seen on deck, and it all seemed to make sense.

Ben wanted to hear every sordid detail of the story, but Isaiah again declined, telling him only just enough—and no more—to know where his papa had come from and how he had gotten to America and ultimately to Fish Springs, Tennessee. Isaiah thought that Ben wouldn't have understood, even if he'd been told, how close his papa had come to dying.

For at more than one juncture in his quest for survival, Nwamaka had prayed for help from the spirits of his ancestors. He had prayed they would help keep him alive until his time came to pass into a new life in the spirit world. Wished, if he entered that world, to come back as an eagle, soaring freely and majestically over his homeland in West Africa.

"You are a fool!" one barely alive man chained near him had shouted as Nwamaka prayed. "None of us will ever get out of here alive. We will die in this dark, filthy place, or the white men above will boil us and eat us. So quit praying. You're wasting your breath. There are no spirits to hear you."

"So, Papa, did you ever begin to lose hope,"

"No, Ben. I always had hope."

But that was a lie.

Isaiah would not tell Ben how he had begun to accept, in those darkest of times, that his life was about to end. And how he had vowed to himself to escape or drown trying, for far better to drown than be eaten. *If only I can slip out of these chains and get up on deck,* he had thought. *Then I'll jump off this ship and swim to shore. I may not live, but I won't be eaten.*

One night, three armed white men from the crew descended the ladder into the hold. The miserable enchained captives shivered and covered their eyes. "Surely," one of them whispered, "he has come to take us to a kettle."

But that didn't happen. Instead the pale-faced ship's mate unshackled Isaiah and three others and took them to the other end of the hold where one of the captives had died. He was a huge man that Isaiah had remembered seeing in his village. It took all four of them to lift and carry the man from the hold to the deck and heave him over the side. Isaiah thought about jumping overboard then, but he knew they would only drag him back aboard.

Isaiah noticed a holding pen near the back of the ship, where they kept the women. He had heard there were women up on the deck, but he didn't know if it was true. He could see fifteen or twenty young women, some standing, others squatting on the floor of the pen. They were all looking through the bars in his direction. Then they all scurried to the back of the pen, as one of the ship's mates walked past Isaiah and the others toward the pen. He boasted to the armed men guarding Isaiah and the others as he passed.

"I think I take a woman to pleasure me tonight!" Isaiah watched as the mate unlatched the barred gate, grabbed a young woman too weak to resist and said loudly, "You pleasure me good or I eat you!"

The slender woman, with fully developed breasts, sensuous lips and shapely hips, couldn't have been over fourteen years old. Even in her decrepit state of being branded and locked in a small pen on the deck in the hot sun, she was beautiful.

But how very frightened she had been! Isaiah had never forgotten the young, helpless woman's piercing dark black eyes—full of fear and dread. On the cusp, back in Africa, of being one of her tribe's most desired females, she had become but flesh to be abused. All the other women huddled in fear as the mate relatched the gate.

He laughed as he tore away her only clothing—a scant animal hide wrap—hoisted her over one of his shoulders and walked back past Isaiah and the others. The young girl reached to Isaiah and the others as they passed. Isaiah instinctively took a step toward the pleading girl, and one of the mates guarding him shoved a musket in his stomach.

"I blow ye guts out, darkie."

Isaiah wanted to forget all this, prayed that he'd never again dream about it—as he had so many times over the years. But it was no use. She had sobbed, cried out for help, pleaded, kicked, pounded her fists into the back of the man who had seized her.

But who would or could have helped her?

She would be raped roughly and repeatedly. And then taken back to the holding pen to be "used" another night.

Such was the fate of a lot of those helpless females in the holding pen of *Wanderer*.

As if reading Isaiah's mind, Ben asked him, "Was there women on the ship, Pa?"

"Yes. Some women. They in a big cage up on deck."

"What happened ta them women, Pa? Did they live?"

"Most of 'em made it alive ta America, Ben. Most of 'em."

Ben, sensing something unspeakably horrible had befallen them, didn't ask any more questions about the female captives.

So Isaiah returned to his narrative about *Wanderer*'s voyage across the Atlantic to America.

Nwamaka had accepted the fact that he might not make it. After weeks at sea any attempt to swim to shore would be futile. The whites had guns, chains, shackles and nets. And although he didn't share this with Ben, he had believed that it was only a matter of time before they ate him.

So he had begun to plan his escape—not for a new, better life because such a thing didn't seem possible on the slave schooner, but for death at his own hands.

I can jump overboard and go into the spirit world, he had thought.

But how to even make it to the main deck of the ship? How to escape the groaning, creaking hold of *Wanderer*?

Nwamaka had told himself that there had to be a way. *If only I can get out of these shackles....*

Nwamaka had learned the rhythm of the ship's crew. *If only I can get free of these chains about half way through the night.*

He surmised that would be the best time to climb up on deck and jump overboard. That was because the crew drank heavily every evening, and by mid-darkness, Nwamaka usually heard no voices, no laughter, no footsteps. Those manning the ship's deck apparently slept deeply until sunup each morning, and only then began to groggily return to their assigned duties. The slave schooner, in effect, was manned by only two crewmates for several hours every night and early morning, one at the helm and one on the bow.

One night, Nwamaka had wedged wet yam peelings between his wrists and the shackles. His hands, slippery now, he managed to pull through the shackles.

The heartened lad did a quick look of his surroundings in the hold. All were either asleep or too weak or sick to care about what may have been occurring around them.

So he slipped the yam peelings between the shackles on his ankles, and rubbed them to slipperiness and freed his shackled limbs. He was now free.

Then he had said a prayer. All was quiet and still up on deck and no one would see him because he would be at the stern, out of sight and hearing of the sleeping helmsman. No one would stop him. It was to be a quick and hopefully painless end to his life when he jumped into the ocean. But Isaiah did not tell Ben that.

He climbed up the ladder onto the deck. Saw no human movement. Heard nothing, save for faint swells lapping against the slave vessel. The snoring of drunken, unconscious crew members told him that he had chosen the right time to do what he had to do. No one would stop him. No one would be there to save him, once he plunged into the ocean. It would be over quickly. Soon he would be in the spirit world soaring as an eagle back in West Africa.

And oh how close I came to dying! he thought now as he stared at his son. *But fo' that one man who talked me out of it.*

Emboldened, Nwamaka had leaned over the side of the deck of the *Wanderer*. Had taken one last look upward and noticed a million twinkling stars in the black, cloudless sky. It had been a windless night, causing the *Wanderer*'s two giant sails to stand still as if at ease. The ship had been dead in the water, with moonlight reflecting off the gentle swells below. Off to the side of the schooner he had noticed two great white sharks—man-eaters that seemed to be anxiously awaiting their prey. The animals sensed their meal, seemed to smell Nwamaka's blood. A bit farther away he spotted a school of playful dolphins, arching up and down in the ocean, maintaining a safe separation from the great whites.

"Don't do it!" said a barely audible voice in Nwamaka's native tongue.

Shocked that someone was awake and had seen him, Nwamaka grabbed a side railing at the last second. Then he looked behind him at one of the largest, most broad-shouldered men he'd ever seen. The man's arm muscles bulged, and he had a barrel chest. He had not a trace of fat anywhere on his massive frame.

What the man said next Nwamaka would remember for the rest of his life.

"I am Jacob but they called me Adaobi in Africa. I am your elder, your savior tonight, the one who will give you hope. Now pull yourself all the way back up!"

"But they are going to eat me, Adaobi!" Nwamaka countered. "I saw the kettles. They will boil me alive in a kettle and scrape the flesh off my bones and feed on me like vultures. The white men are evil. They hate us. I would rather drown than be eaten."

"You won't drown," Jacob responded. "The sharks will make sure of that. You will die a gruesome, painful death. You will be in their belly, never to again be a part of this world."

"So what," Nwamaka said. "If the sharks don't eat me, the white men will."

"You are wrong, boy. I have been on many slave ships, made many trips with the whites from Africa to America, helped the whites survive storms and ocean swells, and I have never seen them eat one of our men. But I have seen many of our people die a senseless death when they jumped overboard.

"You will live to see another day, boy. I promise you that. And no one will eat you. The Bible says, "Be alert and of sober mind, because your enemy the devil prowls around like a roaring lion looking for someone to devour."

"What is this thing you call the Bible, old man?"

"It is part of the white man's religion. You will learn about it soon enough. But for right now you have to stay alive."

As to this part of the story, Isaiah only told his son that he'd come close to jumping overboard and trying to swim to land. But a man named Adaobi saved his life because there were sharks in the water. He told Ben he would go on to survive the long perilous trip across the ocean.

Ben asked, "So what happened when they made you a slave?"

Isaiah told Ben that when they arrived in Charleston, South

Carolina, he was led in chains to the auction block. The auction-eer called him "the finest African specimen you'd ever hope to have for your plantation!"

At that auction, he was poked, prodded and had his mouth opened by bidders checking his teeth so that they could be confident he was healthy and strong. Women in frilly bonnets and hoop skirts, and fanning themselves, gawked while their husbands tried to outbid one another for a strapping Negro. There had been much chatter and shouting and jostling about by the bidders—all of it terrifying and confounding for Nwamaka. He had only known that he would forever be separated from his family in Africa.

What he didn't know was how full of drudgery his new life would be. He would perform backbreaking work from sunup to sundown, mostly tending to crops or livestock on the sprawling plantation in South Carolina. He would not be paid anything and would sometimes be whipped for no good reason. It was as if his first white owner delighted in making him suffer or beg for mercy.

From time to time, he would think about trying to escape. Because he had heard tales of runaway slaves doing anything they could to get to freedom in the North—to faraway places called "Pennsylvania" or "New York"—where colored people got paid for their labor and could live as free men. The runaways cunningly threw off the pursuing dogs by taking to creeks or streams or by dousing themselves with pepper to kill their scent. And some runaways stole horses or stowed away on trains to make it to freedom.

Isaiah shared with Ben how he had toiled for "masta" Robert Henson of Savannah, and then later for "masta" James Ravenell of Charleston for three years. His well-heeled owners changed but not his dreary lot in life.

Both men had cruel "overseers" in the cotton fields who had a singular mission to work Isaiah and those of his ilk to the bone, make them hoe and dig and pick cotton, tobacco, potatoes, corn or tomatoes until their bodies could stand no more.

The slaves were allowed to rest for a few hours in crude, barely habitable shacks before starting the next day anew in the same hot fields. The grind never ended, It only got more intense as the growing season progressed and the market demand for the crops increased. Slaves like Isaiah knew what they had to do, and they did it for one reason—to stay alive and hope that one day they might be freed.

"But dere also be some good white men even back then," Isaiah said. He explained how a few slave owners in Virginia and Tennessee treated their colored workers more like human beings and not like cattle. Some folks, north of the Carolinas and Georgia, sensed that slavery's days were numbered. They believed fervently that the heinous practice of owning another human being ran counter to God's will and committed themselves to helping, not hurting, the Africans who had been abducted from their homeland, separated always from their families and thrust into a strange, hostile world.

"And then along come Mista Daniel Smith," said Isaiah, cracking a smile for one of the very few times since telling about his past to Ben. "He be a godly man from Fish Springs, Tennessee."

Isaiah noted that it so happened that Smith, needing a good, steady, reliable hand to help him on his farm in the mountains of East Tennessee, acquired Isaiah. Isaiah would work for Daniel Smith, the most revered, most charitable and biggest property owner in Fish Springs He would rise from being a slave to a land-owning freed sharecropper. Over the years the two men grew close, Smith as employer and Isaiah as his key employee. Isaiah was with the Smith family through all their family's deaths and sicknesses, triumphs and despair, good times and bad. In the fourth decade of his life, Isaiah had definitely come a long way from the hold of the slave ship *Wanderer*.

"Thank the Lord, Mista Daniel Smith bought me away from that evil slave masta. I'd a'died for sho' but for Mista Smith. He save my life. I still a slave but Mista Smith was kind ta me."

Isaiah explained that such humane treatment stemmed from the goodness of Daniel Smith's heart, because his new "masta" decided soon thereafter that slavery had been wrong. So Smith made him a free man long before the despicable practice was outlawed by President Abraham Lincoln's Emancipation Proclamation.

"That show me dat not all white folks was bad. Some of'em

was downright good."

"And then what happened, Pa? Is that when you met Momma?"

"No, Ben. Prissy'n me didn't meet 'til some time after that. But Mista Smith helped me find her when we went to buy a load'a hay from that mean old Mista Edwards down in Valley Forge."

"Did you love her right from the start, Pa?" Ben asked. His eyes sparkled, and he grinned.

"I was way shy, son, but Prissy be the prettiest woman I ever laid my eyes on."

Isaiah described how had it not been for Daniel making him a sharecropper and deeding him a cabin, he likely would have never been in a position to marry anyone. He credited Daniel's wife Mary, too, with helping make their marriage happen.

But Isaiah reminded his son again that none of those good things would have occurred—and Ben himself wouldn't have been born—had he not survived that voyage across the ocean from Africa.

For the once-proud African boy known as Nwamaka had somehow found the strength and faith to survive—after being captured by slavers—when so many others had not.

Isaiah, a few gray hairs dotting his head, wrinkles forming under his eyes and his shoulders a bit slumped, laughed and spouted, "And you sho' should be glad I made it, 'cause you wouldn't be here, neither."

Isaiah encouraged his son to always notice the beauty of his surroundings in Fish Springs. To never take for granted the cool mountain breeze, blue sky and warm sunshine or the dense, lush hardwood forest that lined the road they were now traversing. It was a forest full of all sorts of majestic leafy trees—maples, birches, oaks, beeches and flowering dogwoods. It was also a landscape blanketed now with daffodils, wild daisies and phlox. He exhorted Ben to value all the critters God had created to roam the wilds of East Tennessee—deer, bobcats, wolves, bears and birds.

All of God's creation was spectacular and amazing, and Isaiah wanted Ben not to get caught up in the painful past.

Ben stared at the mountaintops, today partially covered in a haze of whispy clouds. The wagon bumped along the road. Off to the side was a field full of colorful flowers. The brightest red bird he'd ever seen chirped merrily. Spring was bubbling up in all its glory.

"Why'd God let that happen, Pa, all them awful things they did to you on that slave ship?"

Isaiah smiled and put his big brawny arm across his wide-eyed son's shoulders.

"We don't know what the Lord's plans are, son, but he must have a reason."

About that time three deer dashed across the road in front of them, then bound across a shallow area of the Watauga River, their white flags slicing the air.

Shadow, sound asleep in the back, never stirred.

"Ain't they beautiful, Pa?"

"They are, son. They truly are."

CHAPTER 8

Elijah's Fear

The Rev. Horace Leftwich, founder and head of the Colored Baptist Church in Elizabethton, assured Isaiah that he would have a place prepared for Toby's bones. They would be buried with dignity, the minister promised, in the church's picket-fence enclosed cemetery, and a graveside service would be held following next Sunday's regular service.

The following day Isaiah rose early. Prissy made him breakfast and prepared him a lunch to take on his usual daily duty as a foreman working for Daniel Smith.

Isaiah saddled his horse Charger and rode from farm to farm, checking on other sharecroppers working for Smith. Charger was an American Saddlebred that Daniel had given to Isaiah when Mary had presented Black Jack, a Tennessee Pacer, as a wedding gift to Daniel. Isaiah loved the smooth riding Saddlebred, and even though the horse was twenty years old, he was reliable and spirited. Isaiah had had other horses but he had a real connection to Charger. There were times when the beautiful black horse would respond even before Isaiah gave him a command. He always felt safe on the gentle animal not only for himself but for the boys, too.

As Isaiah checked on the other sharecroppers, he reviewed their progress in getting the fields plowed and made ready for planting, and he often made suggestions if he felt something could be done better.

It was a job that Isaiah was good at. He had the gift of knowing how to get the most out of a plot of land—be it bottomland or rocky hillside. He knew exactly how deep to plow for each crop, exactly how far apart the rows should be and where each crop grew the best.

In the beginning a few of the hard-working sharecroppers did not like taking orders from another colored man, but over time they had developed great respect for Isaiah and welcomed his suggestions. Because being a sharecropper meant they and their family received part of the crop as food for their family and a source of income.

Isaiah headed back home early because he wanted to finish plowing the field where Toby's bones had been unearthed. But just as he arrived, he was met by Sheriff Nave in his buggy, coming from the other direction.

"Afta noon, Isaiah. I was hopin' I'd find you here."

"Afta noon, Sheriff."

"I need your help, Isaiah. I went ta see Elijah Wood yesterdee' and I got nothin' outta him. He was so scared he just wouldn't talk to me. I know you're busy this time'a year but I'd be much obliged if you'd go with me back to his place. I think he'd feel a might more comfortable with you there."

"Sure, Sheriff. I can do that. Let me tell Prissy."

Isaiah told Prissy he would be back before dark. He left Charger with Jeb who had recently taken over the job of caring for Charger at the end of the day.

"Take good care'a him, son. I rode'em pretty hard today," Isaiah said as he climbed in the buggy with Nave.

"Okay, Pa."

Carter County's chief law enforcement officer used the trip time to learn what Isaiah knew about Toby and Jake Edwards' conflict.

"That's how Mista Edwards kept his coloreds from leavin', Sheriff. He made sure they never got their bill paid off at his sto. That's the way he kept Prissy from leavin'. Why, she'd still be there if it wornt for Mista Daniel. Even with the sto gone, he'da found a way to keep her."

About an hour later, they pulled to a stop in front of Elijah's shack at the back of Jake Edwards' farm. It was a crude, ramshackle dwelling, with rotting, weatherworn, warped boards for walls and a pathetic excuse for a porch that looked like it could cave in at any time. Rocks were missing from the top of the chimney, and the only window was cracked.

Isaiah wondered what would happen to the former slave's old structure if it were to suddenly fall victim to a strong wind-storm, of the kind that made trees sway almost to the ground and ripped shingles off the roof of even the most sturdily built home.

Elijah—his back bent over from years of hard work and his face pocked with deep wrinkles—couldn't help but smile upon seeing Isaiah. But inside he was nervous. *I know why that rascal is here,* Elijah thought. *And I got to play it smart.*

Isaiah suggested they sit on the rickety old porch and talk. When Elijah agreed, Sheriff Nave took the only chair, an old cane back, and Isaiah and Elijah sat on a couple of old crates.

"How is Ruthie, Elijah?" Isaiah asked.

The question about Elijah's wife helped put him slightly at ease. Still, however, Jake Edwards' one time foreman sensed the sheriff and his accomplice were up to something, so he kept his guard up.

"She fine, Isaiah. She takin' a nap right now, but she hafta get up soon so's she can go ta the big house and make Mista Edwards' dinner."

Both in their eighties, Elijah and Ruthie did little around the farm anymore. But they did hitch up the buggy and care for the animals. They fed their boss' chickens, gathered eggs, and milked the cow. Plus, Ruthie still prepared Jake Edwards' meals and cleaned his house.

In return, Edwards let the old couple stay in the little shack and have a garden.

"We need your help, Elijah. Our friend ..."As Isaiah beseeched his old acquaintance to assist them, Elijah turned his head to the right, so as to avoid eye contact.

"I don't know nothin', Isaiah. I cain't tell you nothin' 'cause I don't know nothin'. Just like I tol da sheriff hea', Toby left and we's never heerd from 'em again."

Isaiah, putting one of his big roughened hands on Elijah's shoulder, was unfazed.

"We know what he did, Elijah, but we have ta prove it. If you seen what happen, the sheriff here can lock Jake Edwards up. Where he cain't hurt you or Ruthie or nobody."

Elijah just looked at Isaiah but did not speak.

"Please, we need your help."

Several seconds passed. Isaiah could sense his fear.

Elijah, his eyes now meeting Isaiah's, began to speak and the long held words poured out.

"It was 'bout dis time aday. I was settin' on da po'ch with Ruthie, and Mista Edwards rode up on his horse. He tol' me ta hookup da wagon, put two shovels in da back and pick him up at da house. He tol' me to bring Jed wit' me. I found Jed in da barn. That youngin was scared and cryin'. He be just a boy, 'bout fifteen. He tol' me when Jake found out Toby had left, he got real mad. And he made 'em tell where Toby was headed. He told dat boy he would rip his skin clean off wit his bull whip, if he didn't tell."

When Elijah paused as if he didn't want to say anything else, Isaiah urged him on.

"You need to tell us everthing, Elijah. Toby'd want you to help us. You know that. And I know it."

So Elijah resumed his sad recollection. "We caught up with Toby just off the road in that field that runs along da riva. Close ta yo place, Isaiah. Mista Edwards grinned like a possum when we spotted him. Den he tol' Toby if he left, owin' him money, it be da same as stealin'.

"But Toby tol' him he paid off his bill at da sto' and he had a paper signed by Miss Fanny dat said so. Mista Edwards got real mad and said Toby was lyin' and to get in da wagon. But Toby said he weren't goin' back and started runnin'. Mista Edwards fired a warnin' shot toad Toby but he dint stop.

"Mista Edwards look like he had a fire burnin' inside'im. He madder dan' I eva' seen'im."

Elijah closed his eyes, shook his head and began crying.

"He fired agin' dis time hittin' po' old Toby in da back a da head. Toby didn't make a sound; he just fell to da ground. He breathed couple times, like a deer dat had just been shot. Den he just quit an' laid still. Blood come outta his head bad. Real bad. Den, Mista Edwards made us go through everythin' tryin' to find dat paper. He said he knowed there wasn't a receipt 'cause Toby neva' paid off his bill noways.

"I neva' forgit de scary way Jake Edwards look at us. I thought he was goin' to kill us too."

"Den he said if we eva' tol 'bout what happened hea', he'd kill us. He say 'if you want yo sons to live to be men, yo'll keep yo' mouths shut. Dat young boy Jed be so scairt dat he wet hisself, an' dat night he left and I neva' seen'im agin."

Isaiah nodded knowingly, then patted Elijah on the back.

Through it all, Sheriff Nave said nothing. Didn't change his facial expression. Just listened intently.

A now thoroughly contrite Elijah Wood asked the sheriff's understanding, confessing that he knew that he should have told about what happened to Toby a long time ago, but was fearful for his wife Ruthie and for the lives of his children.

"My chillen—dey all moved away now, but he can come afta Ruthie and me."

"That ain't happenin' on my watch, Elijah." It was the first words Nave had spoken since learning about how Toby had died. And he uttered them with confidence, as if to assure Elijah he had nothing to fear for telling the truth—even if it had been a long time coming.

Isaiah noticed Ruthie, wringing her hands and beginning to cry, standing in the doorway.

"I tol Elijah that someday Mista Edwards'd pay for what he done to poor Toby, and I guess dat day is come. But what we gwine do now, Sheriff? Dat evil man'll kill us."

Nave responded that by the time Edwards found out about what Elijah had told them, the man would be in his custody.

But Ruthie seemed puzzled. So Nave clarified, "He'll be under arrest and on his way to jail."

Jake Edwards sat in his outhouse with the door open, grunting and sipping on a jug of whiskey. He wiped his mouth with the back of his hand, squinted his alcohol-glazed eyes and looked toward the back of his property. His stomach had been cramping and he'd suffered bouts of diarrhea, but Edwards, living alone since he'd lost his wife a few years back, had convinced himself he didn't need a doctor.

He suspected his stomach aches stemmed from living a life full of regret, but he figured there was nothing he could do about that now, except guzzle whiskey every now and then and enjoy what good days he had left with Daisy, one of the gals at the Black Bear Saloon in Elizabethton. Agnes Gump, was her real name. She was the oldest and homeliest prostitute at the Black Bear, and the only one that would take Jake's money.

Edwards grunted hard one last time and wiped himself with a wad of lamb's ear, a soft green fuzzy plant that grew in the wild and which the Cherokees had used for the same purpose. His business finished in the outhouse, he squinted his eyes once again toward the back of his land.

What he saw disturbed him. For he was able to make out Sheriff Nave's buggy leaving Elijah's shack. No big surprise, Jake figured, because he halfway expected the always-curious lawman to be snooping around after he'd heard about the bones being dug up.

Now ain't that a sight! That nosy, damned sheriff and dumb nigger prowlin' 'round here. Looks like I might have to get some of the brothers together ta put a little fear in that nigger. Edwards rubbed the stubby beard on his chin and tried to focus.

What he or his "brothers" did had to be done carefully, secretly, quickly. The fear of God had to be put into Elijah and his wife Ruthie and not a day too soon. It might cost him some money, because his "brothers," of late, had been complaining they needed more funds to operate—and to buy off any law enforcement people that might pursue them. Jake Edwards suspected Sheriff Nave could not be bought, but he also figured that every man had his price, and under the right circumstances, and the right amount of cash, anything would be possible.

The "brothers" Edwards had in mind to help him deal with Elijah, and possibly Isaiah, were none other than members of a recently formed local chapter of the Ku Klux Klan. Founded in Pulaski, Tennessee, several hundred miles from the mountains of East Tennessee, the KKK touted itself as a mighty "Invisible Empire" bent on protecting the purity and sanctity of the white race. Critics of the KKK pointed out the white supremacist organization's mission was at odds with the *Declaration of Independence's* "all men are created equal" mandate. They also noted that Klan people conducted their cross burnings and other unseemly business in cowardly shadows—their faces covered with white hoods and their bodies draped in white robes.

But all that aside, the Klan also had its supporters—mostly hard-headed Southerners who would never accept the federal government's abolition of slavery and who couldn't or wouldn't accept that colored folks were just as much human as whites.

One of those defiant, ingrained KKKers was Jake Edwards. He had worked his colored help almost to the bone. Even after they were no longer slaves under the law, Edwards continued several more years to bully those colored people in his employ. When he paid them for their work, it was but a pittance—not even enough for them to have even the crudest roof over their heads or to buy one square foot of their own land.

But they were all gone now. The only ones left were Elijah and Ruthie.

So here he was, confronted with the pesky sheriff of Carter County and, in Jake Edwards' reckoning, his own no-good-for-nothin', triflin' nigger employees who wouldn't let a dead man lie.

Yep, I need tha' help of my brothers, Edwards thought again. Then, as if to justify his take on what he suspected Elijah had told the sheriff, Edwards thought of a verse from the Book of James in the Bible: *The tongue is a flame of fire. It is a whole world of wickedness, corrupting your entire body. It can set your whole life on fire. For it is set on fire by Hell itself.*

For as bad a person as Jake Edwards had been, and for all his hatred of Negroes, he had always gone to church. He knew his Bible, sat with his wife in the front pew as the preacher of their small Baptist church in Valley Forge had railed, Sunday after Sunday, against the sins of the flesh, thievery, debauchery, gluttony, adultery and last, but not least, racial equality.

"Coloreds aint like white folks. They lived in jungles of Af-ree'ca," the Bible-thumping, sweat-drenched preacher had declared again and again. "Keep'em in their place, 'cause you give a Colored an inch, he'll take'a mile!"

And so the church-going, Christian Jake Edwards had taken that to heart. He vowed that he'd "never let a nigger get above his raisin'."

And here now is a nigger consortin' with a white sheriff to take away my freedom—all on account I put a damned nigger in tha ground fer stealin'!

A couple of nights later a nervous group of men gathered in a secluded barn just outside of Elizabethton, not far from the two-story frame house where President Andrew Johnson had died from a stroke a few years earlier. The men paid no mind to the two restless horses and mule stabled in stalls a few feet away. They had more important matters to attend to this evening.

Standing on a platform facing the group, most of whom wore boots and overalls and had holstered pistols, was none other than Jake Edwards himself. Draped on a wall behind him was a large stars and bars Confederate battle flag emblazoned with three letters: KKK.

A lantern gave off a soft glow of light in the barn. And even if the men had been blindfolded, they'd have known where they were. The scent of freshly cut hay, horse manure and chicken poop filled their meeting place.

The men looked annoyed and impatient, as if they had better things to do, as Edwards spoke his piece. "Somethin's come up and I'm needin' a few of you to pull a raid."

"We ain't never pulled a raid before, Jake," said one of the brothers.

"So! how hard can it be?" asked Jake. "They's a nigger that's got above his raisin', and he needs ta be teached a lesson."

"Exactly what you wantin' us to do, Jake?" one of the men groused. "Ya know the law in these parts is sayin' things has changed since the war, and we ain't allowed ta sceer no coloreds—"

"That ain't ever bothered y'all before," the red-faced Edwards snapped. "And just so ya' know, I paid my dues, and then some, a few weeks back. Now y'all goin' ta help me or not?"

"Okay, Jake. We're listening," said another listener, reminded that they needed Edwards' money to keep this new chapter going. "After all, we're your bothers."

"Well, now, that's more like it," Jake said. He grinned and took a deep breath. "I knowed I could depend on y'all.

"This is what I want done. I want five hooded riders to ride over to Elijah Wood's house and make him sa scairt he pees in his britches. I want ya' firing ya rifles in the air and burnin' the God-awfullest, biggest cross right there in his front yard.

"That damned nigger works fer me … lives on my property with his common law wife who happens ta be my house girl. And now, by God, he's runnin' his mouth to Sheriff Nave. Tellin' that uppity lawman 'bout another nigger I had ta kill 'cause he was stealin' me blind.

"I want this nigger Elijah Wood to keep his damned mouth shut. I want 'em ta know right smart good that if he blabs to the sheriff, he ain't goin' ta see the sun come up many more days ..."

As Jake ranted, another of his listeners, shuffling uncomfortably from side to side, interrupted. "But Jake, I know Elijah Wood, and so does some of the other brothers. Ain't nary'a man here can say nothin' bad 'bout 'em."

"He's a nigger! Are you hearin' me?" Edwards screamed. "Elijah Wood's words could land me in jail. I want him ta know that if he talks, the Klan's gonna come down on him like the wrath'a God!"

With that outburst, one of the men in the barn sharply elbowed the defender of Elijah Wood and whispered something about money to him.

"Okay, Jake, count me in!" another man spouted, then spat out a big chew of tobacco. He was loud-mouthed Duke Rayburn, Sheriff Nave's deputy, and he always seemed to be itching for trouble.

"Can we burn his barn down, too?" asked Hank Beeler, Duke's less intelligent partner.

"It's my barn, you dumb jackass! You think I'd burn my own damn barn down?"

Hank was taken aback somewhat but his swagger was still there. He said he was sorry and promised not to harm any of Edwards' property. "I'm your white brother, Jake. You know that."

"Who else can I count on for this raid?" Edwards asked. His eyes darted from man to man.

"When you wantin' it done, Jake?" a man replied. "You know,

we've got our 'backer ta get planted, and my corn crib's about to fall down, an' somebidy's got ta tend our still up in tha' holler."

"Wednesday night!" Edwards demanded.

"I cain't do it Wednesday night, Jake," one of the men meekly replied. "Wednesday night's prayer meetin night. An' I promised my Polly I ain't missin' another prayer meetin."

Another chimed in. "Yeah, Wednesday ain't gonna' won't work fer me neather."

"Okay, dammit. Thursday night."

Duke said, "Thursday night's poker night at the Black Bear Saloon, Jake. Nave wants both me and Hank to work Thursday nights."

Jake held both hands up and rolled his eyes in disbelief.

"Friday?"

All the men looked around at each other nodding their heads, yes.

"You goin' be ridin' with us, Jake?" asked a scruffy-looking, bespectacled, fat man.

"You see this damn cane? It's all I can do just ta get to my damn buggy. How in the hell do you think I can get up on a damn horse, you stupid sombitch?"

Jake Edwards wondered why he had joined the KKK. *Selfish idiots. Nary a one of'ums got a licka sense. All they want is my money, an' then when you need somethun' done, they set there and squabble about it.*

The following afternoon Sheriff Nave pulled his buggy to a stop in front of Jake Edwards' big white two-story farm house, at one time one of the finest homes in Carter County. But after years of neglect it now stood in rundown condition, and Edwards himself wasn't much better.

Jake hobbled out onto the porch with his cane. His clothes were wrinkled and dirty. The only hair he had was on the sides of his head, and it hung almost to his shoulders. His whiskers and beard desperately needed a trim, and, if that wasn't bad enough, he reeked of alcohol.

Jake's wife had passed away a few years before, and it was apparent his heavy drinking had gotten the best of the man, who now was in the autumn of his life.

"What brings you, Nave?"

"Afta-noon, Mister Edwards. I want to ask you about one of your darkies that worked here about thirteen years ago. His name was Toby Jackson."

Dreading but also expecting the lawman's visit, Jake said, "Yea, I remember Toby. He worked for me quite a spell. He was a pretty good worker, for a nigger, but one night he just up and left, like you say, about thirteen years ago. Never seen or heerd from 'im again. After all these years, why you askin' 'bout Toby now?"

The sheriff stared at the unkempt, foul-smelling Edwards, a man he had never liked. Nave knew not to tip his hand.

"Daniel Smith's man, Isaiah, was plowin' down by the river near his place and he plowed up Toby's bones."

"Now Sheriff, how the hell can you tell one nigger's bones from another's?"

"Well, Jake, seems this skeleton was missing two toes. The same two toes you cut off Toby Jackson when he was workin' for you."

So that good-fer nothing nigger Elijah had told this meddlin' sheriff ever'thang, Jake surmised. *The brothers ought ta tie a piece'a barbed wire 'round his damned testicles!*

"Tell me, Sheriff; I'm just curious. How do you come to know all this?"

Edwards tried to remain composed, but Nave could sense the mean-spirited man was nervous. He took a kind of inward delight at making his listener squirm.

"Well it seems Isaiah was a good friend of Toby's, and Isaiah knew about you chopping off Toby's toes after they got frostbitten, Mister Edwards.

"And Isaiah seems to recollect Toby telling him that he owed your store money, and as soon as he paid off his bill, he was leaving for Alabama where his brother lives."

The angry, fist-shaking Edwards snarled, "That nigger Isaiah is lyin' through his teeth! He's just tryin' to stir up trouble for me 'cause I kicked him and Daniel Smith off my property when they took my nigger house girl."

Nave sensed that Edwards, now sweating profusely and with his eyes darting around, was about to break. "Now I ain't got all day, Mister Edwards. I've come a long way out here. It's hot, and I'm tired, and I'm hungry. So you might as well come clean about what happened. I've done talked to Elijah Wood who at the time was your foreman, and he told me everything."

Edwards, leaning on a beam of his porch, said nothing.

Why drag it out? They ain't never goin' ta convict me fer killin' a nigger anyway. He folded his scraggly arms across his bulging stomach and declared, "So what. I shot that thievin' nigger because he stole money from me. Toby never paid off his bill. He owed my store money and he was leavin' without payin' up.

"And, Sheriff, if you don't believe me, I can prove what I'm sayin.'"

When the sheriff asked him to explain, Edwards told him about how his long-time storekeeper, old Fanny May Brown, had kept impeccable records—among them a ledger showing Toby had still owed him money when he left. Edwards also noted that Fanny May had died a few years back after she moved to Knoxville.

But the sheriff was unmoved. "You are under arrest for the murder of Toby Jackson, Jake. "I'm takin' you in."

"For killin' a bald-faced, lyin' nigger that stole from me! My God, what's this country comin' to?"

Sheriff Nave spun his shocked subject around, pulled his arms back and snapped a set of handcuffs on him.

"Damn you, Nave! Do you really have to put handcuffs on me?!"

"No, but I am." The Carter County lawman didn't try to hide his smirk as he put the belligerent, shocked suspect in his buggy and set out for Elizabethton, where he would be put in an eight-foot by 10-foot cell awaiting trial, his only glimpse of freedom afforded by the cell's lone barred window that faced the river behind Nave's office.

This ain't over by a long shot! Nave's captive thought. *My brothers in tha Klan'll see to shuttin' that nigger up for good tonight. This ain't never goin' ta trial and even if does, once the Klan pays Elijah a visit, he'll be too damn scared to testify. Thank God for the Ku Klux Klan!*

CHAPTER 9

A Burning Cross

At first, Elijah and Ruthie thought they were in the midst of the spring thunderstorm that had been building up that afternoon, but they soon realized the loud, crackling explosive sounds were too close together. They rolled off the bed and huddled on the floor.

The old former slave held his terrified wife as close to him as he could. He pulled the edge of a quilt off the bed and draped it over her. Not for warmth but more for a sense of security. At the same time, he put his calloused, wrinkled hands over her ears, trying to block out the sounds outside.

Gunfire and screams pierced the night. Jake's pigs, cows and horses in the barn near their shack were making a ruckus.

"Lawdy Lawdy," Ruthie mumbled. "Is we havin' another war?"

Elijah could see around the room like it was morning. Crawling to the window, he peeked out and saw a burning cross in the front yard. Huge, wicked flames licked the pitch dark. And in the distance clouds lit up as a line of thunderstorms boomed over the mountains, causing the trees outside the couple's old dwelling to sway. In the midst of it all, as if sent from the devil, were the wicked flames—a reminder that just when you might have thought things had settled down after the Civil War, racism in the mountains of East Tennessee occasionally still reared its ugly head.

Ruthie, crouching on the floor, asked, "What be goin' on out dere, Elijah?"

Her husband tried to console her. "You just stay where you be," Elijah said. "Dey be gone soon'nough."

"Who be gone? Who dey be?"

He didn't answer but swallowed nervously. He kept peeking through the window at the flames and at the hooded and masked men on horseback circling the cross and firing their rifles into the air.

"Nigger, keep yore damned mouth shut!" one of the riders yelled.

"We ain't cottonin' to a nigger that's rattin' on his boss!" another of the horsemen threatened.

"Cause if he keeps on blabbin' to the sheriff we'll cut off his tongue and kill his wife and younguns!"

Elijah felt helpless. He didn't even own a gun, and the nearest neighbor was at least a 30-minute ride away. The Klansmen could burn their house down and kill them and nobody would know until it was too late.

"Our father, which art in heaven, hallowed be thy name..." Ruthie began to pray, for now she had heard the racist venom right outside their bedroom window. The KKK had descended on them with a vengeance. Only God could save them if the Klan was bent on destroying everything they owned and killing them.

Still at the window, keeping a helpless vigil, Elijah cursed himself for not having a gun. Then he heard his wife praying and said a prayer to himself, *Dey is some bad men out dere tonight, Lawd. Please make dem go away and leave us be. We need yo' son Jeezus hea' tonight, Lawd. Amen.*

He crawled back to Ruthie and cuddled her in his arms, sitting up against the wall by the bed.

"It's dat Ku Klux Klan, Ruthie." Elijah held his wife closely.

"Is dey gwine ta kill us, Elijah?" Ruthie was crying and wringing her hands. Another angry racist chant could be heard from just outside their bedroom window. A big stone came banging through, shattering the window and splaying shards of glass everywhere. Gunshots fired at rapid succession. Horses neighed loudly.

"Nigga, we warnin' you! Keep yo' mouth shut!"

The sound of hooves and the men on horseback hollering continued.

"Dey's fixin' ta kill us, Elijah! Lawd have mercy on us!"

"We be okay, Ruthie," Elijah assured her. "You just close yo eyes. Dey be gone soon."

He pulled his weathered, frightened little woman close and patted the top of her gray haired head while softly humming a few lines from "Yes, Jesus Loves Me." The song was the old couple's favorite hymn, and tonight, maybe the worst night of their lives, they needed its comfort more than ever.

"Yes, Jeezus loves me, dis I know. Fo' de Bible tells me so," Elijah whispered into his wife's ear.

When Elijah paused, as if trying to remember the rest of the words to the old melody, Ruthie squeezed his hands, mustered a slight smile and continued, "Little ones to Him belong. Dey is weak, but He is strong."

Meanwhile, the commotion outside had subsided. All they could hear was the crackling sound of flames from the burning cross in the dark.

Duke Rayburn, who considered himself the leader of the raiding party, had told his hooded brothers that was enough—for the time being. And the masked men on horseback, their ranting and railing over, had left.

"Dat mean snake Jake Edwards must be in da Klan, Elijah. We should'a never said nothin' to da sheriff. We might be killed 'cause what we told. I'm scared, Elijah."

"It be okay, Ruthie. Dey be gone now," said Elijah, looking out into the haunting quiet.

Clouds which had previously covered the moon now had parted, and a big yellow orb cast its light on the mountainous landscape. The farm animals had returned to their slumber. A solitary wolf howled from high atop a hill off in the distance.

Elijah, too, feared the wrath of the KKK. For as inept and unorganized as Jake Edwards' chapter of the KKK was, they were still feared by local Negroes. The KKK inflicted pain and suffering, especially in the Southern states where many raids and killings had occurred. The Civil War might have had the effect of abolishing slavery but some die-hard racists had seen to it that the "Invisible Empire" stayed viable.

Outwardly, the KKK portrayed itself as a Christian group of men and women devoted to preserving the fundamentals of democracy and freedom. The organization, their members mainly recruited from the South, had even been known to sponsor festivals, hold community picnics, and tout baby christenings. But Elijah, as did other Negroes in East Tennessee, also knew of the KKK's more sinister side—the beatings and burnings and taunting and fear mongering.

KKK members liked to portray themselves as law abiding, upstanding Christian citizens; but they still, in Elijah's mind, were up to no good, lurking as they did in their white robes and hoods in the shadows. "Go to church on Sunday and hang a nigger on Sunday night," seemed to be their motto.

News of the Klan raid made its way to Sheriff Nave the next day, and the lawman was none too pleased. He felt bad that he had not kept the old colored couple safe. He had not seen this coming. He had heard rumors that a new KKK chapter had started up in Carter County, but this was the first cross burning under his watch.

"Mornin', Sheriff," Duke said upon reporting for work the following Monday.

Nave rose uneasily from his cluttered roll-top desk that sat in a corner of the room with a huge wanted poster on the wall. He gave Duke a stare that could have killed.

"Where were you Friday night?" he asked sternly.

"Why, I was outna' woods coon huntin', Sheriff. Why you askin'?"

"Because there was a Ku Klux Klan raid at Elijah and Ruthie Woods' shack Friday night. Some cowards with sheets pulled over their damned heads burned a cross at their place and threw a big rock through the window scaring that old couple ta death."

Duke tried to control his smirk and said nothing at first, but the sheriff was savvy.

"Now you damned well better fess up, Duke, 'cause I ain't standin' for no shenanigans from my deputies!"

"I don't know nothin' 'bout no Klan raid, Sheriff. That's tha' God's honest truth, so help me. I swear it on my mother's grave." Duke shifted uneasily, sweat ran down his forehead and his eyes darted from side to side.

Sheriff Nave sensed he was lying. "Lookie here, Duke. You need to think of this as a come-ta-Jesus meetin', and you better damned hear me straight!" Nave got nose to nose with his chief deputy. He gripped Duke's shoulders hard with his big, strong hands.

"If I ever hear tell that you or any of my other deputies are members of the Klan, your asses are outta here. We got that straight?" Nave gave his deputy a hard shake. "Because they're just a buncha' hooligans who hide behind their hoods and manage to stay one step ahead of the law."

"So help me, Moses, Sheriff, I ain't got nothin' ta do with the Klan. This is the first I heard 'bout a raid."

"Yea, sure it is," Nave responded sarcastically. "Get on over ta the Black Bear Saloon. Burt Grindstaff wants ta file charges on a couple'a trouble makers that busted up some furniture in a fight last night. Just go do your job."

Duke, rubbing his shoulder from where his boss had so fiercely squeezed it, went out the door and headed to the Black Bear Saloon.

In his jail cell behind the sheriff's office, Jake Edwards could not see Nave and Duke but heard the exchange and was pleased to know that the raid had taken place.

"Sheriff! Hey, Sheriff! When in the hell am I gonna get some breakfast in here? You a plannin' ta starve me ta death?"

Sheriff Nave at first just ignored Jake.

More angry and impatient by the minute, Edwards picked up the metal pan in his cell that he'd eaten his supper from. He began loudly banging it against the bars and demanding his breakfast. Clang, clang, clang!

"Hold your horses, old man, it's comin'. Ain't no need ta cut such a shine!"

"I'm tellin' you I want somethin' ta eat right now, Sheriff!"

Nave warned his only prisoner that he best be quiet, or else.

"So whaddya gonna do if I don't stop, Sheriff? Put me in jail?" Edwards laughed. Then he kept banging the pan against the jail bars.

About that time, another one of Nave's deputies escorted a

middle-aged man in handcuffs past where the sheriff had sat back down at his desk and toward the cell in the back. The man was accompanied by a crying, nervously twitching woman. Both of them were pleading for mercy.

"Whaddya bringin' him in for? And who's that woman?" Nave asked Deputy Oliver Hardin.

"He stole from a Baptist church outtin' the county here, Sheriff," Hardin replied. He wore a tin star on his chest emblazoned with the words DEPUTY SHERIFF OF CARTER COUNTY, had a red bandana draped around his neck and a 32-calibre pistol in a holster on his right hip. "And she's his wife. She wanted to come here with'im."

"So you really stole from the Lord?" Nave asked, raising his eyebrows.

The deputy explained that the culprit's duty at the church had been counting and depositing the offerings, but he had gotten greedy and stolen over a hundred dollars over a period of several months. The thievery had been discovered when a few of the church's deacons, wanting to buy new pews for their house of worship, asked to see the church's bank account. When they found hardly any money in the account, they confronted their trusted fellow church member at his home. At first he had denied any wrongdoing, but under pressure from his wife to "come clean with the Lord," he had confessed to the plundering.

"I didn't mean it, Sheriff! Honest I didn't!" the man in handcuffs begged. "I'm just a hillbilly bookkeeper and the devil got ahold'a me."

"Sir, you'll just have to tell all that ta the judge. Lock him up, Oliver."

The wife became hysterical and began weeping and clutching her husband.

"Sorry, ma'am. You can't go with him," Nave said.

After Oliver pulled the woman from her husband, she ran crying from the jail.

"Nave! I don't want that damn heathen in this cell!" Jake hollered from the back as the deputy locked his prisoner in the only cell in the jail. "Nave, you hear me, damn it!"

About that time a tall, dignified-looking man, wearing a derby and with a handlebar moustache, entered the office holding a folded paper.

"Sheriff Nave?"

"Yes, I am Sheriff Nave."

"My name is L. Ross Roberts. I'm the defense attorney for Jake Edwards."

"Yes, I know who you are. What can I do for you Mr. Roberts?"

"You can release Mr. Edwards." As he spoke, the bespectacled lawyer with black penetrating eyes, bushy eyebrows and thick sideburns that stretched to his jaw, exuded an air of importance and authority.

"Like hell I will! He's not goin' anywhere," the lawman snapped. "He's under arrest for first degree murder. He shot a Negro in cold blood in the back of the head."

"With all due respect, Sheriff, that's not for you to decide," Roberts replied, grinning. Then he pulled a cigar from inside the breast pocket of his suit jacket and smoothed his tie.

"Smoke, Sheriff?"

"I ain't wantin' no cigar and I'm not releasin' nobody that's facin' a murder charge!"

Roberts took a match from his vest pocket and struck it on Nave's desk top, lit his cigar and took a big drag, letting the smoke out slowly. He glanced at the fancy watch attached to the gold chain on his belt.

Then he spoke sternly. "Sheriff, I have a document signed by Judge Emmett Stone. Mr. Edwards is to be released on a bond posted this morning. And you are sworn to uphold the law of Carter County and the Constitution of the United States of America."

His sweat-stained hat propped toward the back of his head, Nave shot back, "Who posted this bond? And why am I the last to hear 'bout all this?"

"That is none of your concern, Sheriff Nave."

"You heard the man, Nave!" Jake Edwards shouted from the back. "You let me outta here! Now!"

The lawyer, handing the release order document to Nave, grimaced as if he were running out of patience. "I was in here yesterday, Sheriff, and Mr. Edwards filled out the proper paper work then. Your deputy Duke Rayburn, I might add, was kind enough to assist us."

Nave read the piece of paper quickly, getting angrier by the second. *That damned Duke and the Klan! I know they're in on this. I'm gonna fire him the first chance I get. He's not only a liar. Now he's consortin' with a murderer.*

"Mr. Roberts, my deputy did not have the authority to let you talk to my prisoner, so this here paper's not worth nothin'."

Roberts chuckled, yanked on his fine, tailor-made trousers, shuffled from side to side in his finely polished, black shoes and gave the lawman his most determined "I mean business" stare. "Now see here, Sheriff Nave! You can't keep Jake Edwards from having legal counsel. Surely you know that. You've taken an oath to uphold the law, and the law says a man's presumed innocent until proven guilty. My client is innocent."

Nave had heard what he considered this legal mumbo jumbo before, on many occasions. And he had managed to deflect it, reminding anyone who made a demand that he release a prisoner that his elected duty was to protect the public—at all costs.

But L. Ross Roberts wasn't just anyone. He was one of Carter County's most successful and experienced lawyers and one of its most expensive. He wouldn't be deterred. The more he talked to Nave about the judge's order of release, the more adamant the immaculately dressed attorney became. The sheriff' knew he was fighting an up-hill battle. And he sure as hell didn't want to get on Judge Emmett Stone's bad side.

"Unlock this damn cell now, Nave, or I'll have the judge find you in contempt of a court order!" Edwards hollered. He resumed the irritable banging on the cell bars with the metal eating pan, now causing an even louder distraction.

"Let Edwards out, Oliver," said Nave, handing the document back to defense attorney Roberts. "Then go fetch Deputy Duke. He and I are gonna have another little talk."

"Get me outta this damned cell before I starve ta death!" The demand came loud from the cell behind the office. Sheriff Nave knew when he had to give in. He didn't like it one bit but he had no choice but to free a man he considered to be a full-fledged member of the KKK.

As the deputy went to release a gloating Jake Edwards, Nave

turned to Roberts. "You might inform your client that if any harm comes to Elijah Wood, his wife or anyone else involved in this case, I will personally hold him responsible, so help me God. And we don't take lightly to scare tactics used by the Ku Klux Klan."

"I can assure you, Sheriff Nave, Jake Edwards has been wrongly accused and he's an upstanding, law abidin' citizen who'd never be associated with any unlawful activity such as you describe. In fact, I intend to prove that my client's actions were justified."

"You heard my lawyer, Nave!" said Edwards. "This ain't nothin' but a trumped up charge from a lyin' nigger!"

"Take your upstanding client, and you and your twenty-dollar suit, and get outta my office, Mr. Roberts. I've heard all the outright lyin' I can handle in one day. But I'm warnin' you, he makes one wrong move or tries to harm or scare Elijah and Ruthie Wood, I'll throw him back in my jail faster'n greased lightnin'. Nave had one hand on his big-holstered firearm and the other hand in his bullet-strewn belt. It was as if he were itching to catch the scheming Jake Edwards in the wrong.

Roberts, knowing that the no-nonsense sheriff meant business, assured him that Edwards would stay clean.

Later that day, Sheriff Nave paid a visit to the office of Daniel Smith's son, Charles Smith. He was the newly appointed and popular prosecuting attorney for Carter County.

"What can I do for you, Sheriff?" Smith asked. The handsome young man with a warm handshake was dressed in a neatly-pressed, gray suit with a black vest. One of the community's most eligible bachelors, he sported a red bowtie and puffed on a pipe. He asked the sheriff to take a seat.

The two men exchanged pleasantries about Charles' father and stepmother, Daniel and Mary Smith. Then Nave got down to business: "Has the Jake Edwards case been turned over to you yet?"

"Got it this morning, Sheriff. Why do you ask?"

The sheriff leaned forward in the huge oversized oak chair in front of Smith's desk.

"Well, it's likely the only eyewitness to what happened to Toby Jackson is Elijah Wood. And frankly, I'm worried that something bad could happen to him. The old man and his wife came to see me early this morning. They are scared to death, downright terrified, after that Ku Klux Klan raid on their little shack last night. You mighta heard about it."

"Yeah. News and gossip travel fast in Carter County, Sheriff." The young prosecutor reloaded and tamped his pipe with tobacco. Nave at that moment could see a striking resemblance between him and his father. Young Charlie had giant shoes to fill. The sheriff hoped that Daniel's oldest son had inherited his father's integrity and sense of good will.

Sheriff Nave continued, "I promised Elijah and Ruthie Wood that no harm would come to'em, and I intend to keep that promise. That's where you come in."

"So how can I help, Sheriff?"

"Find'em a place to stay. Get'em off that farm and away from Jake Edwards. Keep'em safe. They's a big murder trial comin' up and we need their testimony. We cain't afford nothin' bad to happen to'em."

Charlie Smith said he'd ask Isaiah and Prissy—his parents' longtime loyal employees—to take the Woodses in. "I'm sure they will do it, They are good people who take care of their own."

Nave thanked him profusely. Then the two men shook hands, and agreed to stay in close contact.

"I'll personally see to it that Elijah and Ruthie are taken good care of," Smith promised. "Because, as you say, we're gonna' need'em at the trial. I took a look at the evidence and we need all the help we can get bringin' Jake Edwards to justice."

The next day, Isaiah with Prissy pulled their wagon to a stop in front of the Woods' shack, and Elijah and Ruthy walked out on their porch.

"Isaiah, you come ta visit us?" asked the stooped over old man. "Why you comin' dis way taday? I know y'all have a lotta work ta do."

Before Isaiah could answer, he and Prissy noticed a big black bear hanging in a giant, sprawling beech tree about twenty yards from Elijah's porch. The bear was sniffing and clawing at a bees' nest in a hollowed place in the tree, about fifteen feet off the ground.

Prissy pointed and Elijah and Ruthie also noticed the bear. "I bet that old bear has found a honey bees' nest," said Prissy. Sure enough, as the four of them watched spellbound, the hungry animal started reaching in the hole.

Meanwhile, bees started covering the bear; but only a few stingers penetrated the thick fur.

Bent on finding the honey, the bear seemed to ignore the attacking bees. He reached into the hole and into the nest, pulling out a hunk of the honey comb and devouring it. After pulling out another comb, aware of the humans and feeling threatened, he slid back down the tree with the comb in his mouth and disappeared back into the dense Tennessee forest.

"I wish a big ol' black bear get a hold dat evil Jake Edwards, Elijah," Ruthie said, her head dropping. He gonna' kill us."

"That ain't gonna happen, Ruthie," Isaiah objected. "Cause me an' Prissy come hea today to fetch you and Elijah. Jake Edwards has been let outta jail, but—

"Oh! Lawdy!" Ruthie hollered.

"Now Ruthie, he ain't gonna lay a hand on you. You stayin' with me an' Prissy."

"Oh Lawdy!" Ruthie cried again, clutching her elbows.

"You will be safe with us, Ruthie," Prissy assured her.

"But you an' Isaiah ain't got room for us, Prissy," Ruthie said. Her husband wrapped his arms around her and dabbed her tears with a handkerchief.

Finally, the old wrinkled colored woman got a hold of herself. But she noted again that while Isaiah and Prissy had good intentions, they had just a little cabin and barely enough space for themselves.

"We will make room, Ruthie," Prissy said. "You are coming with us. Let's get your stuff loaded in this wagon. And don't leave nothin' you need. 'Cause you ain't comin' back anytime soon."

"The Lawd must be havin' a hand in dis, Ruthie," Elijah implored his wife. "I b'leve we sposed ta go with Isaiah an' Prissy. We have ta pack our things."

And so, the two old, former slaves, longtime employees of Jake Edwards, set about deciding what they'd take with them from the dilapidated shack they'd lived in, and birthed two sons in, for the past fifty years. It wasn't much of a place to live, with missing shingles on the warped roof, rotting, creaking floors and a porch that sagged to one side, but it was their home. In it were their few scant possessions—old chairs with wobbly legs, a scattering of dented pots and pans, hand-me-down dishes and glasses, a scratched up little table in their eating area, a long-ago stained and worn-out feather bed, a few blankets, raggedy bed-sheets and the best of practically worn-out clothes, the faded quilt that Ruthie had made using scraps of cloth the Edwardes had thrown out.

So what to take with them to Isaiah and Prissy's little abode a few miles away in Fish Springs, and what to leave behind?

After packing the essentials, Ruthie and Elijah took one last sorrowful walk through the three-room shack, making sure they didn't leave anything they would need or want later.

"You want dat old 'bacca can, Elijah? Ain't you got some nails in it?" Ruthie asked. She pointed to a rough-hewn shelf just above her head.

"Nah, I don't reckon I be doin any nailin'."

"Isaiah! You needs any nails?" Ruthie hollered.

"Sho'. A man can never have too many nails."

Elijah reached up and got the Old Virginia tobacco can, and he and Ruthie walked, hand in hand, out of the shack for the last time. Seeing that the wagon seat had only enough room for three people, Prissy found a little empty spot just behind the seat.

As they pulled away and started toward the road, the Negroes found their path blocked by none other than Jake Edwards standing in the path beside his buggy. Isaiah's first impulse was to speed up and hope that Edwards wouldn't move out of the way fast enough. But his good judgment forced him to pull to a stop.

His anger boiling over, Edwards looked like a man obsessed.

"Where in the hell do you think you're goin', Ruthie! You need to get up to the big house and make me some supper."

Then, looking at the loaded down wagon full of wares, cloth-ing, blankets and a few sticks of furniture, Jake hollered, "What in the hell's goin' on here?"

"We be leavin', Mista Edwards, fo' good, and we ain't comin' back," Elijah said bravely. "The Lawd and de sheriff be takin' care of us."

"Like Hell you are! You get your nigger asses off that damn wagon right now!" Edwards demanded, shaking his cane in the air.

Isaiah acted as if he had heard nothing. He snapped the reins and his mule Sue trotted off, causing the enraged, red-faced Edwards to step to the side and lose his balance, falling on his butt.

"You will pay for takin' my help, Isaiah!" he said. He got up and brushed the dirt from off his overalls. "By God, this time, you will pay!"

All four were aware of what the enraged man meant by, "This time you will pay."

Isaiah could barely hear Edwards' cursing as the wagon rolled over the rocky and bumpy road to Fish Springs. But it was clear to him that Edwards had made the threatening reference to this time. That brought back fateful memories of a time some fifteen years earlier; Daniel Smith and Isaiah, on a visit to buy hay from Jake Edwards, had rescued Prissy from practically being a slave girl to the hateful man and his mean-spirited wife. Edwards had threatened them then—all those years ago—when Prissy had thrown her few belongings in their wagon and left his employ forever, and now he was threatening them again. With a vengeance.

So be it, Isaiah thought, Prissy's arm around his big broad shoulder as he again snapped the reins and bid the horse and wagon onward toward Fish Springs and home.

As the wagon bumped along, Ruthie, feeling safe for the first time in several days, looked up at Prissy and Isaiah smiling. "Old Jake has a hard time keeping help don't he?"

No one said anything for several seconds. Then they all burst out laughing.

CHAPTER 10

A Proper Farewell

As word spread around Carter County about the arrest of Jake Edwards and why he was being arrested, the colored community rejoiced. At the same time, however, some Negroes knew full well that it would be an uphill struggle to have Edwards convicted of murder in a "white man's court."

Regardless, the Rev. Horace Leftwich of the Colored Baptist Church in Elizabethton—the founding "Mother Church" of Negros in East Tennessee—figured it was high time to give Toby Jackson a proper farewell. His remains had been interred, quietly and without ceremony, a few days earlier in the church cemetery, but no one had yet had an opportunity to pay their final respects to "brother Toby."

The Rev. Leftwich, founder of the church and himself a former slave, let it be known that a proper funeral service would be held for Toby following the regular church service as he had promised Isaiah. Leftwich said that all who had known the deceased—and even those who had not—were invited to attend and say their godly farewells.

Attend they did. The size of the congregation swelled as word of Toby's funeral service had spread through the community. The pews of the Colored Baptist Church were packed. Many of the men came in scuffed boots, muddy overalls and ragged shirts. Women made more of an effort to look their best, with several of them in bonnets and plain, but clean and neatly-pressed dresses and recently store-bought footwear.

Heads were bowed; prayers were said and hands linked. When the attendees—some old, some young, all of them colored—solemnly sang a few Negro spirituals, bodies swayed and hands clapped. A few cried and hugged.

Leftwich, a leader in the Negro community in Carter County, offered a serious but hopeful message. "We come here today, brothers and sisters, to honor and say good-bye to one of our own. His name was Toby Jackson and God only gave him thirty years on this man's earth," Leftwich preached.

"We don't know why these things happen. We don't understand why God allows evildoers to do sinful, awful deeds. And we will never know.

"What we do know, brothers and sisters, is that Toby Jackson was a decent, Christ-believin' man, and he never hurt nobody in his whole life. He was a gentle, kind soul, who only wanted what we all want—a chance for somethin' better, maybe a wife and family, his own piece'a land, his own crop and a few cows'n chickens and pigs.

"But brother Toby, the son of slaves and a slave himself before the Emancipation Proclamation, never got that chance. He never even got a chance to buy himself a new suit'a clothes or to sleep in a real bed or be served a meal," Leftwich added.

"A evil man took his life!" a grieving old woman from the back of the church shouted. "Thangs is gonna have ta change 'round hea'!"

"Amen!" yelled a man sitting a few rows in front of her.

Mumbling and a sense of unease and anger filled the sanctuary. Tensions seemed about ready to boil over.

Leftwich held up both his hands for calm. "Yes, we all know that there are sick, bad people in this world, but this is a time for grieving and prayer, ladies and gentlemen. And we should pray for the soul of the man who took our dear Toby's life. We should ask that he be forgiven, so that he doesn't spend eternity in the lake of fire—"

"Why should we do that?" an old codger, standing up, blurted out. "He murdered Toby in cold blood, and now he ain't even in jail!"

Again, the Rev. Leftwich beseeched his listeners to remain calm and prayerful. Then he spoke passionately about justice and righteousness. "There is a fight to be fought. We all know that. But believe this with all your heart, folks. Toby Jackson did not die in vain. And his death shall be avenged, if not by a judge and jury in a court of law, then by our Almighty Heavenly Father!

"But in the meantime, we have to give the court a chance, believin' that Toby will get his justice and that even white folks'll see sin for what it is—ugly, mean, evil, vindictive."

"What he mean by dat vindictive?" a young girl whispered to her grandmother seated next to her.

"Shush," the old woman, elbowing the youth, said. "I 'splain' ta you later."

"The Bible says that because Toby Jackson was a believer, he's not dead. He's only asleep in Christ," Leftwich reassured them. "And soon he will be with Jesus in eternity, because, at any moment, in the twinklin' of an eye, Jesus could come again—ridin' a cloud and wrappin' his arms 'round all of us.

"So today, as we go out these church doors and return to our homes and families, pray for Toby Jackson's soul and pray for the man who took his life. And be in a relaxed state of mind. Let go of your burdens. Let justice take its course. Rest peacefully."

Meanwhile, a few miles away, in the heart of busy Elizabethton, life churned on. Dozens of loggers, who worked in nearby sawmill camps—with cookhouses, dining halls and bunkhouses—had come to town to drink, carouse for women or otherwise have a good time. Likewise, the bustling little town's leather goods shops, cobblers, general stores, post office, boarding houses and livery stables had a higher than normal number of patrons.

Two elderly, wide-eyed men on a whittler's bench took it all in and wondered where all the people had come from.

"They's a lot of em from all them iron mines and timber camps out'en the county," one man opined. "They've got a pocketful of money and they've come ta town ta spend it."

"Yeah, I bet tha Black Bear'll sell a buncha' whiskey taday," the other said. "And them gals workin' there'll get a workout upstairs."

The two whittlers noticed a nervous-looking Jake Edwards

climbing down from his buggy across the street and walking to the law office of L. Ross Roberts.

"Right there goes a man in a heapa' trouble, but he ain't neva' gonna' be found guilty of killin' no darkie. No sir. No judge in his right mind'll send old Jake up tha' river."

"They say they's a strong case against 'em," the other whittler said.

"It don't make no nevermind," said the first, spitting a stream of tobacco. "Mark my words. Sure as I'm whittlin' on this stick here, old Jake'll never serve another day in jail. The Klan'll save him, and he'll laugh all the way home when this court business is done."

But Edwards, as he approached the law office, didn't look confident. He seemed bewildered, unsettled. He had not shaven or bathed in days and his hair, what little of it he had left, was scraggly.

A small, middle-aged man greeted Jake as he entered the waiting room. "Can I help you sir?" asked the bespectacled man whose dark hair was parted down the middle.

"I'm Jake Edwards, and I am here to see L. Ross Roberts."

"Please be seated, Mr. Edwards," he said, pushing his spectacles slightly higher on his nose. "Can I bring you a cup of coffee?"

The unkempt, sullen Edwards just snarled, saying he had come only to speak with L. Ross Roberts and not to drink coffee.

"In that case, sir, Mr. Roberts will be with you shortly."

The man tapped on Roberts' office door then stepped inside. A couple of minutes later he came out and and returned to his desk while Edwards fidgeted in his chair. A big grandather clock ticked loudly from one corner of the room. A half hour later, still no L. Ross Roberts.

"Clerk, I ain't waitin' much longer," Edwards growled. "I've come all the way from Valley Forge. Now is Mr. Roberts gonna' see me or ain't he?"

The clerk said he would peek inside and remind his boss that someone was waiting for him.

"And tell'im I ain't waitin' no longer!" Edwards barked. "My time's worth as much as his!"

About five minutes later, the clerk said Edwards could go on inside Roberts' private office.

And enter he did, but not without angst.

The two men, one Elizabethton's richest, most expensive lawyer, and the other a big land owner from Valley Forge who hated coloreds, shook hands.

Roberts told his client to have a seat in one of the two cushioned chairs in front of the lawyer's massive oaken desk.

As Edwards plunked down, he noticed bookcases, from floor to ceiling, built into one wall of the office. Books, more books than Jake Edwards had seen in his entire life, filled those shelves. On the opposite side of the office was a sprawling fireplace. Above it, a mantle with fine pottery and porcelain vases. Above the mantle mounted on the wall was an Elk's head with large ten-point antlers.

Huge majestic oil paintings and tapestries hung from the other three walls. One was a picture of a snowy mountaintop; the other a beautiful rendition of two wolves howling beneath a foggy, yellow moon; the final painting was of L. Ross Roberts, his wife and their two children.

On Roberts' long, oversized desk were two brass oil lamps, a magnifying glass, more books and the blindfolded Roman goddess of justice with her scales standing on a marble base. A red oriental rug, with an even darker red floral pattern and a gold fringe, covered most of the floor.

Everything about Mr. L. Ross Roberts' office spoke of grandeur, success, intellect, elegance, the best that money could buy.

Edwards took it all in and had the nagging feeling that very soon some of his own money would be in Roberts' bank account.

"Mr. Edwards, sorry to have kept you waiting. What can I do for you today?"

"Well, first of all I preciate you gettin' me outta that jail cell an' all."

"Not to worry, Mr. Edwards. I was glad to do it—for a fee, of course," the smiling lawyer replied.

Edwards said, "So what's your fee, Mr. Roberts? I don't reckon we ever discussed that. I ain't 'spectin' you ta hep me fer nothin'."

"That's good, Mr. Edwards, because you've been charged with

a very serious crime—first degree murder—and you will need the best legal representation possible. And I should warn you, my services will be costly."

"Just how costly? What ya' meanin'?"

"Mr. Edwards, how much money do you have in the bank or in your savings?" Roberts asked the question, not making eye contact with his client. Instead, he stared at the oil painting, directly behind Edwards, of the snowy mountain.

"Now that ain't none'a your business!" Edwards snapped. "We ain't here ta talk about how much money I have. You're spposed ta be defendin' me."

"Yes sir, but at a price, Mr. Edwards. And my fee is very high in a capital murder case."

"I killed a lyin' no-good nigger, for God's sake!"

L. Ross Roberts seemed to ignore that statement, returning instead to the prickly subject of his legal fee. "My services will cost you, at the very least, a thousand dollars. And that number could very well be higher, depending on the complexity of your case."

Jake Edwards grew silent, numbed at what he had just heard. Then he spoke, "They ain't nary a man in Valley Forge, maybe in all 'a Carter County, that's got that kinda' money saved up. You ain't nothin' but a high fallutin' thief in a suit!"

"And you, Mr. Edwards, face a charge of murder for shooting an unarmed man in the back of the head. If you desire my services but don't have the necessary cash, then I will require you to sign over to me the deed to your property. I will hold such deed in trust until you can come up with the necessary funds to pay me—within a reasonable time, of course."

"You are insane!" Edwards, standing up, shot back.

"In that case, Mr. Edwards, good day. Jenkins!" Roberts called out. "Please see Mr. Edwards out." Roberts spoke calmly, coolly, confidently, as if he had better things to do than try to persuade Jake Edwards to hire him.

"Wait just a damned minute," Edwards, jittery, countered. "Let's say I'm found guilty of killin' that no-good worthless nigger. What's the worst thing could happen ta me?"

Jenkins stood at the door ready to escort Edwards out.

"Never mind, Jenkins."

"You could be sent to the gallows, but more than likely you would be sent to the Tennessee State Prison in Nashville," Roberts said. "Either way, your life, as you know it, would end quickly."

"Whaddya mean?" Jake sat back down.

"Because even if you escaped the gallows, Mr. Edwards, you would spend the rest of your days rotting in a prison cell and working on a chain gang. You are sixty-eight years old. You're a white man. You killed a colored man. You wouldn't last long in prison."

"What makes you so sure of that?" Edwards squirmed in his chair.

"Because very many of those in the Tennessee State Prison are Negroes, and they're mean. White people in a white court of law put them where they are. They will absolutely have their way with you, Mr. Edwards.

"And have you ever heard what it's like for a white man to be shackled on a chain gang—with colored prisoners, no less? To have to eat, sleep and work with Negro men? It's brutal, Mr. Edwards. It's torture. You will wish you were dead."

The fear of God descended on Jake Edwards. His knees went wobbly and he started breathing faster.

"Gimmy that damn paper. I'll sign it." he said. "And you hafta do all you can to help me beat this charge. I'm dependin' on you, Mr. Roberts."

"That's more like it, Mr. Edwards," Roberts said, grinning and smelling a windfall of money. "Get me that deed to your property by the end of this week. Good day. I will be in touch very soon. Jenkins will escort you out." Roberts opened his office door and nodded to his clerk.

Meanwhile on the outskirts of Fish Springs, Daniel Smith and his son Charlie, the prosecuting attorney for the case against Jake Edwards, pulled their buggy to a stop in front of Isaiah and Prissy's cabin.

"Hi, folks!" Daniel said, waving to the four Negroes.

"Hello, Mista Smith!" The four responded in unison. Isaiah and Prissy sat in a porch swing, and Elijah and Ruthie were in rocking chairs.

Isaiah said, "You folks come set a spell on the poch with us, Mista Daniel, Mista Charlie."

Prisssy instructed her husband, "Get'a couple of those chairs from the kitchen."

"I suppose you hea' to talk to us about Mista Jake Edwards and what's gonna happen now," Isaiah said as he brought two chairs to the porch.

Charlie, taking a chair, nodded, yes. "Dad and Sheriff Nave told me everything you told them. But I need more. I'm the prosecuting attorney for Carter County. That means it's my sworn duty to gather enough evidence against Jake Edwards to convince the jury to find him guilty of murder and put him in prison or sentence him to death. But—"

"Yea!" a smiling Prissy hollered.

"Hang dat devil!" Ruthy chimed in.

Charlie let the four enjoy the excitement of the moment. Then he said they should listen to him carefully. "I know it's not fair but the cold hard fact is that it's not likely that a white man would be hanged for killing a Negro."

Charlie paused to let that sink in.

Ruthie whispered in Elijah's ear.

"Mista Charlie, Ruthie would like you to explain how a jury works."

Charlie smiled and looked Ruthie straight in the eye. "Twelve men will be picked by drawing lots to hear the case. They are called the jury. They will listen to the evidence …"

He stopped talking when he could tell by Ruthie's expression she didn't know what evidence meant. "Things that people heard or saw that will convince the twelve men that Toby did not owe Jake Edwards any money and that Jake killed Toby Jackson out of pure hatred. Then if the jury finds Jake guilty of murder, the judge will decide his punishment."

"But all twelve of those men have ta say he's guilty. Ain't that right, Mista Charlie?"

"That's exactly right, Isaiah," Charlie replied, surprised that one of his listeners would be so well versed in the law.

Elijah asked, "Lawdy Lawdy, does you think we has a chance?"

"Yes, Elijah, we have a chance, but I need all the help I can get."

The oldest son of Daniel Smith paused again to make sure what he said next would be clear. "All we have now is your word, Elijah, that Toby told you he'd paid off his bill at Jake's store. That's called hearsay, and you can't use it as evidence against Edwards. So we have nothing really. If only we had some physical evidence, like that receipt that showed Toby paid his bill off. Then Jake would not have had the right to try and keep Toby from leaving."

Daniel, who had been listening in silence, spoke up. "I saw the remains, and if there had been a receipt hidden anywhere on Toby it surely would have rotted away. It's really unfortunate that old woman died. She could've won this case for you, son."

The others looked puzzled at that statement but said nothing.

"Yes, I know, Dad," Charlie agreed. "But we'll just have to come up with something. If we all put our heads together somethin'll come up. And all four of you, anything you can think of, I don't care how small it is, tell me about it. I know you want justice for your friend, and I'll do my best, so help me God, to build a case against Jake Edwards."

"Mista Charlie, I have a question."

"Sure, Isaiah."

"Even if Toby did steal from Mr. Edwards, and I know he didn't, could Jake've shot Toby in the backa' his head and be found innocent of murder?"

"No, not normally. But Jake Edwards will make up a story. You can count on that, Isaiah. Like he feared for his life because Toby threatened to kill him with his bare hands, which I am sure he could have done.

"I will be truthful with you, Isaiah. If it had been a white man Jake Edwards killed it'd be easier to get a guilty verdict. But we still have a chance."

"Thank you, Mista Charlie. All'a us will do anything we can to help you. And thank you, Mista Daniel," Prissy said "Me and Isaiah know that you would be the man to go to if we wanted to get anything done. Looks like your son will be walkin' in his father's footsteps. I bet you are right proud a'him."

"Who? This rascal?!" said Daniel, mussing Charlie's neatly combed hair and slapping him on the back. "Truth be known, he's a lot smarter than his old man. Got bigger feet, too." Daniel laughed along with the others.

"Well, we better be goin', folks. Mary's cookin' a big pot of tater soup and some'a that cornbread Prissy taught her how to make."

Charlie, smacking his lips, asked, "Do you have enough for your starving young'in?

"Maybe. Depends."

"Pa!"

"Come on, son. Let's go. Mary's waitin' for us."

As father and son said their goodbyes to the four Negroes, Isaiah began shuffling from side to side. Something had been bothering him and he couldn't keep from speaking up.

"Excuse me for keepin' you, Mista Daniel, but I need to ask you somethin'."

"Sure, Isaiah. What's on your mind?"

"What old woman were you talkin' about that died?"

Daniel turned to his son. "The elderly woman that ran Jake's store. What was her name, Charlie?"

"Fanny May Brown."

Isaiah looked at Prissy and the others, then back at Daniel.

"What is it, Isaiah? Spit it out."

"When did Fanny May die, Mista Daniel?"

"Shortly after she moved to Knoxville to live with her daughter."

Isaiah looked at the other three Negroes who were shaking their heads, no.

"Mista Daniel, Fanny May ain't dead! She's old but she ain't dead!"

"No, she ain't!" the others chimed in.

Daniel scratched his head. "How do y'all know this?"

"Mista Daniel."

"Yes, Prissy."

"About two weeks ago at our church in Elizabethton, Reverend Leftwich told the congregation he got a letter from Fanny May's daughter, Mattie. She said her mama was doin' good and that she'd be 100 years old on her next birthday. Don't rightly remember just when that was."

"In July," Isaiah said.

There was a long pause. Then Daniel and Charlie cracked big smiles.

"Glory be! Fanny May Brown is alive?" Charlie exclaimed. "When you told me she was dead, I had no reason to doubt it."

"Well son, Sheriff Nave is the one who told me. I took him at his word."

"And I bet I know where he heard it," Charlie said. "He shoulda' verified something that important. That's not like Sheriff Nave."

Daniel grinned. "Charlie, looks like your chances of winning this case just went from ten percent to fifty percent."

"That's a good chance. Right, Mista Daniel?"

"A very good chance, Isaiah. A damned good chance!"

The Negroes could barely contain their excitement.

But Charlie reminded them that he first had to find Fanny May Brown, and that might not be so easy—Knoxville being a big town and about 150 miles away. Plus, he noted that the old woman probably was living among colored folks, in a part of the community that might not be so welcoming to a white prosecutor. It might not be so easy, to say the least, to locate Fanny May.

But Daniel Smith refused to believe that the potential star witness couldn't be found. "You'll get her, son. We have confidence in you. Right, folks?"

Isaiah, Prissy and Elijah—all of them smiling and hugging—nodded, yes.

Ruthie, who wasn't quite sure what confidence meant, had a conflicted expression—part happiness, part reservation which elicited a burst of laughter. "If anybody can find Miss Fanny May," Ruthie said, "I guess it be Mista Charlie."

CHAPTER 11

Finding Fanny May

Two days after learning the elusive Fanny May was alive and living somewhere in Knoxville, Tennessee, Charlie went to see the Rev. Horace Leftwich at the Colored Baptist Church. Charlie remembered the first time he had seen Leftwich. It was when he married Isaiah and Prissy on his dad's farm fifteen years earlier.

He had made an impression on the then young and brash Charlie because he was so well-spoken. Daniel Smith's son had from time to time seen the former slave-turned-preacher around town and at various functions. The Rev. Leftwich, looked up to by Negroes throughout East Tennessee, always asked about Isaiah and Prissy as well as Charlie's father and mother.

The bespectacled colored man with graying temples and a slightly hunched back answered the door of the modest wood frame house next to the church and greeted Charlie with a big smile.

"Mista Smith, how nice to see you," said the reverend, extending his hand.

The two men mentioned that it had been too long since their paths had last crossed.

"Is this business or social? I'm not being prosecuted for anything am I? If I am, the devil made me do it."The preacher's tone was jovial as he asked the handsome young prosecutor to sit down in an old canebrake chair.

"No, you're good for now, Reverend. I'm working on Toby Jackson's case and I'm here to see if you can help me locate Fanny May Brown. I'm leaving for Knoxville in the morning."

Leftwich, leaning forward slightly, looked at Charlie with renewed interest.

"She could be a very important witness in bringing Jake Edwards to justice, and I was told you received a letter from Fanny May's daughter."

"That would be Mattie," Leftwich replied. "Yes sir, I heard from her not long ago."

The jovial minister's demeanor became more serious. "Mattie said that they was moving soon, because the home they were rentin' was bein' sold. She told me they would let me know their new address after they moved."

Charlie frowned and dropped his head slightly. "That's not good. Do you have any idea at all where they are now?"

"I wish I had kept that letter. I think their street address was Oak or maybe Elm, some kinda' tree. I shoulda' kept that letter. I knew I shoulda kept it! I'm so sorry."

Charlie stood up and consolingly put his hand on Leftwich's shoulder. "Did she say anything in the letter that might'of given any clues as to where I might find them? Anything at all?"

The reverend closed his eyes. "I DO remember somethin'! Mattie said they had visited a church in a community called Beartown. Darn! I wish I could tell you more, Charlie." The venerable clergyman gritted his teeth and shook his head in frustration.

"Don't be so hard on yourself, Reverend. I know a lot more now than I did when I came in here. I'll find her. There can't be that many ninety-nine-year-old women visiting a church in a place called Beartown."

Leftwich said, "I'd gladly go with you if wasn't for Wednesday night prayer meeting. Toby was a good man, Charlie, a godly man. The last time I talked to him was the Sunday before he was to leave for Alabama. He was so excited about seein' his little brother.

"Please let me know if I can help you with your investigation. I mean that with all my heart. And give my best to your folks, Charlie. They are good people."

Charlie thanked the reverend and bid him farewell.

The young Mr. Smith rose at five in the morning the next day, drank a cup of coffee and ate a piece of cornbread he had salvaged from the meal at his parents' house two nights ago. *When outta biscuits a piece a' cornbread goes good with coffee,* he thought.

This early in the morning was when he did some of his best thinking. *Sure as my name's Charlie Smith, I'll find Fanny May Brown. If I have ta turn over every blamed rock in Knoxville or Beartown or wherever she is, I'll find her. So help me God. And I know it might not be easy, me bein' a white man an' all, prowlin' through a colored neighborhood, but I'll do it. I just needa' break. One person to put me on the right path. Just one lead and I'll find her. And then I'll bring Jake Edwards to justice!*

After packing a bag for the overnight stay in Knoxville, he also made a lunch for the trip. Then he found his way to the depot in Elizabethton, where at 6:30 a.m. he would board the train, affectionately called the "Tweetsie" in reference to the sound of its steam whistles. It carried freight and passengers through the rugged Southern Appalachian mountains and regularly ran on the tracks of the East Tennessee and Western North Carolina Railroad.

After a short trip to Johnson's Depot, Charlie stepped off the train and sat in the depot for two and a half hours before boarding another train that ran on the East Tennessee, Virginia & Georgia Railroad. Charlie's ride would leave Johnson's Depot at 9:40, then make stops at Jonesborough, Greeneville, Rogersville and Morristown, along with nine other small communities.

Along the way, he was struck by the magnificent scenery of East Tennessee—especially its rocky, gushing creeks, where trout and other species of fish thrived, and its meandering rivers where giant water birds seemed to enjoy being perched on boulders. Occasionally up high on the steep cliffs Charlie could make out what he believed to be eagles' nests.

Along the way were plenty of barns, fences, livestock and houses—some of them crude cabins, but others grand, stately dwellings that anyone would be proud to live in.

This part of Tennessee, Charlie thought, was no longer the wild, untamed frontier that his parents and grandparents had found when they settled here decades ago. It was fast being discovered and settled by immigrants, by Indians who had adopted the ways of the white man, by former slaves yearning for a better life, who had migrated here from plantations in Virginia, Georgia and the Carolinas, and by others who were drawn to the soothing beauty and spiritual aura of these mountains.

Finally, the train's shrill whistle signaled that it had arrived in the outskirts of Knoxville, right on schedule. Charlie guessed that it would come very close to reaching its final destination by the appointed time of 8:52 p.m.

As the train slowed and chugged along for its last few miles, Charlie mused that he was a long way from Elizabethton. Knoxville, one of the bustling hubs of the Old South, seemed to have everything—from street preachers, saloons, whore houses and gambling dens, to churches, cotton spinning factories, mercantile stores and fine hotels. Hotels where a person could rest their bones in comfort and leisure, soak in a huge tub of hot sudsy water, and have their fill of fine cigars, imported wines and delectable foods.

Just a few years earlier, during the Civil War, Knoxville had been controlled by troops from the South, but then had fallen to the Union.

But that seemed like way in the past, as Charlie stepped off the train with his suitcase in hand and took in the surroundings. Everywhere, it seemed, people were scurrying here and there. Some were walking. Others were in buggies or on horseback. Still others sat in chairs or on benches in front of their businesses. Here and there peddlers hawked their wares from carts. Women in bonnets and long, full skirts held their little ones in tow. There, too, in abundance, were business men clad in suits, along with others wearing buckskins or overalls.

He waved down a carriage, and, on the ride to his hotel, Charlie made arrangements with the driver to pick him up the next morning at 9. The driver was an elderly man with thick gray hair, a long thin nose and squared-off shoulders who was good at his job, guiding his horse through the heavy congestion at the depot and arriving at the Oliver Hotel in a matter of minutes.

When Charlie checked into the hotel, considered one of the most elegant in Knoxville, he was disappointed to find that the well-regarded establishment's dining room had stopped serving dinner. But the determined-to-please staff, impeccably dressed in their red uniforms and "drummer boy" hats, were kind enough to bring the attorney from Carter County a smoked ham sandwich. He devoured it, washing it down with a cold beer. *Looks like Carter County saved a little money tonight. Maybe I can make up for it with a big breakfast.*

The prosecutor bathed that evening in a huge porcelain tub beneath a portrait of President Abraham Lincoln and slept well in an oversized bed with the finest linens and blankets that money could buy. The next morning he went down to the hotel dining room where the eating areas had candles, white table cloths and exquisite crystal and china. There he enjoyed a delicious breakfast of scrambled eggs, grits, bacon and biscuits with gravy on the side. And, of course, a large cup of hot black coffee.

Looking around the room as he ate, Charlie noticed well-dressed men sitting in groups. Obviously some were in town on business. Others were having breakfast before work. A few women sat with the men. Others, mostly couples, dressed more casually. Charlie guessed they were visitors bent on taking in a few of the popular tourist spots in Knoxville.

He pushed his plate back and opened the *Knoxville Sentinel* newspaper. He read until 9 a.m. then headed to the main entrance, walking through the well-appointed, tiled lobby with its splashing fountain in the middle. Oversized rocking chairs and a dazzling chandelier added to its elegance.

Finally, out the front door, he boarded the carriage he had arranged for the night before.

"Good morning, sir. Where can I take you?"

Charlie surmised that his driver, wearing black boots that reached almost to his knees, had lived and worked in Knoxville for many years.

"Good morning. I need you to get me to Beartown, driver. And I have no idea where that is."

"The only Beartown I know 'bout is where all them coloreds live, sir."

"That's it. Take me there," Charlie instructed the driver, who seemed a bit uneasy.

"Sir, I can take you but I cain't be ridin' around in there. Some of them darkies don't take kindly to a white man in a carriage in their neighborhood. I ain't sayin' they's all bad folks but ..."

"I understand. Just take me as close to the edge of Beartown as you can. I can walk in."

"Are you armed, sir?"

"No. Should I be?"

"Well, like I said, I ain't sayin they's all bad people, but now if it was me and goin' there ta walk around, I'd have a gun."

That observation startled Charlie. He had never felt unsafe around colored people any more so than any other group of people. But he had to admit he had never been a lone white man in a strange city surrounded by hundreds, if not thousands, of Negroes.

A short ride later the carriage pulled to a stop at the edge of Beartown.

Charlie paid the driver and climbed down.

"Sir, carriages for hire often travel this road, so you should be able to flag one down later. And sir, I think to be on the safe side, be out of here before dark."

"I intend to. Thanks for the advice."

As Charlie looked around, he again realized he was a world away from Elizabethton. Beartown was all row houses or dingy buildings. A few small groups of colored people sat on their front stoops, talking. One old colored woman pulled a little wagon with a child in it. A bedraggled, sad looking, droopy-tailed dog followed. A bent over street sign at the corner read Old Town Road.

It was a crowded place where Negroes, many of them down on their luck or just barely able to make ends make in menial jobs, came to lay their heads, raise their families, worship God.

He was sure these were people who daily confronted fear, deprivation and poverty. Whose lives were hard, and who, even if they were no longer slaves, toiled, for the most part, for greedy, heartless white employers. They were colored folks who dared not be "uppity," lest those who paid them their scant wages took even that away from them.

These same Negroes cleaned the rooms and changed the sheets in Knoxville's palatial hotels or cooked the food in the city's fine restaurants, or labored day in and day out in the quarries and mines just outside Knoxville. Others of this exploited class of coloreds curried and stabled and shoed the horses of those privileged whites who conducted business in Knoxville or who had come here to sightsee or enjoy themselves.

Some shouting and commotion caught Charlie's attention just ahead. A crowd of onlookers had formed, and many craned their necks in curiosity. A sobbing woman and her three little children were being put out of their home.

A sheriff and his deputy stood close by as the white landlord ordered his four colored helpers to remove all her possessions and place them at the edge of the road. The middle-aged, fat and balding landlord was obviously reminding the distraught soul that she hadn't paid her rent. The landlord, pointing at her spitefully, yelled that she had been warned time and again about the consequences of not paying up.

The light-skinned woman bawled, and then ranted and cursed and shook her fists at the landlord. Her husband, *or was it just a gentleman friend of hers?* Charlie wondered, pleaded for one more chance at scraping up rent money. But the hard-hearted landlord kept shaking his head, no, and ordered his men to continue removing the family's meager possessions.

"You devil!" screamed the woman. She lunged at the landlord, rolls of fat sagging over his belt, who fell backwards on his butt. Then the deputy grabbed her as she was about to pounce on him.

"I want that woman arrested, Sheriff!"

"You ain't hurt, fat man. Just get that house emptied. I ain't got all day to be here. I've got more important things to do."

"And woman," the exasperated, sheriff warned. "One more outburst like that and I'm haulin' you off to jail. You've been served an eviction notice, and you have to abide by it. For the sake of your children, sit down there and keep your mouth shut."

Charlie took the scene in and concluded that this occurrence, painful and humiliating as it was for the young family, was probably something that played out again and again in a place like Beartown.

He felt sympathy for her, but his time was limited so he kept walking deeper into Beartown.

Soon he sensed that he was being followed. Glancing back several times, he finally noticed a small figure gaining on him. The man from Fish Springs stopped and did an about face, looking down on the scruffiest little boy he had ever seen.

The dark skinned lad was covered with dust, like he had been rolling in the dirt. He was barefoot, wore short pants and a tattered red shirt. He had big dark eyes, lots of curly black hair and skinned up knees, as if he'd been playing one too many games of marbles,

"You got's a penny?"

"Why should I give you a penny?" Charlie, slightly amused, figured the kid for more than a street beggar. He seemed somehow smarter, ill at ease at having to ask for money.

"Cuz I need one really bad."

"If I gave you a penny, what would you do with it?"

"I would buy me some candy. I ain't had no candy in two years."

When Charlie asked the youngster what his name was, he replied "PJ."

And when he asked what "PJ" stood for, the little boy gave him a blank stare.

"It stands for me. That be my name—PJ."

"I mean like Phillip James? Or Paul Johnson?"

"No. just PJ. You gonna g'me a penny or not?" The kid, not taking his eyes off Charlie, was determined to leave the encounter with a penny.

"Look, PJ. I have a job, so I have to work to make my pennies. You still think I should give you some of my money?"

"Yep."

"Why?"

"Cuz I ain't got a job. If I did, I'd give you some a' my pennies."

Charlie, reaching into his pocket, had a hard time not smiling. "You know what, PJ? I think you would. Here's two pennies."

He handed the youth two coins and asked him his age.

"I be seven years old." PJ didn't take his eyes off the pennies.

"Where do you live?"

"Waaay way down dere," PJ said, pointing down the road.

"Why are you so far from your house?"

"I gwine to my mamaw and papaw's house."

"Where do they live, PJ?"

"Waaay way down dere." PJ pointed the way Charlie was walking.

"It's okay with your mom that you walk there by yourself?"

"She wouldn't let me when I was little, but now she do. Afta she go off ta work in da mornin, I walk ta mamaw's house."

"I see. And where does your mother work, PJ?"

"She do house work for some white folks. Waaay over dere." The boy pointed back toward town. "My ma says only white folks dat come to Beartown is bill clecktors. Is you a bill clecktor?"

When Charlie assured him that he wasn't a "bill clecktor" and was instead merely looking for someone, PJ wasn't convinced.

"Ain't NO white folks in Beartown," PJ said emphatically.

"I know, PJ. I'm looking for a colored woman."

"Who she be?"

"Her name is Fanny May Brown," Charlie said. He searched the lad's face for any hint that he might have heard of her.

"Nope. Ain't ringin' my bell," the boy said, after scratching his head and palming the two pennies in one hand, then the other.

"Maybe my mamaw knows her. She old an' she know everbody in Beartown."

"You seem to be a pretty smart fellow PJ, Le—"

"Yep," PJ interrupted, his eyes sparkling.

"Let me ask you somethin' else. Is there an Oak Street or Elm Street in Beartown?"

"Only'est street I knows is mine. Dis'in, O Town Road."

"Any churches in Beartown?"

PJ put his hand on his chin. "Mmm, I thank dey be one close ta mamaw's house. I can show you where."

As Charlie and PJ headed toward the church, two young scowling men, full of themselves and trying to act tough, cut them off at the street corner. They were about 17 or 18 years old.

"Who dis white man, PJ?," one of them asked menacingly. "He a bill clector?"

"Nope. He tryin' ta find somebody."

"Who it be, mista?" the other young man, equally sullen, demanded. "Me an' ma friend knows everbody in Beartown."

"Ain't nobidy here we don't know," the first one said.

"I'm lookin' for Fanny May Brown." Charlie tried not to seem intimidated by the two. "She has a daughter named Mattie."

"Oh yea. We know dem," one of the young men snarled.

"Yea. Dat right. We know dem both." The other youth, his belligerence more pronounced than that of his friend, then demanded to know the reason why this strange white man was looking for Fanny May Brown and her daughter.

Charlie ignored the question. Instead, he asked for information. "Can you tell me where they live? I've come a long way to find them. And I promise you I'm not a bill collector. I need their help. It's very important."

The two young men took this in and began seeing dollar signs.

"Sure, we can hep ya, but it's gonna cost ya a dollar. We ain't heping no white man for nothin'."

Charlie was skeptical and a tad fearful, but for a dollar he was willing to take a chance. *What choice do I have? I have to trust them.*

What surprised him was how fast he would lose his money. And that's exactly what happened when the trusting prosecutor from Carter County reached inside his jacket and pulled out a leather pouch. In a flash, one of the cunning youngsters grabbed it, and the two youths ran like jack rabbits—faster than any humans Charlie had ever seen move.

He chased them for two blocks before conceding defeat.

And when he finally stopped, he noticed JP was still in pursuit, though trailing a block behind the thieves.

Charlie's heart was pounding and his clothes were drenched with sweat. Disgusted and angry at himself and at the two thieves, he considered what had just happened. He realized he had not only lost his $20 of expense money. He had also lost his return train tickets and other important papers.

He sat down on a patch of grass at the edge of the road. *How could I be so stupid? I'm tired, I'm hot, I'm thirsty, I'm broke, and I still don't know where Fanny May Brown is. But I'll be damned! Here comes PJ with my pouch!*

"I think dey took yo' money, but dey threw yo' bag down,"

PJ said, handing the pouch to Charlie.

Charlie checked the contents and found only the money gone. Then he put his arm around the little Negro and gave him a hug. They smiled at each other.

"PJ, we got a church to find," said the prosecutor, now feeling better.

"I heps you find dat place," PJ said. "Foller me."

PJ kept Charlie entertained all the way to the other end of Beartown which seemed to be about half a mile.

"Der be da church" said PJ, pointing down a side street. "And right dere be where my mamaw lives."

"That place there?" Charlie asked. He pointed to one of the better kept row houses with a picket fence in need of repair.

"Yep dat's mamaw an' papaw's."

"You go on to your mamaw's, PJ. I'll come over there in a few minutes, okay?"

"Okay, I tell mamaw you is comin'." The rambunctious youngster took off to his grandmother's like a racehorse out of the gate.

Charlie started to the little white church that was just a few doors down on a side street. When he got close, he noticed that it was by far the nicest, and possibly the newest bulding in Beartown. The top part of a sign out front read "Beartown First Baptist Church." Under that, "Rev. Jackson Jones."

Charlie walked up the wood steps and through the front door. The rough wood floor squeaked as he stepped inside.

Rows of six pews on each side, which looked much older than the church, faced the pulpit. On the back wall was a large weathered cross. And on the cross hung a brown Jesus.

"Can I hep you, sir?"

Charlie turned back to face an old bent over man with gray hair. His face was full of pockmarks, and he trembled slightly—as if suffering from some sort of nerve disorder.

"Yes. Are you the Reverend Jones?"

"No suh'. The Reverand be outta town. He had a death in his family, and he ain't comin' back 'til this Saturday. I'm wachin' over things while the Reverand is gone. Some'um I can hep you with?"

"I am trying to locate Miss Fanny May Brown. She has a daughter by the name of Mattie. And I was told they visited a church in

Beartown. Is this the only church hereabouts?"

The old man studied him.

"Is you a bill c'lector?"

When Charlie assured him he was not, the stand-in for the Rev. Jones told him that this was the only church in Beartown. Then he asked Charlie a question. "This Fanny May. She be really old?"

Charlie, his pulse quickening, replied yes, the woman he was trying to locate was very old—99 in fact.

"Ha, ha. Yep. Dat mus' be her. 'Bout'a month ago dere was dis old lady with her daughter, came ta Sunday service. But I ain't seen'um since then."

"And you have no idea where they live?"

"No suh. But I might knows somebody who do. Come hea."

Charlie followed the old man, now shaking even more, out the front door and to the street.

"See dat little white house wit the picket fence?" He pointed back down toward the end of the street Charlie had walked from.

"You mean PJ's grandmother's house?"

"How you know PJ?" The old man's eyes widened. He seemed flabbergasted.

"PJ is the first person I met in Beartown."

"Well I'll be! Da Lawd mus' be hepping you find dat Fanny May. Ain't dat sometin'? Now you go talk to old Miss Green. She know 'bout everbody in Beartown."

Charlie could hardly contain his excitement as he thanked the old Negro and scurried along.

The old man hollered. "That PJ! He some'um else, aint't he?!"

"Indeed he is!" Charlie hollered back.

It only took a minute or two for the young prosecutor from Fish Springs to reach PJ's grandmother's house. Though a small, ancient dwelling, it had been taken good care of. Someone had planted flowers near the porch, and the house itself appeared to have been freshly painted. He knocked on the screen door.

"Dat man's hea, Mamaw!"

Charlie heard PJ running to fetch his granny.

She was drying her hands on her apron when she got to the

door. Charlie figured she'd been in the kitchen.

But the squat, chubby woman with short curly gray hair and a round face couldn't have been more gracious to the strange white visitor at her front door.

"May I help you?" she asked politely. PJ clutched her apron.

"Miss Green, I'm Charlie Smith, and I am not a bill collector. I give you my word on that. And I want to say that your grandson PJ is a fine boy. I know you're quite proud of him."

The woman flashed him a toothy grin and patted PJ on his head. He smiled up at her, proud of himself.

"Yes, I know. He be a good grandson. That be for sure. And he love his mamaw."

Charlie smiled at her and asked if she could help him find Fanny May Brown. "It's very important, Miss Green. A Negro man was killed in Carter County, where I live, and we want to bring his killer to justice. And we think Miss Brown can help us do that."

"See dat big yella' house? The one dat looks like it ain't parta Beartown? Dat's were da street name change from Old Town Road to Oak Avenue. It didn't used to be Beartown but Beartown's growin' and taken over some of the big houses da white folks owned. So da owner made it into four apartments. Fanny May and her daughter live dere in apartment A."

His heart beat more rapidly as Charlie took all this in.

Then he thanked PJ's grandmother profusely and told her she'd surely made his day, as well as the day of so many others praying for justice in East Tennessee.

The woman told him he was welcome and added. "And may the blessings of the Lord be with you, young man."

"Thank you again, Miss Green! And thank you, PJ," Charlie gleefully shouted back over his shoulder.

As he neared the large yellow house, Charlie noticed all the row houses came to an end on both sides of the dirt street. Then bigger two-story houses filled both sides as far as he could see. Charlie assumed that at least a few colored people lived in these homes. Perhaps they were coloreds like Mattie who, as a school teacher. could afford the higher rent.

Farther down the street he saw a white lady tending to her

flowers in the front yard. The first two story was the house where he hoped he'd find Fanny May Brown. It was huge with a big front porch and big floor to ceiling windows. Apartment A was in the front downstairs portion. So the door was the original front door to the home.

When Charlie knocked on the door and Mattie opened it, he was startled at how old she appeared. *But of course, she would have to be in her 70's at the least. What was I thinking?*

Mattie was an attractive, dignified-looking woman with salt and pepper hair and perfect posture. She had on a blue print dress and radiated energy and friendliness.

"May I help you, sir?"

"Yes ma'am. My name is Charlie Smith, I am a prosecuting attorney from Elizabethton, Tennessee. And I need to speak with Miss Fanny May Brown."

Then came the sweetest voice he had heard in the last two days.

"Who it be, Mattie?! He really be from Elizabethton? Where your manners, girl? Tell him to come in."

"Mama loves company. Please come in, Mista Smith."

"I'd be delighted to, ma'am," Charlie said, smiling and extending his hand.

He shook hands with both of them, was seated at a table in Fanny May's kitchen and served a glass of cold lemonade. The two women couldn't have been friendlier and were eager to know why he'd come so far from Elizabethton—and to Beartown of all places.

So Charlie told Fanny May and Mattie about the gruesome discovery of Toby's bones in a plowed-up field and what Jake Edwards had claimed.

"Dat man's a liar!" Fanny May said, beginning to cry.

Charlie found old Fanny May to be hard of hearing and to have fading eyesight. But she was of sound mind. And her memory was sharp. "As sure as I be sittin' hea, I 'member the day Toby Jackson paid off his bill at Jake Edwards' store. And she recalled clearly how she gave Toby a receipt because Jake was inflating the balance on Toby's account to keep him from leaving.

"Yes, Mista Smith. I be glad to come to Elizabethton to testify, if it will help put that mean man Jake Edwards behind bars. Long as Mattie get me dere, I testify."

"You will travel by train and we will cover all the expenses," Charlie assured them.

"But where will we stay, Mista Smith? It ain't dat easy to find lodgin' for colored folks," Mattie said. "And I bet dey be some people not wantin' us to testify."

"You leave that to me, Mattie. And by the way what is your last name?"

"Daily. Mista Daily passed away two years ago shortly after he retired from the road department. He was a good man."

"I see. I'm sorry for your loss."

"Dat man took good care of my daughter," Fanny May said.

"Miss Brown and Miss Daily," the handsome young attorney said, "it has been a pleasure talking to both of you. And I am pleased and honored that you are willing to help us win this case. We will be in touch with you just as soon as the dates are set."

"You jus' let us know, Mista Smith and we be comin' to Eliza-bethton. Now give an old lady a hug before you go."

"Mama! Maybe Mista Smith don't want no hug."

"Sure I do," said Charlie, laughing and wrapping his arms around the frail little woman who had agreed to be a key witness in one of the biggest trials in the history of Carter County.

CHAPTER 12

Charger

Charlie got back to Elizabethton a day later and caught up on some paper work in his office at the Carter County Courthouse. The next day he worked on his plans for prosecuting Jake Edwards. He researched stacks of binders, case after case. To his amazement, he didn't find one single case where a white man had been convicted for killing a Negro.

I'm sure glad and thank God I have Fanny May Brown. I wouldn't have a chance without her. Still it won't be easy.

Early in the afternoon the prosecutor let Sheriff Nave know that he had found Fanny May Brown and she was willing to testify against Jake Edwards.

"Good for you, Charlie," Nave said. "So you didn't run into any trouble in Knoxville's Beartown?" The sheriff couldn't hide a smirk.

"How'ed you know about my misfortune in Beartown?"

"All I know is that you needed more money."

"How in the hell did you know about the money?"

"I have friends at the courthouse, Charlie. So why'd you need the money wired?" Nave, stroking his mustache, looked him straight in the eyes.

But Charlie decided the less said the better. "No need talking about that, Sheriff. I'm sure you'll hear about it soon enough."

"Well, go see your dad, son. Save him a trip from Fish Springs. 'Cause he didn't come last night, and he'll show up tonight, sure as a bear shits in the woods.

"Your dad was worried sick. He's been coming to Elizabethton almost every night wantin' to know if I'd heard from you.

117

When I told him you wired the courthouse for some more money, he really got worried."

"Oh boy. Okay, I will," said Charlie chuckling. "I need something good to eat anyway. It's hard going from a five-course meal at the Oliver Hotel in Knoxville to what they serve me at the boarding house."

"What you need is a good woman to take care of you, Charlie." The sheriff smiled, trying not to come across too preachy.

"Got one," said Charlie. "My stepmom Mary. And if she starts fussing at me, I can just go home."

"You know what? You may just have something there."

The two men laughed and bid each other good day.

Charlie saddled his horse, Star, and set out on the 90-minute trip to his dad and stepmom's house, his home place in Fish Springs where he had been born and raised with his brother Peter and sister Izzy.

Along the way, as his mount trotted, Charlie reflected on his life. He did so while traveling the road through scenic meadows near a dense forest and beside the rushing waters of the Watauga River.

A lot of time had lapsed since those early formative years in the remote mountain community of Fish Springs. And it hadn't always been easy. His beloved mother Polly, the light of his father's life, had died in a black measles epidemic when Charlie was 17. And his dad, after sinking into deep depression, had finally snapped out of it, thanks to the beautiful, caring Mary Clemmons White.

Mary was a widow who had had to conquer her own demons and who had long been a close friend of Charlie's parents. She had been there when Daniel Smith's life was shattered by the loss of his long-time wife Polly.

But for Mary and the former slave girl Prissy, whom Daniel and Isaiah had rescued from her hateful former employer, Jake Edwards, Charlie, Peter and Izzy would surly have lived a more dismal life. Mary and Prissy had fed and cared for Daniel's three children, making sure they had a decent, tidy place to live in, clean clothes on their backs and home cooked food on the table.

And so, in due time, when Daniel Smith had gotten stronger and more like his old self, he and Mary Clemmons White had become attracted to each other. After a somewhat awkward court-ship, with Daniel not knowing exactly how to pop the question, he and the coy Mary decided to get married. The most beautiful woman in Fish Springs—"pretty as a mountain wildflower," folks called her—had gotten hitched to what many considered was the most prominent and respected man in the community.

Mary had a baby boy, Danny, fathered by her deceased hus-band, Alfred White, who had been killed by a rattlesnake bite. So the three kids got a little step brother when Mary became part of the family. Daniel treated little Danny as his own, and the children—Charlie, Peter and Izzy—couldn't get enough of him. Even Daniel's sharecropper couple, former slaves Isaiah and Prissy, loved Little Danny as if he were their own son.

It had been a joyous, celebrated union from day one, with Mary and Daniel falling even deeper in love. They constantly hugged and kissed and laughed and held hands. In one happy, impromptu moment in the kitchen, when the frisky newly mar-rieds had thought their children had left the house, the kids caught them dancing.

In another instance, Daniel and Mary had squeezed into the family bathtub and sudsed each other up, only to be discovered by Charlie on his way to the kitchen for a midnight snack.

Everything they did, Charlie fondly recalled now as Star kept trotting toward their destination, they did together. Whether it was worshipping, buying items for the home, tending to the live-stock, cooking, gardening, making trips to Elizabethton … it had been a marriage seemingly made in heaven. And Charlie, Peter and little Izzy had no longer been just Daniel's children; they had become Mary's children, too. They cherished their stepmother, who always made time for them. And Daniel couldn't have been more appreciative. For Mary, it seemed, had been sent to him from angels. She had saved his life and become part of the family.

So the big white frame house that for so many years had been home to Daniel and Polly—and then Mary—and their young ones was a place rich in memories. A place that Charlie Smith always came back to, not only for a visit but when he had some-thing on his mind, or faced, as a prosecutor.

It was as if re-touching his Fish Springs roots made him appreciative of where he'd come from and made him stronger, more confident, more prepared for whatever might come his way.

Charlie pulled lightly on the reins to steer Star down the entrance to the old home place, and the animal obliged. But Charlie knew that he needn't have done so because the reliable horse would go straight to the farm unless he turned him in another direction.

Dismounting, Charlie threw his arms around Daniel who was elated to see his son back home safe.

"I found'em, Pa!"

"Hallelujah!" Daniel hollered.

"Yep! I found Fanny May Brown and her daughter Mattie!"

Daniel, cracking a big smile, acted like it was the best news he'd ever heard. He patted his son on the back.

"We ain't won yet, Dad," Charlie said, tempering the news. "Not by a long shot."

"I know, son, but you've got a chance, a good chance. That's all you can ask for, and Fanny May Brown's givin' you that."

When Daniel asked him what the money was for, Charlie fessed up but asked him to keep it to himself.

"They know at the courthouse?" Daniel asked.

"Sure. I had to tell em why I needed more money."

"Then it's too late, Charlie. You know how those men that work in the courthouse gossip."

Charlie swallowed hard. He would have preferred more discretion.

"News spreads like wildfire in Carter County, son. You know that."

"I know, Dad. It's just that—"

Before Charlie could finish his sentence Mary yelled that dinner was ready.

"Come on, son. A man's gotta eat." Daniel put his arm across his son's shoulders.

The two men and Mary sat down to a big delicious meal of fried chicken with all the fixings—cornbread, green beans, mashed potatoes and gravy. For dessert, they feasted on Mary's blackberry pie. When everyone had pushed back from the table, there was time enough for catching up on the latest news about the trial.

"People don't know the least bit about the case, but they talk an' gossip about it anyway. Folks are sayin' we don't have any evidence, and it'll be a cold day in hell before Jake is found guilty of killing a Negro."

"You know how it is, Charlie," Daniel said. "Tongues wag where there's big news, and you've got yourself one humdinger of a murder case. They'll be gabbin' about it up to and all the way through the trial."

"If there is a trial," Charlie, his head sagging, noted.

"What are you sayin'?" Mary asked.

"Well, seems like Jake's high-priced attorney, L. Ross Roberts, is tryin' to get the charges dismissed," Charlie said. "Claims we don't have a shred of proof to convict Jake Edwards of maliciously killing anyone. He said his client was arrested on hearsay. He's threatenin' to bring charges against the sheriff and to st op me from even pursuing this case. Wants a full apology from me and for the county to pay all of Jake's legal expenses. The upside of it is, I don't think Judge Stone is buying any of it."

"Well, he shouldn't. Jake Edwards is guilty as hell!" Daniel insisted. "I know he murdered Toby in cold blood, and now he's got the Klan riled up and folks a' claimin' he did nothin' wrong and he's goin' after you and the sheriff. That's crazy! That hotshot lawyer thinks he can walk on water."

"You've got God and the law on your side," Mary reassured him. "And now you've got Fanny May, Charlie, and the truth'll come out. 'Sides, folks know deep down that Jake's a mean, lyin', no-good-for-nothin' scoundrel. I promise you, Charlie. You'll beat him."

Charlie smiled at his stepmother, hugged her and his dad and said his farewell.

The following evening, Daniel mounted his prized Tennessee Pacer Black Jack and headed to Isaiah and Prissy's to give them and the Woodses the good news about finding Fanny May.

As he skirted the river he became aware of a rumbling off in the distance. The day had started off hot and this time of year was the worst for a sudden thunderstorm. Daniel gave Black Jack a slight getty-up with his whip, and the horse responded.

Luckily for Daniel, it was a short ride to Isaiah's.

And, as expected, Isaiah and Prissy and their temporary guests the Woodses were on the porch. The kids, however, were scattered about.

"Good news, folks!" Daniel announced as he dismounted. "Charlie found Fanny May Brown and she'll testify against Jake Edwards!"

They all hooted and hollered with joy and patted each other on the back.

"Come set down, Mista Danicl," Isaiah said. He offered Daniel his rocking chair. "That's mighty good news, all right."

"Only for a few minutes, Isaiah. "I'd like to get back before this—"

K-boom!! A lightning strike lit up the area. Both women screamed and Black Jack danced around shaking his head. Daniel calmed his horse by grabbing hold of the halter, stroking his neck and speaking softly to him. Then there was total calm as ominous, fast-moving dark clouds drifted in over the mountains. In only a few seconds it began turning as dark as night.

"Well, looks like it's coming fast. Y'all may have company for a little while," said Daniel, gripping the arms of the old chair.

Prissy, who had practically jumped out of her shoes when the lighting flashed, hardly had time to worry about the kids.

But thank the Lord, she thought, upon seeing Benjamin carrying little Willie along with Leroy. All three children were on the porch before the rumbling from the incredible strike quit echoing through the mountains. Shadow, who ran up with them, scooted under the porch and out of sight.

"Where's Jeb, Ben?" Prissy asked nervously.

"He gone ta check on Charger, Ma. He'll be okay. He can get in the barn if it gets too bad."

Eleven-year-old Jebediah had come to love the large black gelding and considered himself Charger's protector.

He would give the big, beautiful black horse a good brushing, fresh water and sweet feed when his father returned home after checking on sharecroppers. And every chance he got he'd take a little ride around the farm.

Jeb had expected to find Charger in the barn lot or the barn.

But the animal was nowhere to be seen. Then noticing one of the rails to the lot fence was broken, the boy figured that lightning had spooked Charger and he had bolted through the fence—which is exactly what had happened.

And there Charger stood up the hill in the pasture. It wasn't the first time Jeb had to round up the elusive animal, but he hoped to get Charger back in the barn before the storm hit. Jeb grabbed a heavy rope lying across the barn lot fence. He figured the rope, used for pulling stumps, might help him catch the fleeing, scared horse.

Each time Jeb got near Charger he'd run away—not very far but just far enough so that the boy couldn't rope him.

Finally, after several fruitless attempts, the boy walked slowly and spoke softly. The jittery horse stood still, as if responding to Jeb's calm voice; and the lad managed to slip the looped end over Charger's head. Then he pulled the other end of the long rope through the loop. By now, horse and boy were at edge of the field lined with poplar trees.

Now if' I can jus get him to the barn.

But Jeb only managed a few steps before the storm hit. It came suddenly and viciously. Rain pounded. A furious wind bent trees and snapped limbs. Jagged lightning began to streak across the pitch black sky, and Charger started prancing about.

The desperate boy, unable to lead the spooked horse without a halter, decided to tie the heavy rope to a tree. He pulled the gelding to within five feet of the tree and tied the rope about four feet off the ground. Just a simple knot, one that would be hard to untie if pulled taut.

Then, as Jeb sprinted in a driven, cold rain toward the barn for the horse's halter, a burst of wind knocked him down. And when he looked back, there was Charger, dancing around, high stepping, his eyes full of fear.

A blinding bolt of lightning hit a nearby tree, and the exploding fireball caused the already frightened horse to go into a frenzy.

With all his might, Charger pulled back on the heavy rope, digging his hooves into the ground. His neck was stretched and his rump, weaving from side to side, was almost touching the ground.

Jeb hollered his name over and over as he ran back, trying to get him to stop. But the struggling, flailing, terrified horse was oblivious to the boy's cries. The harder Charger pulled and stomped and thrashed about, the tighter the deadly noose tightened around his neck, cutting off his air and causing him to pull even harder.

Now in a panic, Jeb attempted to calm the animal, and when that didn't work he tried to untie the rope. He worked at the tight, stubborn knot until his fingers bled, but it stayed taut.

He remembered that he had a small pocketknife in his coveralls.

Hollering and crying, Isaiah's distraught son sawed at the thick, unyielding rope with the pitiful little knife that had been dulled by too many mumblety-peg games with his brothers.

"Pa, help me, please! Somebody help me!"

Jebediah screamed over and over, as he worked on the unyielding rope, for his dad, for anyone, to help him. Then the spent horse, his head still held above the ground by the unforgiving rope, went limp and fell lifeless to the ground.

But the horrified boy, a lump in his throat and his heart beating violently in his chest, would not give up. He sawed at the heavy rope and yelled for help but the howling wind and downpour muffled his cries.

His sawing made little progress, only cutting through a few strands of the thick, tightly twisted hemp. But Jeb, exhausted and horrified, his hands raw and bloody now from so much sawing, kept at it.

Meanwhile, back at the house, Isaiah for the second time looked out a back window toward the barn. The first time, not seeing Jeb or Charger, he had assumed his son had taken refuge in the barn with the horse until the squall passed.

But he now sensed something might have gone wrong, because the sudden, violent storm was over and only a hard rain lingered.

Jeb should be comin' to the house. But where is he?

Isaiah got part of his answer when he stepped onto the back stoop and heard a blood-curdling scream from his son.

"Jeb!" he yelled back. "I'm coming, son!"

Isaiah ran as fast as he could across the open hay field toward the woods that framed it—all the while hollering his son's name. To his horror, he saw Charger on the ground. Beside the horse was his defeated son, his fingertips blooded. Soaking wet and crying, he was sawing at the unrelenting rope.

Isaiah retrieved his own pocket knife, one that he kept sharp, pulled his son away and cut through the heavy rope. But the rope didn't yield easily, and it took him an agonizing minute to saw through it. Then he loosened the rope around Charger's neck.

Isaiah checked the completely still Charger for any sign of life, but found none.

He put his cheek on the horse's nostrils, hoping for a breath of warmth. But he felt nothing.

He laid his head against Charger's wet, frothy chest, praying for a heartbeat. But he heard nothing.

Jeb stood motionless, crying.

"He dead," Isaiah said.

"No, Pa! No! Do somethin', please!" Rainwater and tears mixed and ran down Isaiah's son's bewildered face.

Isaiah stroked his dead horse's neck as tears welled up in his own eyes.

"It's too late, Jeb. There ain't nothin' I can do."

The devastated Negro lying in the mud, his arms now around Charger's neck and his big hands cradling the horse's head, looked up at Jebediah, and what he said next he would regret for the rest of his life.

"My God, Jebediah! What have you done?!"

Isaiah watched his crushed son back away. Jeb's eyes focused on his own. They were the eyes of a defeated, somber boy who had let his father down terribly.

Jeb fled toward the woods.

Remembering then that he was a father, and that no son was perfect, Isaiah felt that in the heat of his anger and loss he had ripped Jebediah's heart out.

"Wait, Jeb! Come back!"

"Jebediah! Come back, son!" Isaiah screamed at his running boy until he could no longer see him. He had disappeared into the woods.

Then the grieving Negro walked back to the house slowly, through the pouring, relentless rain.

"Isaiah, what's wrong?!" Prissy asked her husband. He had stepped up on the porch soaking wet and covered with mud.

She screamed the question again but her husband, his head down, said nothing.

By this time, Elijah, Daniel, Ruthie and the other three children had overheard Prissy's frantic tone, and they all stood there waiting for Isaiah to tell them what had happened.

And he finally did.

Sparing them the horrific details, Isaiah told everyone that Charger was dead and that Jeb had run into the woods.

"I made a mistake. I was way too hard on that boy. I need to find'em and make sure he's all right."

"You need any help finding the boy, Isaiah?"

"Thank you, Mista Daniel, but I think he'll come back home. He's got no place to go."

"Well, let me know if I can help."

Isaiah thanked him again and said he should get on home to Mary. Daniel hugged his friend, told him how sorry he was about Charger, mounted Black Jack and headed home.

"Give the boy a little time alone ta let his heart mend. Maybe it's best ta wait 'til mornin' to do anything else," Isaiah told Prissy.

Amidst the tears, thirteen-year-old Benjamin said that he felt it was his fault because he had never gotten around to teaching his younger brother how to tie a slipknot.

But Isaiah wouldn't let Ben bear the blame. Instead, he tried to comfort his oldest son, telling him that he himself had not taken the time to show Jeb how to care for the horse.

"What he knew he only learned from watchin' us. It's my fault more than anybody's," Isaiah said. "That boy is only eleven years old. I'm the one that let this happen."

"It's okay, Dad," said 9-year-old Leroy. The boy wiped his tears. "You den't mean fer it ta happen."

Prissy tried to ease the grief of those gathered on the porch. She reminded everyone that sometimes bad things just happen—for no reason—and that a family in so much pain had to remain strong and close together.

She drew from her knowledge of the Bible to help give the

children and her husband a sense of comfort. "We all need each other," Prissy said. "We are just like sheep. And God wants us all ta be a shepherd for each other, in good times and bad times. Right now, for sure, we all need to be shepherds for Jebediah."

Isaiah put his arms around his wife. "We all need to give Jeb lots a love and forgiveness. He loved Charger more than we did."

That night, Isaiah and Prissy slept fitfully. Isaiah hoped that Jeb would go to the barn where the three older boys had been staying in the loft after giving up their room to Elijah and Ruthie. *Jeb's hurting right now. He needs his family. He needs his brothers.*

Prissy prayed fervently and silently for much of the night. *Dear Jesus, we ask that you send your angels to take care of our son Jeb. And let him know we all love him very much and want him to come home. Amen.*

Early the next morning, when Jeb was still missing, Isaiah knew he had to go after him.

"Please fix me some food and a jug'a water ta take with me, Prissy. I need to saddle up ol' Sue. I'm gwine find our boy"

At the barn, he put a saddle on Sue, his old work mule. It had been several years since the animal had been mounted, but she did just fine as Isaiah rode her back to the house to get the food and water.

Before he left, he instructed Ben and Leroy to start digging a deep, wide hole near Charger's favorite spot—in the shade of a big tulip poplar tree in a lush green pasture. The family would gather and say a few words at the gravesite later.

Elijah said, "I can hep da boys diggin' a grave, Isaiah."

"We can all work together doing that." said Prissy, handing her husband a jug and sack. "You just bring my boy back home, Isaiah.

"You hear me, Isaiah?" Big tears ran down Prissy's cheeks. "Bring my Jebediah home."

Isaiah put his brawny arms around his heartbroken wife and patted her head.

"I will, Prissy. I promise you. I will."

"Ben! Go get Shadow! I need to take'em with me."

"Sure, Pa."

Isaiah called Shadow and started out, but the dog was reluctant to leave his master.

So Ben had his mom bring him one of Jebediah's shirts he had worn and rubbed it on the hound's nose.

"Go, Shadow," Ben hollered, pointing up the hill.

The canine must have figured out what was expected of him because he took off up the hill.

Shadow darted to the last place Isaiah saw Jebediah run into the woods. He put his nose to the ground and ran, yelping. Isaiah followed on Sue. The earth was soft and mushy from the hard rain the night before, and Isaiah could see his runaway son's tracks. So the former slave knew that Shadow, one of the best hunting dogs in Fish Springs, was tracking Jeb and not a rabbit or some other critter. The dog eventually led him back to the road and headed away from Fish Springs, north toward Mountain City.

Several hours into his ride, as Isaiah and Shadow neared the Watauga River crossing, he came upon a small shack. There, sitting on the porch, was an old Negro in a cane back chair.

"Good aftanoon, suh," the amiable fellow said. His calloused hands gripped the staff of a butter churn. A few animal pelts dangled from the ceiling of his porch. Quite an impressive rack of deer antlers were nailed above the door.

"Aftanoon. Have you seen a young boy walkin' this road today?"

"Well suh, der was a boy in my barn dis mawnin'. Found'im der asleep in my hay when I went to milk old Betsy. He ax me where dat road went, an I tod him, ta Mountain City. He say a city is bigger den a town, ain't dat right, and I said dat's right. Den he ax me if he could get a job der. I said maybe, but don't you try ta cross dat riva, 'cause da wata be too high wit all dis rain we's been havin'. I tol' him to wait 'til da wata went down, and he say he would."

"So he didn't leave?"

"No suh. Not den. But when I went to da barn at lunch time ta take him some'um ta eat, he done gone. I sho' hope he di'nt try ta cross dat ol' riva. Dat be your boy, suh?"

"Yes, he's my son. Thank you," said Isaiah hanging his head.

Fretting even more now, Isaiah slapped Sue on the rear with the end of the reins and headed toward the Watauga River crossing. When he got to where the road forded the rushing whitewater, the worried man climbed down and studied the sandy soil.

He saw boy-size foot prints everywhere and some seemed to go into and disappear in the river.

Shadow stood at the water's edge barking and pawing the ground. Every few seconds the dog looked as if he would venture into the current, but then he backed up.

Isaiah lifted Shadow to the saddle and mounted Sue, and they crossed the rushing river. Shadow jumped down and ran up and down on the other side—his nose glued to the ground. But he could never pick up Jeb's scent. Isaiah also looked for any sign of hope but found no footprints. Then he ventured back across with Shadow, and as he reached land a rabbit dashed across the road in front of them. The dog jumped down and ran yelping into the woods in pursuit.

Isaiah dismounted and sat dejected on a log facing the water. He sat for a long time, fear overwhelming him. His boy had probably tried to swim the raging river and drowned. He took off his hat, pulled out a handkerchief and wiped the sweat from his forehead and covered his eyes. *He drowned in this river. He died with a broken heart. He left this earth alone—without his family. All this because of me.*

Isaiah dropped his head down between his legs and sobbed. "O Lord, please help me. I can't lose my boy. How can I tell Prissy? What can I do? Why is this happenin' ta me, Lord?"

Shadow, panting and his tongue hanging out, returned and laid his head on Isaiah's knee. The heartbroken man stroked him as tears ran down his cheeks.

Along with the sound of rushing water, Isaiah thought he heard his name being called but figured he had imagined it. Then he heard it again.

"Pa," came a whimpering, unsteady voice from behind him.

Isaiah turned around, and there stood his disheveled, whimpering son.

The boy ran to his father's open arms.

"Ya came after me, Pa. I didn't think you'd come after me afta I kilt your horse."

"How could you think that, son?"

"I didn't think you could love me no more. I knowed how much you loved Charger."

As the boy talked, he bawled, and he and his ecstatic dad

hugged even tighter.

"Yes, that's true. I loved him, but I loved him like you love an animal, not like you love a son. You're a part of me, Jebediah. You're my flesh and blood, and I'd give my life for you, son. I have lost animals before, and I'm sure we will lose more. I can get over that, but I could never get over losin' you, Jebediah. I know you loved Charger just as much as I did, maybe even more, and—-"

"I did, Pa! I loved him with all my heart! He was my favorite horse in the whole worl'." Jeb wailed as if he had lost his best friend.

Isaiah dabbed his son's eyes with the handkerchief. "It was my fault more than yours. Don't blame yourself, Jeb."

"I'm glad ya came after me, Pa."

"I'm glad too, son. I'm also glad that ole' river didn't get ya."

"I didn't try to swim cross the river, Pa. I was to a'scared to. I was looking for a safe place to cross down river and old Shadow found me," said Jeb, hugging the dog's neck.

Shadow returned the favor with a big slobbery lick of his tongue on Jeb's face. And for the first time since they'd reunited, Jebediah smiled.

"You ready ta go home, son?"

"Yes, Pa! And I am really really hungry, too!"

Isaiah grinned as he mounted old Sue and pulled Jeb up to sit on the saddle in front of him.

"Take us home, Shadow. Reach down in that saddle bag, Jeb. Your mama made you a biscuit with some ham on it."

Jeb devoured the food. And when he asked for more, Isaiah smiled and pulled another biscuit out.

"I figured you'd be ready ta eat."

As Isaiah headed down the road toward Fish Springs, with his beloved, wayward son safe and alive, he passed the little shack nestled among the huge chestnut trees. Jebediah waved at the aging colored man sitting in a rocker on his porch, and Isaiah tipped his hat and nodded to him.

"Thank ya, Lawd, fo' answerin' ma prayers," mumbled the old man, nodding back.

CHAPTER 13

Push Comes to Shove

The talk all around town was that a star witness, Fanny May Brown, and her daughter Mattie would soon be paying a visit to Elizabethton. Word was she would be testifying for the prosecution against Jake Edwards.

"Who's Fanny May Brown?" asked an oldtimer at the dry goods store.

The clerk, bagging a new shirt, replied, "She's that ol darkie that ran Jake Edwards' store in Valley Forge."

"Oh yea. Lordy, that store closed might nar ten years ago. She must be really old."

"Pert near one hunert, they say. I heared she's gonna be the main witness for the proscution in the murder case'gainst old man Jake Edwards. Folks say Charlie Smith's gonna bring her by train from Knoxville to Elizabethton. She wants ta testify. Said she cain't get here fast enough. Said she'd do anything to put Jake Edwards behind bars for killin' her friend Toby Jackson."

The more people gabbed—at the Black Bear Saloon, the Post Office, at church, at the barber shop, and elsewhere in Carter County—the more nervous Jake Edwards became.

Why cain't folks keep their damned mouths shut? Edwards wondered. *It's like they ain't got nothin' better ta do than gab 'bout somethin' that's none'a their damned business!*

Edwards knew Prosecutor Charlie Smith would do everything in his power to win a guilty verdict. The prosecutor was tightly connected to the family whose sharecropper, ex-slaves had befriended Toby Jackson, and both that prominent family and their Negro employees wanted more than anything for Charlie to get a conviction. If ever Charlie Smith had deep motivation to win a case, this was it. *Lucky me. Why'd it have ta be me that Daniel Smith's boy's tryin' ta nail ta the cross? And all over a nigger, no less!*

Edwards had taken to drinking more and more—and even to "whoring around," as some gossipers put it, at the Black Bear Saloon more than ever. But the alcohol and sex—mostly with his long-time gal Agnes Gump but also with other ladies of the night at the Black Bear—had done little to lessen his anxiety.

The man accused of murdering Toby Jackson was one worried, anxious, irritable, depressed soul. And he was angry and scared as he rocked back and forth in the old chair on his front porch. Angry because it had occurred to him that he just might be the first white man in East Tennessee—maybe even in all of Tennessee—to be convicted of killing a Negro. Scared because, if that happened, he could be sent to the gallows, or, maybe even worse, spend the rest of his life in prison.

He thought again about the fate that his pricy, self-serving attorney, Mr. L. Ross Roberts, had said surely awaited a white man being shackled to Negroes on a chain gang. He kept trying to put that dreadful outcome out of his mind, but to no avail. Even if he escaped the gallows he'd likely end up on a chain gang. Nights would be spent in a nasty prison cell. He'd maybe even take his last breath in a smelly space not much bigger'n a smokehouse.

But it wouldn't be alone. Behind bars, he'd surely be in the company of coloreds who despised white men—and who especially would hate a white man who murdered a Negro. What would prevent the big, nigger, sex-starved brutal bucks—as Edwards imagined they'd be—from raping him?

Come hea, whitey. You be my wife. You git nekkid when I say so. You pleasure me 'cause I be your masta now.

And what if he screamed to the guards for help? Nothing would happen, Jake sadly concluded, because rape comes with being in prison. *Feelin' is that convicts deserve all the misery and abuse and assault they get 'cause they done wrong. Real wrong! And who'd believe a prisoner anyway who claimed he was raped? Who'd give a damn? And what if another prisoner told a guard of the rape and who done it? That poor wretch'd be a snitch, and no one puts up with a snitch....*

Jake, who had hardly slept last night, kept rocking and brooding. And the more he rocked and dwelled on what surely lay ahead of him if Roberts lost the trial—the gallows or misery in jail and unmitigated hell on a chain gang—the more he fretted.

Rock, rock.

Creak, creak.

He rested his weary, limp hands on his knees, and, as he sat there slumped over in the rocker, he tried to come up with a plan—any plan to save his life, his freedom, everything he owned. But it was looking very bad. Maybe even hopeless.

Rock, rock.

Creak, creak.

He cast his eyes out toward the mountains—towering creations of God that had always seemed, somehow, to give him peace and escape from his worries. A spectacular vermillion sunset lined the horizon. A few puffy red tinged clouds would soon disappear into the cool Tennessee night. And he could hear, far off, the high pitched howling of a lone coyote. The morning would bring a magnificent sunrise—a bright and warm, yellow ball of light painting the mountains a soft hue of purple.

But none of that seemed to ease his mind right now. Because Jake Edwards sensed that all his selfishness, his unkindness, his lifelong greed, his penchant for making others around him—especially colored people—suffer and loath him, was somehow coming back to get its due.

Rock, rock.

Creak, creak.

He recalled the haunting words of his preacher last Sunday. "We'll all appear before the judgment seat of Christ! There ain't nothin' covered up that'll not be revealed. Everything'll be known. God's keepin' a record and remembers everything. He don't forget. He sees all."

But then, from the depths of despair, came a dose of plucky determination and anger. "I aint dead yet!" he yelled to no one except a few chickens, a cow and an old sow that was in the barnyard not far from his porch. "They ain't nary a nigger gonna send me ta jail!"

He rose from the rocker, grabbed his cane, hobbled back into the house and fetched a pint of whiskey from the kitchen cabinet. Jake took a big swig, wiped his mouth with the back of his hand, and emphatically swore again—out loud—that he'd never give up. With every ounce of energy he could muster, he pledged himself to fight the charges against him.

Tomorrow, I'm gonna pay that fancy dancy blood sucking lawyer man a visit and come up with a plan. Ain't nobody seen the last'a this old sly mountain man!

That night—thanks to several gulps of Tennessee straight whiskey—the man accused of shooting an unarmed Negro slept deeply. But he also had the same nightmare he'd been having over the last few weeks.

The recurring dream focused on a rattlesnake—the kind that was all too common in East Tennessee. A deadly venomous creature, that if Jake Edwards had his druthers, he'd slip somehow into Charlie Smith's room at the boarding house to do away with the one man determined, come hell or high water, to send him to the gallows or to prison. He'd seen such rattlers, with their needle-sharp fangs that could almost instantly kill any living thing they encountered. They were up to seven feet long. And there were plenty of them crawling about not far from where he lived.

What to make of the rattlesnake dream? Jake Edwards hadn't the slightest clue. But dream or not, the next morning he awoke fresh as a daisy. He rubbed the sleep out of his eyes, peeked out the window at the big blazing sun, stretched his arms, slipped on his clothes and made himself a pot of coffee. Then, not having Ruthie to fix his breakfast like she had ever since Prissy had been taken from him, he fried two eggs and a few slabs of bacon. He capped it all off with a couple of leftover crusty biscuits from the morning before. Fresh strawberry jam—that he'd bought from a sale at his church—went well with the biscuits. *I'm doin' just fine, thank ya, without nigger help.*

It all seemed to make Jake Edwards stronger and more resolute. No way, he told himself again, would he be convicted for killing a nigger man. *No damned way!*

He struggled with harnessing the horse, with no Elijah to help, but soon enough he was on his way to Elizabethton in his buggy. Time enough to think about the scheme he intended to share with Mr. L. Ross Roberts.

He arrived in town in short order, first going to the general store to stock up on flour, coffee and dried beans. But there on the walkway to the store was a sight that stopped him in his tracks. It was Isaiah and Prissy with little Willie in tow. Willie, the mulatto child that had been handed over to the two former slaves, had a stick of rock candy in one hand and held his mother's hand with the other. He was smiling and skipping gleefully as Prissy and Isaiah, not yet noticing Edwards, entered the store.

Edwards, spewing with anger, waited a few minutes, then shuffled inside.

Willie, who could have passed for white, stood at the counter waiting for Prissy and Isaiah to finish their business.

"Now ain't that somethin'?!" Edwards growled, loud enough for everyone to hear him. "A little half-breed nigger boy thinkin' folks don't know better 'bout where he come from!

"And there's his lyin' nigger daddy and momma with'em, pretendin' his real momma an' daddy didn't defile the white race."

"Jake, now that's enough," the startled storekeeper said. "They've got a right ta be here just as much as you. Leave 'em be."

But Jake Edwards was having none of it. "It makes my blood boil that you're tradin' with these niggers. Not only that—they've gotta half-breed!" he spouted to the sheepish clerk. "Ain't ya' got no morals a'tall?!"

"Their money spends as good as yours, Jake. By the way, you're way behind on payin' your bill here. When you settlin' up?"

"Just you don't worry 'bout that!" Edwards snapped. "I always pay, and you know it!"

"Yeah, but word 'round town is you've spent your last dollar on that high priced lawyer."

"Gimme' five pounds'a flour, five pounds'a beans and that can'a coffee, and I'll be on my way! And good luck tradin' with these triflin' niggers!" Edwards cursed.

Prissy and Isaiah tried to avoid eye contact with her former employer as he cast them one last evil stare, then stormed out the door. Little Willie clutched Prissy's hand more tightly and looked up at his pa.

Two eavesdropping women in the store whispered to each other while they covered their mouths with their fans.

"It's okay, Willie. You didn't do nothin' wrong, son." Isaiah patted him on the head reassuringly.

Jake Edwards crossed the road to L. Ross Roberts' office building and burst into his waiting room. "Clerk, I need to see Mr. Roberts right now!"

"Mr. Edwards, I'm afraid you don't have an appointment, sir."

When he protested and declared that he'd come a long way over a bumpy, winding road from Valley Forge, just to have a talk with his attorney, Jenkins still didn't give in.

"Sir, you don't have an appointment, but I will schedule one for you."

"Listen, you little runt! I want to see your damned boss right now!" he demanded.

"Jenkins, send Mr. Edwards in," came the calm voice of L. Ross Roberts through the open door to his office.

"That's more like it," Edwards said,

The overruled clerk ushered him into Roberts' office and shut the door.

"Now what can I do for you today, Mr. Edwards? My time is very valuable and short, so speak your piece."

"I come ta talk to you 'bout my case," Edwards responded.

"Well, unfortunately, there's not much to talk about at this point. Judge Emmett Stone was not inclined to dismiss the murder charge against you; and you might have also heard that the prosecutor, Charlie Smith, has located a witness who will make this case more difficult for us to win.

"That's old news, I know all about that."

"Well! I have to tell you that Charlie Smith is destined to be one of the most well-liked prosecutors ever in the history of Carter County. He comes from good stock—from a family that has strong character and solid integrity. A family that's helped many a down and out man or woman in our community."

"So."

"So that won't be lost on a jury, Mr. Edwards. They'll feel beholden to Daniel and Mary Smith and to their prosecutor son Charlie. That does not portend well for you, I'm afraid."

L. Ross Roberts leaned back in his chair, yawned, as if he'd just awakened from a nap, and stretched his arms out. "To be perfectly honest with you, Mr. Edwards, you better come up with something—anything that might sway the jury."

"I have."

Roberts, lighting a cigar, put his hands behind his head and grinned. "I'm listening."

"Suppos' I was tryin' to reason with Toby Jackson, to pay me the money he owed me before he left. But he was bein' unreasonable. He got real mad hollerin' and cussin' at me. Said he wer goin' to kill me with his bare hands. Then he done attacked me. He wrassled with me, tryin' to choke me ta death. Had me down on the ground, and I could hardly breathe, but somehows I got away from'im and got ma gun—all the while he kept comin' afta me with far and hatred in his eyes. I was sceered ta death. So I had to shoot'em . It were self defense."

"So that's what you're saying happened?"

"Yes sir. It's all coming back ta me now," said Jake, pleased with his contrived story.

"But how did you come to shoot Toby Jackson in the back of his head?"

"He must'a spun round as I far-ed off the shot."

Roberts said nothing for a few seconds. He seemed intrigued but skeptical.

"Your story will help, Mr. Edwards. But it will be disputed. 'Cause the prosecution's plannin' on callin' a whole bunch of colored folks, includin' Fanny May Brown to testify against you. And I know of no way to keep them off the stand."

By God, I do! Edwards thought. *I'll put the fear of the KKK in em!*

"And you know what they'll say, under oath, Mr. Edwards? They'll swear, through tears some of them, that their beloved friend Toby Jackson never hurt anyone in his entire life. That he was killed by a bad man who had no conscience."

"You sayin that jury will swaller the word of'a darkie over the word of'a white man?"

"In this case, they could. I want to help you, Mr. Edwards, but you have to give me something to work with. We need witnesses we can call to the stand on your behalf—who'll testify to your honesty and fairness and goodness as a human being.

"Do you know anyone that will do that, Mr. Edwards? How many people can we count on?"

Roberts' client just sat there with a somber, stone-like hopeless expression.

"You shot a man in cold blood, Mr. Edwards. A Negro that had lots of friends. You better be ready for the worst when we go to trial. You best practice what you'll say."

"A damned triflin' nigger!" Edwards shouted, rising from his chair and balling his fists in front of Roberts' big desk.

But the lawyer's expression didn't change. He sat there impassively. "I will work for your freedom, Mr. Edwards, but you will have to come up with some answers. And you need to have people to speak on your behalf."

I have the brothers. Hell yes, I do! Edwards thought. But he was getting angrier and more desperate by the second. "By God, I'll get you some people who will speak for me," Jake said.

"Good. And, most importantly, don't forget my fee, Mr. Edwards. As the case gets more complex, my fee will increase. The thousand dollars you've already paid me might be just a pittance of what you really will owe me."

"You'll get your money! You just be damn sure you win this case." *He ain't nothin' but a blood sucker! But I need the best lawyer I can get and that's what they claim he is. So I'll have to put up with'im.* Edwards stormed out of the office.

Roberts looked out his window. He watched as his perturbed client snapped the reins on his buggy and left in a cloud of dust. *That old coot has a nicer buggy than mine.*

"Mr. Jenkins, don't you have a friend at the courthouse who works in the property tax office?"

Roberts' clerk stepped in his office and replied that he indeed did have a relative who worked on the tax rolls.

He instructed Jenkins to ask that person to ascertain the taxable value of Jake Edwards' farm.

"Yes, Mr. Roberts."

"And be discreet about it, Jenkins, because there might be something in it for you."

Jenkins smiled and promised to inquire quietly about the farm. Then he asked, "Is there anything else I can find out for you, boss."

"Yes.

"While you're at it, see if you can find out how much a buggy like his is worth."

Roberts turned and looked back out the window.

"Yes sir, Mr. Roberts," he said. "I will gladly do that."

As Roberts' beleaguered client traveled the bumpy road back to Valley Forge, he mulled over his strategy. *There'll be a KKK raid on them troublemakers at Isaiah and Prissy's farm. And not just a burnin' cross. This time it'll be a burnin' barn, too. Maybe even a dead nigger or two.*

I want the Brothers to put the fear of the devil in all the darkies 'round here. I want 'em to know what they're up against. I want that nigger Elijah so scairt he won't go near the damn courthouse. And at the trial the Brothers'll testify about what an upstanding and honorable Christian man I am.

Jake Edwards chuckled at the absurdity of the idea of being held up as a God-believing, law abiding, neighborly citizen at the trial. But the more he thought about it, the more he wanted it to happen.

As a dues payin' Brother, I've done give a lotta my hard earned money to the Klan and now it's time fer em to step up and help one'a their own. They'll help me. But if push come to shove, I have a ace in the hole. If they start crawfishin' or whinin' they cain't help me, I'll put the fear'a God in them! I'll swear to em I'll stand on the courthouse floor, the day of my trial, and shout the names of ever' last one of the som'bitches as KKK members. Includin' two of the high and mighty Sheriff Nave's deputies and that holier than thou preacher of mine.

Yes siree, I think they'll be mor'en happy to testify for this old, wise mountain man once they hear my plan. 'Cause I ain't goin' down easy.

CHAPTER 14

Night Sounds

Finally the much-anticipated date for the capital murder case of the State of Tennessee versus Jake W. Edwards was set. The Honorable Judge Emmett Stone, a no-nonsense, hard-nosed judge who had been on the bench for two decades, set the trial date on the docket for June 25th.

It wouldn't be a day too soon for folks in Carter County who'd heard about the case. Many of them despised Jake Edwards and didn't think he should get away with killing a man—even a Negro. Also, most of the community respected Daniel Smith and knew his son Charlie was the prosecutor. Nevertheless, few thought the accused murderer would be convicted.

"Why don't Jake just take his medicine and tell tha' truth that he killed that colored man and be done with it?" one grizzly old-timer at the feed store opined. "He ain't goin' to no prison no way. Ain't no jury gonna' find a white man guilty on accounta he had ta kill a darkie that stol' money from'im. That's what I heerd happen."

But others weren't so sure.

"The times, they's a changin'," said Madge, one of the gussied up gals at the Black Bear Saloon. "Ain't like it used ta be. Old Jake could git hanged if he murdered that Negro. Or the next time we see em, he might be on a chain gang with a buncha darkies. How you supposin' he'd like that?"

"Jake Edwards is 'bout ta get his comeuppance, and he ain't gonna like it one bit. Mark my words," said a blacksmith, sweaty and dirty from head to toe. He leaned up against a post next to the livery stable in the heart of Elizabethton.

And so it went. Folks in Carter County chose sides, the majority of white people predicting that Jake Edwards would emerge from the court proceeding a meaner and more hardened scoundrel than ever. However a few folks, sensing that Jake had committed an unspeakable crime against another human being, thought and hoped otherwise.

Meanwhile, Carter County's chief law enforcement officer— the indefatigable, tough-as-nails Sheriff Nave—tried to go about his business as usual.

"Whaddya bringin' him in for, Cyrus?" the sheriff asked one of his deputies. The deputy had a middle-aged, bearded man, wailing and protesting his innocence, in handcuffs. Behind Deputy Cyrus and the handcuffed suspect was a bedraggled but attractive young woman—perhaps in her 20s. She clung to the deputy like a frightened bird.

The deputy said, "He belongs in a jail cell, Sheriff."

"On what grounds?" asked the curious sheriff, putting his cup of coffee down on his desk.

The woman, full breasted and with specks of straw and dirt on her behind, shrieked, "On them grounds out by tha barn, Sheriff! I just gave him a little kiss but he put his tongue in my mouth. Then he got me pinned down on the ground and had his way with me!"

"Is that so, mister?" the sheriff asked. "Now you come clean with me right now and it'll go easier on you."

"She wanted me, too, Sheriff. She might've said no but her eyes was saying yes.

"And I never hit her, even once."

"Lock'm up, Cyrus." Nave turned to the young woman. "And you, young lady, get on home and keep your skirts clean. We'll send for you when we're ready to take him to the judge."

"How was your trip to Asheville and the weddin', Cyrus?" Nave put the question to his favorite deputy when he returned from locking up his prisoner.

"It was a right good trip, Sheriff. Thanks for givin' me the time off."

"And how is that beautiful ex-wife Martha and that married boy of yourn doing?"

"She's as beautiful as ever, and he ain't a boy no more. He's a twenty-three-year-old married man."

"Time sure flies," Nave allowed. "And you actually stayed in the same house with them?"

"Yep."

"You're a better man than me, Cyrus Weaver," said Nave, taking a sip of his coffee.

"It's a really big house, Sheriff, with servants, even a ground-skeeper."

Sheriff Billy Nave had known Cyrus Weaver from the time he was knee high. He even attended his wedding to beautiful Martha Trivette after a whirlwind romance and the baptism of his baby boy six months later. Then the Civil War broke out, and Cyrus went to fight for the Union. Nave grieved along with Martha and others in Carter County when they mistakenly received word that the young Union soldier had been killed in the Battle at Kennesaw Mountain in Georgia.

Martha took her four-year-old son Jonathan back to Asheville where she had lived as a young girl. In due time, she married a plantation owner from a wealthy family. Cyrus sent letters, but they kept coming back unopened.

And so it was a big shock to everyone when Cyrus returned to Elizabethton after the war. It would take him another six months to find his wife and son. But when he saw the life Martha and Jonathan were living, and how much his son loved his stepdad, he had to walk away.

Cyrus returned to Elizabethton and went to work for Sheriff Nave, vowing that he could never love another woman like he loved Martha Weaver.

Martha's husband promised he'd make sure Jonathan stayed in touch with his father and that he was always welcome to come for a visit.

There had been several such warm, albeit awkward, visits over the years, but this latest one to Asheville would be the most memorable. Cyrus Weaver, the Civil War soldier given up for dead and whose wife had married another, had stood as best man at his son's wedding.

Meanwhile—just about dark, up Fish Springs way—Isaiah, Prissy, Ruthie and Elijah sat on the porch of Isaiah's cabin.

"Monday June twenty-fifth, three more weeks. That's when the trial starts," Isaiah said. "We should have all the hay put up by then. And everything else'll be in the ground growin'."

"How you know dat, Isaiah?" Elijah asked.

"The governa tol me when we were havin' a beer at the Black Bear Saloon today." Isaiah flashed a gap-toothed smile and laughed.

"Isaiah, you tell that man the truth!" Prissy demanded.

"Okay. I's just funnin' you, Elijah. My boss, Mista Daniel, told me when we was havin' a root beer at the general store."

"You drinking beer, Isaiah?" Elijah asked, raising his eyebrows in wonderment.

"Root beer, Elijah. It's made from sassafras root. Don't have alcohol in it. They make it right in the sto."

Little Willie ran to the porch, climbed up on Prissy's lap and handed her a dandelion.

"Thank you, Willie. You are such a sweet boy."

Then he scampered back to his brothers; they were playing mumbly-peg below the house.

The four Negroes began talking about little Willie.

"Why that youngun' be so light skinned?" Ruthie asked.

"Cause the Lord made 'em that way," Prissy said. "Just like me. I'm light skinned too. Just like my mama was."

"Somewhere dey was a white man in the woodpile!" Elijah chortled.

His attempt at humor didn't work, because Prissy, Isaiah and Ruthie grew silent. But Isaiah did look at Prissy and gave her a half smile.

And then the silence was broken.

"Ma-ma! Can Willie sleep with us in the loft tonight?" Benjamin asked, as he held little Willie's hand. Jeb and Leroy stood eagerly nodding their heads, yes.

"Oh, I don't know, baby? He is so little…." But as Prissy eyed the children, her heart began to give in.

"He can sleep tween me an' Jeb. He's been askin' me every night. Please, Mama," Benjamin pleaded. "He be a good boy."

Prissy looked at Isaiah who nodded his head.

"Okay, Ben, but you make sure he stays between you all night."

"Yes mam! We will take good care'a him."

Isaiah, grinning at Prissy, said cheerfully, "G'night boys."

"Night, Pa. G'night, everbody."

The three rambunctious boys and little Willie headed to the sagging, old barn in the bright moonlight. Some nights Isaiah would take them to the barn loft by the light of a lantern but this time they had no trouble finding their way.

"That was really nice of the boys takin' care of their little brother like that. I love little Willie but he don't need to sleep in our room every night," said Isaiah, smiling at Prissy.

"You can just wipe that big grin off your face, Isaiah. I'm doing this for the boys, not for you."

Elijah shot a knowing glance at Isaiah and had a hard time not laughing.

"Why don't y'all let little Willie sleep in our room? Der won't be nothin' goin' on in der," Ruthie said.

"Der could be."

"No dey couldn't, Elijah."

Isaiah looked at Elijah, grinning from ear to ear.

"Everything fine the way it is, Ruthie, but thank you anyway."

Getting a little more information than she wanted to hear, Prissy decided to change the subject. "Listen. Y'all hear that?"

"What?"

Prissy put her finger to her lips.

The Negroes detected the barely audible sound of a hoot owl off in the distance. "Who … who who!"

"Yea, I hear it," said Isaiah. "A hoot owl. He say who."

"Who," Elijah said.

"Da hoot owl," Isaiah responded.

"No, I jus say, who."

"Da hoot owl!"

"Hush. You two can make a sane woman crazy," said a giggling Prissy.

When the chuckling over the owl sounds ended, Prissy said she loved what she heard after dark.

"The night sounds are the best. The crickets and the tree

frogs, the red headed woodpecker when he pecks on a hollow tree. I even like ta hear wolfs when they howl at the moon. Long as they ain't too close. Is that what they really howlin' at, Isaiah?"

"I don't know, Prissy. They could be howlin to go on a hunt."

Ruthie, clutching her elbows, said, "I don't like ta hea wolfs. Dey too scary."

Elijah asked, "Mo scary den a mouse?"

"No! Nothin' mo' scary den a mouse," said Ruthie, sheepishly causing another burst of laughter.

The now barely discernible night sounds, the gently swaying treetops in the soft breeze and the thousands of stars twinkling in the black sky soothed the four of them.

And then off in the distance.

"What's dat?" Ruthie asked.

"Sounds like a lot'a horses on the road," said Isaiah, a hint of alarm in his voice.

"O Lawd! Dey's comin' again. It's dat Klan!" Ruthie exclaimed.

They saw what looked like two balls of fire floating hideously behind the trees along the road.

Closer inspection revealed ghostly looking white hooded riders as they left the road and moved across an open field toward the cabin. Two hooded men carried torches lighting the way, and the other six fired rifles into the air as they hollered warnings.

"Stay away from that courthouse, niggers, if you wana stay livin'!"

"And if you want your boys ta not lose their hands or feet to our axes, you better never testify!" another of the Klansmen shouted. "We ain't gonna warn you again!"

Then the window beside Prissy shattered as a bullet whisked past her head.

"Everybody in the house! Hurry!" Isaiah commanded.

They all rushed in.

"Get on the floor!" Prissy shouted at Ruthie who was curled up in a chair screaming hysterically. Elijah crawled over to Ruthie and pulled her out of the chair and lay on top of her.

"The boys, Isaiah!"

"They be okay, Prissy. Ben'a make sure they stay down."

Their rants meaner and uglier by the second, the intruders

circled the cabin firing random shots that splintered window frames and furniture. Shards of glass splattered on Elijah's back as he lay there protectively over his terrified wife.

It went on for several grueling minutes while the foursome lay flat on the floor.

Elijah mumbled a prayer. "Oh Lawd, dis ole world is wicked and the devil is out dere tonight. But we know dat Jesus'll save us. Please send angels down ta be with us."

Then the firing stopped.

Isaiah assumed that the Klan had shot enough bullets and spouted enough hatred that they would be on their way. But when he crawled to the back of the house and looked out a shattered window toward the barn, he found out otherwise.

The two Klansmen carrying the torches were in the barn lot. One, on a jittery horse that seemed on the verge of bucking him off, threw his torch into the barn through the open doors. Shadow ran out barking at the men but retreated to the house and crawled under the porch when a shot fired off near him.

The torch landed in hay at the bottom of the ladder to the loft and in a matter of seconds flames started spreading through the dry hay.

The other Klansman reared back to throw his but hesitated when he thought he heard a child crying.

"Let's go, preacher!" the other said as Sue the mule ran past, followed by a bunch of squawking chickens.

Then high above the barn entrance a door flung open and two of the boys looked out.

"Help us!" they hollered, their necks craning and their arms waving.

"Oh my God! They's youngins' up there!"

Hank Beeler, none other than Sheriff Nave's deputy, yelled, "That's too damn bad, preacher! Ain't no time fer Bible thumpin' now! Let's go!"

"I ain't got no stomach fer killin' children no matter what color they are!" protested the one called preacher.

"Your gonna get your ass shot off! I'm outta here!" Deputy Beeler slapped his horse on the rear, putting him in a flat out run. He was soon out of sight, engulfed in the darkness.

Meanwhile, Isaiah, a 30-30 hunting rifle in his hand, headed to the barn, followed by Elijah and Prissy. The big Negro stopped just long enough to draw a bead on the Klansman who was still holding his torch, making himself a lighted target. Isaiah never thought he could kill another man. Taking a life was against every instinct in his body. But nothing or nobody would keep him from protecting his children.

The preacher, atop his horse, a confederate flag attached to his mount's saddle, was lit up like a lantern. He was about 50 yards away as Isaiah steadied himself and and put his finger on the trigger.

"Shoot him, Isaiah! We have to save our children!"

But then his target went dark as the preacher dropped his torch to the ground and dismounted.

Isaiah started running again, followed by Prissy and Elijah. When he got to the barn, he realized the Klansman was attempting to coax the children into jumping out the loft door. But Jeb and Leroy were too afraid to make the leap.

So the hooded man ran inside the open door and pulled on the tongue of the hay wagon.

No one could go in the barn to push because heat from the fire was too intense. Isaiah got a hold of the tongue alongside of the Klansman and together they managed to pull the partially filled hay wagon out enough to be below the door where the children gathered above.

The flames had gotten bigger and more deadly by the second.

Feeling the heat, the boys had begun to panic. They were screaming for help and hadn't even looked downward toward the hay wagon.

Crying and shaking, Prissy yelled, "Jump, Leroy!"

There was only enough hay in the wagon to soften their landing. But, mercifully, it did the trick.

Leroy, flailing his arms, jumped into the hay, landing hard on his bottom. Followed by Jeb.

Then they climbed down off the wagon and ran crying into Prissy's arms.

The Klansman watched but said nothing.

Benjamin stood, silhouetted against the increasingly bigger

flames, in the opening. He held Willie who was terrified and screaming for his mom.

"Ben! You be okay, son?" Isaiah hollered over the roar of the inferno.

"It's gettin' awful hot, Pa!" Ben yelled back.

"Hold Willie out as far as you can and drop'em. I'll catch'em," said Isaiah, climbing up on the wagon. "You can do it, son. I promise he be okay, Ben."

Ben followed his dad's instructions and dropped the screaming child. Isaiah caught the terrified little boy, then he gently handed him down to the Klansman who set the crying child on the ground where he, like the others, ran to Prissy.

Benjamin jumped last, landed hard, then rolled off the wagon to the ground but jumped right up and ran toward the house to get buckets to bring water from the spring.

Isaiah and the Klansman pulled the wagon clear of the barn, as the inferno raged.

The Klansman looked at Isaiah like he wanted to speak. Isaiah looked back waiting for a word but none came. Isaiah could see the man's eyes through the holes cut in the white hood that covered his head and face. They were blinking and full of tears. *Was it from the smoke or the guilt?* Isaiah wondered. Still he did not speak; he locked eyes with Isaiah for a few more seconds, and then mounted his horse and rode away.

A few minutes later Ben returned with two buckets of water, but he knew it was futile—as did the others, so they all walked away toward the house.

Prissy and the children huddled together—away from the intense heat and flames that pierced the darkness.

Isaiah watched as his barn collapsed in sections and wicked red and yellow flames carrying fiery embers rose high in the sky.

The barn he had lost, but not Prissy, nor his children, nor his friends, not even his animals. They had been spared. And for that, he thanked Almighty God. He also thanked God that he had not squeezed the trigger on his 30-30 rifle.

CHAPTER 15

Casket for Elijah

At best, Isaiah had only a few hours of fitful sleep. He rose several times during the night and looked through the broken bedroom window at the smoldering ruins of his barn. He even walked out onto the porch to make sure the invaders had not returned. Normally, he would be readying himself for another day of tending to livestock and working the rocky but fertile ground. But this was no normal day. He slipped into an old, faded blue shirt and overalls and strapped up his boots.

Making another trip to the porch, he stepped over one of the boys. He wasn't sure which one, because they were wrapped like cocoons against the cool morning air drifting in off the river.

Isaiah was amazed at how soundly the boys slept after all they had been through the night before. He thanked God again for keeping his family and friends safe. And as he stood on the porch eyeing the mountains and fog hanging over the Watauga River, he wondered how there could be so much hatred in such a beautiful place.

Golden, bright sunbeams came into view over Pond Mountain. It was a cool, crisp morning, full of the promise of a new day in rough but enchanting Fish Springs. It was as if God had intended the little remote mountain community to reflect His grandeur and to give Isaiah some peace of mind among all the turmoil.

Isaiah would normally be rising about this time. So rubbing the sleep out of his eyes and stretching, he made his way back to the kitchen. He brewed a big pot of coffee in one of the few pots that hadn't been pierced by a bullet.

He liked to get his bearings each morning, so, sipping his coffee, Isaiah sat on the porch, contemplating what to do next.

Shadow crawled out from under the porch and joined Isaiah. While he lingered there stroking Shadow, he heard the scream of a hawk way off to the West. The sunshine got brighter and warmer, but along with the normal fresh scent of pine was the smell of lingering smoke and burnt wood, bringing back the anxiety from the night before.

Soon Prissy, holding her own tin cup of coffee, joined Isaiah on the porch. Isaiah noticed the stress on his beautiful wife's face. The close call from the KKK and the fear of almost losing her children was taking a toll.

"It's nice having my coffee waitin' fo me when I get up," she said, trying to sound cheerful.

"Well, you've been havin' mine waitin' for me all these years." He hugged his wife, kissed her softly, and caressed the back of her neck. "I'm so sorry all this is happenin', Prissy. I know it's so hard on you."

"What we gonna do, Isaiah? I am really scared. For my boys and us and Elijah and Ruthie."

"I been tryin' ta figure that out, Prissy."

A frazzled Ruthie interrupted them out on the cabin's porch. "Has Elijah been out hea?"

"No. I thought he was still in the bed," said Isaiah, putting his coffee down.

"Oh! Lawdy! He tol' me sometime in da night he gwine to da outhouse house. Where could he be?"

"You set down, Ruthie," Isaiah said. "Don't worry. I will find him." He was scared but didn't want to show it.

He knew Elijah could have been dragged off by the Klan and beaten to death. Or the old, gentle man he had grown so close to could have had his hands tied behind him, his neck fitted into a noose and hanged from a tree. All while the KKK "Brothers" laughed and celebrated. Isaiah thought about such as he scoured the area, looking in the outhouse first.

But Isaiah couldn't find a trace of Elijah anywhere.

He got more anxious by the time he returned to the porch to Prissy and Ruthie. But somehow he had to stay composed. Because the last thing Isaiah wanted to do was add to their worry.

"Y'all stay here," he said. "I'll find Elijah. I promise. Prissy, wake the boys up please, and have them do their chores. I'll be back as soon as I find him."

"Okay, Isaiah. You be careful. You want ta eat something before you go? You haven't had anything but coffee."

When Isaiah said he didn't have time for breakfast and had to leave right then, Ruthie began rocking and crying. Prissy wrapped her arms around the old woman, patted her on the back and whispered comforting words from Scripture.

But Ruthie kept bawling. "We should neva talked to dat sheriff!" she cried. "Now my Elijah be gone! Dat Klan took him. I knows dey did."

Isaiah started to say something to Ruthie, but Prissy motioned for him to go.

Isaiah mounted his old mule Sue and headed to the road. He wasn't sure which way to go but decided to head away from town, thinking that's what Elijah would probably do. If the KKK did take him, the frail old man would probably be hanging lifeless from a tree along the road.

Riding along the dusty road, Isaiah thought of how before the war Negroes were somehow safer because they were valuable property. But an old man like Elijah would have been worthless then.

If his friend Elijah had been taken by the Klansmen they would have done their dastardly deed under the cover of darkness, ignoring his pleas for mercy and stringing him up almost before he could say a prayer. The execution would have been quick, heartless and efficient—as if Elijah were less than nothing, let alone an innocent human being.

He felt bad having convinced Elijah, fearful and reluctant from the outset, to tell Sheriff Nave what he had witnessed between Toby Jackson and Jake Edwards. He had put Elijah's life, as well as Ruthie's, at risk. *Why'd I have ta drag him inta this?*

Every corner of the twisting road he rounded he expected to see the lifeless form of his friend hanging from a tree. As he rounded yet another, a magnificent buck sporting a huge rack with 12 points stood in the road frozen for a few seconds. Then he leaped off the road, crossed the river and bounded up Pond Mountain.

When Isaiah turned back, barely visible in the distance was the figure of a man. Could it actually be Elijah? His heart pounded and soon enough he realized it was.

The old, stooped-over gray-haired man walked like he had lost his last friend and expected to die any minute. Elijah barely gave his pursuer a glance.

"Where you headed, old man?" Isaiah asked the question gently as he stopped the mule.

"Go back home, brother Isaiah." Elijah didn't break stride. He cast his forlorn eyes downward.

"I can't do that. I've been lookin' for ya, Elijah. We were worried somethin' awful about you. Ruthie's havin' a tizzy."

Elijah continued sauntering along. "Well, you found me. So you can jus' go back home."

"Come on, Elijah. Ruthie is worried sick."

"I cain't be dere, Isaiah. Cain't you see dat? I is da reason dat Klan came to yo place. Dey burn down yo barn 'cause'a me. Dey almost kill the young'uns."

His eyes watering up, Elijah stopped and stared at Isaiah. He brushed a swath of mud and some briars from his raggedy clothes. "Thank da Lawd dat yo children didn't burn up in dat fire. Oh Lawdy, Isaiah, what I gonna' do? Everbody 'round me get killed if I stay." The old man, feeling as if he poisoned those near him, dropped to his knees.

"Dat Klan'll do anything ta keep me from testifyin'. Dey will kill all us. You know dat, Isaiah. Save yo-self and Prissy and yo' younguns. And tell Ruthie I love her, but I got to be gone. Now leave me be, my friend."

Isaiah climbed down off Sue. "So where you think you are goin', Elijah? There ain't no use runnin' away. We have ta trust in the Lord and the law."

"The white man's Lord and the white man's law," Elijah shot back. "Always the colored man gettin' the short end'a the stick. Always the colored man gettin' throwed off on. Always the white man crowin' and struttin' like a rooster and the colored man hidin' ta keep from gettin' hanged. Dat jest da way it is, Isaiah."

Isaiah said nothing. Just stood there, one hand on the bridle of his mule, listening and wondering how he could reason with such a defeated, hopeless man.

"I is the only one dat can testify, 'cause I was da only one who was dere. I needs ta go away, Isaiah. Then da Klan will leave yo' family be. Cain't you see? It be the only way."

Elijah sat down on the road, his head and hunched shoulders drooped, and he cried. At one point, Isaiah thought the aging Negro might be better off if he left without a trace. But that would surely break Ruthie's heart. And he, Prissy and even the children had come to love the old man. And on top of that, Jake Edwards would surely go free without Elijah to testify at the trial.

There had to be another way.

Isaiah pulled him up, patted him on the back and whispered a few encouraging words. "You know we all love you, Elijah. And we will make sure the law protects you. I promise. Now come back home with me."

"But how you goin' keep dat evil Klan from coming back, Isaiah? And what 'bout Ruthie and Prissy and da chilen? How you goin' keep'em safe?"

He's askin' some hard questions, Isaiah thought. *Maybe Mista Charlie Smith can come up with somethin'.*

"I ain't goin' back, Isaiah." Elijah sounded more determined then ever.

"Here's what we gonna do, Elijah. I gonna take you back—"

"No!"

"Let me finish," Isaiah said.

"I gonna take you back ta my place. Then I am going to see Mista Charlie and tell him what happened last night and see what we need to do. If he can't help us, then we'll send you on your way, but with food and water and a bed roll. If you have ta leave, you can at least be able to live in the woods for a while. Okay?"

Elijah studied the idea for several seconds. He said nothing. Then, with the back of his hand, he wiped his eyes dry.

"Okay, Isaiah, but you has ta promise. I ain't stayin' at yo house tonight. I be goin' somewhere else."

"Okay. I promise."

Isaiah had no intention of letting Elijah sleep on the ground among snakes, bears and mountain lions in the woods. But for right now it was the only way to get his old friend to come back home—at least until someone could come up with another solution.

Isaiah cupped his hands for Elijah's foot and helped him climb up on Sue. Then he, too, mounted the mule, and the two headed back to Isaiah's farm.

He dropped off Elijah—tired, dirty, bitten by insects and hungry—to an elated and grateful Ruthie, told Prissy of his plans and headed toward Elizabethton with a couple of biscuits and a jug of water.

Along the way, he stopped under a thick canopy of trees to let Sue drink from a cold mountain stream. On the other side a flock of wild turkeys made a nervous fuss, flapped their wings and then scattered. Trout thrived there; Isaiah had seen them in the rushing, gurgling waters between the mossy rocks and in the occasional deep pool at the foot of a waterfall. He wished right now he could linger here beside the cool blue water with a fishing pole and catch a few for his family. But it wasn't to be. *Why dis ole world have ta be so mean? Why cain't colored folks and white folks get along?*

Later that day, back in Fish Springs, Prissy, Ruthie and Elijah sat on the porch.

They gave thanks that their beloved friend and husband had been found and brought back after spending those frightful hours in the dark alone. Just days earlier, they'd heard about how a neighbor in Fish Springs had encountered a big black mother bear. The man had been hunting alone, had somehow come between the bear and her cubs and had made the big, romping animal angry and protective. When the bear charged at the man, his rifle jammed. The bear knocked him down and clawed the hunter's neck, face and stomach. But then the unpredictable animal, just as fast as it had attacked, ran off, leaving the hunter severely injured and covered in blood.

They knew this surely could have been Elijah if he'd been in the wrong place at the wrong time.

Just then, coming into their view in a cloud of dust, was a wagon driven by Charlie Smith. Beside him was Isaiah. A canvas covered a crate or something in the back. Tethered behind the wagon was Sue.

Charlie pulled the wagon to a stop at the porch, set the brake, and he and Isaiah climbed down.

No one spoke. The porch sitters just looked at Charlie for an explanation.

Isaiah broke the silence. "Where are the children?"

Prissy said, "They are off fishing, except little Willie. He's takin' a nap. They be gone for a while." She was obviously curious about what was on the back of the wagon and what her Isaiah and Charlie might be up to.

"Good. We need to keep this from them," Charlie said. "I need you to promise me. No one talks to the children about this."

"What we gonna keep from the children, Mista Charlie?" Prissy asked.

Charlie looked at Isaiah and nodded.

Isaiah reached up and pulled the canvas off a rather plain looking pine casket with brass handles.

"We have a plan," Isaiah said proudly.

"Good, long as dat casket not fo me," Elijah grunted.

"But it is for you," Charlie said.

"Oh, Lawdy!"

"We gonna fake your death," Isaiah said.

"As a matter of fact," Charlie intervened, "we already started. We spread the news all around town that because of all the stress brought on by the Ku Klux Klan, you had a heart attack during the night and died."

"So Isaiah gonna hide me 'til the trial?" Elijah asked incredulously.

Prissy and Ruthie got wide eyed. And they couldn't keep from staring at the casket.

"No!" Charlie commanded. "We can't take that chance, Elijah. Reverend Leftwich is going to have a funeral service in a couple of days at the Colored Baptist Church. Where you will be mourned over and viewed in that casket."

Elijah looked at Charlie, wondering if he heard him right.

"But only for a few minutes, Elijah," Isaiah noted.

"Oh, Lawdy! You mean I has ta get in dat casket?!"

Charlie explained that once they got Elijah to the Colored

Baptist Church, he'd be hidden in a back room, and there he'd
stay, safe and sound and out of sight until the trial.

"Except for the funeral. We have to have a funeral for you, Elijah. We'll explain everything better later, but for now we need to
go. We want people to see us hauling the casket through town
while it's still light," said Charlie.

"But folks'a see me in da wagon. Where you gonna hide me?"
Elijah asked.

Neither Charlie nor Isaiah answered. They just looked at each
other, then Elijah, while Prissy and Ruthie both covered their
mouths.

Elijah, now grasping the plan, dropped his head and mumbled, "Lawdy, Lawdy, Lawdy. You won't have'ta fake ma death. I be
dead by da time I get to da church."

A grinning Isaiah remarked, "Ain't just any man can be alive
for his own funeral, Elijah. And besides, you will be doing' this ta
get justice for our good friend, Toby."

When the old Negro seemed to be at a loss for words, Charlie
Smith spoke up. "Elijah, I know this won't be easy for you. But it's
the only thing we could come up with. Will you do it?"

Elijah studied the plan a couple of minutes.

He flashed a hint of a smile. "I do it fo' my friends and dey
chilin and fo' my old friend Toby. I do the best I can. Yes, I do it."

Prissy and Ruthie hugged and kissed him and pledged they'd
be there with him—through the funeral, through the trial, through
the guilty verdict (they hoped) for Jake Edwards—every step of
the way.

And Charlie Smith assured Elijah that what he would be doing would make it safer for everyone—with the Klan thinking
he had died and that giving them no more reason to torment
him, his wife, Isaiah and Prissy and their children. *I just hope I'm
right*, Charlie thought.

Elijah, his brittle bones not working as good as they once did,
nevertheless willed himself to climb up on the back of the wagon with Isaiah. He studied the inside of the casket after Isaiah
opened it. The cushioned bottom was red with gold trim. He
fidgeted with the soft round pillow for several seconds.

"We need to go now, Elijah," Isaiah said firmly.

But Elijah didn't want to be rushed so. "I needs to take ma boots off, Isaiah. I don't want to get dat nice cloth dirty."

"He's right, Isaiah," Charlie said. "We should keep it clean for the next fellow."

Elijah took off his boots, and they stuffed them in a feed sack under the seat.

"Maybe we could leave dat lid open 'til we get to town?" said Elijah, putting one foot in.

"Can't take that chance, Elijah," Charlie said.

Elijah eased his other foot into the casket and stood frozen.

"You have to lie down in the coffin, Elijah," Charlie said.

"Lawdy, Lawdy," he said, sitting down.

Isaiah put his hand on top of Elijah's head and pushed him down into the casket. Then he put the lid on and secured it with a length of rope.

"Elijah! Elijah!" Ruthie called out.

"You need me, Ruthie?" asked Elijah in a muffled voice from the box.

"I bring yo' nice Sunday clothes to da church. I want you to look real nice fo' yo' funeral."

"Okay," he called out.

"Let's move out. We need to get to town while its still light, said Charlie

Then came a desperate cry from the box.

"Wait! Wait! How I gonna breathe in hea' wit dat lid shut?"

"We drilled the bottom full'a holes."

"Oh." Then after a pause, "How many?"

"'Nough," said Isaiah, snapping the reins and moving out.

"Lawdy, Lawdy, Lawdy."

CHAPTER 16

A Death Wagon and a Funeral

The horse-drawn "death wagon" containing what was believed to be the corpse of Elijah Wood rolled into Elizabethton a short time later.

Low-lying clouds hugged the mountains framing the east Tennessee town and the sun had begun its downward path. But it was still daylight, just as Charlie Smith had hoped, and the courthouse square near the center of town where the wagon passed was a beehive of activity.

He grinned at Isaiah as he stepped down from the wagon at his office. "You sure you don't need me to go to the church with you, Isaiah?

"I be fine from here, Mr Charlie."

Two women standing on the courthouse steps were galking at the casket. Charlie, noticing the women, spoke loudly.

"You better get Elijah's body to the church, Isaiah. Poor soul."

"Okay, Mista Charlie," Isaiah said, clucking to Sue and pulling out.

As Isaiah headed to his destination people lined the road in front of the feed store, dry goods store, post office, and the Silver Spoon, one of the eating establishments. A few took their hats off and bowed their heads. Isaiah wasn't sure if news that Charlie's star witness in the Jake Edwards trial died had gotten around, or if folks were just showing respect for the deceased.

On one corner. as Isaiah passed, a bearded jowly man in buckskins played a fiddle while a couple of smiling drunks danced to his tune. They stopped and stood silent.

A couple of well-perfumed, dolled up ladies of the night from the Black Bear Saloon craned their necks, just outside the saloon's entrance, to see what everyone was looking at.

One of them yelled "Oh my!" when she spotted Isaiah and his haul. "That casket must be holdin' that darkie was going to testify 'genst Jake Edwards. They saying the Klan scared him to death."

Nearby, under a massive oak tree not far from the courthouse square, more genteel women, in bonnets and long flowing dresses, stopped knitting and gossiping and watched as Isaiah's wagon passed.

Regardless of what they were doing or who they were, all eyes seemed drawn to the mysterious coffin in back of the wagon driven by Isaiah.

A wide-eyed Negro shouted, "Who dat be in the coffin, Isaiah?!" The inquisitive fellow happened to be in town that day picking up supplies for his family.

"It be my old friend, Mista Elijah Wood!" Isaiah yelled back, loud enough so that everyone within earshot could hear him.

"I knows Elijah! What happened ta him?" The curious Negro ran toward the wagon.

"That Ku Klux Klan raided my place, scared him so bad he didn't make it through the night. His heart just gave out. God bless his soul!"

As Isaiah spoke, others—colored folks and whites—gawked and drew closer to the wagon. Many had heard that Elijah was to be a key witness in the murder trial of Jake Edwards.

"So! Looks like poor old Elijah ain't sayin' nothin' to nobody, right?" came a loud voice just outside the sheriff's office. It belonged to Deputy Duke Rayburn. Rayburn had a tough time hiding his smugness.

"I reckon not, Mista Duke," Isaiah answered. "Only person Elijah be talkin' to now is Jesus in Heaven."

"So where you takin'em, Isaiah?" the sullen, grinning deputy asked.

"The Colored Baptist Church where the Reverend Horace Leftwich will be givin' Elijah a proper Christian funeral and burial."

"Well, ain't that somethin'?" The deputy mocked him. "Too bad he didn't live long enough to testify. I guess some things just ain't meant to be."

Isaiah's worst fear began to play out as Rayburn walked toward him and the casket, figuring to get a glimpse at the corpse.

"Don't you move, Elijah," whispered Isaiah, his back to the approaching Klan member. "Deputy Duke is comin' this way. I'm sure he is gonna open the casket."

A fearful Elijah braced for convincing Duke that the man in the coffin was dead. Holding his breath and clinching his mouth shut, he prayed, "Lawd, please make me look da'ed."

"Duke! Get your ass back to the office, and leave that man be!" The loud, insistent command came from Sheriff Nave. He had heard the exchange as he exited the office on his way to see Charlie Smith to get all the details about the Klan raid.

"Ok, Sheriff," said Duke, stopping in his tracks. But his eyes stayed glued to the coffin.

Isaiah whispered, "It okay, Elijah. The sheriff stopped him."

Elijah, who had done his best to look like a dead man, started breathing again as Isaiah snapped the reins and Sue plodded off. Isaiah kept his eyes straight ahead on the road as he guided the wagon past Duke toward the Colored Baptist Church.

When Charlie Smith's loyal helper rolled up to the entrance of the church, founded by the Rev. Horace Leftwich, the preacher was there to receive him and his cargo.

"Come around here, Isaiah." Leftwich motioned him to drive the wagon around to the back. "I think you and I can get this coffin to the back room."

Isaiah heard a few gasps inside the coffin when he and the preacher lifted it off the wagon and hauled it inside the church.

"Shoosh!" Isaiah ordered. "You s'pposed ta be dead."

"We takin' you in the church, Elijah. You'll be out soon." Leftwich whispered as he and the muscular Isaiah strained, lifting the coffin.

"Dat's good, 'cause I needs to pee real bad."

"Okay. We have you a pot in here 'cause you can't go to the outhouse."

"Lawdy, Lawdy, I knowed I should'a run away."

Once inside the safety of the church's back room, Elijah squirmed out of the pine box, used the chamber pot in the corner and began breathing easier.

Isaiah and the preacher, dressed like you would expect a clergyman to be dressed—in a white shirt, black pants and shiney black shoes—then hatched their plan with him.

They said the viewing and funeral would be at noon the next day in the church sanctuary. That way they wouldn't have a big crowd, because it would be over before a lot of folks got the word. They were relieved that the news probably wouldn't get to Elijah's two sons who lived in Nashville. It would be a fairly small affair, with only Elijah's wife and a few close friends attending; and of course, members of the Colored Baptist Church who had heard about Elijah's passing and would want to come by and pay their respects. A few songs would be sung, Scripture recited and prayers would be said. Leftwich would deliver the eulogy, keeping it meaningful and uplifting—but most importantly, for Elijah's sake, short.

"And folks be lookin' at me in dat coffin?" Elijah asked nervously.

"Yes, but not many and not for long. I promise," said the preacher who had founded his church, not only to worship God, but also as a safe haven for Negroes caught in the crosshairs of hatred and prejudice in East Tennessee.

"Lawdy, Lawdy, Lawdy! I's goin' to my own funeral. But what if dey touch me or stay dere at da casket starin' at me a long time?"

"They won't," said Isaiah, grinning. "They will think you are rottin' from how bad you smell. They'll hold their noses and get away from you fast."

"Isaiah! You sayin' I smells bad?"

"You will, 'cause we gonna' put a dead rat in the casket with you."

"A rat! Lawdy, Lawdy! I knowed I should'a run away."

Just thinking about lying on a dead, stinking rat made Elijah's stomach turn. He worried that he wouldn't be able to stand it.

"You can do it, Elijah. You have ta do it for Toby," Leftwich said.

"And then you be takin' me to the cemetery?" he asked.

"That will be the next day, when we have a grave dug for you in the church cemetery, but don't worry. Nobody will be in the casket, Elijah." Leftwich spoke confidently and calmly, trying to ease the anxious man's fears.

Isaiah said, "We ain't puttin' you in the ground. We just actin' like we are. You will be hidin' in the back room, and you will stay there 'til Mista Charlie sends for you to testify at the trial."

"How long I has ta stay in dere, Isaiah?"

"It's about three weeks 'til the trial, Elijah,"

"Lawd, please hep' me. Three long weeks."

Leftwich told Elijah his wife was a good cook. He also said he would visit him often and try to slip Ruthie, Isaiah and Prissy in every now and then.

The following day, the handful of expected mourners—Elijah's friends and a few long-time members of the Colored Baptist Church—filed dutifully by his casket. They glanced at the "deceased," many pinching their nose from the putrid smell and hurriedly returned to their place in a rough-hewn pew.

It all worked as planned until old Bo Brown, a blacksmith in town stepped up to the casket to get a quick look in spite of the smell. Just as he did, a pesky fly landed on Elijah's nose, and he twitched it. Bo, his eyeballs almost popping out of their sockets, flinched, as if he'd seen a ghost, and jumped back.

"Reverend, did you see dat? Elijah just twitched his nose."

"Oh, that happens sometimes with the departed. It's just a reflex, Bo. Nothing to get riled up about. I once had a man set plum up in his coffin during his eulogy. Folks screamed and gasped and carried on somethin' terrible. Almost emptied the church out."

"Well I'll swear. That's a boogerish thing, Reverend," said Bo as he returned to his seat.

"Last up was Ruthie who was unaware of the dead rat. She bent over into the coffin and kissed Elijah on the forehead. "You looks real nice, Elijah, but, Shoo! you sho' do smell bad. You sho' you ain't da'ed?" As the pretend "grieving widow" spoke, she clamped her nose shut.

"I will be if dey don't hurry and get me outa hea," he whispered. "Ruthie, is dey a lot 'a people at my funeral?"

"Dey sho' is, Elijah. Da church be filled up." Ruthie figured one little white lie couldn't hurt. "But don't smile. You da'ed."

The Rev. Leftwich, wearing a black robe and brandishing his Bible, walked to the pulpit and recited a few verses of Scripture. At Elijah's request, the preacher had selected the words from Ecclesiastes. "Brothers and sisters, the Good Book says this, 'There is a time for everything … A time to be born and a time to die. A time to plant and a time to uproot … A time to mourn and a time to dance.'"

He figeted and crossed his fingers behind his back. "Our beloved Elijah is in Heaven! He has gone on to that Big Mansion in the sky to be with Jesus! He never has to worry again about bein' beaten down or treated like a slave or ex-slave or barely havin' clothes on his back or food in his mouth.

"That's because God has called him home—away from torture and misery and not havin' nothin'.

"Elijah's where nobody can hurt him. Where they ain't no colored church or white church, where they's only angels and glory and Jesus and where nobody's sick or old or ailin'."

A thunderous chorus of "Amens!" came from those at the service.

After the eulogy, as was the practice for funerals at the Colored Baptist Church, there was weeping, but it quickly gave way to singing, swaying, clapping, hugging and more *amens*.

"Don't he look right peaceful, Amos?" said an old lady to her husband, her eyes watering up.

"He sho' do. He almos' look like he smilin'."

A few members of the congregation took turns standing up and publicly mourning the one whom they'd come to pay their respects to. One of those was a wrinkled, frail elderly woman, herself, like Elijah, a former slave who had been captured in Africa. Like Elijah, she had endured the long miserable voyage across the Atlantic Ocean, only to be bought and sold like an animal at an auction in South Carolina. "Elijah, he be happy to be finally goin' home to his family and to Jeezus Christ!" she shouted with jubilation. Her fellow mourners clapped with joy. And again the little sanctuary was filled with hearty "amens!"

The man in the casket took it all in and would have enjoyed listening to the praise heaped upon him if it were not for sharing the small enclosure with his rotting rodent companion.

At times the stench became overwhelming and he fought to keep from throwing up. He dared not move a muscle, trying hard not to swallow or to twitch the least little bit. Instead, he lay there in the pine box as stone cold "dead" as possible.

The scheme seemed to be working perfectly.

But then Deputy Duke Rayburn, a half sneer on his face, showed up during the last stanza of "We Shall Gather at the River." Removing his hat, he said he had come to pay his respects and asked to view the corpse.

"He ain't very pleasant smellin', Deputy Rayburn. You sure you want to see him?" Leftwich said. While trying to stay calm, he laid his rumpled old hymnal down and asked the congregation to sit.

"Just the same preacher, I'd like to have a quick look," the deputy countered sternly.

"Okay, Deputy, step on up and take a look but don't say I didn't warn you." The minister spoke loud enough so that Elijah would be ready.

The "dead" imposter swallowed hard one last time, slowly took in as much air as his lungs would hold and held his breath before Duke got to the casket.

The lawman approached the open coffin mindful that about 25 sets of suspicious eyes on dark faces watched his every move. For several seconds, he looked at Elijah's pallid face, made that way from flour dabbed on it by Leftwich. Then he got a whiff of the most repulsive, rotten odor he'd ever smelled. He gagged, turned up his nose as if it had taken in something so foul it was beyond belief, and quickly did an about face toward the church's exit.

"Okay, that's enough respectin'," Duke said on his way out. "Preacher you need to get'im in the ground just as quick as you can."

Leftwich nodded, then with his back to the mourners, whispered "good job, Elijah" and shut the lid.

Minutes later, Duke plunked down at a table in a back room at the Black Bear Saloon, where Jake Edwards and three of his "KKK Brothers" were sitting.

"He ain't only dead. He's done dried out and smells like a dead rat," Duke announced.

"And you're damned sure it was him?" Jake Edwards asked.

"As sure as my name is Duke Rayburn and as sure as I'm gon-na' bed me another whore tonight. Ain't no doubt about it, Jake. The man in the coffin is Elijah Wood. He's the deadest darkie I've ever seen. And he's the nastiest, rottenest thing I ever smelled."

"How can you tell it's him, Duke?" one of the KKK brothers asked. "All them niggers look alike to me."

"It's him, damn it! I know what I saw, so shut the hell up."

Jake Edwards raised his hands like a peacemaker.

"Now boys, settle down. Old Duke here knows a dead darkie when he sees one. Looks like to me that Klan raid at Isaiah Wash-ington's farm paid off. So y'all did somethin' right for a change.

"Now you'ins skedaddle. I'll get in touch if I need you. Me an' Duke need ta talk."

Out the saloon's swinging doors the three "Klan Brothers" shuf-fled—satisfied that for a change, they'd gotten some good news.

Once outside, one of the Brothers growled, "Now we can get on back to our own affairs. I'm 'bout tired of old Jake callin' the shots. You'd think he was the Imperial Wizard just 'cause he pays his dues like the rest of us."

"He might be 'bout broke anyways —with havin' ta pay that fancy dancy lawyer an' all," said another.

"Don't kid yourself. That old bird's got money stashed every-wheres."

Back inside, Duke ordered a shot of straight whiskey. "Make it a double, darlin'!" he yelled, gesturing to the bar gal.

Meanwhile, a relieved Edwards took a gulp of his beer. Then he laughed and clapped his hands with glee. *One nigger dead and one to go.*

"What you wantin' to tell me, brother Jake?"

Jake held his hand up gestering for Duke to wait a minute.

"Here you go sweetie," said the bar girl giving Duke a seduc-tive wink.

Duke chugged a big swig of his drink and said "Ah!" as if what had slivered deliciously down his throat had hit the right spot. He smacked his lips and sat the glass back on the table.

Jake Edwards looked around then spoke. "Duke, I wanted to talk to you alone because some of the brothers are weak and quite frankly, I don't trust em. This is for your ears only."

"I'll take it to my grave, brother Jake. You can trust me. You know that," Duke said, gulping the rest of his whiskey.

Edwards said nothing for a few seconds, as if trying to size up, one more time, the man he was with. *He's a scoundrel. Ain't no two ways 'bout it, but he's all I got.*

Then he spoke—in a low voice. "We need to shut that old nigger woman up."

"Fanny May Brown?"

"Yep. She can cause me a heap'a trouble. She worked in my store thirteen years ago. She'll lie about that no-good nigger Toby Jackson payin' off his bill, 'cause she was a friend of his and she hates me."

Edwards, his expression dead serious, took another sip of his frothy brew.

"If she testifies and they believe her, I could end up in prison or worse. So as a Klan brother, I'm askin' you to shut her up for good. And if you need to get rid of her daughter, too, that's just fine."

Duke studied what Jake was proposing for a few seconds. *I've got that bastard right where I want 'em. He's as nervous and worried as a whore in church.*

"Thousand dollars, Jake."

"What?! Ain't no way! For God's sake you're my Klan brother. We stick together!"

"It's a damn risky job at best, Jake. She'll be in protective custody from the time she leaves Knoxville. And on top'a that, Sheriff Nave's gettin' a little suspicious 'bout me and Hank. "

"Okay, dammit! Five hundred now and the rest when it's done."

"Deal."

"Don't cross me, Duke. If I go down, your'a goin' down with me."

The deputy, sensing a big windfall, tried to hide his delight.

"You just get me the money, old man," Duke ordered. "She'll be dead and in the ground before the trial starts."

Smiling, he raised his glass to clink it.

The anguished man accused of murdering Toby Jackson at first hesitated, then participated reluctantly in the toast.

CHAPTER 17

Two Boys in the River

Back at the church after all the mourners had left, Elijah, Ruthie, Isaiah, Prissy and the Rev. Leftwich congratulated one another in Elijah's back room sanctuary. They had pulled off a well-planned, carefully-crafted deception. And now, the five Negroes would let the wheels of justice take their course.

After hugs and pats on the back, they thanked Leftwich for all his help and promised to return for the worship service and a short visit with Elijah.

In the meantime Isaiah would get back to farming and supervising the other sharecroppers for Daniel Smith. Prissy and the boys would be salvaging anything that was left from the barn fire, while Ruthie watched over little Willie and took care of the house chores.

Eleven-year-old Jebediah asked, "Mama, is we gonna build a new barn?"

"Make that 'Are we,' Jeb," his mother corrected him. "And yes we are. But we have to tend to other things right now, sweetheart."

"Why'd those bad men burn our barn down, Mom?"

"They were trying to scare us. They didn't want Mr. Wood to testify in court."

Then, realizing she was saying way too much for Jeb's young ears, Prissy added, "It's all very confusing, son. But I promise that when you are older, I will tell you the whole story. Okay?"

"Okay. They sure scared me, Mom."

"Me too, Jeb," Prissy said, wrapping her arms around her inquisitive, easily frightened boy. "But we all have to be strong like your father. Life'll never be easy for us, son. We just have to have faith in the Lord and do the best we can."

"I know, Mom. The Lord'll take care'a us."

Before they knew it, Sunday rolled back around, and Isaiah, Prissy and Ruthie were on their way back to Elizabethton, leaving the children at home until after the trial.

The warmth of the sun also brought a sense of hope and divine continuity. God, mountain folks believed, was again looking out for them. How could it be otherwise with such a magnificent sunrise?

In due time, after their wagon had forded streams, traversed lush meadows and climbed hills, they arrived at Leftwich's church.

The Colored Baptist Church in Elizabethton, Leftwich's pride and joy, was a solemn sanctuary where Bible-believing colored folks turned for divine reassurance, guidance and comfort.

Many of the churchgoers worked day in and day out on sprawling farms owned by white people. Theirs was an endless task of laboring from sunup to sundown tending to their white employers' crops and animals. Others had become sharecroppers like Isaiah, which meant they planted, worked and harvested crops on someone else's land and got a share of what they harvested. Then there were those who had their own little cabins back in the mountains, where they worked their gardens so they could feed their family and cut firewood for cooking and heating.

Most had a cow for milk and chickens for the eggs. The women made a lot of their own clothes and their children's clothes, and the men hunted the forests around them for wild game, squirrels, pheasants and quail for the meat. And the bigger the game, the better. Prey like deer and elk. Also a nice speckled trout could be pulled from the Watauga River. Many set traps for beavers for their pelts. A bear would not only put meat on the table; his hide would make a warm fur coat. The children helped out scouring the woods and fields for blackberries and blueberries for jams, jellies and pies. So when they worshipped the Almighty, they gave thanks for all these blessings and for the safety and well being of their loved ones.

On this particular glorious Sunday morning, Leftwich had a

good turnout. Negroes, seeking solace from the Holy Spirit, arrived on horseback, on the backs of mules, in work wagons or on foot. A few came in buggies, and one big burly man showed up today, as he did every Sunday, on the back of an ox he called Goliath.

Colored churchgoers in and around Elizabethton had risen early, bathed and put on clean clothes and spruced up their mud-caked boots or shoes. They had dressed in their Sunday best because it was the Lord's Day and to do otherwise was to send a message that they didn't think enough of the Almighty to look presentable for Jesus.

Many of them exchanged brief pleasantries and handshakes with Leftwich on the front steps of the Colored Baptist Church. Then, when a bell high up in the steeple tolled that the service was about to begin, they squirmed into the sanctuary's well-used but serviceable pews. These, and that precious bronze bell, had been gifted to Leftwich from a white sympathizer preacher who'd worked years earlier on the Underground Railroad.

Sitting there in the pews, some of the parishioners swapped the latest news and stories with a little gossip mixed in. The main topic of conversation was still Toby Jackson along with snippets of gossip about the KKK, Jake Edwards and the trial.

Flanked on her left by two handsome young men, young attractive Eula Sanders noticed that Maurice had brought a friend along to the service. Eula, with an eyecatching figure and bright brown eyes, was a bit perplexed that Maurice had not wanted to know her better, for she had tried on several occasions to appear interested in the well-spoken young man. She knew little about Maurice other than the fact that he came to church every Sunday and he worked as a waiter in the dining room at the Snyder House Hotel.

Most young men would relish a chance at courting the beautiful mahogany-colored woman. *Why wouldn't Maurice?* She got her answer when she reached across Maurice for a hymnal and caught a glimpse of the two young men holding hands, out of view to anyone else. Eula saw the fear in the young man's eyes—like he had been caught at some horrible indiscretion. But she put his mind at ease when she smiled and said, "Why don't you introduce me to your friend, Maurice?"

The introduction ended just as a balding, beefy colored man of the cloth, a glint in his knowing eyes, took his place at the altar. Just below and to the side of the altar was a big pail of cool mountain spring water and a dipper. The good-natured but serious-minded Leftwich had long ago tired of losing his speech and his throat drying out during a long sermon. In his right hand the preacher clutched a well-worn Bible. He gazed at his congregation from above his thinly framed spectacles which had slid down to the middle of his nose. He began to speak but then stopped suddenly to dab a bead of perspiration from his forehead.

And then, having sufficiently collected himself, the black-coated man of God made sure that he had his audience's attention. "Good morning!" said Leftwich, tugging on suspenders that stretched over his sagging belly.

"Good morning!" the worshippers replied. And a few of them added a fervent "Amen!" or two for good measure.

"Before we get started today, in case you were not here last Sunday, when I announced it, I know some of you knew Elijah Wood. He was not a member of our flock but he was a believer, a good Christian. Mr. Wood went to be with our Lord Thursday before last and was laid to rest in our cemetery the following Saturday. So be sure to say a prayer for his widow, Ruthie Wood, and her family.

"This is the day that the Lord has made! We will rejoice and be glad in it!" the reverend exhorted his listeners.

"There's nothing more uplifting than a good hymn to get started, so let's all stand and sing, "Amazing Grace." The song leader rose to lead the hymn for the congregation. "And my flock, put your soul into it! Sing it like you feel the presence of the Holy Spirit!"

After the hymn, everyone sat back down. Leftwich cleared his throat and opened his Bible.

"My message today comes to you from the Book of Philippians. That part of the Bible says that God's workin' on us and never, ever gives up on us! He wants us ta go to Heaven.

"But, brothers and sisters!" Leftwich shouted, shaking his right fist, "It also says that we're condemned to eternal fire and damnation if we don't obey the Lord's commandments!

"Our Almighty God has beseeched us, through his son Jesus Christ, to obey all His commandments! That means we must put away our wickedness and lyin' and stealin' and gossipin' and adulterous ways!" The preacher's voice was now so loud it could be heard beyond the church's doors.

He cleared his throat a couple of times. He stopped speaking for a few seconds and a woman on the front row, as if on cue, brought the water filled dipper to him. Leftwich wiped perspiration from just below his nose, gulped the water, returned the dipper to her and resumed—almost without missing a beat—his message.

Near the end of his sermon, a few of the congregants shuffled nervously. Some had heard enough. The reference to gossip, lying and adultery hit a bit too close for comfort on this Sunday morning.

"If he keeps dis up," one grimacing old man muttered to his wife, "nobody gonna have'im over fo' dinner. He 'bout gettin' too high'n mighty."

But then Preacher Leftwich, just as suddenly as he had warned his listeners about the wages of sin, shifted his message. With his handkerchief, he wiped perspiration from his forehead this time, closed his Bible and stared straight at his parishioners. A few of them grew even more uneasy and began rustling about as if threatening to leave.

"Now, everybody just sit still and listen. I can't let you go today," Leftwich said, "without telling you a true story that I only heard myself this very morning about one'a the members of our flock. His name is Isaiah Washington and there he happens to be sitting today with his gracious and loyal Christian wife, Prissy."

Grinning, he pointed to the couple. They were sitting, as they always did during the church service, in the second pew from the front.

Both Isaiah and Prissy were at odds as to why they were singled out. *Surely,* Isaiah thought, *this don't got nothin' to do with the trial.*

"There ain't no better Christians than Isaiah and Prissy!" Leftwich said.

Indeed, Isaiah and Prissy had seemed always to be extending a helping hand to those most desperately in need in Fish Springs—Elijah and Ruthie being good examples of that. They had also taken in another, when a loveable little mulatto child named Willie became part of their family.

Perhaps following the example of Daniel and Mary Smith, their long time employers, Isaiah and his wife never turned a blind eye to the less fortunate souls of the community.

Caught unaware that he'd be singled out in church, Isaiah tried to deflect attention from himself. He closed his eyes and lowered his head, but it was useless. People in front and in back and to the side of him stared and wondered what would happen next.

"Isaiah, bless his heart, would never tell you this, but I will!" the preacher holding his head high, announced emphatically. "That's because he don't like to draw attention to himself or Prissy. But God wants you to know that he an' Prissy saved the lives of two young white boys, ages six and seven, children of the Oliver family here in Elizabethton.

"This all happened three days before this past Christmas, right at the start of that terrible cold spell we had last winter. Snow had just started fallin' and of course all younguns have to go outside to greet the first snow. So Sara Oliver bundled her younguns up and let them go out, and she warned them to stay clear of that river."

Leftwich closed his eyes for a few seconds and said nothing, as if for effect and to make sure everyone was listening.

In fact, they seemed to be hanging on the preacher's every word.

"Well, boys will be boys so they had to check out the quackin' comin' from the place where they weren't supposed to go, the river. So while they were fixin' their eyes on a mallard swimmin' in the cold icy river, the bank caved in and they both fell in. It was in a slow deep part of the river so at least they were not goin' downstream too fast.

"So here's these two boys screamin' and thrashin' about in that icy, river and they're gettin' colder and more numb by the second, and they're even turnin' blue.

"And who happens along just in the nick'a time like two

guardian angels? None other than our very own Isaiah and Prissy Washington!"

All spellbound eyes in the church looked toward them as Isaiah and his wife tried unsuccessfully to shrivel from the limelight.

"It just so happened that Prissy, by the grace of God, had to get to the dry goods store for a few Christmas gifts for the boys. And when they set out from Fish Springs, the weather looked good for the trip, but when they got close ta Elizabethton the storm hit and it started snowin' really hard. Ridin' along the cold Watauga River, they could only see a few feet ahead so they had to go really slow."

Again, Leftwich stopped speaking for a few seconds.

An old man in the back of the church, leaning on every word coming from the pulpit, yelled, "Say it, preacher! Tell us what happened!"

Leftwich grinned and tried to take his eyes off the cracked big window on the right side of the sanctuary. He reminded himself to replace the glass.

"Well, bein' so close to the river, Prissy thought she heard screamin' comin' from just beyond the trees along the bank. So she an' Isaiah pulled off the road and got over closer to the river. And there to their horror they discovered the two boys thrashin' in the icy water.

"And this is where the good Lord had a hand in helpin' Isaiah and Prissy save them boys.

"There was no time to think. No time to go get help. And the boys were strugglin'. But then, by the grace'a God, they remembered they had a long rope in their work wagon. So Isaiah tied one end around him, and Prissy took the other end and tied it to the wagon. Then he swam out into that deathly cold river! Cold'n icy! He's shiverin' and his teeth are chatterin' something awful but he's swimmin' just the same!

"He mustered all his strength and willpower and reached Paul, the seven-year-old who's clingin' to a limb of a dead tree in the middle of the river.

"And what does Paul do? Why, he hollers above the howlin', bone-chillin' wind to Isaiah, to please save his little brother first.

About this time, Mrs. Oliver heard the boys hollerin' and came running up screamin'. Isaiah swam a little farther out to reach young Peter, who's fightin' somethin' awful and thrashin' about and gaspin' for air.

"Isaiah's about to freeze to death, himself, but he grabs a hold of Peter, and Prissy and Sara Oliver pulls them both to the bank.

"And Prissy? She's scared Isaiah could drown or freeze to death, so she starts to go after the other boy herself. So does Sara, but Isaiah pushes'em back. What then does the shiverin' Isaiah Washington do?

"Folks, remember, he'd used up all his energy. He didn't know if he could even keep his own head above water."

The congregation was now even more spellbound. No one moved. All eyes and ears were on the preacher.

"Isaiah swam back out to Paul, who's about frozen to death by now. He's so God-awful stiff he can't let go of that limb. So Isaiah pries the boy's hands from the branch and wraps his big arms around the lad. Then Prissy and Sara pull Isaiah and the boy from the water."

Amens and gasps of relief rang through the audience.

Leftwich now had them in the palm of his hand. And he thoroughly liked that finally, on this Sunday morning, he had delivered a message that no one could turn away from.

"Brother and sisters, I was told by Sara Oliver that it was so cold that Isaiah and the young boy had ice on their face and hair. Isaiah carried Paul, and the two women carried Peter. Praise the Lord, they got the half frozen boys to the Oliver home.

"Let me put this question to you this morning: How many of us would be so brave and good and godly to risk our own lives to save two total strangers? How many Isaiah Washingtons are here amongst us?"

Amens thundered throughout the church.

Prissy, tears of pride in her eyes and a huge smile on her face, hugged her shy, embarrassed husband, his head still lowered and his big muscular frame trying to hide itself.

But it was useless. The congregation applauded him.

"Stand up, Isaiah! You is a hero!"

Some came over and shook his hand and patted him and Prissy on their backs. Others gave them a hug.

"Those two blessed, selfless people—Isaiah and Prissy—are what Christianity is all about!" Preacher Leftwich boomed.

"And we're proud to claim them as part of our family here at The Colored Baptist Church!

"Indulge me a few more minutes, brothers and sisters," said the preacher, holding his hand high and slowly lowering it, as they all sat back down in their pews. "Case you probably wonder why we just heard about this, seems our heroes after gettin' the boys in the Oliver house, were thanked, then asked to leave by Mrs. Oliver's inebriated husband.

"He was drunk," said the Reverend, noticing several confused expressions. "Mrs. Oliver wanted me to tell you this story just as she told it to me. So that's what I did. Sara Oliver wanted to come forth and tell everyone how Isaiah and Prissy had saved her children, but she was afraid. She hopes that the Washingtons will forgive her for her weakness. Without going into details, Mrs. Oliver was afraid to tell what Isaiah did, because her bossy husband told her not to. That's all I am going to say about that. But I will tell you this. After eight long, years of being told what to do, Sara Oliver mustered the courage to take her children and leave."

Amens rang through the church.

"That was a few weeks back. Sara's brave son Paul recognized Isaiah when he was bringin' Mr. Woods' body through Elizabethton and followed him here to the church. He was so excited about finding the man who had saved his life, that he ran as fast as he could all the way home to tell his mom.

"As fate would have it, Mrs. Oliver showed up here at the church with her two boys this very morning, asking if I knew the man who had brought a casket here about ten days ago. Well, of course I did! And I remembered that, three days before last Christmas, I opened the door at the parsonage to see two half frozen souls, one wet and one soaked. Said he fell in a deep snow drift and I believed him."

A few in the congregation giggled.

Leftwich, a twinkle in his eye, said, "Who am I to doubt a true Christian?"

Everyone was laughing. Even Isaiah was snickering.

"Brothers and sisters, please welcome Mrs. Oliver and her sons Paul and Peter!"

Amid the cheering and clapping, Sara and her two boys waved to everyone, and the proud, smiling preacher motioned for Isaiah and Prissy to approach the front.

Isaiah reluctantly stepped up and Prissy followed. He offered Sara Oliver his hand thinking she would want to shake it, but she insisted on hugging him. Then she hugged Prissy, and the boys heartily followed suit.

Joyous, loud clapping and "Amens!" echoed from the congregation.

One parishioner started singing a Negro spiritual, and everyone joined in, singing, clapping and tapping their feet to the music.

After a closing prayer, the emotionally moved parishioners streamed out into the churchyard, many of them wiping away tears of happiness and hugging Isaiah, Prissy, Sara and the boys.

The reverend pulled Isaiah off to the side.

"Fell in a snow drift? Boy, you sure had me fooled. Tell me, Isaiah, beins' that we're good friends an' all, why didn't you' tell me about saving them boys?"

"Because I knew you'd talk about it in church. You said it yourself, reverend. Me and Prissy don't like all that attention."

Leftwich flashed him a big smile.

"Isaiah, if you insist on pulling children out of the river, you'll have to suffer the consequences."

A few yards away, Prissy watched the good-natured bantering between the preacher who had married them all those years ago and the man she was so proud of. The selfless, proud man she loved with all her heart. The man she would die for if need be. And the man she was sure would readily give his own life for her if it ever came to that.

Prissy reflected on what a great day it had been. *What a wonderful Sunday, seein' Mrs. Oliver smilin' and happy after gettin' the courage to leave a bad husband. And it was beautiful seein' my Isaiah acknowledged for what he had done. But most of all, it was wonderful seein' two little boys still breathin'—two of God's children who almost died in the cold Watauga River.*

CHAPTER 18

Ride on the Tweetsie

A small-framed man in a dark blue suit and a black vest looked at his gold plated pocket watch. He closed the cover on the watch attached to a chain and returned it to his vest pocket.

"All aboard!" he announced loudly. Wearing a flat top conductor's cap, he stepped into the station's waiting room.

"Morristown, Mooresburg, Bulls Gap, Rogersville, Johnsons Depot and Elizabethton—now boarding!"

It was Friday, June 20th, three days before Jake Edwards' much-anticipated trial would begin in Elizabethton. Carter County Prosecutor Charlie Smith wasn't taking any chances. He wanted his star witness in Elizabethton two days before the proceedings started on Monday, June 23rd. He'd need time to prep Fanny May about how she would be questioned by an aggressive, shrewd, determined L. Ross Roberts. And he wanted the 99-year-old woman well rested after her trip from Knoxville.

"Mattie, I be a hunnert years old on my next birthday and I ain't never rode on a train. Ain't dat something?" said Fanny as her daughter helped the old woman up from a bench.

"I know, Mama. You told me."

"I did?"

Mattie handed her mother her cane and helped steady her on her feet. Fanny May clutched the old wooden walking stick tightly—as if she would surely fall without it. She held her daughter's hand, Mattie held her mother's hand, picked up their bulging battered suitcase, and the two of them slowly made their way to the platform along the track where they'd board the train.

Steadying her mom with one hand and dragging the large suitcase with the other was proving to be a challenge. And she was about to stop to rest when a colored porter ran up and offered his assistance.

"Let me hep you folks," the tall, slim, gray-headed porter, his skin the color of ebony, instructed them. It seemed like he couldn't wait to greet them. "And welcome to the Tweetsie, the best little steam locomotive in Tennessee. Step right up here. Y'all just find yo-selves a seat and get comfortable."

Lifting Fanny May gently while he helped her hold onto her cane, the porter helped them board.

The two women—one a pivotal witness in the upcoming murder trial of Jake Edwards—found a seat near a window, among the rows of seats, and got ready for a 10-hour ride they'd never forget. This wasn't traveling the dusty and bumpy road by horse drawn wagon or on horseback. Instead, it was going all the way to Elizabethton in comfort and luxury. Comfort in that the ride would be smooth, clean and quick compared to cutting a meandering swath through the rugged mountains of East Tennessee in a wagon. Luxury because humble service-minded porters, many of them former slaves, would cater to their every need.

A few minutes later the Tweetsie sounded two long blasts, alerting conductors and passengers alike that the little passenger train, its brakes released, was pulling out. The train jerked and began slowly chugging away from the depot as thick black smoke belched from the smoke stack.

"Hea we go," said Fanny May. She gripped Mattie's hand and the bench hand rail while grinning like a 10-year-old about to sled down a mountainside.

Her excitement and wonderment warmed Mattie's heart. Because a simple train ride that most people would take for granted was the most excitement that Fanny May had experienced in years. It made Mattie ashamed that she hadn't taken her mother on a train trip before, when she was less feeble.

"Are ya'll ladies thirsty, 'cause we can wet yo whistles with a—"

A high-pitched piercing sound boomed from atop the locomotive, interrupting the porter. The whistle blew two blasts, one short and the other long, alerting everyone crossing the tracks on the road ahead that the Tweetsie was coming through and nothing would alter that.

The dark-jacketed porter smiled broadly. "Dat not be the kind of whistle I mean. I can bring you somethin' to drink from the galley."

When Fanny May let it be known that they had very little money, the porter told them not to worry. That was because a "Mista Charlie Smith of Elizabethton" had made arrangements that they were to be served—at no charge.

Fanny May and Mattie looked at one another incredulously. They realized now that the ride of their life, Fanny May's first aboard a train, would not only be fun, interesting and exciting. It would be free.

"Well, in that case, please bring me a ice cold lemonade," the old woman said.

Mattie said she'd have the same.

"Coming up, ladies," the porter replied. "I be right back."

When he left them, Mattie quietly told her mother that she'd heard that such a porter amounted to being a paid servant of the railroad. Furthermore, Mattie said railroad porters—always clean, well groomed and polite in their dapper jackets and flat-topped hats—relied on tips to help make ends meet.

"So that means we should give him some money, Mother."

"How much?" Fanny May asked.

When Mattie said she had no idea, Fanny May got uneasy.

"But we find out somehow, Ma. We find out."

He returned with two glasses of lemonade on a tray. Along with their beverages, the kind, genteel porter had placed two cookies.

"In a few hours, we be servin' dinner in the dining car," so y'all ladies just rest and enjoy the ride. And ain't no need to tip me. Mista Charlie Smith done took care of that, too."

When Fanny May and Mattie thanked their gracious host, he again broke out in a big smile. His teeth, the two women noticed, seemed perfect—white as snow and not one of them missing. They had noticed, too, that the broad-shouldered man stood proud and erect and his hands bore no scars or deformities like many former slaves. Mattie thought that if he had been a slave, he must have been a house servant.

In due time, as the train kept chugging along—past cabins,

barns, cows and sheep, split rail fences and chickory filled pastures—Fanny May and Mattie got more relaxed to the point of knodding off. But both were awoken at the sound of a whimpering baby.

"Lookie there, Mama. That woman has a little baby."

Across the aisle and several seats ahead, a young white lady held a tiny, fussing baby. She patted its back and rocked the infant back and forth, while its little pink head bobbed left, then right.

"It looks like it's only a few weeks old," Mattie remarked. "It's so little. So helpless."

"Mattie, did I ever tell you 'bout my mama puttin' Aunt Sadie's baby in the oven to keep it alive?"

"Mama! A baby in a oven?! Now I ain't believin' that."

"It be the truth, Mattie. I was there."

When Mattie sighed and protested that she was still skeptical, Fanny May recited the strange story to her. "My aunt Sadie, that be your great aunt, was visitin' Mama and us. I was just a little girl, 'bout ten. Sadie was only sixteen and she was seven months along. Well it was in da dead of winter and cold as a witch's tit."

"Mom!"

"Sorry. And wouldn't you know, that baby girl decided she was comin' out. It be so little that mama's weddin' ring would fit on that little one's arm—just like a bracelet."

Fanny May's daughter, now speechless, just stared at her while the old Negro kept talking.

"Mama swore that surely that baby would die if it warn't kept warm. So what did mama do? She carried that little helpless infant, still sticky, with blood from bein' birthed and put it on a pillow in her wood burnin' cookin' stove."

"No!" said Mattie.

"I tell you this be the truth, sure as my name be Fanny May Brown. I swear it."

"So did that baby die, Mama?"

Fanny May seemed to ignore the question.

"Well, Sadie started screamin', causin' she's thinkin' her big sister's goin' to burn her child alive. But of course that didn't happen, 'cause mama laid it gently down on that pillow in the top part of her stove—in somethin' they called the warmin' oven. That's how they be keepin' their food warm after they cooked it.

"And not only did that shiverin' little baby girl live! She's still alive today, last I heard. Cousin Matilda Martin be 'bout ninety now.All on account'a my mama puttin' her in that warmin' oven."

Mattie grinned. "You never told me that story.You amaze me, Mama. Sometimes you can't remember a word the preacher said when we're havin' dinner later that day, but you can remember a story from when you was ten years old."

"When I saw dat tiny baby, it just all come back to me."

Mattie hugged her mother and reminded her about why they were going so far, on a train no less, to participate in a murder trial.

When Fanny May assured her anxious daughter that she had not forgotten why they were aboard the Tweetsie, Mattie breathed a little more easily. Because on occasion her almost century-old, steadily declining mother had a hard time remembering her own name.

"Mama, Mista Charlie Smith say that with your help that old mean Jake Edwards goin' to be found guilty. He say that evil demon 'bout to lose it. He say Toby finally be gettin' his justice."

Fanny May nodded her agreement but then cautioned Mattie that a beast is probably most dangerous when it's wounded or flailing or thrashing about desperately.

"Ain't no tellin' what that mean, schemin' devil try," she said. "He know now that the law might be finally catchin' up with him."

Mattie decided to change the subject. "Look how this train snatches them mailbags, Mama. Ain't that somethin'?"

About that time, the Tweetsie slowed and retrieved a big bag of mail, attached to a hook on a pole next to the tracks. The sweet, shrilling sound of the train's whistle blared again as the locomotive picked up speed.

A few minutes passed and a white-jacketed steward from the galley announced that dinner was now being served in the dining car.

He went on to proclaim that he and his staff had prepared a delicious meal and they should get to the dining car now—before it filled up.

Fanny May and Mattie quickly made their way to that car, wafting with the odors of warm, tasty food. They chose a table offering a picturesque view of the passing Tennessee countryside. On the table were a white tablecloth, cloth napkins, silver eating utensils, fine china plates and crystal glasses, and a vase of freshly cut flowers.

Reviewing the menu made mom and daughter even hungrier.

Fried chicken, baked ham, mashed potatoes, gravy, green beans, biscuits and fresh tomatoes. For dessert, passengers would have their choice of blackberry pie, apple pie or fresh strawberries. Beverages included hot coffee, hot tea, ice tea or cold lemonade. And if they so chose, they could top their meal off with a glass of fine imported wine.

"At your service, ladies," said a soft spoken waiter, also a Negro. "Just tell me your pleasure and we will see that you are served the best food this side of the Smoky Mountains."

Fanny May Brown and Mattie again couldn't believe that they were being taken care of in such elegance, splendor and with such keen attention to detail. All while the little green locomotive clickety clacked and steamed eastward toward their imminent rendezvous with destiny.

Yes, Fanny May's first ever ride on a train and Mattie's most enjoyable—which just so happened to be on the much-loved steam locomotive Tweetsie—was truly going to be unforgettable.

Meanwhile, in Elizabethton, after meeting with Charlie Smith, Sheriff Nave pulled all his men together and told them he needed their full attention.

"Just think of this as a 'come ta Jesus' meetin', gentlemen. I need you to remember every word I say." Nave knew from experience that a few of his men weren't Carter County's brightest or smartest—that their attention was prone to waver. So for this meeting he had decided to proceed slowly and meticulously. *And if I have to tell 'em more than once what I want 'em to do tonight, so be it. Can't have no mistakes.*

Sure that his deputies understood that what he was about to share with them was of the utmost importance, he began. "The star witness in the Jake Edwards trial, Fanny May Brown and her daughter Mattie, will be arriving tonight on the 8:20 Tweetsie. Deputy Weaver, I want you to oversee their protection. Charlie Smith will have a buggy at the station to transport the two women. You and Harden will ride your mounts alongside the buggy to the Snyder House Hotel where they will be stayin'."

"Sheriff, they allow darkies to stay at the Snyder House?" one of the deputies interrupted.

"I'm not finished." The sheriff scowled and again made sure all eyes and ears focused on him. "Now none of y'all get whoppy-jawed on me. Just listen to what I'm sayin'. I'm going to explain everything. Listen up and listen right good!"

Five heads nodded and five sets of eyes didn't blink as Nave paused for effect. Then he proceeded. "Charlie Smith convinced the owner of the Snyder House to make an exception. So tonight Fanny May Brown and her daughter are bein' allowed to stay at the hotel. The owner only agreed to it if the two colored women stayed in their room, where none of the white patrons could see'em. But that is privileged information. No one, and I mean no one, is to know two colored women are stayin' at the Snyder House Hotel. Not your wives, your sweethearts, not even your mama. Y'all got that?"

"Got it, Sheriff," they mumbled in unison.

"Mr. Smith will pick them up from the train and drive his buggy to the back of the Snyder House where you, Cyrus, and you, Oliver, will take them up the back steps located outside, to the second level—then inside to room 201.

"Am I clear so far?"

Both deputies said, "Yes sir."

"After the women are in their room behind a locked door, the back entrance door at the top of the stairs will be locked and dead bolted from inside. One of you will then be posted at the bottom of the main stairway near the entrance. The desk clerk, Ed Timbs, will be there also just in case you need to take a quick break. I will post someone there every night until Fanny May testifies. Ain't nothin' gonna happen to those two witnesses under my watch. Not a hair on their heads is to be disturbed and no one gets up to their hotel room without my personal say-so.

Do y'all understand that?"

Sheriff Nave's deputies again signaled that they understood his orders loud and clear.

"Harden, you take watch the first night."

"Okay, Sheriff."

"Just in case, any of you wonder why we are taking such precautions, you need to understand that there's already been two KKK raids at two farms. Now I wasn't born yesterday. I know damn well that somone—and you and I can guess who that scoundrel would be—got the Klan to scare the daylights outta Elijah Wood, one of the colored witnesses. Those hooded cowards wanted him scared so bad that he'd refuse to testify. In fact we think the raid caused his heart attack, which killed him."

"I knew old man Elijah," said Deputy Henry Robinson. "He was a kind soul. Never hurt nobody in his whole life. Worked hard. Went to the Colored Baptist Church with the resta them darkies. Never, ever tried to crawfish outta anything folks'd give him to do."

Sheriff Nave, speaking somberly and softly, agreed that Elijah Wood was an upstanding, hard-working, law-abiding citizen who didn't deserve to be tormented by anyone.

Then the sheriff returned to his "I mean business and there damned well better be no mistakes" message. "We have no proof of this but some of us think Jake Edwards is a Klan member himself. I will not be intimidated by the Ku Klux Klan. I repeat: I will not be intimidated or scared off by the Ku Klux Klan.

"I don't care what your views are. The law is the law in Carter County, Tennessee, and we are here to see that it is obeyed! Are we clear on that, men?"

When no one said anything, Nave put more emphasis into what he had just said. "Are we clear on that, gentlemen?"

All the deputies nodded their heads yes, even Duke Rayburn and Hank Beeler who, unbeknowst to their boss, had their own agenda.

"I want all of you to be on your toes. Keep your guns loaded and keep your eyes and ears wide open. Watch out for anything suspicious. Let's keep the witnesses safe and get through this trial. I'll be sleepin' in my office until after this trial. And during the day I plan to stay close to the courthouse. So, whatever happens, just know that I'm close. You know where to find me.

"Again, am I perfectly clear?"

One by one, they nodded their heads and responded, "Yes sir."

"Okay, good," Nave said. "That's all, men. Just do your jobs, and don't let anybody get hurt."

Several hours later, Cyrus Weaver, Oliver Hardin and Charlie Smith stood on the platform at the Elizabethton train station. It was 8:28 p.m. when the Tweetsie, as regular as rain, rolled in to the practically deserted station. The little locomotive had made all its stops along the 150-mile or so journey from Knoxville, had picked up passengers and had let others off and had done all of this without missing a beat.

Tonight at the Elizabethton train station only a few folks—one a mousy, lonely-looking woman with a dog and a big trunk full of belongings—were there to board for points north or east. Another was a big strapping Negro who apparently had heard of money to be made at a kinder, more accepting community somewhere in North Carolina. He carried only a small tattered bag, and he put that down to help the woman, startled that a stranger would lend her a hand, get on the train.

When Fanny May Brown and Mattie stepped off the Tweetsie, there to greet and hug them was a smiling, happy Charlie Smith.

"How was your trip, ladies?"

"Thanks to you, it be the best trip we ever took, Mista Charlie," said Fanny May.

Smith introduced the deputies and informed his guests that they'd be headed, under armed escort, to the Snyder House Hotel.

"Mista Charlie, they don't allow colored folks to stay at the Snyder House, do they?"

"I took care of all that, Fanny May. That's where you're stayin'. But I hope you understand you will have to stay in your room when you are at the hotel. I wish it wasn't that way."

Mattie said, "We understand that, Mista Smith. You ain't needin' to apologize. You have made us very comfortable."

"I did the best I could. I promise you will be treated with respect. Just think of yourselves as our honored guests."

"Well bless my soul. How 'bout dat, Mattie?"

As the two women and their escorts made their way to the Snyder House, they noticed that Elizabethton was quiet, even still and almost lifeless in the lingering twilight. A few lanterns and candles still flickered in the town, and a pale yellow moon had begun to break through the clouds. But Elizabethton, a bustling center of activity during the day, was quite different right now. The county seat of Carter County, Tennessee, was on the verge of going to sleep. Quietness and peacefulness had begun to descend on one of East Tennessee's most thriving little communities.

Across town in a back room of the Black Bear Saloon, Duke and Hank were having a deep, frank discussion. They sat alone at a small table. And they had made it clear to the bar gals at the Black Bear that they didn't want to be disturbed.

"Okay, I want'a go over this one more time," said Deputy Duke. He stroked his chin and focused on his very nervous Klan brother, Hank Beeler.

"You go up the back steps. They are on the outside. And at exactly thirty minutes past midnight, you kick the back door two or three times, loud enough to be heard at the front desk. Then bust out a pane in the door, hurry back down the steps and get outta sight in the dark.

"Ten minutes after you hear the gun fire, get back to the front'a the hotel. People'll be gatherin' by then. Say you heard gun shots and then two minutes later, you saw a man come from behind the buildin' and run down the street. You went after him, but lost 'em in the dark. That's all you have to do. So don't mess this up. You hearin' me, Hank?"

"I hear you. But don't you ferget. Your'a payin' me two hunnert dollars fer my part in this."

"You'll get your damned money!" Duke barked.

Satisfied that they had planned down to the last detail the murder of the two innocent women who would help bring Jake Edwards down, the two Klan brothers set their watches. Then they emerged from the back room of the saloon and hovered among the drinkers and gals in the smoke-filled, beer-smelling main room, hoping to give everyone there the impression that they were just two deputies doing their jobs of making sure that no one broke the law.

Across town at the magnificent Snyder House Hotel, Fanny May and Mattie were escorted to their room by Charlie Smith and Oliver Harden. Then Deputy Harden went downstairs and Charlie showed the women around their accommodations. They were struck by the handsome, comfortable furnishings—including a solid mahogany, huge canopied four-poster bed, a walnut armoire, a mirrored dresser. On top of a small side table next to the bed were flowers and a box of candy. It was as if Charlie Smith—and Carter County—had spared nothing to make the two colored ladies feel special.

They were dazzled, for they had never seen, much less stayed in, such a grand place. Everything about the Snyder House was elegant and spacious. Its ceilings were ornamental plaster. Its walls were laden with paintings. There was a marble fireplace for heat in the winter months. On their floor a gold fringed imported rug made them feel like royalty.

But the attractions didn't end there.

Off to the side was their own private bathroom with a marble-tiled floor and a huge, claw-footed tub.

Charlie told them that if they needed anything to pull the cord on the wall and a servant would knock on the door a few minutes later. But they were not to open the door unless the servant knew the pass word, Dixie. When asked, he or she was to say they were from Dixie. Mattie said she understood.

Goodnights were said, and then the witness and her daughter shut and bolted the door. Charlie went downstairs to the lobby to see if Harden needed anything. Then he called it a night and left as Harden, taking the first watch, sat in a chair near the main stairway. He had been in the Snyder House before, but this time he had a chance to study his surroundings. The first thing he noticed was the massive crystal chandelier, the biggest he'd ever seen, hanging in the center of the room. Also in the room was a huge wood-burning fireplace with a white marble mantle. Above the mantle was a large mirror, fit for a king, with a decorative gold frame. As he relaxed in the overstuffed highback chair, Oliver thought, *How in the world am I going to stay awake all night?*

A few minutes later Ed, the young, pony-tailed night clerk behind the desk, struck up a conversation with Oliver. *If nothing else,* the deputy thought, *he can help me stay awake.*

Upstairs, the ladies were settling in.

"I ain't never stayed nowhere like this, Ma!" Mattie exclaimed as she hoisted their suitcase on the bed and stared at her surroundings. "This is like heaven!"

Fanny May Brown was speechless. She, too, had never been so pampered in luxury and grandeur. A slave most of her life, she had lived in crude, primitive dwellings, most of them run-down shacks. Drafty, sagging structures, many of them had been barely fit for an animal, let alone a human being. Even after slave times, Fanny May had had it rough, at least until she moved to live with Mattie, residing in what could barely pass for a habitable little cabin. She had heard of big bathtubs—knew about such things—but had never soaked in one in her entire life.

As they stood in awe, they heard a rap at the door.

"Room service," a feminine voice from the other side harkened. "I'm here with a beverage for you two ladies."

Mattie asked, "And where are you from?"

"Well, I am most certainly from Dixie," said the maid, mocking a Southern belle.

"Well then please do come in," said Mattie, giggling as she unbolted the door.

The maid, a pretty young Negro with hony-colored skin and bright, friendly eyes, served them a tray with a pot of hot tea. Two roses and two cookies were placed next to the pot and two matching cups made of fine china.

The maids and servants, who were mostly colored, took it upon themselves to make sure their first time ever colored patrons got extra special service.

Fanny May and Mattie finished unpacking. Then they each put on their night clothes, poured themselves a cup of the hot brew and reminisced about their trip. They talked about what would be expected of Fanny May when the trial commenced.

"I sho' hope I don't let Mista Charlie Smith down," the old lady said. "Cause he done be treatin' us like queens."

"Just tell the truth when you get up on the stand, Ma. That's all they is to it. You be fine," Mattie said.

Then, around 10 p.m., no longer able to hold their eyes open, they climbed into their sprawling, canopied bed—with luxury linens, fluffy, feathered pillows and the most beautiful embroidered coverlet they'd ever seen.

They were soon fast asleep and had no idea what danger lurked just ahead. For at precisely 12:27 a.m. a sly and scheming Duke Rayburn walked into the main entrance of the Snyder House Hotel.

"Just thought I'd check on you, Oliver. You need anything? I could bring you some hot coffee."

"No. I'm good, Duke."

"How are you, Ed?" Duke asked the night clerk who had busied himself behind the desk.

"Young Ed here's been tellin' me about his love life. Which up ta now ain't been too exciting," Oliver, snickering, said.

"Well maybe not for you but for—"

Their conversation suddenly stopped—interrupted by a barely audible banging and the unmistakable sound of glass shattering.

"You hear that?" Duke, acting shocked, asked.

Oliver, who had broken off his bantering with the night clerk, said he definitely had heard something—and it didn't sound good.

"Stay here, Oliver. Stop anybody that comes down these stairs and keep your gun ready."

"Okay, Duke. Sure enough, anybody comes down them stairs is riskin' gettin' a bullet in 'em. But you be careful, Duke. Somethin' just ain't right."

Duke turned his attention to Ed Timbs, the night clerk with just a slight fuzz of a mustache, who looked aghast.

"Ed! Run to Sheriff Nave's office and bang on the door. He's sleepin' there. Tell 'em we got trouble."

Sure that Ed had heard him loud and clear and was now leaving the hotel, Duke headed up the stairs. And once he got to the top, it was only a short distance down the dimly lit hallway to the door to the outside steps. The wayward, conniving deputy, intent on earning his money from Jake Edwards, unlatched the dead bolt and slung open the heavy door, making it appear the killer had made a fast exit.

He heard the broken glass crunch beneath his feet as he hustled down the hallway to room 201.

He pulled his Colt 45 from the holster, then tried the door.

As expected, the door was locked, so he leaned back and kicked as hard as he could. The door, not being able to stand such a mighty force, burst open taking part of the jam with it.

Duke, grinning and feeling he was getting ever so close to a big payday, entered the room, lit dimly by a wall lantern turned low. *This'll be as easy as takin' candy from a baby. Them two darkies is not long for this world.*

He walked up to the big canopied bed, lowered his colt 45 pistol, and fired into the covered head of one of his victims.

Duke knew as soon as he fired the shot he had been set up. Because there had been no screaming, nor a last desperate request to God from the other intended victim, also covered up, on the other side of the bed.

Only silence.

He pulled the sheet back, revealing only lined up pillows.

"Oh Shit!"

"Drop your gun!" Cyrus Weaver commanded. His voice came from a dark corner behind Duke.

But the corrupt, would-be-murderous deputy wasn't going down so easily. Duke swung around and fired at the dark shadow in the corner.

Cyrus fired back, hitting Duke in the middle of his chest.

One shot would be enough, because the man who had tried to murder Fanny May Brown and her daughter Mattie died almost instantly from the slug in his torso—falling on the bed and then sliding to the floor.

He exhaled loudly and went disgracefully to eternity.

Cyrus had not realized, until that very moment when he looked into the open, fixed eyes of the murderous-minded Duke Rayburn, that he had just killed one of his fellow deputies. He knew that Duke had his faults and didn't take kindly to coloreds. But to kill another person out of pure hatred or for money? That was another thing entirely, and it caught Cyrus by surprise.

As he took in the death scene, a sharp pain gripped Cyrus' shoulder, and when he touched the spot, he felt warm blood oozing from a wound. Then he became nauseous and he sat down on the bed.

"Cyrus!" Sheriff Nave hollered as he ran into the room and knelt down over his friend.

"I'll live, Sheriff." The injured deputy applied pressure to his wound with his own hand.

Sheriff Nave stripped a pillow case from the bed and gave it to Cyrus to use as a temporary bandage to help stop his bleeding.

About that time, as the sheriff consoled Cyrus and explained that Duke had been a bad apple, Deputy Oliver Harden arrived on the scene and felt for a pulse on Duke's neck. Then he looked at Nave and declared, "He's dead."

"I killed him, Sheriff. I killed Duke," said Cyrus, crying and his body shaking.

"You had no choice, Cyrus. We know that. I didn't want to believe Duke was involved with the Klan, but I had my suspicions."

Then Nave gave his emotionally rung deputy a pat on the back. "Can you walk, son?" the head lawman asked.

"I think so, Sheriff." Cyrus, with Sheriff Nave helping him stay on his feet, hobbled toward the door.

"Oliver! Let's get this man over to Doc Godfrey's."

"Yes sir, Sheriff."

Oliver, helping the sheriff guide Cyrus down the inside stairway, noted to his boss that Duke had to have help because "somebody broke that window out."

"Yep, and I have a good idea who it was," Nave replied.

The sheriff told one of his deputies who showed up on the scene to check on Fanny May and Mattie in room 210. He also instructed the deputy to post himself in the hallway. "Those two are still in our protective custody until and throughout the trial. We can't take no chances," Nave said. "Now get yourself right outside room 210 and keep a sharp eye out. I'll be back shortly with the coroner."

"Ok, Sheriff."

"Oliver, can you get Cyrus over to Doc's by yourself?" Nave

asked as they stepped into the street.

"Sure thing, Sheriff."

"I need to stay here. Let me know what the doc says."

A few inquisitive people who had heard the shots gathered in front of the Snyder House under the coal oil lamp post. They were mumbling and rumors had already started flying.

"Who got shot, Sheriff?" an old timer asked.

"I can't talk about that right now. You folks just go on home."

"We got a right, Sheriff!" the rough-looking man, a bit under 6 feet tall and with scraggly hair, demanded.

Nave threatened to have them arrested for disturbing the peace if they didn't disperse.

"Well ain't that the dog," one of the mean-spirited gossipers grumbled. "We got us a sheriff who's plum fergot who put em in office. We'll see what happens come election time."

Just as Sheriff Nave expected, a couple of minutes later Hank Beeler ran up and asked what happen.

Nave decided to let it play out. He thought it best to let Hank hang himself.

"Someone shot our witness and her daughter. Both are dead."

"I was afraid'a that," said Beeler, acting distraught. "I saw a man come from behind the hotel and run down the street after the shots was fired. But I lost him in the dark."

Sheriff Nave said nothing for a few seconds. He sensed that Hank Beeler was squirming.

Then he let him have it with both barrels. "Sure you did, you bald faced liar!" said Nave, gripping Hank by the neck. "Deputy Cyrus Weaver, I'll have you know, killed the man who tried to kill our witness. You and Duke planned this murder sure as I'm standin' here. Duke is dead, and you are gonna burn in Hell for what you did."

"Now wait a minute, Sheriff," Beeler said meekly. "All I did was break out that window."

"You are under arrest; damn your sorry self, Hank Beeler, for breaking into the Hotel, if nothing else," Nave said. He spun the now forlorn deputy around and snapped the handcuffs on him.

A few minutes later Oliver Hardin returned and told Sheriff Nave that Doc Godfrey got the bleeding stopped. Cyrus would be okay, but he would be out for a while.

"I can't believe I let those two lowlifes work as Carter County law men," Nave said. "What in the world was I ever thinkin'?"

"Don't beat yourself up, Sheriff," Cyrus said. "They had us all fooled."

Later, when Sheriff Nave met with Charlie Smith, the two men surmised that Jake Edwards was behind the attempted murder of Fanny May Brown and Mattie. It would now fall to Nave to try to get Hank Beeler to testify to it.

But far easier said than done, because word soon got to Hank Beeler that if he implicated Edwards in any way, he'd end up a dead man.

That no count coward Hank'll never squeal on Edwards, but we can put him away nonetheless, Nave thought wearily.

CHAPTER 19

A Pleading Request

News travels fast in the mountain communities of Carter County. So when Isaiah picked up some supplies at the general store in Fish Springs, he heard all about the foiled murder attempt on Fanny May and Mattie's life at the Snyder House Hotel. He also learned about the ill-fated demise of Deputy Duke Rayburn.

"They's'a saying Deputy Duke could end up in a grave at the Colored Baptist Church cemetery," said Clarence Simerly, one of several old geezers sitting on crates around the pot belly stove in the center of the store. The old timers sat there in the winter to stay warn. They sat there in the summer from force of habit.

"Wouldn't he just hate sleepin' forever there with all them darkies?" said another of the local news harbingers. "Why would they put em there?"

"Cause nobody else'ed want him in theyrn," Simerly replied, cackling. "Duke warn't much for havin' friends, 'ceptin' for a few of them bar gals at the Black Bear Saloon. "They say them saloon gals is takin up a collection to hire a preacher to say a few words over his grave, ifen he ever has one. And if that Reverend Leftwich won't take'im, no tellin' where Duke's body'a end up. Maybe in an old, stinkin' outhouse hole."

"And don't forget Duke's sidekick, Hank Beeler," one of the listeners added. "He's in a heapa' trouble hisself for helpin' Duke try to kill them two coloreds."

None of this hearsay escaped Isaiah who had come to the store to stock up on feed, flour, salt, sugar and a few sticks of hard candy for his four sons. The big Negro paused not far from the gossipers to get all the news.

Waiting in line behind two women trying to pick out material for a dress, Isaiah closed his eyes and prayed silently, *I'm askin' you, Lord, please keep Fanny May, her daughter and my friend Elijah Wood safe and forgive me for not prayin' for Duke Rayburn's soul.*

The Good Book says you should forgive those who sin against you. But when it came to Deputy Duke Rayburn and his sidekick, Hank Beeler, Isaiah had a hard time doing that. He figured Duke got what was coming to him. Hank'd likely get off with paying for the window, since nobody was around to testify against him. *But when his day comes, he'll likely end up with Duke in a lake of fire.*

Isaiah had to smile at his next thought, *It sho' is hot today, I wonder if it's because some more fuel got throwed on the fire down there.*

Back in Fish Springs early that afternoon, Isaiah, Prissy and Ruthie sat on the porch of their little cabin and Isaiah rehashed what he'd heard about the murder attempt on Fanny May and Mattie in Elizabethton at the Snyder House. He also told them about Deputy Duke Rayburn being shot and killed by one of Sheriff Nave's deputies.

The women listened attentively. Then the conversation turned to Elijah.

"I wants ta go to church tomorrow, Isaiah. I want to see my Elijah, and besides, we has a lot to be thankful for. Will you take us?"

"Sho, Ruthie. We can go."

The three talked about how fortunate they were that no one was hurt in the Klan raid and that Fanny May and Mattie were saved by Sheriff Nave. Ruthie was grateful that she still had her beloved Elijah.

Prissy, anxiety in her voice, asked, "Who is that coming?"

A one-horse buggy carrying a white couple was approaching down the path from the road. A well-dressed man with a neatly trimmed beard wearing a wide-brimmed hat sat at the reins. A petite, dark-haired woman in a long blue dress and a bonnet sat beside him. Soon Prissy realized the bearded man was none other than Barnard McFarland, Little Willie's lost father.

Things had changed dramatically for Barnard McFarland after he had literally given his only flesh and blood son, Willie, to Isaiah and Prissy. But before that, he had reached rock bottom, ending up in jail in Jonesborough, Tennessee—about 40 miles from Fish Springs. The charge: public drunkenness and theft. At that point Willie's father had begun to turn his life around. He had done his penance in jail, given up the bottle, had earned an honest living in a lumber camp and found a church.

He had also met and married a good, upstanding, devoted Christian lady, Ida Pearl Tester—who kept him straight. They had become two of the most stellar, loyal members of their church.

Prissy fought back tears, even before a word was spoken, as the buggy pulled to a stop only a few feet from the porch.

"Good afternoon, folks. I am sure you wonder why I'm here. But I must ask you first: I heard about the Ku Klux Klan raid on your farm. Is my son all right?"

Isaiah said, "Willie is fine, Mr. McFarland."

"Thank God."

Then, Prissy, her eyes moist, her body trembling and with a commanding voice, stated emphatically, "I know why you are here, and the answer is no!"

Isaiah pulled his wife closer to him and tried to calm her.

"Leave me be, Isaiah! He's here to take our son away from us!"

Barnard McFarland and his wife, Ida Pearl Tester McFarland, got out of the buggy. He took her by his hand, removed his hat, and the two of them walked slowly and humbly toward the porch, stopping at the steps.

Then he said his piece. "Things have changed for me, Mrs. Washington. I got my life straightened out. I have a good woman for a wife. I found the Lord. I ain't drinkin' no more."

Prissy by now had regained her composure.

"That's all well and good, Mr. McFarland," she said. "But things have changed for us, too. "Little Willie is now part of our family. A loving family. He has brothers that he dearly loves—that love him. He is our son now. You can not have him back!"

Little Willie's birth father stared at the ground for a few seconds, and with a pleading, somber tone, he asked Prissy to be reasonable and fair "because me and Ida Pearl can give our son a good life. You have my word."

Isaiah, who had been holding his tongue, spoke up, "You heard my wife, Mr. McFarland. Now please leave us be."

Acting like he had heard nothing that Prissy or Isaiah said, McFarland became more adamant. "What kind of life can you give Willie, Isaiah? Where will he go to school?"

"Prissy will teach him. She's a good teacher. She taught our other three boys how to read and write and work with numbers."

"Dat's right. Prissy be a good teacher," injected Ruthie—wanting to get her two cents in.

Prissy shouted, "You asked us to take Willie and we did! We gave him a good lovin' home, and now you come ridin' in here all gussied up after almost three years, and you gonna take Willie away from us? That's just not right!"

"Please leave us be, Mr. McFarland," Isaiah said again.

"Now you look here! And listen to what I'm sayin'. Legally you ain't got a leg to stand on, Mr. Washington. So I want my son and I want him now!"

McFarland's wife whispered in his ear to calm down.

He took a deep breath and shook his head fron side to side. "I was hoping it wouldn't come to this."

"Come to what, Mr. McFarland?"

The desperate father walked to his buggy, pulled a rifle from behind the seat and pointed it at Isaiah. "I'm tellin' you one more time: give me my son."

"Barnard! No! You promised me, you would only ask for your son back!" Ida Pearl protested.

Barnard thought Isaiah was complying when he stepped inside the cabin. But when the angry, protective man returned, he had his own gun. He cocked the lever action rifle and aimed it at his adversary.

"Oh! Lawdy," Ruthie yelled.

"No! No! No! No more violence!" Prissy screamed, dropping to her knees.

Isaiah laid his rifle down, went to Prissy and wrapped his arms around her.

About that time laughter and hollering caught everyone's attention. All four boys, along with Shadow, were running across the bottom near the river where they'd been searching for arrowheads.

The two older youths ran with Willie between them—each holding a hand.

The four-year-old couldn't keep up so he raised his feet. He squealed happily as he dangled above the ground while they ran toward the house.

Barnard quickly put his rifle back behind the buggy seat.

And likewise, Isaiah emptied the chamber on his own weapon and placed it inside the door.

Prissy stood up, pulling herself together. She straightened her dress, wiped the tears from her face and forced a smile.

"Ma! Wait'll you see the arrowhead Willie found!" Ben yelled.

"Show her, Willie," Jeb said, as they ran up on the porch.

"It's in dat pocket, Willie," Leroy chimed in. He pointed to one on the bib of his dirt-stained overalls.

"Leroy!" Prissy scolded.

"Sorry, Ma! That pocket, Willie."

Barnard and Ida Pearl smiled at the exchange.

Willie, with a big toothy grin, reached into his pocket and pulled out a perfectly shaped arrowhead. It almost completely covered his little palm and fingers.

Ben, for the first time, acknowledged the white couple.

"Excuse me. I'm sorry, you must'a been talking," he said, realizing he had interrupted them.

"It's okay, Benjamin," Isaiah said. He glanced at Barnard who no longer looked angry. "We was finished."

Prissy, giving him a big hug, said, "That's the best arrowhead I ever saw, Willie."

Willie turned to Isaiah showing him his find. "Look, Pa."

"I think that's the biggest one I ever seen," Isaiah said.

McFarland and his wife took this all in, but said nothing.

And then, Barnard, his eyes watery, stared at Ida Pearl, took hold of her hand and smiled. She smiled back and squeezed her husband's hand, giving him a knowing look.

Prissy sensed that the two visitors had made a heartbreaking but correct decision: Little Willie wasn't going anywhere.

So the woman who had cared for the child for the last two years scooped him up, wrapped her arms around him and kissed him on the cheek. Then, addressing her three other boys, she declared: "Children, this is Mr. and Mrs. McFarland. Mr. McFarland is Willie's father and—

"That's right. I am Willie's father, and since Willie lives here now, I wanted to come by for a visit and see how he was doin'. And it looks like he's doin' just fine. I can see you boys is takin' really good care of your little brother."

When Barnard asked Prissy if he could hold Willie for a few minutes, she said of course he could—if that was okay with the youngster.

With a little coaxing, Willie let his father take him. Then he studied his face for a few minutes, touching his beard.

"You like my beard, Willie?"

Willie nodded his head, yes, and then he held out his hands for Prissy to take him back.

McFarland was sad, but he reminded himself that he had abandoned Willie—some two years ago, when he'd been little more than a baby. *Lord, if it be thy will, I just hope he'll get to know me again and love me as much as he does Prissy and Isaiah.*

Isaiah invited the McFarlands to "sit a spell" on the porch while Ruthie made a big pitcher of cold tea with water from the spring box.

And the two couples started working out all the details of how to best raise Willie. It was agreed that the McFarlands would come as often as desired to visit Barnard's son and he could go to their place for short visits. They agreed, too, that when Willie reached his teens he would make his own decisions about where he wanted to live.

Both men, shaking hands, apologized for their actions. They vowed in the future to base their decisions on what was best for Willie. The McFarlands and Washingtons would go on to forge a lifelong friendship.

As their visitors returned to their buggy and began making their way back toward Jonesborough, a relieved and happy Isaiah, Prissy, Ruthie and the four children waved them good-bye.

"We sho' is hungry. Mama, are we gonna be having supper

soon?" Ben asked.

"You always hungry, Ben. You sho' do eat a lot," Isaiah replied.

Prissy, smiling said, "Okay, I guess we need to feed this poor starving boy Ruthie. We havin' a special meal tonight. Anybody like fried chicken, cornbread, mashed potatoes, fresh corn and apple pie for dessert?"

The boys yelled a joyful "Yes!" in unison.

Things had been tense. And now everyone was more than ready for a good meal.

Meanwhile, a gentle breeze had whipped up and caressed the pastureland framing the little cabin. In the nearby Watauga River two beavers busied themselves building a lodge. A turtle, on a big moss-covered rock near the soon-to-be-completed lodge, stealthily slid off his resting place into the water. Overhead, eagles soared, and the old-growth forest—haven for bears, deer raccoons and wolves—gradually grew more quiet.

Soon a magnificent red sunset would magically pop out from behind clouds and over the mountains surrounding Fish Springs. Later a close-knit family in the Carter County little mountain community would sleep soundly.

CHAPTER 20

Sunday Surprise

Sunday morning, June 24th—one day before the murder trial of Jake Edwards—the pews at the Colored Baptist Church were packed. Some folks couldn't find a place to sit. So they stood shoulder to shoulder down both sides and across the back.

Taking his place at the altar and before opening his Bible, the Rev. Horace Leftwich looked out at his audience and noticed his usual congregants. But he also spotted a good many strangers, some white. *Quite unusual for my little church,* Leftwich thought.

They were at his church to show their support for all who desired justice for Toby Jackson, at least that's what he hoped. This community didn't need any more trouble from the Klan.

Ruthie, sitting up front, wished Elijah could be there with her. But the ruse of his death, at least for the present and maybe for the next few days, had to continue. So he could not show his face, let alone be seen breathing and talking.

Isaiah, Prissy and their four boys all sat in the same pew as Ruthie and took in the heartwarming scene of so much support for Toby and were uplifted. *Maybe, after all, there's good, carin' Christian people in this world—folks who'll be there when you really need'em. Folks not afraid to take a stand,* Prissy thought.

"Good morning, all!" the Reverend declared exuberantly. "It is truly a wonderful day to be in the Lord's house. And we especially welcome all our visitors! What a great testament to the power of our Lord Jesus Christ!"

A tall white gentleman standing with 8 or 10 other white

people in the back of the santuary raised his hands, as if asking Leftwich for permission to say something.

The minister got the message and motioned for the stoutly built man to speak.

"We's all here to pay our respects to Toby Jackson and to honor his memory," he said calmly. "And we want y'all to know that we're prayin' for a good verdict for Toby at the trial. It ain't just coloreds that want justice for Toby. We want it too.

"But we're sorry we interrupted your service, preacher."

On seeing the women standing in the back with the group, several of the colored men near them offered them their seats.

Leftwich said there was no need for an apology "'Cause we're all God's children and we want the same thing! We all want truth and righteousness and justice!"

That spirited declaration elicited a loud applause and cheering from the congregation, with several shouting "Amen!"

It also caught the attention of Fanny May Brown, who up to that point had begun nodding off—even before the church goers had been seated. Her daughter Mattie had gotten her very old, frail mother to church, but it hadn't been easy rousing her and helping her get dressed.

And then there was the trip to the church—on the outskirts of Elizabethton about half a mile from the Snyder House Hotel. Sheriff Nave and Prosecutor Charlie Smith had been uneasy about it since one attempt had already been made on their lives, but Fanny May insisted that she be at the Lord's House on Sunday morning.

They relented when Fanny May agreed to let one of Nave's deputies and Charlie Smith accompany her to the service. So there they sat, right on the front row—Oliver Harden, Fanny May Brown, her daughter Mattie and Charlie Smith.

In the midst of the hearty chorus of "Amens," Fanny May Brown stood and looked back, spouting her own exhortation. "My daughter and me come all da way from Knoxville on a train ta make sho' Toby Jackson get his justice! And we ain't'a leavin' 'til he get it. And Mista Smith hea' gonna make dat happen!"

Thunderous applause rose from the congregation—this time accompanied by the joyful stomping of feet and hands raised high in the air. A man in the pew behind Charlie patted him on the back.

The Rev. Leftwich allowed the outburst for a few moments, and then made a sign for everyone to be seated.

He opened his Bible and read Scripture about redemption and forgiveness. The preacher said Toby Jackson had been a gentle, caring, godly man with a pure heart. Had been a light in a dark world and had not deserved to die so young or in such a vicious way. But because he had been a Christian, his soul was never at risk.

"He was born a slave and even when slavery was over, they still treated him like a slave," Leftwich said. "But brothers and sisters, he's no longer a slave today to anyone. He's gone home. He's in paradise!"

Mattie nudged her mom, who again had threatened to doze off. And the little prodding with her elbow worked. For Fanny May, her eyes wide open again, had heard the preacher's every word.

"That be right!" Fanny May, managing to stand, boomed. "Ain't nobidy can kill Toby's spirit! 'Cause the Lawd says we might be weak and we might be lost and we might be done wrong, but we as God-believin' people ain't helpless and we're never hopeless or forsakin'!"

"Mama, sit back down," said Mattie, speaking softly and tugging on Fanny May's dress.

But the preacher and others didn't seem to mind at all that the almost 100-year-old woman from Knoxville had been speaking her piece. In fact, a good many of those present—folks who'd usually be dozing off themselves by this juncture in the service—delighted in her being among them and talking so sincerely and excitedly.

Leftwich embraced it all. He grinned. He listened. He raised his hands high above his head, as if invoking the sprit of God. He clapped. He yelled "Amen!" And, laying his Bible down, he walked down from the altar and put his arms around both Fanny May and Mattie, sparking another thunderous, tumultuous outburst of emotion from the worshippers.

And a solemn pledge—this one uttered loudly by a white visitor in the back—that no one in Carter County should rest until Toby got his justice.

Again, Leftwich took it all in. Then he returned to the altar and asked everyone for quiet and to be seated. His message this time was that he had been praying for calm, patience and good behavior in the courtroom.

"They'll be watchin' and listenin' to all of us at the trial, ladies and gentlemen," Leftwich warned. "And so we can't be actin' out or shoutin' or doin' anything to turn that judge or jury against us.

"I'm pleadin' with all of you to be on your best behavior—for Toby's sake and for the sake of justice. 'Cause we're gonna hear some things we won't like—things that might not be true. But we all got to remember that Jake Edwards is innocent until proven guilty.

"And do you really want him to be found guilty, ladies and gentlemen?"

"Yes!" came the unmistakable, in-unison response from the congregation.

"Jake Edwards be a mean, evil devil!" a young, angry colored man interjected. "He gonna' get what he got comin' to him!"

A wrinkled old woman muttered, "Ain't likely a buncha' white men on a jury'll find him guilty. That's just the way things always is in this old world."

"Folks'll not hear us anyways!" an upstart middle-aged fellow yelled. Short in stature, he had a grizzled beard, humped shoulders and a pot belly. "That's causin' they's herdin' all us coloreds up to the balcony. We ain't even 'loud ta sit where we can hear good."

The Rev. Leftwich listened and admonished those in his sanctuary that they would best honor the memory of Toby Jackson if they held their tongues in the courtroom tomorrow and stayed calm. He recited a verse from the Book of James in the Bible: "Everyone must be quick to hear, slow to speak and slow to anger."

Out of nowhere Prissy's middle son, Jebediah, turned to her and said, "Ma, I smell fried chicken."

"You just hungry, Jeb."

An old gospel hymn and a fervent prayer—for justice, peace and forbearance—closed the service.

"Part in peace," the reverend said, "but you may not want to part when you hear what I am about to tell you. When my wife found out Fanny May Brown was coming back to Elizabethton for the Jake Edwards trial she got all excited. Fanny May was a long time member of our little church and we love her dearly. We were heart broken when she left to live in Knoxville with her daughter Mattie. I found out just last night that Fanny May will be turning one hundred years old tomorrow. God bless you, Fanny May Brown."

Clapping and *amens* resounded through the church.

"My wife Martha and some of the ladies here at the church been cooking all morning. We are having a birthday party for Fanny May Brown today.

More clapping and *amens*.

"It's all spread out on tables they set up while we been worshipping. We've got enough fried chicken and fixin's and birthday cake to feed everybody. So come on out on the church grounds, under the trees, and celebrate Fanny May's birthday with us."

In the midst of the hearty chorus of amens, Fanny May Brown stood with Mattie's help and looked back, waving her hands.

"Thank you Reverend. You sure made this old woman happy."

More thunderous applause rose from the congregation, this time accompanied by joyful singing, amens stomping of feet and hands raised high in the air.

"I knew I smelled fried chicken," Jeb said.

"What're we waiting for?! Let's eat!" Ben yelled.

And eat they did. Some from out of town had brought picnic baskets of food with them, so there was plenty to go around. Oliver Harden and Charlie stood under a tree and munched on a couple of chicken legs while keeping a watchful eye on Fanny May. She had several old friends around her— one of those being Prissy—catching up on the last 12 or thirteen years.

"Fanny May! Do you remember me?" Prissy asked.

The old lady studied the face of the mother of four for several seconds. "Are you Prissy?"

When Prissy said yes, Fanny May hugged her tightly. The old woman then harkened back to a time years earlier.

"Lawdy, child you as beautiful now as you was when you was a young'n. I remember da day I heard dat a man from Fish Springs rescued you from dat devil Jake Edwards. Dat was a happy day fo me."

"For me, too, Fanny May. That man was Daniel Smith and I married one of his workers—Isaiah Washington. We have four boys now."

"Well I'll be. Dat attorney I be workin' with, his name is Smith."

"That is Daniel Smith's son, Charlie."

"How 'bout dat? Dey sho' is good people."

Noticing Oliver and Charlie, the Rev. Leftwich made his way to the shade of a large oak. There, among the tree's gnarled roots, he asked, "How is your day going, gentlemen? I would think tryin' to keep up with Fanny May Brown could be exhausting."

"She has a lot of energy for an almost one hundred year old," Oliver said. "That's for sure."

"So how is Deputy Cyrus Weaver doing?"

"Better than expected, Reverend," Oliver replied.

"Please tell him he is in our payers and we are extremely thankful for the two lives he saved."

Leftwich then spoke with the man who the next day would be front and center as prosecutor at the upcoming murder trial. "What do you think, son? Can you put that scoundrel Jake Edwards behind bars?"

"With Fanny May's testimony, I'd say we have a good shot at it, Reverend."

"Good. I suppose your dad'll be comin' to town for the trial?"

"You can count on that, Reverend. My step mother, too."

Leftwich nodded approvingly, then encouraged them to help themselves to more chicken.

"I need to get on about and save some more sinners," the grinning preacher said.

Isaiah, Prissy and Ruthie, along with the four boys, sat on an old army blanket enjoying the surprise lunch when Leftwich approached.

"So nice to see all of you in church this mornin', and I bet Ruthie had a little something to do with that."

When Prissy, smiling, acknowledged that the preacher was correct, Leftwich asked Ruthie to come with him because "someone wants to see you."

"Yes'sa. I be comin', Reverend," Ruthie said. "I'll bring along a little chicken just in case they's hungry." She gathered up some chicken and a couple of biscuits in a basket and joined Leftwich.

Ben noticed and wondered aloud to his mother where Ruthie was headed with the chicken.

"I don't know, Ben. But she must know someone who needs it worse than us."

Leftwich, with Ruthie following, went inside and to the back of the sanctuary.

He tapped on an old wooden door three times and an anxious voice on the other side said, "Who it be?"

"It's Reverend Leftwich, Elijah. There's someone here to see you."

There was the sound of a sliding latch and the door opened.

"I sho' be hopin' it was my Ruthie," said Elijah, grinning from ear to ear.

"I is so happy ta see you." Ruthie threw her arms around her husband of some 50 plus years and kissed him. Then she backed off just a bit to see how he was looking. "You just happy 'cause I bringin' you some chicken. You always thinkin' about food."

Leftwich chuckled.

As Elijah feasted his eyes on the fried chicken, Ruthie told him she hated that he'd missed the church service that morning because the preacher had had a timely, good message.

"I didn't miss it," he said, a hint of slyness in his voice. "I cracked da door and listened. It was fo sho' excitin' and somethin' we all needed to hea."

"Well, I'll leave you two alone. I best be gettin' back out in the churchyard," Leftwich said.

"Think you fo bringin' Ruthie in, Reverend."

Elijah bolted the door, and he and Ruthie sat down at a little table. She told her husband about all that had happened in the last few days while he devoured the chicken and biscuits.

When he had finished eating, the old colored man just sat and looked at his wife. She hadn't been able to take her eyes off him and had enjoyed every second they'd had together—in this, a little dusty back room of the church.

"What is it, Elijah?"

Then he said something that he had not said in many years. "I loves you, Ruthie."

"Elijah! Is you okay?"

"I fine, Ruthie. I been settin' hea day afta day, night afta night and I had a lot'a time to think."

"'Bout what, Elijah?"

"'Bout you, Ruthie. All dem yeas of house cleanin' and cookin' for Jake Edwards, den comin' home and cookin' a meal for me and da boys and never complainin' 'bout doin' it. I ain't never gave you nothin' but a hard time, Ruthie. You should'a got better. And to tell you da truth, I dint spect' to miss you so much. I thought I'd be just fine without you. And I was—fo' 'bout a week. Then I started to miss that sweet voice of yourn. I tried to remember the last time I told you dat I loved you, and I couldn't remember."

Ruthie, her old eyes tearing up, said, "It was da day our youngest son, Abraham, was born. But I always knowed you loved me, Elijah." She reached across the table and took her husband's hand.

"But I should'a tol' you."

"Well I could'a said it too, Elijah. With da' Lawd's help, we got some mo' years left ta say it."

Elijah got up, bent over his wife and gave her a sweet, kiss. When their lips parted, Ruthie said, "I be so happy when dis' trial over and you can come back to us."

"I be glad too, Ruthie. I sho' do miss bein' wit' you."

Meanwhile, outside on the church grounds, Mattie almost had to drag Fanny May away because she was enjoying the gathering so much. But pull her away she did, because she knew her mother needed some rest. Plus, it was a good bet Charlie Smith would want to spend some time with her before the trial.

All made their way back in Charlie's buggy to the Snyder House Hotel where Fanny May was told about what was expected from her on the stand. Then Mattie tucked her exhausted mom in the bed for, hopefully, a good long nap. Oliver went downstairs to stand guard, and Charlie headed to Fish Springs as he did most Sundays to visit his folks.

As Charlie, alone now in his buggy, rode along, he fretted about the next day. The long-awaited Jake Edwards murder trial would start at precisely 8 a.m.

For weeks, Charlie had studied, researching other cases and planning his strategy. If he wasn't ready now, he figured he never would be. Still, he kept thinking about how he would proceed.

The ride along the Watauga River to Fish Springs helped calm him. And what he needed more than anything right now was calm.

CHAPTER 21

Truth and Lies in the Courtroom

At long last, the day was here: Monday morning, June 25th, 1883. And the man charged with murdering Toby Jackson found himself in the Honorable Judge Emmett Stone's courtroom in Elizabethton.

After many hours of huddling with his lawyer, L. Ross Roberts, Jake Edwards was about to face his time of reckoning. He had dreaded it. Feared it. Had tried to delay it. Had hoped it would somehow never occur. Nevertheless, this was the day.

Across the aisle to Edwards' right was the man determined to win the jury over to a guilty verdict. Prosecutor Charlie Smith had already made a name for himself in a number of criminal cases. And rumor had it that higher office awaited him in East Tennessee—and possibly statewide—if he chose to pursue it.

Sitting nervously next to his lawyer, Edwards heard a murmuring and scuffling behind him. When he turned around he saw throngs of people—young, old, some of them dressed as if for church, but others in their work clothes— easing into their seats and craning their necks for a better look at what promised to be one of the most historic trials in Carter County.

Everyone seated behind him was white. But the courtroom's balcony was jam packed with colored folks. And in the middle of the front row of the balcony, as if he were there to make sure his flock behaved, sat the Rev. Horace Leftwich. Alongside Leftwich sat Isaiah and Ruthie. Prissy was in the witness room near the front across from the jury box along with the only witness to the killing.

The courtroom itself was a sight to behold. It had maple-paneled walls heavy with big framed paintings of presidents, governors, senators, and noteworthy judges. The ceiling, ornate with alabaster carvings, towered over the proceedings. Statues—each of them with figures representing truth, fairness, justice or some such ideal—were sculpted from marble; these graced each side of the expansive courtroom.

The wooden floor had been polished to a high sheen—as had every chair, desk, railing and pew.

"All rise!"

Everyone dutifully stood up as the judge entered magisterially and walked to an elevated platform and took his place in a large leather chair.

"Presiding Judge, The Honorable Emmett Stone!"

"Be seated!" the bailiff barked, upon receiving his signal from the judge.

The balding, bespectacled judge was an imposing man who wore a black robe. He had dark, knowing eyes, bushy eyebrows, thick, wide sideburns and a splotch of gray hair dangling from the front of his head.

Behind the judge, a huge American flag, and a few feet off to His Honor's right—behind a railing—was the jury box. Twelve men—all of them white—would hear the case.

Judge Stone noticed a juror had his hand cupped over the ear of a grimacing fellow seated next to him. He was whispering incessantly. The judge instructed the bailiff to put the man on notice to keep his mouth shut, which the bailiff promptly did.

The judge pounded his gavel twice and asked for everyone's attention. And then, satisfied that all were listening, he spoke, "Gentlemen of the jury, we are here today to decide a very important case. A man's life has been taken, and another man has been accused of taking that man's life. I want you all to listen carefully to defense lawyer L. Ross Roberts and the testimony from his client Mr. Jake Edwards, and his witnesses—and to the prosecutor, Mr. Charlie Smith, and his witnesses.

"Mr. Smith represents the State of Tennessee in this case. He will be trying to obtain a guilty verdict against Mr. Edwards, who is charged with first degree murder in the death of the late Mr. Toby Jackson."

Judge Stone took a drink of water from a cup he had at the ready. He swallowed, paused and tried to make eye contact with every juror. "Members of the jury, you have a solemn responsibility to remember that there's a presumption of innocence until found guilty in every case. That means you cannot return a verdict of guilty unless you are persuaded beyond a reasonable doubt that Mr. Jake Edwards did indeed murder the late Toby Jackson.

"You will hear all manner of testimony and you must exercise your best judgment to determine if what you hear is true or is false. That is your sworn duty. If, after hearing all the testimony and after careful deliberation on your part, you return a guilty verdict, you the jury are saying that the presumption of innocence for the defendant no longer holds water. And again, if you decide Mr. Edwards is guilty, you are saying that the prosecutor—Mr. Charlie Smith—has proved Mr. Edwards' guilt beyond a reasonable doubt. If that is your verdict, Mr. Edwards will face sentencing according to the law. I will determine what that sentence will be, based on testimony of the trial.

"On the other hand, if you find Mr. Edwards not guilty, he will be free to return to his home and get on with his life."

Judge Stone paused. After a few seconds, he spoke again—this time more slowly and more emphatically, "Members of the jury, have I made myself clear?"

The jurors nodded, yes.

Dead silence for a few seconds.

"Now I have a few things to tell the spectators in this courtroom. Do I have everyone's attention in the audience?" The judge glared outward toward the packed room; then he glanced upward to the balcony.

Hoping that all ears were open, he proceeded—loudly, "This is an open, public trial. That's according to the Constitution of the United States of America and to the laws of the State of Tennessee. And I promise you I will do everything in my power to make sure it is a fair trial. Everyone who wants to speak—from either the defense or the prosecution—will be heard. That's as it should be, because the law of the land says that every defendant is entitled to a fair, public, impartial trial.

"But what I won't allow in my courtroom is yelling or cursing or any other shenanigans that'll interfere with this trial! Do I make myself clear?"

When no one in the audience spoke and several heads nodded yes, Judge Stone took another sip of water and tapped his gavel.

"You may now read the charges from the docket, bailiff."

The bailiff was a freckled man with a receding hairline. What hair he had, he brushed across the top, trying to hide his bald spot. He stood as if at attention, threw his shoulders back, cleared his throat, held up a piece of paper and read loudly: "State of Tennessee versus Jacob Lee Edwards! In the case of Jacob Lee Edwards, accused of killing Toby Jackson!"

He passed the document to Judge Stone, who tapped his gavel again.

"Are counsel ready to proceed?" the judge asked.

"Ready your Honor," Charlie Smith said.

"Ready your Honor," L. Ross Roberts said.

"You may proceed with your opening statement, Mr. Smith."

"Thank you, Your Honor." The prosecutor got up from his desk and walked as close as he could just outside the railing of the jury box and scanned every pair of eyes looking back at him.

Confident that he had the attention of the twelve men who would decide the defendant's fate, he began: "Good morning, gentlemen. My name is Charlie Smith. I have been entrusted to represent the People of the State of Tennessee in this important case. My purpose this morning is to help you anticipate what you will hear. But before I continue, I want to publicly commend all of you for your service as jurors. I know serving on a jury is a big sacrifice because many of you, if not all of you, have work to do, families to provide for, wood to cut and stack, crops to tend, animals to feed and far more enjoyable things you could be doing. I thank you, on behalf of the State of Tennessee, for your presence, for your undivided attention and for your patience. and service. Were you not here today, we could not have this trial, could not consider the testimony, and justice could not be achieved.

"Today, tomorrow and maybe even over the next few days you will be listening to testimony. This is considered, in a court of law, the evidence; and I ask that you take all of it into account.

"On behalf of the state, I fully understand what we have to prove in this case. I am certain that by the conclusion of all the testimony you will know that we have more than met that burden of proof. The only conclusion you will be able to reach is a guilty verdict.

"Please know right now that the state will present reliable, indisputable testimony. This will be solid, strong evidence—all of it pointing to a guilty verdict. Gentlemen of the jury, there is no doubt, in my heart, mind and soul, that the criminal defendant Jacob Edwards did in fact murder Toby Jackson in cold blood.

"Do not be misled by the defendant's high-paid, clever attorney—Mr. Roberts. He will try to have you believe that no man should be convicted of murder by a colored man's testimony. He may not say that, but believe me he will imply it. Well, let me say right up front, our eyewitness to Mr. Edwards' vicious crime is a colored man—a good, God-fearing Christian man. If our eyewitness was a white man, we probably wouldn't be here today. There would likely be no trial. It would have been a clear, open-and-shut case. The defendant would have pleaded guilty and began serving his punishment. He would have already been behind bars."

As Charlie gave his opening statement, he scanned the jury box, doing his best to make eye contact with every juror. "Along with our eyewitness, gentlemen of the jury, we have very compelling circumstantial evidence—in the form of sworn testimony—that Mr. Edwards committed the act of murder.

"A word of caution: you may hear the defendant's attorney, Mr. Roberts, assert again and again that self defense was the reason Jake Edwards killed Toby Jackson. That is not true. Toby Jackson was a gentle man who never raised his hand against anyone. Jake Edwards killed Toby Jackson out of pure hatred. Hatred of losing ownership of his slaves after the Emancipation Proclamation along with a hatred of all colored people. He still thought of himself as a slave owner, and one of his slaves was leaving and he could not stop him.

"Jake Edwards will tell you that Toby was leaving owing him money, and that's why he tried to stop him. Also a bald-faced lie! We have a witness that knew Toby paid off his bill before he left to go work for the railroad in Alabama. Please don't be taken in by Mr. Roberts' slippery, questionable, tricky strategy. He will try to confuse. He will try to cast doubt. He will have you wondering if the sky is blue or if there are mountains in Tennessee. He will try to argue that the defendant is an upstanding, law-abiding, respected citizen of Carter County.

"Nonsense!" the prosecutor, waving his hands, shouted. "Even if Mr. Edwards were an upstanding, respected citizen of Carter County, which he is not, that would have very little bearing on this case. Guilty verdicts have resulted in the past—for folks who had mistakenly been thought of as fine, law-abiding citizens of their community. After hearing all the testimony, you'll have no choice but to return a verdict of guilty. Thank you again, gentlemen of the jury."

Charlie Smith looked at the judge who nodded slightly. As he returned to his chair in the front of the courtroom, he caught a glimpse of his proud father and mother a few rows back. They were smiling. Charlie winked at his mom and took his seat.

A woman in the balcony whispered to her husband, "Zeke, who dat colored eyewitness be dat Mista Smith talkin' about?"

"I has no idea. Less it be dat boy I heard 'bout dat run away."

Judge Stone instructed L. Ross Roberts to give his opening statement.

The skilled, silver-tongued defense attorney had been listening intently to the prosecutor's opening statement. He stood up, smiled at the jurors, straightened his neck tie, cleared his throat and began pacing slowly. "Members of the jury, I am L. Ross Roberts. I have been practicing law in Carter County for more than twenty years. I have been retained by the defendant, Mr. Jacob Edwards, to represent him. I do so with honor and pride. And with the strong, unshakeable conviction that my client is not guilty. I am sure you will reach that same conclusion when you have heard and carefully considered all the testimony in this case.

"You may know my client simply as Jake. He is a good man who has been wrongly accused of a horrible crime. A man of God. A faithful churchgoer in the Valley Forge community of Carter County. A farmer who had been married to his beloved, loyal wife for forty years before she died tragically and suddenly from the consumption. A man who owned a store and who employed coloreds there. A man who provided food, clothing and shelter to the coloreds who worked for him. A man who, before his unfortunate false arrest in this case, had never been charged with any crime at all. A man who had never harmed anyone or anything.

"One thing that the prosecutor and I can agree on is that we are all here today because of a horrible tragedy. It should have never happened. No man should die over a few dollars. but he did. A good man, who did not deserve to die, was the victim of his own anger. He was killed, and we all grieve about that, and we pray for his soul. Toby Jackson—may you rest in peace."

Roberts stopped talking, closed his eyes and bowed his head.

Then he looked straight at the jurors. "But imagine this, gentlemen of the jury. You are falsely accused of murder. Your life is turned upside down. Some of your friends and neighbors, even some of your fellow churchgoers, suddenly become cold and distant. You have trouble eating, and what few morsels you swallow you can't keep down. You toss and turn all night, unable to sleep. You lie awake wondering why you are being punished for trying to defend yourself. Your life is threatened. You wonder if God has forsaken you. And you try to remember the last time you saw the man who senselessly lost his life—and who you are now accused of murdering.

"What would you do if you were in Jacob Edwards' place? How would you get through the next hour, let alone the next day or next week? How would you go about proving your innocence?

"That is the nightmarish situation my client, who has done absolutely nothing wrong, finds himself in. And that, along with Mr. Jackson's death, is another horrible tragedy.

"Gentlemen of the jury, this case should have been dismissed. It should have never gotten this far. But here we all are today. One side trying to convict an innocent man of the worst crime imaginable, the other side asking you to consider the facts. Yes, Mr. Edwards went after Toby Jackson because he owed him money. A decision he truly regrets. But that is no proof that my client committed murder. After hearing all the testimony in this case, any reasonable jury would conclude that Mr. Edwards feared for his life and was only trying to defend himself after Toby Jackson turned on him.

"If only we could bring Mr. Jackson back from the grave and know the real truth, but we cannot do that. So here we are—about to hear testimony, much of it from the prosecutor's side, unreliable or false. And we will be presented with so-called evidence that was gathered shoddily by our sheriff.

"Remember, as we proceed, that there are always two sides, maybe even three or four sides, to every story. You will not hear the whole story from the prosecutor's witnesses, nor from him. His job, the job he is handsomely paid for by the citizens of this county, is to get a guilty verdict—regardless of the unfortunate defendant's innocence. Prosecutor Smith, who will never admit he is wrong in this case, has all of the State's resources at his disposal. My client, Mr. Edwards, has only me and a few of his close friends who still believe his side of the story.

"Lastly, I want to say that my client is far from being a perfect man. But who among us is? Haven't we all gotten angry at someone at one time or another? Haven't we all said things or done things we later regretted? The Bible says 'Let him who is without sin among you be the first to throw a stone!' No, my client, Mr. Jacob Edwards, is by no means perfect, but he is not a murderer. Please do not wrongfully convict an innocent person who was only trying to defend himself."

L. Ross Roberts tugged gently on the lapels of his dark blue suit and gave the jury one last look—this one serious and long. Then he returned to his chair.

The judge tapped his gavel lightly and announced that the trial would continue.

Are you ready to proceed with your first witnesses, Mr. Smith?"

"Yes, Your Honor."

"Very well. You may call your witness.

"Your Honor, I call Elijah Wood to the stand."

Gasps and confusion erupted in the court room.

Judge Stone hammered his gavel several times as a shocked L. Ross Roberts sprung to his feet.

The bailiff opened the door to the witness room and Elijah walked out, adding to the commotion. The bailiff led the confused old man to the witness stand where he took a seat.

The judge, banging his gavel, shouted, "Order in this court!"

After several seconds the room settled down.

"I object, Your Honor!"

"I'm sure you do, Mr. Roberts."

Locking eyes with the prosecutor, the judge asked, "Mr. Smith, is this not the witness that supposedly died of a heart attack a couple of weeks ago?"

Smith, obviously ready for the question, responded, "Your Honor, it's my understanding that friends of Mr. Wood—a key witness in this trial—faked his death, fearing for his safety, after two Ku Klux Klan raids. One at Mr. Wood's home and one at the home of his friend, Isaiah Washington, where Mr. Wood was staying. Then there was the recent murder attempt at the Snyder House on the lives of Fanny May Brown and her daughter—also key witnesses."

The judge, reviewing his list of witnesses, said, "So why then did you not take Elijah Wood off the list of witnesses, if you thought he was dead, Mr. Smith?"

"That was just an oversight, Your Honor. I apologize to the court and to Mr. L. Ross Roberts for that."

Clearly not liking that his court had been deceived, the judge issued a stern warning. "Mr. Smith, I know you are well liked in this community. You come from a good family with a highly respected father. It has been said that you have a bright future ahead of you. But that does not give you license to get away with stunts like this. One more shenanigan like this and I will have you reprimanded. Do we understand each other, Mr. Smith?"

"Yes, Your Honor."

Judge Stone, pointing toward the balcony, said angrily, "Reverend Leftwich, you ought to be ashamed of yourself!"

Then the judge instructed the baliff to swear the witness in.

"I object, Your Honor!" Roberts protested.

"Mr. Roberts, is Eljah Wood's name on your list of witnesses?"

"Yes, Your Honor, but we assumed Mr. Wood was deceased."

"Well then, you should have questioned Mr. Wood's name being on the list. And saw to it that it was removed.

"Therefore, overruled. Bailiff, please continue," the judge said.

"You are Elijah Wood?"

"Yes, suh."

Instructing Elijah to place his left hand on the Holy Bible and to raise his right hand, the bailiff asked, "Do you swear to tell the truth, the whole truth, and nothing but the truth, so help you God?"

"I do," Elijah nervously answered.

Then Charlie asked Elijah to tell in his own words what happened the day Jake Edwards killed Toby Jackson thirteen years earlier.

Elijah set silent for a few seconds, then started. He told how Jake Edwards killed Toby Jackson thirteen years earlier also. He said Jake found out Toby paid off his bill at his store and was leaving to go to Alabama. "He made Jed, a young boy who worked wit us, tell where Toby be headin'. Mista Edwards told dat boy he would rip his skin off wit his bull whip if he didn't tell."

L. Ross Roberts, springing up from his chair, shouted, "Objection! Hearsay!"

"Sustained." The sudden outburst startled Elijah and he stopped.

"Its okay Elijah. Please continue," said Charlie.

"Jake tol' me to throw two shovels in da wagon and pick up Jed and him at da house," Elijah testified. "Then we headed out ta find Toby.

"We found Toby walkin' cross a'field a short piece from Isaiah's house. Mista Edwards tol Toby he couldn't leave 'cause he owed his sto' money. But Toby say he paid dat money and done had a receipt ta prove it. Jake said 'you lyin' and you ain't leavin'.

"You stop now or I'll blow yo head off.' But Toby don't pay him no mind. Jake had a rifle wit him and he fired a shot over Toby's head, but Toby, he just kept walkin'. Toby said 'I'm gwine to Alabam and I ain't comin' back.' Jake fired dat rifle again and dis time he hit poor ol Toby in da back of da head."

Elijah apologized as he started to weep when he got to this part of the story.

Charlie Smith told him it was all right and he could take a moment to collect himself.

"I be okay now, Mista Smith."

"Then proceed with what you recall, Elijah. Take your time," said Smith.

"I ran to Toby and looked down at him. He breathed a couple'a times and dat was it. I seen blood spillin'out dat hole in the back'a his head and I knowed he was dead. Dat devil Jake Edwards killed my friend."

The prosecutor gave him a sympathetic look. "I'm sorry about your friend, Elijah. What happened then?"

"Mista Edwards made us go through everythin' tryin' to find dat paper. He said he knowed there ain't a receipt 'cause Toby neva' paid off his bill no ways.

"Den Jake looked at us mean like and said if we eva' tol' 'bout what happened he'd kill us. He say 'if you want yo' sons to live to be men, yo'll keep yo mouths shut.'

"Dat young boy Jed be so sceered' dat he wet hisself, an' dat night he left and ain't neva' come back.

"We buried Toby right dere where he died. He was on his way to see his friend Isaiah befo' he left to go to Albama. But that be as far as he got. I knowed I should'a told somebody, but I was 'fraid for my boys and Ruthie."

"Thank you for your testimony, Mr. Wood."

When Judge Stone asked L. Ross Roberts if he wished to ask Elijah any questions, he hesitated for a moment, then said, "Yes Your Honor. Mr. Wood. Mind if I call you Elijah?"

"No suh. Dat's my name."

"How old are you Elijah, if I may ask?"

"I be eighty-four dis March."

"You seem to have a pretty good memory, for a man your age. But if your wife is like my wife, I bet she says, Elijah, you can't remember from one day to the next."

"Yes suh, she sho' do."

"It's hard, though, remembering every word someone said on a particular day, thirteen years ago. Isn't it, Elijah? But then again, I suppose Mr. Charlie Smith helped you remember some things didn't he?"

"Yes suh, he--"

Charlie jumped up and tried to stop Elijah from answering but was a second late.

"Objection! Mr. Roberts is leading the witness."

"Sustained!"

"No further questions," said Roberts.

"Call your next witness, Mr. Smith."

"I call Prissy Washington to the stand."

Prissy, in her Sunday-best, blue dress and shiny black shoes, was sworn in.

"Mrs. Washington, may I call you Prissy?" the prosecutor asked.

"Please do."

"Prissy, I understand that you live in Fish Springs with your husband Isaiah and four boys. And one of those boys you took in, out of the goodness of your heart, because he had no home of his own. Is that correct?"

"That's right," said the attractive, soft-spoken woman who as a child had been a slave on a plantation in Virginia.

"Takes a godly person ta do that," whispered a wife to her husband five rows back.

"And your husband is a foreman for Mr. Daniel Smith of Fish Springs?"

"Yes sir. Isaiah has worked for Mr. Smith about twenty years now."

"Sounds like your Isaiah is a good Christian man and you and your sons have a good life."

"Yes sir. We sure do."

Isaiah, leaning over from his pew in the balcony, was beaming.

"Take me back Prissy before Isaiah Washington came along. What was your life like back then?"

"Get on with it, Mr. Smith," the judge demanded. "This seems to be going nowhere."

"Sorry, Your Honor." Smith, trying to put her at ease, said, "Please continue with your testimony, Prissy. You were saying?"

"I was workin' for Mr. Jake Edwards in Valley Forge as his housekeeper. And I also helped feed tha' chickens and the pigs and did some sewin' and cannin' for his wife."

Charlie gave her a knowing look. "That was after the Emancipation Proclamation, was it not? And you were free to leave. Did you want to stay and keep working for Mr. Edwards?"

"No Sir," Prissy said adamantly. "Mr. Edwards wouldn't let me leave. He said I owed money to his store but I didn't. He kept addin' money on my balance. He did that to all of us that worked for him."

"I object!" L. Ross Roberts, jumping up, interjected. "Hearsay—witness cannot speak for others."

"Sustained," Judge Stone agreed.

"So Mr. Edwards kept you there against your will? Is that correct, Prissy?"

"Yes sir. I hated bein' there but I couldn't leave." Prissy fidgeted with one of her soft black curls.

"So how did you finally leave?"

"Mr. Daniel Smith arrived one day with Isaiah to buy some hay from Mr. Edwards. That was when I met Isaiah. Mr. Edwards heard me talkin' to Isaiah and Toby Jackson in the barn, and he rushed in the barn and slapped me hard in the face. He woulda' hit me again but Isaiah stopped him."

L. Ross Roberts again rose and demanded to know what possible bearing any of this had on his client's case. "Your Honor, do we have to listen to Mrs. Washington's life story?"

"Mr. Smith, I told you to get on with it."

"I will, Your Honor. Just a few more questions and I'll be done with this witness." He promised not to waste the court's time and that what he was asking was relevant.

The judge took a drink of water, nodded reluctantly and motioned for him to continue.

"What happened then, Prissy?"

"Mr. Daniel Smith showed up in the barn. He was plenty mad at Mr. Edwards. He told me I could go with him and Isaiah because I was a free woman. That I didn't have ta stay there another hour.

"That made Mr. Edwards fightin' mad. He got real mean. Said I couldn't leave because I owed his store money. But I didn't. Mr. Smith believed me. He knew Mr. Edwards was lyin' about the money."

"Objection!" Roberts shouted.

"Sustained."

"Mr. Smith paid Mr. Edwards the money that he said I owed him. Can't remember exactly how much. Coulda' been about eight or ten dollars. Then we left."

"Who do you mean by 'we,' Prissy?" Smith asked.

"Me, Isaiah and Mr. Daniel Smith."

The prosecutor shifted to another line of questions.

"What was it like working for Mr. Edwards and his wife?"

"Objection! Not relevant!"

"Sustained," an increasingly irritated Judge Stone said.

"I once saw a young colored girl almost whipped to death—

"Objection!"

"Sustained!" the judge growled loudly. "Strike that from the testimony. Gentlemen of the jury, you are directed not to consider those parts of this witness' testimony in which I have sustained Mr. Roberts' objections.

"And as for you, Mr. Smith. That's quite enough."

"That's all, Prissy," said Smith, trying not to break out in a smile. "Thank you."

"Do you want to cross examine this witness, Mr. Roberts?"

"Yes, Your Honor."

"Mrs. Washington," said Roberts, in a soft respectful tone. "May I also call you Prissy?"

"Yes," Prissy said coldly.

"You stated that Mr. Edwards would not let you leave because you owed his store money. Is that true?"

"He said I did. But I didn't," Prissy insisted. "He just wanted to keep me as his servant."

"Well, if you did not owe Mr. Edwards money, why on earth did Mr. Smith pay him so you could go with them? Why not just leave?"

The question caught Prissy off guard, but after a few seconds she responded, "I guess he wanted to be sure."

"So he thought that maybe you lied?"

"No sir. I don't think so." She had become jittery, uneasy. *What else is this man gonna' ask me?*

"You don't like Mr. Edwards, do you Prissy?"

She did not respond.

"In fact you hate him so much that you lie about things he has done. Isn't that right? Isn't that the honest to God truth?"

"I don't lie!" Prissy stated loudly.

"Excuse me."

"I said I don't lie."

L. Ross Roberts stared briefly at the jurors—as if beseeching them to pay extra close attention to what he was about to say. "Mrs. Washington, did you not tell your friends and your own children and even some folks that attend the Colored Baptist Church that your good friend Elijah died of a heart attack? That's a pretty serious lie, Mrs. Washington. Wouldn't you say?"

"That was—"

"No further questions."

Judge Stone, along with Charlie Smith, the jurors and many of the spectators had been hanging on every word of Prissy's testimony.

Next up was Carter County Coroner Doc Reuben Bowers. At the court's request, Bowers stated his credentials:

"My grandpa was a coroner. My pa was a coroner. My uncle was a coroner, and I've been a coroner for pert near thirty years, and I'm a damned good one."

Questioned by Prosecutor Smith, Doc Bowers confirmed that he investigated the bones found in a plowed field in Fish Springs by Isaiah Washington.

"And who was with you that day in that field, Doc Bowers?" Smith asked.

The gray-headed, squinty-eyed coroner said that it was Sheriff Billy Nave, Isaiah and his son Ben and Deputy Duke.

"So what did you find, Doc? Please tell the court."

"Well, they wasn't much left of whoever it was, 'cause them bones been in the ground 'bout thirteen years. Of course, maggots, worms and all kinds of bugs, even ants, woulda' cleaned all the flesh off that cadaver the first couple of years. But there was enough left that I could tell that this man was a victim of foul play."

"What brought you to that conclusion, Doc Bowers?"

"There was a hole in the backa' his skull. Big enough to put your thumb in. And while emptyin' all the dirt out'ta that skull, a slug dropped out. Probably from a 30-calibre rifle, accordin' ta Sheriff Nave."

"And what did you conclude from that?"

"It appeared to me and Sheriff Nave that the man was fleein' since he was shot in the backa' his head."

"Objection!" L. Ross Roberts thundered. "Witness is engaging in speculation."

Judge Stone waited a few seconds and stroked his chin. Then he spoke. "Overruled, counselor."

"Whose bones were they, Doc?" Smith asked.

"They sure wasn't no Indian's bones—like Deputy Duke was tryin' sa' hard to have us believe. Me an' Sheriff Nave concluded they was the remains, at least what was left of em, of Toby Jackson."

"And what led you to that conclusion, Doc?" Smith asked.

"Well for one thing, we found a tiger's tooth with the bones and Isaiah said he'd given that to Toby."

"Objection! Hearsay!" L. Ross Roberts shouted.

"Sustained," the judge ruled.

Charlie Smith asked, "Okay, Doc. Did you find any other evidence that helped you identify whose bones they were?"

"Yes sir. One of the feet was missin' two toes. Appeared to me they'd been sawed off."

"So, how was that evidence the remains were those of Toby Jackson?"

"Well, sir," the coroner declared. "Isaiah said Toby'd suffered frostbite on two toes while workin' for Mr. Edwards and Jake sawed'em off."

Objection! Hearsay again!" L. Ross Roberts yelled.

"And sustained again," Judge Stone ruled. "Mr. Smith, please confine your questioning to what the witness knows or has seen firsthand, not to what he has heard."

"Yes sir, Your Honor."

"So, Doc Bowers, would it be fair to say that you reached a conclusion that Mr. Jackson died from a gunshot to the back of the head?"

"Yes."

"Objection!" Roberts screamed. "Coroner only knows it was a skeleton found in that field. He hasn't presented solid evidence of the identity of that skeleton."

"Overruled," the Judge said.

"That's all the questions I have. Thank you very much, Doc," said Smith, trying to suppress a grin.

"Do you wish to question this witness, Mr. Roberts?" Judge Stone asked.

"No questions, Your Honor."

Judge Stone tapped his gavel twice. "Then we will take a brief recess and reconvene at one o'clock."

While Charlie put papers in a satchel, his father, Daniel, tapped him on the shoulder. "How about me and your mom take you to lunch at The Snyder House, Mr. Prosecutor?"

"Sounds good to me, Pa."

CHAPTER 22

Deadly Encounter

While on a break from the trial, Charlie and his parents enjoyed a meal at the Snyder House where the conversation soon turned to the trial.

Daniel asked, "So I suppose you're saving your most important witness, Fanny May Brown, for last?"

Charlie finished off his buttered cornbread and and wiped his mouth with a linen napkin.

"Yep. As a matter of fact, she'll be my next and last witness. I've sent Deputy Oliver Hardin to bring her to the courthouse. She should be in the witness room by now. I'm letting her stay there, safe and sound, 'til we need her. I wasn't wantin' too much stress put on her. After all, the woman is one hundred years old today."

Charlie took a bite of delicious roast pork—one of the hotel's specialties—and took a sip of iced tea.

"So exactly what is it that she knows that'll help your case, son?" Charlie's mom asked. For the most part, she had been silent leading up to the trial, but the question had been nagging at her for the last several days.

Her prosecutor son took one last gulp of his iced tea, pushed away from the table and looked into his stepmother's beautiful green eyes.

Charlie said, "She knows Toby paid off his bill at Jake Edwards' store. She took his money and gave him a receipt. You see, Jake Edwards claims that Toby was leavin' owing him money. That's why he says he went after him."

"What about that receipt?" Mary asked.

"Never been found," her son said.

Mary Clemmons Smith, sensing Charlie's uneasiness, tried to reassure him. "Well, if you want my opinion, even without a receipt, I think with Fanny May's testimony, you're going to win this case."

"Sure hope you are right, Mom."

The conversation ended abruptly when an out-of-breath Oliver Hardin suddenly appeared at their table.

"What is it, Oliver? What's wrong?"

"It's bad, Charlie," the long-faced, frowning deputy replied. "You need to get up stairs to Fanny May's room right now. Mattie's waitin' for you."

Fearing the worst, Charlie leaped to his feet and rushed out of the dining room. He took the hotel stairs two at a time, while Deputy Oliver stayed and told Daniel and Mary what Charlie was about to find out.

What in God's name could have happened? Right when she'd come so far and I had her ready to testify.

The first thing he noticed in the room was Mattie sitting on the bed with her head on Fanny May's chest crying. Fanny May, her eyes closed and her hands folded peacefully at her waist, was a ghostly pale color.

Charlie put his hand on Mattie's shoulder.

She ran her fingers through her mom's silver hair.

"She was fine this morning, Mr. Smith. They brought us a nice breakfast of flannel cakes covered with blueberries. Mama loved it. Then a little later she said she thought she had ate too much and was goin' to take a little nap. In about an hour or so, she was sleepin' so peaceful like. I just let her be and I started readin'. I fell asleep. I woke up when the deputy knocked on the door. That's when I tried to wake her up and I knew she was gone."

Mattie wept as Charlie held her. He felt bad for putting the trial ahead of a woman's life. *What can I say to a daughter who's lost her beloved mother? I shoulda' never brought Fanny May to Elizabethton in the first place. Just too much stress on the poor aging woman.*

He tried to find the right words. "I am so sorry, Mattie. It's all my fault. It was just too much to expect of a one hundred-year-old person. It woulda' been hard for a woman half her age. The stress of the long trip, her busy day at the church, I should not have—"

"You hush, Mr. Smith. Don't you fret about that. You gave Mom the best three days of her life. You know what she told me last night? She said she'd done things she never dreamed she'd be able to do. The train ride, staying here at the Snyder House in this big wonderful bed, the fine meals, the people she'd met, bein' able to see her old friends at the church, visitin' with Reverend Leftwich…

"I just hate that she wasn't able to help you get justice for Toby Jackson."

Against the way the wind now was blowing, Charlie Smith tried to stay positive. He told her the court case wasn't over by a long shot.

Mattie, drying her tears, had an idea. "Could I say in court what Mom told me about Toby payin' off his bill?"

The young prosecutor said he appreciated that offer but it wouldn't work, as it would just be considered hearsay. "You stay here with your mom, Mattie. "I need to get back to the courthouse. And remember, I'm here for you. I'll be glad to help you with any arrangements for your mom. She was truly a wonderful lady."

Charlie gave Mattie a hug, but as he started to leave, the 75-year-old colored woman broke down crying again. Charlie put his arms around her one more time.

"I loved my mama so much."

Charlie fought back his own tears. "I have to go, Mattie."

"I know, Mr. Smith. I'm sorry. You go."

The now late prosecutor ran down the stairs to his waiting father.

"My buggy's out front, son! We need to go now."

Outside the Carter County Courthouse, on a whittler's bench beneath the shade of a huge oak tree, three grizzled, tobacco-chewing old-timers offered their predictions.

"Jake Edwards is the stinkin'nest, lyin'est, meanest man in Valley Forge," one of the chewers said. "He's likea' big old rattle-snake wantin' ta bite somebidy.

"But no way he's gonna get hanged for killin' a darkie," the spitting prognosticator added.

"They oughta give him a good whuppin' and let'im be," said another.

"Don't make no difference no way," the third fellow grunted. "Life ain't nothin' but a slow death. Even if Jake's found innocent he ain't long for this world."

By and by, the three bench sitters noticed a stirring on the courthouse steps. People were eagerly making their way to the huge front doors. A bell rang. A man waving his arms shouted from the entrance that the trial was about to resume. Folks hurried to get back to where they'd been sitting inside.

At 1:05, a bailiff announced loudly, "All rise!"

The Honorable Judge Emmett Stone entered, sat down at the bench and motioned to the bailiff for everyone to be seated.

Charlie Smith and his parents traveled quickly back to the courthouse in their buggy, leaving a trail of dust behind them.

In just a few minutes, they arrived, with Daniel pulling to a stop at the courthouse steps.

"You go, son. We'll be in, in a few minutes."

Mary gave her son a quick peck on the cheek and wished him good luck.

And with that, the tardy and increasingly worried prosecutor hurried up the steps and through the big doors.

"So nice of you to join us, Mr. Smith," Judge Stone growled sarcastically. But His Honor's demeanor changed when he saw the devastation on Charlie's face.

"Do you have something to share with this court, Mr. Smith?"

"Sorry, Your Honor. But I just found out that Fanny May Brown died in her sleep. Her daughter tried to wake her up about a half hour ago. But she was gone."

A few muffled cries were heard in the courtroom, especially from the balcony.

Judge Stone tapped his gavel and called for order.

"Your Honor, if it please the court, I would like to recess for a couple of days," Charlie requested.

Judge Stone lowered his head as if considering this, then replied.

"Mr. Smith, I am sorry you have lost your star witness. I offer my condolences to friends and family of Fanny May Brown. But a recess or delay of this trial because a witness died is just not acceptable."

The judge tapped his gavel. "This proceeding will continue. Do you have any other witnesses to call, Mr. Smith?"

Charlie studied the question for several seconds.

"Mr. Smith?"

"Yes, Your Honor. I call Daniel Smith."

"Objection!" L. Ross Roberts stated loudly. "Daniel Smith is not on our list of witnesses."

"Overruled!" the judge responded. "Under the circumstances, I will allow it this time."

A somewhat surprised Daniel walked to the witness stand and was sworn in by the court clerk.

I've got somehow to paint a true picture of Jake Edwards. My only hope is to convince the jurors what a vengeful, hateful person he was—and still is, Charlie thought as his father prepared to testify.

"Dad—I mean Mr. Smith—a few chuckles from the courtroom—try to think back some thirteen years. It's my understanding that you and your helper, Isaiah Washington, took a trip to Valley Forge to buy hay from Jake Edwards. Tell us in your words what happened that day."

Daniel Smith stared at his son, trying his best to intuit what Charlie wanted him to say.

When Daniel said nothing for a few seconds, Charlie asked him again just to tell—in his own words—what he recalled about that visit.

"Okay. I'll do my best. After I was greeted by Mr. Edwards, I sat on the porch with him and we talked about the weather and farmin' and how things'd changed since the Civil War. I told him I thought for the better. But he cussed and said for the worst.

"Isaiah drove the hay wagon on down to the barn, where he and Toby Jackson started loadin' it. Mr. Edwards commenced to rantin' and ravin' about how lazy colored people were and—"

"Objection!" L. Ross Roberts snarled. "Not relevant!"

"Sustained. Get on with it, Mr. Smith, but we don't need any side stories from the witness."

Charlie instructed his dad to continue with his testimony.

"Well, Prissy, Mr. Edwards' house girl at the time, went to the barn to take Toby his lunch. And a few minutes later Mrs. Edwards sent Jake after her—on account Prissy was takin' too long."

"And then what happened?"

"I remember it clear as a bell," Daniel Smith answered. "Mr. and Mrs. Edwards got madder'n a hornet, and Jake said he'd be back dreckly, that he had to go after that stupid nig—"

"Objection!"

"Sustained. Mr. Smith, please make your witness understand. We are only interested in what happened and not what Mr. Edwards called his help."

"Yes, Your Honor."

"Please continue, Mr. Smith."

Daniel Smith squirmed in his chair, dabbed his forehead with a handkerchief and wet his lips with his tongue—as if what would come next was of the utmost importance. "I heard terrible screamin' and cryin' comin' from the barn, so I ran to see what was happenin'. Mr. Edwards had struck Prissy and was about to do it again but Isaiah grabbed his hand and stopped him. Prissy's face was red and there was blood comin' from her nose and from the corner of her mouth."

"Objection!" L. Ross Roberts screamed. "Your Honor, this is all irrelevant. Besides, we have heard it before and it has nothing to do with Mr. Edwards' guilt or innocence."

"Sustained! I agree. Wind it up, Mr. Smith."

"If I may, one more question, Your Honor."

"Make it fast and to the point, Mr. Prosecutor."

"Yes sir, Your Honor. So, Mr. Smith, would it be correct to state it is your opinion that Prissy Washington was being kept against her will, by Jake Edwards, claiming that she owed money to his store? That she in fact did not owe? That, in fact that is the very same way he kept Toby Jackson from leaving? And furthermore, would it be correct to state it is your view that there was no reason in the world for Mr. Edwards to go after Toby Jackson other than hateful, mean vengeance on the part of Mr. Edwards?"

"Yes, that is my opinion!" Daniel Smith declared loudly.

The prosecutor had rattled off the words so fast that L. Ross

Roberts had no time to respond.

But now Roberts did—and with anger.

"Objection! Objection! Nothing but conjecture and speculation!"

Judge Stone said, "Sustained! That is quite enough, Mr. Smith."

"I have no further questions, Your Honor."

The judge tapped his gavel. Shuffling and a few murmers were heard from the balcony.

"You wish to cross examine, Mr. Roberts?"

"No sir, Your Honor."

"You have other witnesses, Mr. Smith?"

"No, Your Honor."

The judge, glancing impatiently at his time piece at the end of a chain attached to his belt, said, "Very well. Call your first witness, Mr. Roberts."

"I call the accused, Mr. Jacob Lee Edwards, to the witness stand."

The defendant, using a cane, hobbled nervously toward the witness box. Jake Edwards was not the same unkempt looking Jake Edwards that Sheriff Nave had arrested several weeks earlier. He was well groomed and had the demeanor of a Southern gentleman, wearing a white suit with a gray vest and a red bow tie.

After being duly sworn in by the court clerk, the jittery sweating Edwards sat down. His nose twitched and his beady little eyes, which folks had called snake eyes all his life, blinked again and again.

L. Ross Roberts whispered to him to try to remain still and calm.

"Mr. Roberts!" the judge shouted. "Speak up so the jury can hear you!"

"Yes, Your Honor."

He asked his client to state, for the record, his full name, age and place of residence.

"My name is Jacob Lee Edwards. I'll be sixty-nine years old come December. I live on my farm in Valley Forge, and I am a charter member of the Valley Forge Baptist Church."

"So then, Mr. Edwards, I am to assume that you are a Christian and try to live by the Good Book?"

"Yes, we are all sinners but I aim to do right in God's eyes."

"Mr. Edwards, you know, of course, that you have been accused of committing a horrible crime. But I don't think you are capable of such a crime."

"Objection, Your Honor!" Charlie Smith said. "No one here is interested in counsel's opinion of his client."

"Sustained," the judge ruled. "Ask your questions, Mr. Roberts, but keep your opinions to yourself."

L. Ross Roberts told his witness to continue.

"No sir, I'm not," Edwards said. "I ain't never hurt nobidy in my whole life."

"Very well," Roberts said. "How do you think those who know you best in Valley Forge or elsewhere in Carter County would describe you?"

"Objection!" Prosecutor Smith interrupted. "Question is asking for the defendant's opinion. This is speculation. It has nothing to do with the facts of this case."

"Overruled," Judge Stone said.

"Thank you, Your Honor," Roberts said, bowing ever so slightly to Judge Stone. "Please answer my question, Mr. Edwards."

"Well, I don't rightly know for sure, but I'd say them that knows me best'd say I'm an upstandin' Christian man who ain't done nary a thing wrong in my whole life. Ain't even swallered much whiskey. Ain't never been in trouble with tha' law. Ain't never hurt nobidy. Never even done nothin' bad ta any'a my niggers…"

L. Ross Roberts flinched and gave Jake a hard look.

"Sorry. I mean my coloreds," Edwards, taken aback, corrected himself. "And I'd say even them'd say I'm a good man that ain't deservin' ta be lied about and ain't deservin' any of this trouble with tha' law."

"Okay, Mr. Edwards. One last question about yourself before we bore down into the heart of this case: Would you call yourself an educated man? By that, I mean can you read and write?"

Edwards squirmed and wiped his forehead. "I can read writin' but I cain't write readin'."

"So you never had a chance to go to school because you worked so hard as a young man and even now, into your old age, because you were so busy on your farm and helping your church. Is that right, Mr. Edwards?"

"Objection, Your Honor!" Smith shouted. "Defendant's ability to read or write has absolutely nothing to do with the crime he's charged with."

"Sustained," His Honor ruled. "Mr. Roberts, please get on with it! Enough of these pointless questions about the defendant's reputation or past."

"Yes, Your Honor."

"Mr. Edwards, tell us what happened in that field in Fish Springs thirteen years ago—the day you tried to keep Toby Jackson from leaving."

"Well, I recollect it bein' in the afternoon. Sun was shinin'. Warm and no wind and if I'd been in my younger years, I'd a been rock skippin' across the creek."

"Mr. Edwards, just please tell us what happened in that field that day," L. Ross Roberts said. "But I will have to say you seem to have a good memory. Is that correct?"

"Objection!" Charlie Smith shouted. "Counsel is trying to put words in his client's mouth."

"Your Honor, if it please the court, my question about Mr. Edwards' memory goes straight to the heart of this case. He's about to tell us what he recalled about that day thirteen years ago."

"Overruled then," Judge Stone snapped.

"So tell us again, Mr. Edwards, what you remember about what took place in that field in Fish Springs."

"Well, I done went to my store, like I did most days, to check on things. Fanny May Brown—God rest her soul—told me Toby Jackson added some things to his bill, then said he was runnin' off to Alabama 'cause his brother had'im a job on the railroad down that ways. Fanny May told me she tried like the dickens to make him do right. Said she told him he cain't rightly leave owin' money to the store 'cause that'd be like stealin'."

"Objection again, Your Honor!" the prosecutor yelled. "Witness' testimony is nothing but hearsay."

"Overruled, counselor," Judge Stone said. "Wrap it up with this witness quickly, Mr. Roberts."

"Yes, Your Honor. And thank you. Mr. Edwards, please continue with what you remember Fanny May Brown telling you that fateful day."

"Well, she said Toby got all high and mighty and claimed I owed him money anyways. Claimed his debt at my company store had done been paid. Said he weren't a slave no more and they wasn't nothin' I could do ta stop him from leavin'. Fanny May said Toby acted way above his raisin', kindly like he could do any damned thing he wanted and was glad to be sheda' me."

"Mr. Edwards!" His Honor exclaimed from the bench. "I don't hold to any cursing in my courtroom. Do you understand?"

"Yes sir," the witness said meekly.

"So what happened next?" Roberts asked. "Please tell the court."

"Well, I took off to the farm hopin' to stop him before he left and talk some sense into him. But when I got there he'd already flew tha' coop. Jed, he bein' the young man that worked fer me, said Toby was on his way to see Isaiah before he left for Alabama. So me, Jed and Elijah took off in the wagon. We was wantin' to see if we could persuade him to do the right thing and come back.

"We caught up with Toby 'bout'a half mile from Isaiah Washington's place. I got down outta the wagon and asked Toby, real polite like, to come back causin' he still owed me money and waren't s'posed ta leave 'til he got his bill paid.

"Well, he got hateful and mad and started kickin' up dirt and cussin' somethin' awful and shakin' his fists at me. I tried to reason with'im but it waren't no use."

"What happened then, Jake?" Roberts asked.

"That's when he commenced to chokin' me with them big brown, calloused hands 'round my neck. Them killin' hands made three'a mine and his arms was thickern' my legs. I knowed I waren't standin' a chance. And he was tryin' ta squeeze the life plum outta me. Spittin' in my face while he did it. Baring his big white teeth like he was 'bout to bite my nose off. Hollerin' 'I'll kill ya'!' Like he'd lost his everlastin' mind."

"I see," Roberts responded. "And then what happened?"

"He done pushed me ta the ground. And he kept comin' at me fulla' hate and spitefulness. And he put his big rough hands 'round my neck agin, but somehows I got loose, grabbed my rifle and shot that big bad, lyin' nigger…"

"Witness will not use that word in my courtroom!" the judge ordered. "Mr. Roberts, please control the language of your defendant!"

"I meant ta say colored man," Edwards sheepishly said.

"So you are saying that you killed Mr. Jackson in self defense because he was trying to kill you? Is that correct, Mr. Edwards? The only way you could save your own life was by taking his?"

"That's the plain, whole truth, so hep me God," Edwards, feigning a sniffle, said. "It was either him or me. Any man woulda' done the same thing."

"Thank you, Mr. Edwards. That will be all."

Judge Stone asked, "Mr. Smith, do you wish to question this witness?"

"Yes, Your Honor."

"Mr. Edwards, mind if I call you Jake?"

"Most do." *What's this sneaky nigger-lovin' bastard up to?*

"Your young helper Jed that ran away that very night. Was it because you threatened to rip his skin clean off with a bullwhip unless he told you where Toby was headed?"

"Objection! Hearsay!" L. Ross Roberts yelled.

"Sustained."

"When you told Elijah to put two shovels in the wagon before going after Toby, was that so you could bury his body in a shallow grave after you shot him?"

"Objection! Speculation!"

"Sustained! I'm warning you, Mr. Smith," Judge Smith said harshly. "No more such purely speculative questions."

Jake Edwards, scowling, shot back, "Those shovels was already in the wagon! That's why they call it a work wagon. Course you probably wouldn't know that."

That got a few chuckles from some of Jake's supporters, causing the judge to pound his gavel.

The judge demanded, "Quiet in the courtroom!" "Just answer the questions, Mr. Edwards."

Prosecutor Charlie Smith tried to move in for the kill. "Mr. Edwards, you claim you shot Toby Jackson in self-defense and yet you shot him in the back of the head. How can that possibly be?"

The witness, wiping the sweat off his forehead, asked for a drink of water before answering, and he was given one from the clerk. Then he spoke:

"By the time I got ahold of my rifle to shoot, he'd spun around. Then I seen I'd shot him in the backa' his head. I waren't very fast in seein' where he was standin', not like a young man woulda' been. I shot fast as I could ta try ta save my life. You just cain't move as fast when you get old."

"But that was thirteen years ago, Mr. Edwards."

"So what. I was fifty-six years old and slow and askeered. I've always been slow on the trigger. That's why I never kilt' a pheasant or a duck in my whole life."

"Okay, I understand," Charlie Smith answered. "I have another question for you, Jake. After you shot Toby in the back of the head, why did you have Elijah and Jed looking through everything for that receipt?"

"They worn't looking for no receipt. They worn't none. They was lookin' for the money he owed me."

"I see," the prosecutor said lukewarmly. "Almost done here, Jake. Can I ask you another question?"

"You ain't needin' my permission and you know it."

Charlie Edwards grinned, took a few steps toward the jury, then walked back toward the witness stand. "I noticed you walked with a cane, Jake. Have you always?"

"No, just for the last few years," Edwards said insolently.

"That's quite a nice cane. Is that an animal's head on the handle, Jake?"

"It's a wolf's head. My father carved it. This was his cane."

"May I see it?"

"Sure," Jake said uneasily, handing his treasure to Charlie.

"How nice!" the prosecutor glowed. "I wish my dad could make stuff like this. He can't make anything."

Laughter broke out in the courtroom. Daniel, sitting near the front, held both hands up. Even Judge Stone had to chuckle before tapping his gavel.

"That's quite enough, Mr. Smith."

After inspecting the cane Charlie held it out for Jake to take back. But before Jake got a hold of it, Charlie let it go. Jake swiftly lunged forward and grabbed the falling cane.

"Wow, Jake. What a move! You must be faster now than you were thirteen years ago." The prosecutor faced the jury when he made that observation.

"Yea, just 'a lucky ca—"

"No further questions, Your Honor."

"You may step down, Mr. Edwards," said Judge Stone. He looked at Charlie with a slight grin and shook his head from side to side.

"Do you have any other witnesses, Mr. Roberts?"

"Yes, Your Honor."

L. Ross Roberts went on to call several character witnesses, mostly folks from the Valley Forge Baptist church who painted a picture of a good Christian man who cared about others.

Roberts' most compelling witness, however, was Jake Edwards' neighbor, Eli Elliotte, a simple farmer with a large family. Most knew the long, thin nosed Eli as a respected deacon at the church. But very few knew of his darker, more sinister side as a dues paying member of the Ku Klux Klan. Eli swore that he was in Jake Edwards' store the day Toby Jackson said he was leaving.

L. Ross Roberts asked, "So, you knew Mr. Jackson?"

"Well, not personly, but I knowed who he were. I'd seen him at Jake's farm and ever now and then in the store. He worn't like most coloreds. He was a mean looking fella. He acted kind of uppedy and quare like he didn't quite understand the peckin' order, and he had the biggest hands I ever seen."

Charlie shook his head at the statement.

"So tell us what you overheard on that day, Eli."

"Well sir, I remember it like it were yesterdee. Toby told old Fanny May that he didn't care if he did owe the store money. He was leavin' for Alabama and if that old man tried to stop him, he'd ring his neck."

Roberts said, "Old man, meaning Jake Edwards?"

"That's what I figgered."

"Thank you, Mr. Elliotte. No further questions."

"Would you like to cross examine, Mr. Smith?"

"Yes, Your Honor."

"Mr. Elliotte, just where would you place Toby Jackson in your pecking order?"

"Objection!" Roberts shouted. "Question is not relevant!"

The judge, frowning, said, "Come on, Mr. Smith."

"Sorry, Your Honor. I just get tired of all the bigotry."

"That's quite enough, Mr. Smith," said the angry judge, pounding his gavel.

"You have any more relevant questions for this witness, Mr. Smith?"

"No, Your Honor."

"That's good, because we're all gettting a little testy here—this late in the day," the judge said.

"You may step down, Mr. Elliotte. We will adjourn now and start closing arguments when we reconvene tomorrow at 9 a.m."

He tapped his gavel one last time that day, and everyone in the courtroom began leaving. Some of them stretched. Others hugged or shook hands or bantered with folks they hadn't seen in quite some time—but who had come here, like everyone else, to see for themselves what fate would befall Jake Edwards.

Prosecutor Charlie Smith wouldn't sleep well that night. *If I had to speculate as to how all this'll play out, it all boils down to one man's word against another's. One a colored former slave, who had reason to hate his former owner, and the other a white man, who hated the fact that he no longer was a slave owner. Will a jury of all white men believe the word of a colored man over the word of someone like themselves? Then there was Eli's testimony thrown in on top of that.*

That night, Isaiah, Prissy, Ruthie and Elijah—who Sheriff Nave thought was now safe after he had testified—sat on the porch. A million stars twinkled beautifully far above the mountaintops. Crickets, frogs, cicadas and hoot owls filled the night with nature's music. A soft, warm breeze seemed to caress, even soothe. But the atmosphere was one of defeat. Because Charlie had told them not to get their hopes up; without Fanny May Brown's testimony, it was a long shot at best.

Ruthie decided to make a pitcher of refreshing tea—with cool water from the nearby spring house. But on her way inside she tripped on a board that had come loose on the porch.

Prissy asked, "You okay, Ruthie?"

"I be fine, but dat boad hea' at the door needs to be nailed down," Ruthie said.

When Prissy asked Isaiah to take care of it—because someone could get hurt—he promised he'd tend to it tomorrow.

But then he noted it might take longer, as all his nails had been in the barn when it burned down.

"They's a little tobacco can with nails in it on the kitchen shelf," Prissy reminded her husband. "Elijah gave it to you, remember? There's a hammer there, too."

"See all the trouble you cause me, Elijah," said Isaiah, kidding his friend.

"What I do?"

Isaiah fetched the Old Virginia tobacco can. It was tall with an oval lid—perfect for holding cut nails. He took off the top and pulled out two nails. After he nailed down the loose board, he laid the hammer on a rail that ran across the porch from post to post and stood the can beside it. When Elijah saw the can on the rail, he remembered where he got it.

"Dat 'bacca can was Toby's."

Isaiah, scratching his head, asked, "How'd you come by it?"

"Afta Toby was shot, we was lookin' fo dat receipt. We found dat 'bacca can. Jake Edwards took it and shook all the 'bacca out. Dat devil looked in it, then throwed it on da ground. I picked it up later. I just wanted somethin' of Toby's."

Everyone got quiet.

"Way back, on eavnins' like dis, Toby and me'd set in the barn loft and talk 'bout bein' free and what we'd do if we was. Toby said he'd go fishin' ever day. Dat be his dream. Poor Toby—he never did get free."

Prissy, who had been listening closely, had her say. "Oh no! I think you are wrong, Elijah."

"What you mean, Prissy?"

"I think Toby is free now. I know Toby is free."

Everyone got quiet taking in what Prissy had said, then swirling tree tops near the river in the moonlight caught everyone's attention. Even Shadow jumped up and barked at the intrusion.

242 Michael Manuel & Larry C. Timbs, Jr

The swirling continued along the river, then into the river bottom pasture. The wind gust in the tall grass moved across the bottom below the house. Then up the hill toward the house and across the porch, blowing out the porch lantern and knocking the tobacco can off the railing. When the old, tarnished can hit the porch floor, the lid popped off and the nails fell out. Then all was calm again.

Isaiah relit the lantern then begun scooping up the nails. "Where did that come from?" Isaiah asked. But before putting the nails back in the can, Isaiah took a closer look. Holding it under a lighted lantern, he turned the flame up high. "Is that somethin' in the bottom?"

He shook it vigorously, but nothing fell out. Then he tried, without success, to put his big hand in the can.

"Prissy, reach in this can and see if there is somethin' in the bottom."

Her eyes wide now with wonder, Prissy reached in and pulled out a small folded up paper wedged in the bottom. She carefully unfolded and read the old, partially torn and stained document.

"Glory be, Isaiah!" she said excitedly. "Do you know what you've just found?"

"Is that a receipt?"

Prissy just looked at him and nodded.

Ruthie hollered, "Praise the Lawd! Halleluia!"

Isaiah, hugging his overjoyed wife, said: "Do y'all believe in angels?"

"I do now," Elijah said. "I sho' do now."

"All rise for The Honorable Judge Emmett Stone!"

The judge gazed out on his courtroom, including at the packed balcony where the Rev. Horace Leftwich stood vigil.

"Be seated."

Prosecutor Charlie Smith said, "Your Honor, may I approach the bench?"

"You may."

Charlie told Judge Stone that he had a critically important piece of evidence that needed to be presented before the closing arguments. It was evidence, the prosecutor noted, that Fanny

May Brown had traveled over 100 miles to share with the court.

"This is highly unusual, Mr. Smith," His Honor replied in a soft voice. "But I guess we owe Fanny May Brown that much."

The young prosecutor turned to the jury box.

"Charlie."

Charlie looked back at Judge Stone.

"Sir?"

"This better be good."

"It is, Your Honor. Thank you."

"I call Elijah Wood back to the stand," Charlie announced.

"Objection! I don't understand, Your Honor?" said a confused, pacing L. Ross Roberts.

"Overruled, Mr. Roberts. I know this is unusual, but I'm allowing this testimony out of due respect for the deceased, Fanny May Brown.

"Continue, Mr. Smith."

There was dead quiet in the courtroom as the old man made his way to the witness stand.

"Mr. Wood, remember you are still under oath. Thirteen years ago, after Jake Edwards killed Toby Jackson, you were searching through everything for a receipt. Did you find anything you forgot to mention when I last questioned you?"

"Yes suh. I found a 'bacca can."

"Then what happened, Mr. Wood?"

"I gave it to Mista Edwards. He took da lid off and shook all da bacca out. Den he looked in it and throwed it down. I picked it up later. I kept nails in it fo the last thirteen yeas. Then I give the can to Isaiah Washington a while back. Last night we's settin' on Isaiah's poach and he needed to nail a boad down. That's when Isaiah found a piece a paper stuck in da bottom'a dat can."

"Would this be that tobacco can, Elijah?" Charlie held up the can.

"Yes suh. Dat be it."

Charlie, unfolding the receipt and holding it above his head, pressed on. "And would this be the paper Isaiah found in the can, Mr. Wood?"

"Yes'sa. Dat be it." Elijah broke out in a big white toothy smile.

"Thank you, Mr. Wood. You may step down."

The prosecutor stared at the judge. "Your Honor, with your permission, I would like to read this document."

"Permission granted, Mr. Smith."

Charlie faced the twelve members of the jury and read the receipt. "July 25th 1870. Toby Jackson's bill of $8.75 at Jake Edwards store is paid in full."

Charlie held the document up and added, "And it is signed by Fanny May Brown."

Cheers, joyous hand clapping, and back patting erupted in the balcony of the Carter County Courthouse.

Judge Stone allowed it for about a minute. Then he hammered his gavel three times. "Order in the court!"

Jake Edwards hollered, "That's a forgery! That damn lyin', thievin' nigger didn't pay his bill off! Ain't no way!"

"Mr. Edwards, one more outburst like that and I'll have you gagged and found in contempt!"

Finally, it seemed that the moment had arrived. A moment dreamed of by Prosecutor Charlie Smith—along with the late Fanny May Brown, her daughter and the entire colored community of Carter County.

"Your Honor, this signature can be authenticated," Charlie Smith said. "I have letters from Fanny May Brown."

"Thank you, Mr. Smith," His Honor said. "Gentlemen, are you ready with closing arguments?"

Both agreed that they were.

Charlie went first, Standing before the jury box the Carter County Prosecuting attorney gathered his thoughts and started. "Even after being threatened and intimidated by, not one but two Ku Klux Klan raids, our witness Elijah Wood still testified. He wanted the truth to be told. He saw his good friend gunned down by Jake Edwards. Shot in the back of his head not because he was leaving owing Jake money. Jake knew Toby paid off his bill at his store.

"As we have proven, Jake Edwards had no reason to go after Toby Jackson. Fanny May Brown—God rest her soul—traveled from Knoxville to testify to that fact.

"To Jake Edwards, Abraham Lincoln's Emancipation Proclamation had no meaning whatsoever. Jake still considered himself the owner of Toby Jackson and he could not deal with the fact that he was about to lose what he owned. As to the assertion that Jake Edwards had killed Toby in self defense, that dog won't hunt. Jake Edwards lied through his teeth on the stand, and everyone in this courtroom knows it. Toby's Jackson's dream was to live out his life as a free man but that dream never happened and Toby was murdered by Jake Edwards in cold blood, for no other reason than revenge and pure hatred of all colored people. Give Toby Jackson the justice he deserves. Thank You."

L. Ross Roberts closed, pointing out that the court had been misled by Elijah Wood's fake death and that Jake had simply made a mistake. He had truly thought Toby still owed him money and he feared for his life and had to protect himself. He also noted that Jake Edwards was a good Christian man, who had never been in trouble with the law before and who had never hurt anyone.

After listening to two days of testimony, the all-white jury deliberated only two hours.

"Members of the jury, have you reached a verdict?"

"We have, Your Honor."

"Please stand and face the jury box, Mr. Edwards."

Judge Stone next said, "Mr. Foreman of the jury, read your verdict."

"We the jury find the accused Jake Edwards guilty of first degree murder."

Jubilation exploded throughout the courtroom. Judge Stone pounded his gavel but it was no use. The celebration was especially loud in the balcony, where the back slapping, hugging, kissing and praising the Lord went on and on. It was as if folks had had their emotions pent up for weeks and now they were letting all their relief and joy spill out. Charlie looked out at his proud stepmother and father and smiled. Several rows back in the courtroom sat the Klansman called "Preacher." He also had a smile on his face.

L. Ross Roberts walked over to Charlie and shook his hand. "Good job, Mr. Smith."

In the Carter County Courthouse In Elizabethton, Tennessee,

on June 26th, 1883, justice was served. However, there were a few who would never be convinced that the Declaration of Independence forged in 1776 had it right when it stated "All men are created equal." Among them were members of the KKK, a few stubborn holdout supporters of Jake Edwards, and others who simply would never, ever accept the idea that colored people should have the same rights and protections, under the law, as white folks.

An hour or so later, a defeated, embittered, scared Jake Edwards stood facing the Honorable Judge Emmett Stone.

"Mr. Edwards, do you have anything to say before I pass sentence."

"Yes. You can go to hell! And take all these nigger lovers with you!"

"Mr. Edwards, you are a little man with a big mouth, so full of hate that I am sure it will consume you. I doubt seriously you will live out your sentence. I pity you.

"Jacob Lee Edwards, I hereby sentence you to ten years of hard labor in the Tennessee State Prison in Nashville, Tennessee. May God have mercy on you."

Those in the courtroom all watched the sentencing in silence. They had wanted to see the trial through to the very end, and now here it had ended. The only one making a sound was Jake Edwards who was dragged away—kicking, cussing and screaming. And when the convicted murderer was gone, they stood up and filed out, many of them feeling better about the future.

Outside, there was raucous revelry and celebration, especially from the coloreds of Carter County.

A lot of people felt a ten-year sentence for premeditated murder was not harsh enough. But being one of the first white men to be sent to prison in Tennessee for killing a colored man, it was a beginning.

And the beginning of the end for Jacob Edwards. He died a few months later while working on a chain gang. Some folks said the cause of death was a heart attack. Others pointed to two of his toes being hammered off one of his feet. They said he likely bled to death, painfully and slowly, next to the ten Negroes he was busting up rock with.

Charlie Smith had heard the news from Sheriff Nave and a few days later he paid a visit to Isaiah and Prissy. He found them in rocking chairs on their porch in the cool of the evening. He told them that Jake Edwards had died.

"Sheriff Nave wanted you to have this, Isaiah," said Charlie, handing Isaiah the tiger's tooth once worn by Toby.

"Thank you, Mista Charlie. Tell tha sheriff I said thanks, too."

Prissy invited their visitor to "come sit on the porch a few minutes. I just made some cold tea."

Charlie sat down in a rocker facing Isaiah.

Isaiah studied the tiger's tooth, rubbing his fingers over the surface worn smooth by many years of wear by Toby. Being in the ground for thirteen years seemed to have had no effect on the tooth.

"This means a lot to me, Mista Charlie." Isaiah shed a few tears and said nothing for about a minute while he remembered his old friend. Charlie didn't break the spell. Then Isaiah said, "Everything's not always fair in this old mean world but it seems like the good Lord found justice for Toby."

"Yes, he did, Isaiah, with a little help from you, Elijah and Fanny May Brown."

"And you, Mista Charlie."

Epilogue

A big turnout of colored folks, along with a few white people who had come to know her, paid their respects at the funeral of Fanny May Brown.

The Rev. Horace Leftwich, the former slave who years earlier had made his way up to East Tennessee from Charleston, S.C., preached what he called a "celebration of her life" eulogy at the Colored Baptist Church.

Fanny May, it was said by the mourners, looked at peace. She wore a bright blue and white dress and a bonnet. A large vase of cut flowers stood on one end of the coffin, provided by the Snyder House Hotel, and on the other was one provided by Charlie Smith. Next to her freshly cut rhododendron-lined coffin was a drawing—by one of the youngsters in the church—of the locomotive that had pulled her all the way from Knoxville to Elizabethton.

She was laid to rest, after a graveside prayer by Leftwich, in a little fenced-in cemetery not far from the church's entrance and under a towering, majestic oak tree. Before her body was lowered into the grave, a woman said a prayer for Fanny May's soul. Then she released two doves from a basket.

The birds immediately flapped their wings and took to the blue, sunny sky—like "two angels taking Fanny May's spirit up to heaven," an old colored woman whispered.

A few days later, on a bright sunny morning, Isaiah and Prissy sat on their porch. They noticed a buggy approaching from just over the hill. In it, to Prissy's consternation, were Barnard McFarland and his wife Ida Pearl.

"Isaiah! The McFarlands must be coming for a visit."

Isaiah said nothing.

Both a bit anxious, they then noticed trailing the McFarlands" buggy were at least a half-dozen other buggies along with wagons filled with lumber.

Isaiah said, "Lookie there, Prissy. They're folks from the church."

Prissy, incredulous, asked, "I wonder why they all comin' here, Isaiah?"

A young colored man in a wagon load of lumber yelled, "Hey, Isaiah! We's all come ta build your barn back! You gwine be our foreman today. "

"Where y'all get all that lumber?" Isiaah shouted back gleefully.

"I reckon dis all be taken care of by Mista Daniel Smith," the man answered.

"And Prissy, we brought lots a good food for all the workers," a woman in one of the wagons called. In back of her were baskets full of fried chicken and all the fixins.

By this time, the McFarlands had gotten out of their buggy and were at the porch. Little Willie, seeming to come out of nowhere, ran up and stood near them.

Barnard McFarland, holding his wife's hand, told Isaiah and Prissy that they'd come to help raise the barn—and to visit their little one.

Then the arduous, but fulfilling work on the barn began— the lifting and hauling and hammering and nailing and sawing.

As it took place, Isaiah thought he recognized one of the barn raisers. *Lord have mercy, could that be the Klansman that helped me the night my barn burned?*

Isaiah, getting his nerve up, said, "You look like a man who's been here before. But then I only saw his eyes. Could that'a been you?"

The man briefly stopped driving nails, turned to Isaiah and said, "Could'a been, and if it was, I sure hope he's changed his ways. He grinned while he stroked Shadow who had just ambled up." Isaiah looked at the man and said "God bless you." The man nodded and went back to driving nails.

During a break in the work, they all enjoyed a grand picnic. But not before a fervent blessing was given by the Rev. Leftwich:

"Lord, you are a mighty, just Lord. We thank you for this food and for all these good-hearted men and women who are doing all this labor and for your many blessings. And we thank you, especially today, for the life of Toby Jackson. He was a good, honest, hard-working man. May we never forget him and may your angels keep him in their arms forever. Amen."

Years later, Isaiah and Prissy became grandparents. They loved it when their four sons and their wives came with the grandkids for visits. Grandpa and Grandma enjoyed taking their grandkids fishing, canoeing, hiking and doing other things fun in Fish Springs.

Prissy, always the nurturer and teacher, founded a school for the colored community in Carter County. Isaiah, Daniel Smith's long-time favored employee, went on to expand his own spread of land in Fish Springs; he became one of the most respected and well-off Negro farmers in Carter County.

Before their deaths, Isaiah and Prissy set aside land in their will, guaranteeing that 100 of their 300 acres of land would be protected forever against development. Decades later, a descendant of the former slaves would proudly note that that "the government now be workin' for all our family—past, present and future—till we be sittin' with Jesus."

Elijah and Ruthie Wood lived to be in their nineties. They died and were buried in Fish Springs—not far from their little crude but adequate cabin. Their remains were removed and planted in higher ground—as were the remains of about 1,200 others—when Watauga Lake, which covered most of Fish Springs, was created by TVA in the late 1940s.

Prosecutor Charlie Smith, as had been predicted, was elected to higher office in East Tennessee. He served as a U.S. Congressman for more than two decades. Little Willie, the mixed race child of Isaiah and Prissy—and of Barnard McFarland—had a tough time as a youngster but he prevailed against many obstacles as he grew into an adult, and did well. He met and married a woman who was a top assistant in Congressman Smith's office.

Authors' Notes

Like our first book, *Fish Springs, Justice for Toby* is intended to paint an accurate picture of what life was like in the communities of Fish Springs and Elizabethton, Tennessee in the later 1800s but embelished with imagination.

Many landmarks mentioned in *Justice for Toby* were in place at the time of our story. These include the Covered Bridge in Elizabethton, the Snyder House Hotel in Elizabethton, and the Phillippi Missionary Baptist Church, originally the Elizabethton Colored Baptist Church.

The story of Isaiah Washington's determination to gain justice for his friend is fiction and includes a lot of wishful thinking as well as some intentional manipulation of historical details. We found no record of a white man being convicted of murdering a black man in the 1880s. The court system in Tennessee

The first Carter County Courthouse built in 1852 is featured in the last chapter of *Justice for Toby*.
From courthousehistory.com.

included provisions for a grand jury to determine if enough evidence existed for charges to be brought in the 1880s, as it does today, so the process of bringing Jake Edwards to justice would have been more complex than we presented.

It is true that the Rev. Horace Leftwich, a former slave, was

251

the founder of the Colored Baptist Church. However, all of his actions in our novel are products of our imagination.

The Colored Baptist Church in Elizabethton was re-named the Phillippi Missionary Baptist Church. An historical marker outside the sanctuary in a section of Elizabethton, known by some as "Beartown," notes that it was founded by the Rev. Horace Leftwich as one of the first black churches in East Tennessee. The current minister as of early 2016 is the Rev. Joseph Holifield. He was quoted a few years ago in the Elizabethton Star: "When we get to heaven, there isn't going to be a black or white heaven. It's going to be all of God's people, and if we have a problem with that here we won't make it up there."

The property we've fictitiously described as belonging to Isaiah and Prissy Washington would have been on the outskirts of Fish Springs along the Watauga River that now lies below the surface of Watauga Lake created in the late nineteen-forties.

The slave schooner Wanderer, which historians report as the last ship to bring a cargo of African slaves to the United States in November 1858 (delivering its cargo at Jekyll Island, Ga.), was actually built in 1857—a few years late if ours were a true story.

The ET&WNC Railroad, later known affectionately throughout East Tennessee as the Tweetsie, dates back to 1866. But again we used dramatic license on where it traveled, times and running schedules. We have likewise used dramatic license with the title of the local newspaper, the *Knoxville Sentinel*, which was founded a few years later.

There may not have been a Ku Klux Klan raid with a cross-burning in Carter County, but there was Klan activity elsewhere in Tennessee in 1883.

We trust the reader will forgive us these few manipulations of the historical record and join us in this wishful recreation of a time in our mutual past.

THE *Wanderer* was the last slave ship to reach U.S. shores and was featured in Isaiah's account of his early life in Chapter 7. Image courtesy of the Jekyll Museum Archives. The original color painting, by Warren Sheppard, has been reproduced in black and white.

The Snyder House was the first hotel in Elizabethton, operated from 1850 until about 1900. The hotel plays a crucial role in the story and is the setting for the plotted demise of Fanny May Brown and her daughter Mattie. Photo from the Murrell Family Collection, the Archives of Tennessee.

Michael Manuel

Mike Manuel finished high school on the Mississippi Gulf Coast and attended The University of Southern Mississippi. He and his wife Joyce live on a mountain, with their two cats, overlooking Watauga Lake near Hampton, Tennessee. They like to hike on the Appalachian Trail just below the house and kayak on the lake. The Manuels each have a daughter.

Justice for Toby co-authored with Larry C. Timbs Jr. is his second published novel and is a sequel to their first, *Fish Springs: Beneath the Surface,* published in 2014. Michael is also a screen writer and has written screenplays for both novels. Michael says, "life is good."

For more details about the authors and the story, see the authors' website:
www.fishspringsnovel.com

Michael Manuel and Larry C. Timbs Jr. are available for presentations and select readings.
E-mail them at: bearhavenproductions@gmail.com

Larry C. Timbs Jr.

Larry Timbs is a journalist, a retired journalism professor and a Vietnam-era USAF veteran. His roots are in East Tennessee, but he worked for 27 years at Winthrop University in Rock Hill, S.C.

Fish Springs: Beneath the Surface, published in 2014 with co-author Michael Manuel, was his first novel. *Justice for Toby* is his second novel.

Growing up, he heard many colorful stories about Fish Springs—a mountain community in East Tennessee now almost entirely covered by Watauga Lake—from his father, Lawrence C. Timbs, who died at the age of 90 in January 2012. His father and many of his ancestors were born and raised in Fish Springs—the setting for *Justice for Toby.*

Larry blogs at: http://larrytimbs.blogspot.com

For more details about the authors and the story, see the authors' website:
www.fishspringsnovel.com

Michael Manuel and Larry C. Timbs Jr. are available for presentations and select readings.
E-mail them at: bearhavenproductions@gmail.com

Acknowledgments
of author
Michael Manuel

Many thanks to my family—my sister Marcia, brothers Fritz and Chip, and their wives Lois and Betty, for their never ending support and encouragement. Thanks to my lovely daughters Leigh and Gwen for being there and listening. To Joyce, my lovely wife, an avid reader, for her intelligent suggestions during rewrites and tolerating my obsession with writing, thank you. I love you.

Thanks to Dr. Jim Godfrey for his encouragement of my writing and feedback on the screenplay of *Justice for Toby*. To Betsy Sullenger who works in the film industry—thank you for helping me with my early screen writing, that ultimately led to writing novels. Thanks to Peter Ford for his many hours of computer skills that were invaluable. Thank you, Ben Everette, book buyer for Food City Stores, for helping us launch our novels *Fish Springs* and *Justice for Toby*. Also many thanks to Lisa Johnson of Food City for helping us with book signings.

A heartfelt thank you to my friend and co-author Larry C. Timbs Jr. Larry, a retired journalism professor, who I co-authored with on our first novel *Fish Springs: Beneath the Surface*, convinced me that we needed to write a sequel to *Fish Springs*. Together, I believe we created a novel that captures part of the heart, soul and lore of Appalachia.

Thank you, former IPG Senior Editor Judy Geary, for your hours, days and weeks of editing and your expertise of historical facts and researching. You are the best.

Acknowledgments

of author

Larry C. Timbs, Jr

My work in this book is dedicated to my parents—Lawrence C. Timbs and Dixie Nadine Jenkins Timbs. Both of them were accomplished, gifted writers. Whatever skills I have as a writer derive in large part from them.

Credit, too, goes to my co-author, Michael Manuel. Michael laid out the basic structure, plot and characters, for *Justice for Toby*, and asked me to help him put some "meat on the bones" of the story.

They say timing is almost everything, and Michael had the very good sense, early in 2015 when we started on this novel, to know that race (especially the divisions between whites and blacks) had become part of the national conversation in America. Headlines on race (the Black Lives Matter movement, and movies such as *Selma, The Butler, Twelve Years A Slave* and *Roots*) had come front and center in popular culture. Thus, it was a good bet, Michael and I figured, that the public would want to read a novel about ex-slaves caught up in a controversy in the mountains of Appalachia.

I also want to acknowledge the friendship and help of all my "brown and black cousins" in South Carolina—many of them the descendants of slaves. I learned a lot about their culture, how they cope and how they "stayed in their lanes" (as one close black friend described it) to overcome, survive and thrive.

I was a smarter writer about some of the main characters in *Justice For Toby* because of them.